UNIDENTIFIED FUNNY OBJECTS 3

Edited by
Alex Shvartsman

UFO Publishing
Brooklyn, NY

PUBLISHED BY:

UFO Publishing
1685 E 15th St.
Brooklyn, NY 11229
www.ufopub.com

Copyright © 2014 by UFO Publishing

Stories copyright © 2014 by the authors

Trade paperback ISBN: 978-0-9884328-4-0

All rights reserved. No part of the contents of this book may be reproduced or transmitted in any form or by any means without the written permission of the publisher.

Cover art: Tomasz Maronski
Interior art: Barry Munden
Typesetting & interior design: Melissa Neely
Graphics design: Emerson Matsuuchi
Logo design: Martin Dare

Copy editor: Elektra Hammond
Associate editors: James Aquilone, Cyd Athens, James Beamon, Frank Dutkiewicz, Michael Haynes, Nathaniel Lee

Visit us on the web:
www.ufopub.com

TABLE OF CONTENTS

Alex Shvartsman
    FOREWORD 1

Jim C. Hines
    ON THE EFFICACY OF SUPERVILLAIN BATTLES IN
    ELICITING THERAPEUTIC BREAKTHROUGHS 3

James A. Miller
    THE RIGHT ANSWER. 19

Mike Resnick
    THE GEFILTE FISH GIRL. 29

Jakob Drud
    MASTER OF BUSINESS APOCALYPSE 39

Caroline M. Yoachim
    CARLA AT THE OFF-PLANET TAX RETURN HELPLINE. 53

Nathaniel Lee
    WHY I BOUGHT SATAN TWO COKES ON
    THE DAY I GRADUATED HIGH SCHOOL 59

Robert Silverberg
    COMPANY STORE. 79

Josh Vogt
    THE DOOR-TO-DOOR SALESTHING FROM PLANET X 97

Matt Mikalatos
    PICTURE PERFECT. 101

James Beamon
    THE DISCOUNTED SENIORS. 117

Karen Haber
    THAT MUST BE THEM NOW. 131

Sarah Pinsker
    NOTES TO MY PAST AND/OR ALTERNATE SELVES 149

Tim Pratt
    THE REAL AND THE REALLY REAL. 153

Camille Griep
    INTO THE WOODS, WITH ZOMBUNNY. 163

Gini Koch
: Live At the Scene 179

Krystal Claxton
: The Newsboy's Last Stand 191

Jeremy Butler
: The Full Lazenby 201

Piers Anthony
: Do Not Remove This Tag 213

Tina Connolly
: Super-Baby-Moms Group Saves the Day!.................. 227

Oliver Buckram
: The Choochoomorphosis 245

Kevin J. Anderson And Guy Anthony De Marco
: The Fate Worse Than Death.......................... 249

Cat Rambo
: Elections at Villa Encantada......................... 259

Jody Lynn Nye
: Infinite Drive 275

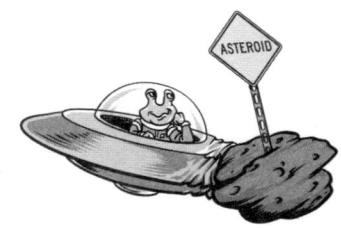

FOREWORD

Alex Shvartsman

Welcome to the third annual installment of *Unidentified Funny Objects*—an anthology series of humorous, light-hearted, wacky, and downright unidentifiable stories.

In this, our thickest volume to date, you'll find a traveling robot salesman and a vampire novelist, a brain-in-a-jar superhero and a jinn trapped in a mattress. You'll visit the scene of an alien invasion alongside a local news team and become embroiled in the board elections at a condo populated by magical beings.

Our regular readers will get the chance to revisit settings introduced in the previous UFO volumes, in stories by Jim C. Hines, Matt Mikalatos, and Jody Lynn Nye. New readers need not worry; each story stands on its own and doesn't require familiarity with the previous episodes.

All but two of the stories in this book are original. Of the two reprints, the history of "Company Store" by Robert Silverberg is especially interesting. This story was originally published in the 1950s and hasn't been reprinted in English since the 1970s. In fact, it's been out of circulation for so long that even the author did not have a digital copy. He photocopied the story pages out of a paperback and sent them for us to type up.

Although "Company Store" may be unfamiliar to most English-speaking readers, this story is very well-known to Russian fans. The translated version (titled "The Contract" in Russian) was published in numerous Russian anthologies, and a short animated film based on it was produced in the 1980s. It was broadcast regularly on one of only two national TV channels during the final years of the Soviet Union, and so is as familiar to that generation of Soviet viewers as ThunderCats or the Care Bears are to their American counterparts.

I invite you to rediscover this lost gem and to enjoy the other fine and varied stories collected within.

Happy reading!

ON THE EFFICACY OF SUPERVILLAIN BATTLES IN ELICITING THERAPEUTIC BREAKTHROUGHS

Jim C. Hines

Patient Name: Tamara "Puff" Jones

Insurance: Silver Shield State Coverage w/Metahuman Rider. Policy 2851-28-H3.

Physical: Tamara appears to be a healthy teenage girl, approximately fourteen years old, with—oh, hell. Who am I kidding? The poor girl is a laboratory experiment, one of Michael "Monster-Master" Manchester's final creations before he was locked up for a decade. In Tamara's case, he spliced blowfish and human physiology together.

As challenging as this has been for Puff, she's adapted better than Manchester's half-man/half-skunk soldier.

Physically, Puff is roughly human sized, heavyset with venomous spines that lay flat against the skin. When frightened or angry, her blowfish instincts take over, something that apparently happened two weeks ago in phys. ed. Needless to say, Puff was mortified. This was when her adoptive parents, both superheroes, brought her to me.

Psychological: Puff presents with low-level anxiety disorder and possible depression. Her relationship with her parents is terse and strained. Given her unique physiology, psychiatric medication is not recommended at this time.

I'm uncertain whether her father's telepathic control over sea creatures allows him to command his daughter. I suspect he knows better, but if he's using his powers to make his kid clean her room or some such, I'll kick his ass myself.

Don't write that down. No, delete that. Delete!

Dammit, I hate this bloody machine.

"IT'S SO EMBARRASSING." Tamara Jones, aka "Puff," sat with folded arms in her wheelchair, avoiding eye contact with her adopted parents. "Other superheroes can fly faster than the speed of sound or punch a hole through the moon. What does my father do? Gossips with jellyfish."

"A telepathic bond with the creatures of the sea is a powerful weapon," said Jarhead. This was his third session with Puff, and the first time he had felt comfortable bringing her parents in for more than a few minutes at the beginning and end. Given the amount of anger emanating from the teenaged mermaid, that might have been a mistake on his part.

"It's like they're stuck in the Silver Age," Puff said. "He hasn't changed his costume since the seventies."

"It's iconic." The superhero known as Triton, self-proclaimed Master of the Oceans, was a tall, broad-shouldered man with umber skin, blue eyes, and bright red gill slits running just beneath his jawbone.

"It's gold and brown." Puff still hadn't looked up from her smartphone. "Your costume is *literally* the colors of an unflushed toilet bowl. And Mom's is worse. It's like she made her outfit from the leftover scraps of his."

"This was the style when I got started," protested Optica.

Jarhead kept his mouth shut. He had been a superhero back then too, before a neck-height tripwire transformed him from the fastest man in the world to a decapitated head in a jar. He had once seen Optica peer into a lead-lined armored car, then use her heat vision to burn through the car and vaporize the mercury switch on a bomb that would have turned the people of Lake City into giant mutant gerbils. After that, he figured she had the right to wear whatever the heck she wanted. He wasn't about to criticize a woman who could kill you just by looking at you.

"She's fifty-three years old," Puff continued, tapping the screen of her phone. "Her costume doesn't even make sense. What do skintight hot pants and all that cleavage have to do with superpowered eyes?"

"You remember the rules," Jarhead said gently. "No phones."

Puff didn't answer, but her tail flapped against the base of her wheelchair, one of many, many ways she signaled annoyance. Unlike her parents, Puff dressed in heavy layers of dark, drab clothing that, in the words of her father, made her look like a homeless person. The only exception was her hair, which was styled into short blue spikes. She made a show of finishing what she was typing, then shoved the phone into her pocket.

"Thank you," said Jarhead. "How have you been doing on the goals we set last week? Homework and chores?"

"I got an A in algebra."

Jarhead waited.

It was Triton who broke the silence. "She failed her biology exam."

"What happened?" asked Jarhead.

Puff shrugged and made a show of studying the carpet.

"She doesn't study," said Optica. "When we remind her, she tells us to stop treating her like a child."

"It's not biology," Puff snapped. "It's *human* biology. I should be taking Intro to Medical Freaks instead."

"You're *not* a freak." Optica reached out.

Puff inhaled... and kept on going. Her body swelled, stretching her clothing tight. Spines poked through her skirts and sweatshirt, and she gripped the arms of her chair to keep from toppling forward. Her cheeks and eyes bulged, and she looked at her adopted parents as if to say, *Oh, yeah?*

While Jarhead hated to see his clients hurting, this was a good sign. At least Puff wasn't locking everything away inside.

Puff deflated and began picking at her clothes, sliding her spines back through newly-torn holes. Optica had jerked back, and now folded her hands in her lap, looking sadly at her daughter with those mesmerizing, all-black eyes.

"There are days she doesn't say a single word to either of us, from morning until bedtime," said Triton.

"What do you want me to say? 'Hey, mom. Guess what! The boy I like has an old cheesecake poster of you in his locker." Puff pantomimed gagging. "You wouldn't understand, Doctor J. You were one of them. Zipping around, punching bad guys and doing commercials for running shoes. It's like they don't know what to do with a problem they can't blow up or feed to a shark."

Before he could take advantage of the moment, someone knocked on the door.

"I'm with clients," he called out.

"This is the Lake City P.D."

"Figures," muttered Puff. "'Duty calls.' What else is new?"

"I'm sorry about this." Jarhead used the microneural circuitry connecting his brain into the technology in the base of the jar to remotely open the office door.

A squad of LCPD's finest waited, guns drawn, with polarized riot shields on their arms. Before anyone could react, they fired a Taser into the room, striking Optica in the shoulder. She seized and fell. Puff screamed and ballooned outward so hard she fell from her chair.

Triton leapt toward the door, but his powers were weaker on land, and another Taser took him down.

"I'm sorry," said a detective wearing a bullet-proof vest over a shirt and tie. "We have a warrant for the arrest of Optica and Triton."

"On what charge?" asked Jarhead.

The detective looked slightly embarrassed. "Tax fraud."

THE ARREST WAS only the beginning of Jarhead's headache. The detective called him later that day ... not to apologize, but to ask for Jarhead's help.

For the most part, Jarhead had come to terms with his lack of body, but some conversations called for a good old-fashioned facepalm. Slapping his jar with one of the mechanical spider-like legs built into the base just wasn't the same. "You're saying that in the two hours since you burst into my office to assault my clients, your men—a task force charged with bringing down supervillains—have managed to lose a mermaid in a wheelchair?"

"There was ... an incident." The speakers carrying the detective's voice through the bionutrient fluid in the jar conveyed both embarrassment and annoyance.

"What kind of incident?"

"Some sort of monkey/goat centaur things. They ambushed us. They'd gotten up onto the ledges of the credit union and the history museum. Damn things can climb like—"

"Like monkeys? Or mountain goats?"

"Yeah."

"Manchester."

"That's my guess. We've got a BOLO out to all units. Manchester's parole officer says he's has been checking in regularly. We searched his apartment, but it was empty."

"Did he capture Puff?"

"We don't think so."

Jarhead blew a thin column of bubbles, the equivalent of a relieved sigh. "Was anyone hurt?"

"You don't understand, Doc. They didn't attack us. Just shot steel lines across the road to stop traffic, and then the lead monkey-goat climbed down to deliver a court order."

"A court order?"

"It was almost cute. She was wearing a tiny suit jacket and tie." The detective hesitated. "I confirmed the order was legit."

"You're stalling," said Jarhead.

"Yeah. With the custodial parents under arrest, Michael Manchester is suing for custody of Tamara Jones."

JARHEAD HAD SPENT several sessions working to build trust and rapport. A text message from Puff was enough to confirm that those efforts had paid off.

Puff's family split their time between land and sea—another source of stress for a teenaged girl looking for stability and identity. Their land-based house was protected by an electronic security system keyed to a series of lasers Optica had designed in her free time.

Puff was too smart to try to hide out here. Between the initial arrest and her disappearance, the police would have searched her house at least three times. The computers had been taken, along with any files that might prove or disprove the allegations of tax fraud.

After turning off the alarm, Jarhead skittered into the

house and maneuvered himself through the doorway of Puff's room, a hybrid arrangement that reminded him of an oversized turtle aquarium. Half the room sank into a pool, while the other half held a small flat-screen TV, closet, and a poster of Albert Einstein sticking out his tongue. Plastic ponies lined several shelves on the wall. A large tank full of goldfish sat beside the pool. Puff had inherited a number of the blowfish's traits, including a voracious and predatory appetite. Those goldfish were the equivalent of a half-eaten bag of chips.

Jarhead retrieved a black electrical cord from the floor. He pulled up the display inside his jar and sent a text message. "At ur place. Got ur cellphone charger."

The response came quickly. "Thx. And don't say 'ur.' You're too old."

Jarhead sent an emoticon of a face with its tongue sticking out. "U know about the court order?"

"I'm NOT going with that creep."

"If the courts decide that using his genetic material as part of your creation gives him a parental claim ..."

"Then they can send a scuba team to try to catch me. Come on Dr. J. U know he framed my parents. Ugh. He's so creepy."

Jarhead paused. "Have you been talking to him?"

"He tried to friend me on Facebook. Like I even use that site anymore. My *parents* are on Facebook. I blocked him."

Jarhead's sensors picked up a faint noise from the next room. He amplified the microphones, trying to pinpoint what he had heard. "Gotta run. Company."

His mics weren't good enough to pick up heartbeats, but the quick breathing of three creatures one room over? No problem. He crept toward the door, then paused. Several of the goldfish in the tank floated upside down on the surface. Swimming over the gravel at the bottom was one of Manchester's spies, a tiny merman, half minnow, half fetus-like person, and 100 percent disturbing. "How long have you been hiding out here?"

It would be just Manchester's style to have installed a camera and transmitter into the merminnow's head. He'd known the instant Jarhead arrived. Jarhead crept into the living room to see what Manchester had sent. "That's new."

From the waist up, the creatures resembled small hawks, but their legs and tail were those of black, chitinous scorpions. One stood atop the sofa. The second was helping itself to butterscotch candies from a bowl on the coffee table. Like most of Manchester's creations, they showed little sign of intelligence. Puff was one of the few exceptions. The third spread its wings and swooped at Jarhead.

He waited for the clink of the thing's tail against the jar to stop. "You know, back in my day, supervillains were a little smarter. That glass will stop a .45 caliber bullet at point blank range. You're only going to hurt yourself."

The creature's tail stiffened, and a pointed flame erupted from the tip. It narrowed to a needle of blue fire.

"That's much better." Jarhead tipped himself forward, trying to crush the animal, but it scampered around the glass, continuing to try to cut through. His temperature sensors spiked. It was hard to say whether the flame would pierce the jar before it heated his biofluid to unsustainable temperatures. "Crap."

The other two flew at him in a cloud of feathers, adding two more blue-hot torches to the mix. One still clutched half a butterscotch in its beak.

In the old days, Jarhead would have moved too fast for them to touch him. He could have plucked every feather from their bodies between one wing beat and the next, and duct taped their tails so their weapons pointed at the backs of their own heads. Sadly, the ability to wiggle his nose at superspeed didn't do him much good now.

He climbed onto the counter and into the kitchen sink. The motors in his legs were strong enough to carry several times his weight. Once there, he used one of his manipulators to turn on the water and grab the sprayer. The water did nothing to stop the flames, but spraying it directly into their faces seemed to annoy them.

A tail slashed out, burning through the hose. So much for that.

Warning: Temperature reaching dangerous levels. His fluid cycled faster, the cooling mechanism trying to cope.

Jarhead pulled up the neurocontrols. His jar was a self-contained, self-sustaining environment, but every mechanical device required maintenance sooner or later, including the ability to change out his nutrient fluid. He mentally unlocked the drainage spout, tightened the valve, and overrode the safeties to increase the pump's pressure to dangerous levels.

The blast of blue biofluid slammed the creature's head against the end of the faucet. It gave a pathetic squawk and slumped to the bottom of the sink. He used his legs to grab the next one, yanked it around, and fired directly into the beak, blasting the butterscotch candy into its throat. It staggered away, hacking and choking.

The third flew away, either out of fear, or because Manchester had ordered it to retreat.

Jarhead tested his jar's metal limbs and checked the status of his systems. He hadn't had a good old-fashioned throwdown since the day he lost ninety percent of his body weight. That had almost been fun.

"You know, legally I'm obligated to report your whereabouts to the police."

Puff had taken refuge in the bay, hiding out in the shadows below the docks. Jarhead bobbed in the darkness beside her. His system was equipped for swimming and diving, using a series of small pumps to propel him through the water. The buoyancy was off, though, thanks to his expending a quarter of his biofluid against those flying scorpions. His eyes and scalp kept threatening to dry out, forcing him to perform rather ridiculous somersaults with his jar every few minutes to rehydrate.

Puff's eyes narrowed. "I'll be long gone before they get here."

"Exactly. So reporting you wouldn't help anyone. But as your therapist, it's my job to help you. The way I see it, our best chance is to prove your parents were set up, and that Manchester was behind it. That should be more than enough to get a judge to rule in your favor."

"How do you expect to do that?"

"I say we take the war to him. He broke into your home, so we break into his. We find the evidence we need, and—"

"You're as bad as my parents," Puff snapped. "Do I *look* like a superhero? What, am I supposed to dress up in spandex and follow you around as your sidekick now?"

"Don't be ridiculous. I'm not—"

"Oh, now I'm ridiculous? All I wanted from you was my stupid cellphone charger."

Jarhead used a claw to remove the charger cable from the compartment in his base. "Here you go. I put it in a baggie so it wouldn't get wet." He waited. "You have what you wanted, and we both know I can't stop you from swimming away."

She snatched it away and rolled her eyes. "I'm not interested in breaking into Manchester's lair and fighting past traps and guards and whatever else he has waiting. It's crazy."

"It's normal to be afraid—"

"I'm not afraid," Puff said, emphasizing every syllable.

"I'm telling you the whole superhero thing is stupid and archaic. Dressing up in costumes, trying to solve everything with your fists, always looking over your shoulder for the day your arch enemy kills your loved ones or banishes you to an alternate dimension. The only winners are the lawyers and the merchandisers selling action figures and movies and 'Super-inspired fashion.'"

"You might be right," said Jarhead. He had been thinking like a superhero, not a therapist. The fight at Puff's house had triggered old memories of a life he thought he'd left behind years ago. He was still feeling the aftermath of the adrenaline rush ... which was fascinating, now that he thought about it. He'd have to do some testing on how the adrenal gland worked when you were nothing but a head. Maybe he could get a paper out of it. "I'm sorry. You have every right to be angry."

"I know that." They bobbed in silence in the darkness beneath one of the docks. "I meant what I said. I'll run away rather than let him take me."

Jarhead started to assure her that he wouldn't let that happen, but that was him speaking as a superhero again. In the past twenty-four hours, Puff's world had been ripped apart.

But *she* hadn't. She had escaped both Manchester's monkey-goats and a team of highly trained police officers. "Why was your charger so important? You wouldn't risk me turning you in just so you could check Facebook."

"I told you—"

"I know, Facebook is for old people. You don't need me to come up with a plan. You already have one, don't you?" He studied her more closely, and smiled. "How can I help?"

Puff took a deep breath, enough to raise her spines slightly. "I could use a beta reader."

It took Puff just over twenty-four hours to bring Manchester down. Jarhead was impressed. Even with superspeed, it would have taken a while for him to find where Manchester was hiding, scout the location, and deal with whatever obstacles were waiting.

Puff didn't bother with any of that. She foiled his plan within twenty-four hours, using nothing but a smart phone, and stopping only to sneak onto one of the ferries to recharge it.

Unfortunately, as any experienced superhero could have warned her, villains were at their most dangerous when their plans were falling apart.

Jarhead and Puff had just picked up her chair from a dockside storage locker and were waiting for a wheelchair-friendly cab to arrive when the commotion started.

"What the hell are those?" Puff whispered.

With his quasi-legal attempt to gain custody of Puff ruined, Manchester had fallen back on his old tactics. Charging down the road were a pair of full-grown bulls with the long, flailing tentacles of a giant squid and the thick armor plating of an armadillo. "Three species in one," Jarhead commented. "He's finally changing things up a little."

A third ... squimadull? ... carried the doctor himself, a middle-aged man who made Frankenstein look like a male model. Manchester had spliced himself back together again and again over the years, until he was a patchwork of different races and species. Only the head and brain were original parts. In that respect, he and Jarhead had something in common.

Traffic screeched out of the way. Cars too slow to move were gored aside.

"Doctor J, I can't control my chair."

Manchester had probably found a way to hack it. Jarhead hoped the nanocircuitry in his jar was advanced enough to ward off similar attempts. He climbed onto the back of Puff's chair as it carried her toward Manchester.

"I tried to be civilized," Manchester shouted. "Once I discovered your home, my creatures could have poisoned your parents in their sleep. As a favor to you, I allowed them to live. And you repay me with slander and libel?"

Jarhead grinned. Puff had started by posting a series of animated gifs on Tumblr, showing clips of some of Manchester's more disturbing experiments. She had included a two-paragraph summary of how, despite being a convicted supervillain, nothing in the law prevented someone like Manchester from suing for custody.

What if it was your baby sister he kidnapped from the hospital? Your newborn daughter he cut and pasted into a monster. Bad enough he creates monstrosities like me, but should the insertion of a bit of his DNA give him ownership over his victims?

The last time Jarhead checked, that particular post had been reblogged six thousand times, with an additional twelve thousand "likes."

Similar clips, images, and pleas had gone live on Vine, Instagram, Superfriends, Twitter, and even Facebook. The results were impressive, and included a petition to the mayor with thousands of signatures; a barrage of Tweets targeting Lake City's elected representatives, three of whom had already vowed to fight any attempt to grant Manchester custody; and more.

It turned out that Puff's various online friend lists included a number of other superpowered kids. One had the ability to telepathically interface with the web. She had begun digging up Manchester's oldest and most embarrassing secrets, and posting them online. Another was some kind of superevolved computer genius, who had hacked the IRS computers to find evidence of Manchester's tampering. He had also provided the location of Manchester's hideout to a third superteen, one who had done some very careful and precise weather manipulation to create a wind that began at the waste treatment plant and ended in a slow-moving circle of air, concentrating the stench at Manchester's front door.

Jarhead amplified his speakers. "It's over, Manchester."

Manchester was experienced enough to have had long ago learned not to waste time with pointless monologues. He shouted a command, and one of the bullsquallos whipped a tentacle forward to pluck Jarhead from the wheelchair. Slimy, dripping suction cups surrounded him. They couldn't hurt the jar, but they blinded him to whatever was happening.

Jarhead jabbed two metal legs into the tentacle and sent an electric charge through his attacker. An instant later, he was flying through the air. He hit someone's windshield, breaking halfway through the glass and leaving a web of cracks around him.

By the time the biofluid stopped sloshing around, Manchester had reached Puff.

Jarhead scurried forward, then grinned. "You didn't think this through, did you?"

Puff had escaped her chair and expanded to her full size. She bristled like a porcupine in the middle of the road. An angry, venomous porcupine. She couldn't fight like that. She could barely move. But neither Manchester nor his creatures could touch her. From the way one of the animals whimpered and cradled a tentacle, they had already tried.

Another tried to carefully sneak a tentacle around Puff's throat. She grabbed the tentacle, pulled it close, and took an enormous bite. Never underestimate the appetite of a blowfish or a teenager.

"There's still time to run away before the police and superheroes arrive," Jarhead said.

Manchester's mount reached past Puff to grab a bystander. It hurled the man at Puff, who deflated to keep from impaling him. The tentacles snaked around her body, squeezing tight to prevent her from inflating again. Manchester laughed, and his mount turned to escape.

"Hey!" Jarhead skittered into the street. "Get your tentacles off my client."

He adjusted the output feed on his speakers and used the one weapon he had left. The weapon he had hoped never to have to use. Not because it was dangerous, but because it was ... embarrassing.

Bubbles filled his vision, but he saw the armasquidull

stumble. The bull head shook angrily, like it was trying to get rid of an annoying insect inside his skull. The other two creatures were already running away.

Jarhead walked toward them. He could hear sirens approaching.

Puff tumbled free as the animal wrapped its tentacles around its head, staggering in pain.

Manchester jumped down and strode toward them, a pistol-sized bioweapon of some sort clutched in his hands. "I don't know what weapon you've got hidden away in there, but we'll see how cocky you are once I've spliced you face-first to the back end of a cow! You'll—"

That was when Puff slapped him in the legs with her partially inflated tail, driving her spines deep into his leg.

He yelped and jumped away. His body wobbled. "Oh, hell."

With that, Manchester's eyes rolled up in his head, and he collapsed.

"I TOLD YOU," Puff said sullenly, sitting in her customary spot in Jarhead's office. "It's the twenty-first century. My parents are stuck in the past with their costumes and their showdowns and their battles in the middle of the city."

"How long have you been fighting crime?" asked Triton.

Puff shrugged. "We've been working as a team for a year or so. We have three other supers, and a few normals. You remember the scandal that killed Maximole's run for Governor? We were the ones who turned him into a laughingstock online."

"It's an impressive power," said Jarhead. "But remember—"

"You're going to give me the 'great power, great responsibility' lecture, aren't you?"

"I don't know," said Optica. "Fighting crime from a smart phone? With no costume, no secret identity—"

"Oh, please. I have six different identities," said Puff. "Neurogirl has thirty-four. And I guarantee my user icon is cooler than a few strips of spandex." She turned back to

Jarhead. "What I haven't been able to figure out is how you stopped Manchester from escaping. I was trapped, and then his animal suddenly went crazy."

If Jarhead's circulatory system had still been capable, he might have blushed. "I'm still a speedster, remember?"

"But you're ..." She gestured at the jar.

"That's right. Pretty much all I can do these days is wiggle my nose at superspeed" He pursed his lips. "However, sound is nothing but vibrations, and animals tend to have much better hearing than we do."

"You can shoot sonic beams out of that thing with your nose?" She covered her mouth and nose, but not before he saw her laughing. "That is so *weird*."

"Says the mermaid to the head in the jar," he shot back. "Now, it's going to take a while to process everything that's happened over the past day. But that doesn't mean we can ignore things like your biology grade."

Puff smiled. It was a dangerous, predatory smile. "I already emailed her about a make-up paper examining the physiology of a hawk-scorpion who choked to death on butterscotch candy ..."

Jim C. Hines

Jim C. Hines' first novel was **Goblin Quest**, the humorous tale of a nearsighted goblin runt and his pet fire-spider. After finishing the goblin trilogy, he went on to write the Princess series of fairy tale retellings, and is currently working on the *Magic ex Libris* books, a modern-day fantasy series about a magic-wielding librarian, a dryad, a secret society founded by Johannes Gutenberg, a flaming spider, and an enchanted convertible. His short fiction has appeared in more than 40 magazines and anthologies. You can find him online at www.jimchines.com.

THE RIGHT ANSWER

James A. Miller

While I certainly didn't plan on an alien encounter, my life had been in such a downward spiral that I had gotten used to expecting the unexpected.

Cheryl, my wife, and Ryan, my friend and boss, had been spending some extra time together without me—nights mostly. I handled this by 1) punching Ryan in the mouth, twice, then 2) spending the rest of the day drinking lunch, and 3) picking up dinner at the liquor store. On the way home, my car expired on the freeway by spewing steam and smoke then finally bursting into flames. I did, however, manage to rescue my bottle of dinner vodka before its fiery demise, but somehow forgot my personal laptop was in the back seat. I eventually reached home only to find Cheryl had gone. Judging by the amount of stuff she had taken with her, it was for good.

I surveyed what little remained in the house. In the living room there was carpeting with clean spots where the furniture had been, and a TV stand with no TV. In the kitchen I was left with one red plastic cup, an unopened box of flexible drinking straws, and a bag of pretzels. In the bedroom I saw a bed frame with no mattress or sheets, wire hangers, and a torn

Sports Illustrated. I grabbed the pretzels from the kitchen and made my way out onto the patio to get away from the heavy absence of material items. I was considering which lawn chair I might sleep in, when I noticed a little green creature standing in my back yard. It took a while for my senses to come into agreement; I was looking at Fonzie. Yes, Fonzie, the character played by Henry Winkler on *Happy Days*.

He didn't look at all like Fonzie in the face, or even his body type. In that regard he was as stereotypically expected: green, about four feet tall, three long fingers on each hand, comically big eyes, with no nose to speak of, and a very tiny mouth. It was the leather jacket, pinch rolled jeans, and perfectly greased jet black hair that gave the general appearance of the Fonz.

The creature leaned coolly against my fence, holding one finger of each hand in the air. I assumed those were the closest thing he had to thumbs.

"Aaaaaaaayyyy."

I am sure most other times I would have reacted with fear and horror, fleeing the situation in order to head straight for the police or psychiatric help, but tonight was special. I had given up caring about a lot of things, including concern for my own well-being. Whether this was an alcohol induced fantasy or plain old reality, I decided I had plenty of free time to roll with it.

"So you're an alien. Sure, why not. Before we get on with the probing, can you tell me why you're dressed like a *Happy Days* character?"

"I am a respected person from your media."

"How clichéd. So why Fonzie? Why not Abe Lincoln or Thomas Jefferson or Scarlett Johansson or Scarlett Johansson as a nurse or Scarlet Johansson as a naughty teacher, or any of the other Scarlett Johansson possibilities that I would be really open to right now?"

"Everybody loves the Fonz."

"I sure can't argue with that logic, but your timing is terrible.

You know that character went off the air thirty years ago."

"Is Arthur Fonzarelli no longer a viable form?"

"Well, let's just say if you're trying hard not to be noticed, there'll be a high degree of failure in your future. Right now, for me, you couldn't be more perfect. But do tell me, tiny Fonzie, what brings you all the way across the galaxy, or universe, or from New Jersey, to my pathetic back yard? Did Mary Beth dump Ritchie again?"

"I am here to share our technology with you."

The little guy didn't seem to be bothered by my sarcasm, which just invited more.

"No kidding? The old technology routine? Well ... okay, I'll take it. So does that come on a disk or some sort of thumb drive? Wait, you guys aren't all Linux, are you? I like that it's open source software but I am just not in love with the whole penguin for a logo thing. I had a bad experience at the zoo once. Those little guys will try to eat anything the size of a sardine."

"As the ambassador for your planet, you will first have to convince me why the human race is worthy to receive our gift."

"What?"

"As the ambassador for your planet, you will—"

"I heard what you said, but how did I become the ambassador?"

"Random pick."

"Out of six billion people? And yet, I can't get more than two right on Powerball. That figures. Say, I hope you don't mind, the ambassador has had way too much to drink, so I am just going to go ahead and urinate by this shrub over here. "

Little Fonz only shrugged. For some reason his indifference made me belligerent. Or, I should say, more belligerent. I stepped up to a rant while watering, or maybe killing, an arbor-vitae.

"You are really too much; you know that, Fonzie? 'Worthy of your gift.' What makes you think your technology is any better than what we've got? You're from the fifties."

"I traveled here. When was the last time *you* left *your* planet?"

"You mean me personally?"

"The question was meant to be rhetorical."

He shuffled across my burnt-out grass and sat in the lawn chair I had just been using before nature called. Clearly his sense of etiquette wasn't tuned for the subtleties of how long you should wait before taking over someone's seat. Once his skinny ass hit the chair, I realized it would be even harder to take him seriously. Past the pinch-rolled jean cuffs were lanky lime-green chicken feet. He was short enough that when he was sitting his feet didn't even touch the ground.

I caught an odor from him that reminded me I should check the cat's litter box.

"Whew, can I offer you something to freshen up with? I'd recommend Lysol."

"You have three attempts to convince me."

"Of what? Our worthiness?"

"Aaaaaaaayyyyy," he said again, with fingers in the air.

"Was that a 'yes'? Because it seemed like it meant 'Hello' earlier."

I zipped up and we looked at each other silently. I noticed that he had a third set of eyelids, and he noticed that I had a bag of pretzels.

"What are the rules on this thing?" I asked.

"No rules," he said, between quick crunching bites of pretzel.

"So I just have to come up with a good enough reason and the gates to your E.T. knowledge will open up for all mankind?"

"Yes."

"Um, okay. So is it something along the lines of 'We are a noble and honorable species, and we would do great things with your technology to benefit all of mankind'?"

"No. You have two attempts left."

"Wait, that was a dry run. I was talking out loud."

"Too late."

"Jeez. Was I at least even close?"

"No."

He started coughing dryly as though something was stuck in his throat. I offered the only liquid I had readily available, his tiny mouth barely fitting over the top of the vodka bottle. He took three quick gulps before throwing up a fluorescent yellow slime all over my patio. Along with the small chunks of pretzel, there were little white insects crawling around in the mess.

"Whoa. I take it you're not a martini man."

Green Fonzie dropped to the ground and started picking the white bugs from the goo. He gathered a handful, and swallowed them. Except for the white bugs, I probably wasn't too far off from having my night end the same way.

Little Fonz jumped back up in the chair and returned to the pretzels.

"Just what kind of technology are we talking about?" I asked. "Because if it's those little white stomach bugs, I'm not so sure we're interested."

He sat up in the chair, let the bag of pretzels drop, and pulled what looked like a switchblade knife from his leather jacket. He pressed a button that should have flipped it open to a blade, or in Fonzie's case, a comb, but instead the device started projecting an intense white beam of light. He fiddled with a tiny knob on the side of it until he had tuned the beam to a dark green. With a wave of his Kermit-the-Frog arm, tiny Fonz ran the beam along the back of my yard, planting a row of thirty-foot tall pine trees that continued through my fence, then into, and up through, the neighbor's garage.

Walt was going to be pissed about that.

Little green Fonzie changed the beam to red, and with another wave, cut down the first few trees. They crashed onto the other fence line, destroying part of Susan Anderson's gazebo and all of her quarter scale wooden windmill.

Susan was *really* going to be pissed. It was, however, an impressive display.

"Ok, so you've got something there," I said.

Susan came running out of her house. Even though it was after nine, she was, as usual, still in a business suit. She had always played that off on "the busy life of a Real Estate Agent," but I think it just made her feel important. It certainly made her act that way.

"Oh, my! Oh, my! Is anyone hurt? Oh, my!"

It was all so ladylike and professional until she got to the flattened windmill. There was a flash of horror on her face that was quickly replaced with an angry sour look as she peered across the felled trees, seeing that they originated in my yard, and yet somehow completely missing the fact that the trees weren't there the day before.

"What in the hell happened to my wind—"

Susan fell to the ground. I turned to see my pretzel-loving friend pointing the device in her direction.

"You didn't?"

"She's only sleeping."

I looked back at Susan. There was a subtle movement of her chest and the sound of a quiet snore. Her leg was bent at an uncomfortable angle, but I could live with that. After what that rumor mill had put me through, oh how I could live with that.

I immediately thought of two other people that I wouldn't mind being able to put to sleep at will or drop trees on. I looked back at the Fonz.

"You're right. I could definitely use that thing."

"Why are you worthy?"

He said "you" as though maybe my situation had something to do with it. Maybe it wasn't random at all, but maybe they had been watching me, or even setting me up. I had seen Star Trek; I knew the classic answer to the question was that the human race has compassion and that we have the ability to love. So maybe Fonz wanted to see if an embittered guy like me could still believe in such a thing.

I thought back on my relationship with Cheryl for a

moment and realized that yes, I still did believe in love. Maybe it wasn't the case anymore, but at one time Cheryl and I were very much in love; I was quite certain of that.

If I was going to be honest about it, the infidelity may not have been entirely her fault either.

As innocent as I wanted to be in the whole her and Ryan thing, the truth was Cheryl and I had been drifting apart for some time. I knew it, I felt it, and yet I did nothing about it. I just didn't think we had quite drifted to the shores of infidelity, not yet anyway. At least I hadn't drifted that far. Maybe the fact that she was the first to find someone else was making me the most upset. Or that it had to be that S.O.B. that used to be my best friend.

Even though I wasn't "in love," anymore, down deep inside I could honestly say I still believed in love. It seemed like the right answer. I kept thinking about it until I had convinced myself that it *had* to be the right answer.

"I think we are worthy because we can love."

"No. One attempt left."

"What? How can love not be it?"

"Love is a participant emotion in the biological imperative for your sexual reproduction."

"No—not always. In fact, thinking back to college, probably not even most of the time. And what about a mother's love for her children?"

"Parental love is a participant emotion necessary for the protection of offspring until maturity."

"You are sounding less and less like Fonzie. He would never say any of that."

"One attempt left."

The little guy was pissing me off. It didn't help that I was incredibly bad at the challenge, and I'd probably lost some respect for him when I realized he couldn't hold his liquor.

I tried to look at the question from another perspective. What could possibly qualify us as "worthy"? We didn't exactly have the best track record. We were constantly killing each other off with some sort of war. And we had no problem messing with our environment until we were now facing an impending global climate change.

Even our leaders were embarrassing: Hitler and his Nazis, Nixon with the Watergate scandal, and then there was that whole Bill Clinton—Monica Lewinski thing.

It seemed that the definition of being human was to make mistakes. Fallibility was the cornerstone of our existence. It occurred to me that maybe the right answer was that we *weren't* worthy of such technology. Even though I wasn't quite sure what their full technological menu had to offer, the appetizer seemed pretty daunting. Hell, Susan was still sleeping, and that ability alone was probably more than most people could handle.

"You know what, Fonz? I don't think we deserve it. That's my final answer; all in. The human race is not worthy of your technology. You heard it right. *Not* worthy."

"You are correct."

"I got it?"

"No, the answer is wrong. You are correct that you are not worthy."

"Oh well, no biggie I guess, I just struck out for the entire human race. Could you just kick me in the nuts before you go? That would kind of finish my week off nicely."

The Fonz stared at me as though he were seriously considering my last statement. I found myself wondering how bad a chicken claw kick to the crotch could really be.

"What was the right answer by the way?" I asked.

"Humor."

"Humor? Why is that it?"

"There is no biological reason for laughter. There is no other species on this planet or in the universe that possesses that ability."

"And how would that make us worthy?"

"It alone does not, but knowledge of its power does. Humor has the ability to cure your planet of its ailments."

"You are going to have to explain that one to me."

"I'll let you think about it."

With that final enigma, Fonzie was gone. No ship, no flash of light, nor vortex of a wormhole, just gone.

Past Walt's garage I could see the lights of his pickup as it came up the driveway. He turned off the truck and got out, surveying the pines sticking through the roof of his garage. He saw Susan sleeping in the yard, listened to a few heavy snores and then turned his to focus to me.

Somewhere in the universe, my little Fonzie was taking off his jacket and jeans, ungreasing his hair, and telling whoever sent him that Earth was not ready to receive their technology. I felt pity for the lot of them, because they didn't possess the sense of humor needed to appreciate the look on Walt's face.

"What in the hell happened here?"

"An alien did it," I said, taking a pull from the vodka bottle.

Walt rolled his eyes, turned, and went into the house.

I guess that wasn't the right answer either.

James A. Miller

James A. Miller is an electrical engineer who lives in a small town west of Madison, Wisconsin. Much of his day is spent programming machines to do the things people want them to do. Much of his night is spent with his family. In the times in between, he reads or writes, and thinks about possibility. And then there is that dang rental property where the tenants are always complaining. That seemed like a great idea before the whole Real Estate meltdown. Stupid. He should have just got a part time job at McDonald's. He blogs at breakingintothecraft.wordpress.com. This is his first published story.

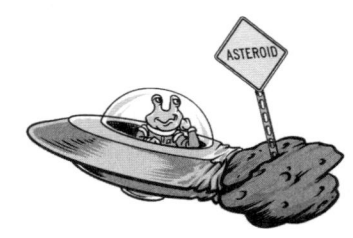

THE GEFILTE FISH GIRL

Mike Resnick

So I walk up to her and say, "Ma, we gotta talk."

And she never looks up from the TV, and she says, "Not during *Homemakers' Jamboree*, Marvin."

And I say, "Ma, I'm Milton. Marvin is your *goniff* brother who is serving six to ten for passing bogus bills." (Which he is. He's a great artist, even the judge admitted that, but he just doesn't do his homework, and printing a bunch of twenties with Andrew Johnson's picture on them is probably not the brightest move he ever made.)

Anyway, she says "Marvin, Milton, what's the difference, and did you know that Liz Taylor is getting married again? What is it for her now—the thirty-fourth time?"

And I say, "You know, Ma, it's funny you should bring that up."

And she says, "Funny? Okay, Mister Big Shot, tell me what's so funny. Are you the one she's marrying? Go ahead, make my day."

And I say, "Lots of people get married, Ma. Some of them even get married to women who aren't Liz Taylor, hard as that may be for you to believe."

And she says, "Lots of *mature* people, Melvin."

And I say, "Melvin is my cousin who ran off with the gay lion tamer from the circus. I'm Milton, and speaking of mature, I'm thirty-four years old."

And she says, "You'd think someone who's thirty-four years old would know to change his socks without being told." Suddenly she curses and says, "See? You made me miss today's health tip. Here I sit, waiting to go to the hospital for a nerve transplant from all the *tsouris* you cause me, and I can't even watch my television in peace."

So I say, "You're in great shape, Ma. Every artery's as hard as a rock."

"*Feh!*" she says. "God has reserved a special place in hell for ungrateful sons."

"I know," I say. "It's probably right next to where He puts all the henpecked husbands."

"Don't you go making fun of my dear departed Erwin," she says.

"I wasn't," I say. "And besides, all we know is that he departed in one hell of a hurry. We don't know for sure that he's dead."

"If he isn't, he should be, that *momser*!" she says.

Well, I can see the thought that he may be alive and God forbid enjoying himself is about to drive her wild, so I try to mollify her.

"Okay, okay," I say, hoping the Lord is otherwise occupied and does not hear what I am about to say. "May God Himself strike me dead if he's not your late husband."

"Well, he was late for most things," she agrees, leaning back in her chair. "Except in the bedroom. *There* he was always early."

I try to change the subject again.

"We were talking about marriage," I say.

"Someday, when you're old enough," she says, "you'll get married and ruin some poor Jewish girl's happiness, just the way your dear departed father ruined mine, and the only good thing that will come of it will be a grandson who, knock wood, won't take after his father and his grandfather but will show me a little respect and compassion."

I begin to see that this is going to be even more difficult than I thought, and I try to come up with a subtle way to break the news to her. So I think, and I think, and I think some more, and finally I say, as subtly as I can, "Ma, I'm engaged."

And she looks away from the television set and takes her feet off the hassock and plants them on the floor, and stares at me for maybe thirty seconds, and finally she says, "Engaged to do what?"

"To get married," I say.

She digs into her sewing kit, which is on the floor next to her, and pulls out a scissors.

"Here," she says, handing it to me. "Why waste all afternoon rushing me to the hospital's cardiac unit? Just stab me now and be done with it."

"Jugular or varicose?" I ask.

"Schmendrick!" she says. "How can the fruit of my looms talk to me like this?"

"I'm the fruit of your loins, Ma," I tell her. "Fruit of the Loom is what I'm wearing beneath my pants."

"All right," she says. "Just stand there and watch me breathe my last."

"Your last what?" I ask.

She glares at me and finally says, "Before I die, at least tell me the name of this female person you're engaged to do whatever with."

"Melora of the Purple Mist," I say.

"Melora of the Purple Mist?" she repeats. "How can I fit all that on a wedding invitation?"

"Just use Melora," I say.

"And what bowling alley or topless club didi you meet Miss Whats-her-name of the Purple Mist at?" she asks.

"I met her at work, kind of," I answer.

"I *knew* it!" she says, poking a pudgy forefinger into the air. "I knew I should never let you take that job with the sewage company!"

"It's a salvage company," I say.

"Sewage, salvage, what's the difference?" she demands. "It's that Gypsy who walks around half-naked with her deathless beauty sagging down to her *pupik*, right? I *told* you she had her sights set on you!"

"She's not a Gypsy, and it's not her. She's just another diver."

"So you're marrying some other girl who lies around on deck with her *tuchus* soaking up the sun," she says. "I should feel better about that?"

"She doesn't lie around on deck," I say uneasily.

"On deck, below deck, big difference," she snaps.

"Bigger than you think," I say. "The truth of it is, she spends most of her time about 50 feet below deck."

"So she's a diver," she says.

"Not exactly," I answer.

"What, then?"

"Try not to get real excited, Ma," I say.

"I'm not excited, I have convulsions all the time," she says. "Just tell me."

"She's a mermaid," I say.

"As long as she's not that Gypsy girl," she says, fanning herself with the *TV Guide*. "Or that lady bartender from last summer. Or the bug woman."

"The entomologist," I correct her.

"Whatever," she says. "So tell me about this Purple Mist person."

"Like I said, she's a mermaid."

"Like what, she has a tail and spends her whole life in the water?" she asks.

"That's right," I say.

"Does she wear a bra?" she says suddenly.

"Ma!" I say, outraged.

"You heard me—does she wear a bra?"

"No," I finally answer.

"Figures," she says.

"What a thing to ask!" I say.

"What do you want me to ask?" she says. "My son comes home and tells me he's marrying someone who's covered with scales and spends all her time swimming in salt water, despite what it must do to her complexion. So can she at least get us a price on fresh fish?"

"It's not something I'm real concerned with," I say.

"Of course not," she says. "You're as impractical as your late father." She sighs. "All right, so where did this female person go to school?"

"I don't think she did," I say.

"Ah!" she says with a knowing nod. "Rich family with a private tutor. What temple do they belong to?"

"Who?"

"Her family," she says. "Try to pay attention, Martin."

"Martin is your nephew who went broke manufacturing the folding waterbed," I say. "I'm Milton, remember?"

"Don't change the subject," she says. "What temple do they go to?"

"They don't," I say.

"They're Reformed?" she asks.

I take a deep breath and say, "They're not Jewish at all," and then I wait for the explosion.

It takes about three-millionths of a second—a new record.

"You're marrying a *shiksa*?" she bellows.

"I'm marrying a mermaid," I say.

"Who cares about *that*?" she screams. "Call my doctor! I'm having a coronary!"

"Ma, try to understand—there *aren't* any Jewish mermaids," I say.

"It's *my* fault?" she demands. "It's bad enough that you want to give me grandsons with fins—and how in the world will the rabbi perform the *bris*?—but now you tell me that their mother's a *goy*?"

"I knew I was gonna have trouble with you," I say unhappily.

"Trouble?" she shrieks. "Why should there be trouble? Your Uncle Nate will come by with a knife and a cracker and say, 'Is this a jar of Baluga caviar?', and I'll say 'No, it's forty thousand of my grandchildren.'"

"Will you at least meet her?" I ask.

"Some conversation we'll have," she replies. "She'll say 'Blub!' I'll say 'Gurgle!' and she'll say 'Glub!' and I'll say 'I'm getting the folds,' and she'll say—"

"That's the bends, not the folds," I explain.

"Bends, folds, what's the difference?" she says. "I plan to be dead of a heart attack in two more minutes."

"She speaks English," I say, getting back to the subject.

"She does?"

"With a beautiful lilting accent."

"I knew it!" she says. "You're too young to remember, but they drove our people out of Lilting before the last war ..."

"Lilting isn't a place, Ma," I say.

"It isn't?" she says suspiciously. "Are you sure of that?"

"I'm sure," I say. "She really wants to meet you."

"I'll just bet she does," she says. "She probably wants to feed me to her pet lobster."

"I don't think lobsters eat people," I say.

"Aha!" she says. "But you don't *know*!"

"We're getting off the subject," I say.

"Right," she agrees. "The subject was my imminent death."

"The subject was Melora."

"What does this fish person who doesn't wear a bra want with you anyway?" she demands. "Why doesn't she go elope with some nice halibut?"

"I met her while I was hunting for treasure," I say. "It was love at first sight."

"So what you're saying is that you went down there looking for gold and what you came up with was a topless person of the Purple Mist?"

"You're making this very difficult, Ma."

"You bring home a cod for dinner, and instead of cooking it I have to give it my son, and *I'm* making this difficult?" she says, just a bit hysterically.

I figure it's time to play my ace in the hole, so I say, "She's willing to convert, Ma."

"Into what—a woman with two or more legs?"

"To Judaism," I say. "I told her how important it was to you."

"How can she convert?" she says. "Do we know any rabbis who can hold services fifty feet under the water?"

"She can come to the surface," I say. "How else would we talk?"

"When did you ever *talk* to a girl?" she says. "You're just like your departed father."

"We talk all the time," I say.

She considers this and finally nods her head. "I suppose there's not a lot else you can do."

"Don't get personal, Ma," I say.

She raises her eyes to the heavens—which are just beyond the lightbulb in the middle of the ceiling—and has another of her hourly chats with God. "He wants me to welcome a lady fish into my family and he tells me not to get personal."

"A lady Jewish fish," I point out.

"So okay, she won't be just a fish girl, she'll be a gefilte fish girl, big deal. What do I feed her? If I give her lox, will she accuse me of cooking her relatives?"

"She eats fish all the time, Ma."

"And when we leave the table to go watch Oprah, do I carry her or does she slither on her belly?"

"Actually, she doesn't watch Oprah," I say.

"She doesn't watch Oprah?" she says, and I can tell this shocks her more than the fact that Melora is a mermaid. "What's wrong with her?"

"She's never seen a television," I say. "They don't have them in her kingdom."

"What are they, some kind of Communists?" she demands.

"They don't have any electricity," I explain.

"You mean she doesn't even have a food processor?"

"That's right," I say.

"That poor girl!" she says. "And no disposal unit in her sink?"

"None," I say, and I can see that suddenly she's working up a head of sympathy.

"How can anybody live like that?" she says.

"She manages just fine."

"Nonsense!" she says. "Nobody can live without a trash masher. My son's wife may be a fish, but she isn't going to slave thirty hours a day just because *I* had to!"

"That's very thoughtful, Ma," I say. "But—"

"Don't interrupt!" she snaps. "You bring her by this afternoon. I'll have some knishes ready, and some blintzes, and maybe a little chopped liver, and we'll watch Oprah and I'll show her my kitchen and ..." Suddenly she stops and re-thinks her schedule. "Bring her earlier and we can watch Dr. Phil, too. And tonight they're re-running that old series with Lloyd Bridges. It should make her feel right at home."

"You'll like her, Ma," I promise.

"Like, *shmike*," she says. "If I have to go through life without ever being able to point to my son the doctor, at least I can point to my almost-daughter the gefilte fish girl. Mrs. Noodleman down the block will be so jealous!" She pauses. "We'll have to put a little meat on her bones."

"You haven't even seen her," I say.

"That's all right," she says. "I know your taste in women.

Cheap and skinny."

"Ma, you think any woman under two hundred pounds is skinny."

"And you think any woman who doesn't ask for ice cubes and a straw with her wine is sophisticated." She gets up, and I can see she's getting set for a couple of hours of serious puttering. "Now, you go get her and bring her back, while I prepare something for the poor undernourished thing to eat. And I think I'll invite Rabbi Bernstein, since we need someone to work with her, and he's always fishing when he should be at Temple, and ..."

As I leave, she is trying to remember which company sells the pens that write under water so she can send out wedding invitations to the bride's family.

Mike Resnick

Mike Resnick is, according to *Locus*, the all-time leading award winner, living or dead, for short fiction. He has won 5 Hugos (from a record 36 nominations), a Nebula, plus other major awards in the USA, France, Croatia, Spain, Japan, Catalonia, and Poland. He is the author of 75 novels, close to 300 stories, and 3 screenplays, and the editor of 41 anthologies. He is currently the editor of *Galaxy's Edge* magazine. Mike was the Guest of Honor at the 2012 Worldcon.

MASTER OF BUSINESS APOCALYPSE

Jakob Drud

For the last one hundred thirty-one years my job at Mundo Perpetuo has been to stop all the probable and improbable apocalypses that people accidentally invoke. I've worked my way up from junior meteor diverter to viral containment specialist, and now, as the most senior staff member, I get to run the Department of Mixed Ends of the World. If the dinosaurs return, or civilization as we know it is threatened by falling anvils, Old Joe steps up to bat.

And still, some days the world takes me by surprise, like the day when Paula Johnson greeted me in the lobby with these words: "Mr. Inflectus. I am to inform you that our new CEO, Mr. Halen, has called a meeting of all department heads at 9:00 A.M., and that you are now five minutes late."

Around the office I just go by the name of Joe, so her salutation stopped me dead in my tracks. "And, eh, a very formal morning to you too, Ms. Johnson. New CEO, you said?"

Paula just cracked her knuckles, a gesture I knew as danger incarnate. Her magic was capable of manipulating physical objects in disturbing ways, which made her the best security chief in the northern hemisphere. She was also an archivist of unrivalled skills, and both abilities had saved my life time and again. If she felt threatened, I did, too.

I power-stepped up the stairs, one flight at a time, wondering what we needed a CEO for. We'd been without a nominal leader for the last eight years since our former director had fired himself for being redundant. But when I entered Conference 2, I knew right away that our new CEO would never reach a similar conclusion. He was a young white guy with flashy teeth, a black Armani suit and a shave so close he must have had his hair follicles surgically removed.

"Joseph Inflectus? From Mixed Ends of the World? Glad you could finally join us," he said, mistaking acidity for authority. "Please have a seat. Now, as I was telling everyone before you chose to show up, I am your new boss, and you may address me as Mr. Halen."

I'm not big on self-imposed authority, and I'm afraid it showed in the way I sat down next to Antonio Suarez from Pandemics: as slowly as I possibly could, I waited until Mr. Halen drew breath to speak again, and then found my most casual voice.

"Have you ever directed a magical department before, Mr. Halen?"

"Of course not. You're the only one in the country."

"That you know of," said Ingrid Blunt from Nuclear Holocausts. "Do you have any experience with enchantments, summoning, or protection spells?"

That got a laugh and a flash of those bright, shiny teeth. "Don't worry, I'm leaving the hokus pokus to the professionals. My qualifications are in leadership. I've got an MBA from Yale. When I was office intern at WaterHome Crunch, I took a BPCD at BPCC and soon graduated to internal office department HoC. After WaterHome Crunch I moved on to—"

Speaking of hokus pokus. I cleared my throat Archwizardly, that is to say, in the way that made people Pay Respectful Attention.

Mr. Halen just looked annoyed. "Yes?"

"Mundo Perpetuo has prevented every conceivable apocalypse in the last seventy-five centuries, saving Earth and mankind at least a thousand times over. Proof of our efficiency: you've not been turned into a vampire, infected with a deadly virus, irradiated, flattened by a meteor, smothered by a vengeful deity, or drowned in an antediluvian tide. We intend to keep you and the rest of the world that way. The question is, Mr. Halen, what you bring to the table."

He showed his teeth and steepled his fingers. "I'm going to increase turnover. Together we'll make profits skyrocket."

The last word made B.S. Belamy, head of Alien Invasions, flinch habitually. The horror I read on the other faces had been conjured by another phrase.

"You may be CEO, Mr. Halen," said Manfred Parsons, head of Undead Outbreaks. "But continue to think that way and you'll be DOA." Working zombie apocalypses for half a century had blunted Parson's sense of humor and situational awareness. Zombies need a firm hand, not subtlety.

"What Parsons means is that we don't need increased turnover." I stressed the last word. "The fewer apocalypses we have to prevent, the better."

"That's where you're wrong," Mr. Halen said. "As of today, Mundo Perpetuo is paid for every alien/nuclear/zombie/rapture disaster we prevent. It's all in the new guidelines from the Board of Directors."

Only Flower Agyll, head of Supernatural Endings, crossed her arms as if to indicate further resistance. "Let me guess," she said. "Your bonus depends on the bottom line."

He beamed. "My PowerPoint presentation will explain everything in detail."

Everybody's eyes glazed over until Chai Chen from Natural Disasters mouthed the words of the 3P protection spell.

FLOWER AGYLL GUESSED right, which became very clear four hours into the presentation when Mr. Halen laid out a long list of expenditure cuts. Those included the demand that everyone put in extra hours, a preliminary 10 percent staff cut, and a plan to use cheaper materials for our spells.

Which was why I made it my first priority to visit Madison Stars, Chairman of the Intact Foundation. The foundation was our meal ticket, a money hoard directed by seven imaginative people, who understood how many different ends the Earth would see if it weren't for Joe and the crew. Madison Stars herself knew just enough magic to do no harm, but her real skills lay in finance and leadership, where she had an efficient yet caring way with people.

But the minute I laid out my grievance, her friendliness evaporated. I suddenly felt like a tool in her presence. Like a coat stand, albeit a specially commissioned, one-of-a-kind coat stand.

"Harlan Burgeson and Tara LeGoff resigned last week to spend more time with their families," she explained. "Instead we got two guys from a bank, and they pointed out that we could save a lot of money and use the surplus to support another charity, like cancer research or new antibiotics. These guys just can't wrap their head around the idea that your organization takes precedence over all others."

"I'd love to wrap their heads around something for you."

"Except we have those pesky rules, don't we?" Meaning the Wizard Code and the death sentence awaiting any out-of-line magic user.

"Look, we can try Halen for a while," I said. "Some of the Vietnamese reagents he's ordered really are a bargain compared to the handpicked organic kind. But I don't see how bringing in a CFO and a HR department is going to save money, and trust me, you don't want to risk us being underfunded."

"It's new times, Joe. Everybody's underfunded."

She put a hand on my shoulder, squeezed it firmly. The encouraging touch of an experienced leader who knew that change could tax an employee, but also the firm grip of a leader bent on her current strategy. For all my respect for Madison, it still felt like being held from the scruff of the neck by a very big hellhound. And trust me, I know how that feels.

Mr. Halen's HR department fired twenty of our two hundred wizards the next week. Fortunately, it was a light week with only one massive meteor impact to prevent and one invasion of an algae-like species that threatened to cover the oceans in a rock-hard surface, and we had advance warning against both apocalypses.

All magical apocalypses siphon off a lot of energy from the magical field that separates the Earth's inner and outer core. It doesn't matter where on Earth the apocalypse is going to start, or who starts it. A trained apocalypse wizard can sense the waning magical field as a weakening in their own powers.

We call it advance warning when the siphoning starts long before the actual spell is called down. That means the energy gathers in a particular area—just where a crazy cult is about to light a bonfire and read out loud from *The Martha Stewart Living Cookbook*, for instance. It's easy to pinpoint the energy, so I can just show up on the night of the bonfire, call up a rainstorm to put out the fire, and voila: the world doesn't meet a culinary end, and the energy is reabsorbed in the Earth's core.

In other cases, we have no warning. That's when we get to stop rifts in the fabric of reality, and that's where having extra magicians on your payroll is usually really handy. And of course, our next six weeks were filled with such incidents.

Flower Agyll and her Supernatural Endings staff worked around the clock to stuff fire-breathing imps back through rifts appearing all over the globe and manipulate people's memory to allow them to sleep again. At one time she even had demons invading her office, and we all had to pitch in with salt and banishing spells before Mr. Halen found out and told her to work from home over the weekend. I also got to spend an eventful Thursday night in the Rocky Mountains where a cult was trying to call down the Rapture using a black cat and a pentagram of albino rats. Their amateur chant would most likely only have ignited Mount St. Helens, but I stopped them anyway on principle.

I attended to my own Ends, too. An evil breed of supervillains summoned from a comic book decided to rid the world of humans. Whacking bad guys with fireballs was great therapy for my frustrations, but then a new species of intestine-eating worms threatened Earth's water supply. For five days straight I teamed up with Chai Chen from Natural Disasters to cleanse every drop of H_2O on the planet, so when the office closed up on the seventh Friday after Mr. Halen's arrival, I felt about as archwizardly as a molten slice of cheese.

Times were when I'd devoted Friday nights to studies, or quizzing librarians and movie critics about what kind of Ends to expect. That Friday, though, I just wanted to sleep. I wasn't even up to power-stepping down the stairs.

As I waited for the elevator, Mr. Halen caught up with me.

"Hey Joe, I wanted to ask you: How do you start an apocalypse?"

"I don't," I said truthfully. "Only idiots call down the End of the world, and most do it unawares. We interpret the signs and set out to stop the Ends before it's too late. Usually a summoning takes a couple of weeks to fully appear, but ..."

I swore inwardly—wizards really shouldn't swear out loud—when I saw in his grin what he'd concluded from that statement: That we had plenty of time.

"But how do those idiots do it?" he asked. "Do they read Lovecraft novels out loud? Look in the mirror and say 'Zombie' five times, or what?"

"Mindless shambling scumbag," I said. "Technical term."

Oblivious to the double entendre, Mr. Halen put an arm around my shoulder and pulled me into the elevator.

"We really need to generate more business, Joe. Since you're in that Mixed department, you can't have much to do. I'm putting you in charge of calling down new Ends of the world, but keep it to one or two a week for now, alright? We must be able to break the records in the next fiscal quarter."

The elevator 'dinged' and he exited. I had to take the elevator up and back down in order to not violate every paragraph in the Wizard Code at the same time.

I could live with saving money. I could live with hard work and sacrifice. But if you have ever stood on the brink of having land-walking squids appear in every city, town and hamlet of the world, no one is going to talk you into summoning a single cephalopod.

When I finally left the elevator, I had made up my mind. Board or no board, Mr. Halen would have to go.

I CAME IN on Monday to find Flower Agyll arguing with Mr. Halen outside his office. I'd made a couple of plans that weekend to get the entire firm behind me, and Flower Agyll had been aboard from the beginning.

"I'm down three wizards," she said rather loudly. "If two of my staff call in sick at the same time, and three Raptures are called at once, I won't answer for the consequences."

"Don't worry!" Mr. Halen beamed. "I'm hiring a secretary for all department heads. That'll give you more time to handle your little disasters. Besides, all companies allow for a margin of error."

"You're saying we should be content with a 5 percent Ragnarok? Ask Suarez. He'll tell you that's the kind of thinking that led to the Black Death."

"You can't," I said. "He called in sick."

"Well, he better get his ass in here, because his department is underperforming by several percent, and I'm not ..." Halen stopped. Doors were opening all along the hallway, and department heads swarmed our little gathering.

"Suarez called in sick?" Belamy asked. "It can't be the L'ln'qi virus. We dispelled every trace last week, and the incubation time is only fourteen minutes."

"It's not a zombie infestation," Parsons said. "And even if it were, I gave him that baseball bat for his birthday."

"Nothing flooded his house, neither sea nor lava," Chai Chen said.

"I watch CNN," Mr. Halen said tersely. "But let me assure you, it's all taken care of. Suarez will be back soon, and if it's long term I'll get HR to find a middle manager to take care of things while he's gone."

"Mr. Halen," I intoned. "It is the first time the head of Pandemics called in sick. Ever."

"I'm sure it's just a cold. Joe, I read your resume. Level sixty-six technically gives you the skills to cover for him."

But he didn't flash his teeth, and I could all but see the worry in his mind. Not about Suarez, of course, but about living up to his contract with the board.

"There's something I'd like to ask your advice about," I said, nodding towards his office.

He closed the door behind us. "What?"

"I can call up the extra apocalypses you asked for. But I looked over some of the newest research this weekend ..." (Like hell I did. The best research was done in the sixteenth century, but guys like Mr. Halen like their research new, not good.) "... and I found something about a condition we call a Cosmic Resonant Simultaneous Conflux."

He looked blank, which was to be expected. After all, I'd made up the Conflux theory myself. However, I needed him to believe it, so I switched to acronyms.

"A CReSiC happens when we have too many different apocalypses at the same time and they start to influence each other. Falling pianos start causing strange new diseases, vengeful deities use nuclear weapons, and meteor impacts bring the dinosaurs back. In short, the cost of dealing with disaster triples."

I had his full attention now.

"And sometimes we have to go to truly extreme measures to save the world," I added.

"Such as?"

I opened my briefcase and handed him the package I had prepared over the weekend.

"Your predecessor left this," I said, lying through my teeth. "I didn't give it to you before because I didn't want to worry you, but I'd really hate for anything like this to happen again. But we're only two disasters away from a potential CReSiC."

I put on my best remorseful smile and stalked out before he could ask any questions.

Back in my office I cast the spell that let me listen in while Mr. Halen rummaged through the package. It contained apocryphal summoning schematics, detailed descriptions of the human sacrifice necessary to dispel a CReSiC, and a diary. The latter, written over the weekend by a couple of very imaginative fantasy writers, purported to show the escalating panic of our former CEO as more and more ends of the world overwhelmed Mundo Perpetuo. In the final entry he pleaded with his employees not to sacrifice him, and the diary ended abruptly, blood smearing the former CEO's handwriting.

It really ought to make Mr. Halen resign.

For a long time I didn't hear a thing—no surprised yells, no nail biting. The only sound was a little scratching, a bit of muttering and humming, and what sounded like the flick of a lighter.

When Mr. Halen finally spoke, he was chanting in a deep, commanding voice: "More middle management. Intern recruitment policies. Armed security guards. Non-disclosure agreements. Internal review procedures."

As I heard that chanting, it dawned on me that Mr. Halen didn't need to work in apocalyptic magic to get to us. All he had to do was use ordinary summoning spells that called in his hordes of managers to smother us all—that, and the deception that he knew no magic at all.

No sooner had I figured it out before two armed security guards burst into my office. "We have orders to escort you from the premises," said the guard on the right. "Your desk will be cleared out, and any personal effects will be sent to you."

I stepped between them and bowed my head, partly in admiration of Mr. Halen's trickery, partly in order to fool the guards. They were armored in Kevlar and force fields that looked capable of withstanding ice, fire, water, air, scalding coffee, and every other basic element, but once I started probing the layers of magic, I found just the kind of weakness I'd expected from an amateur magician: no anchoring. As soon as the guards put their hands on my shoulders, I teleported us all to a pocket dimension where Chen Chai had relegated a particularly nasty invasion of immortal carnivorous plants. Then I teleported myself back, making a mental note to retrieve the guards before their protection spells wore out. If my mood had improved.

When I entered Mr. Halen's office, I found him standing in the middle of a pentagram, blood dripping from his palms in what must be a spell to summon a demon, or perhaps a tax lawyer. His magic was indeed as real as any that my colleagues and I could perform, and I brimmed with anger for not having seen through his sham.

"How clever of you to use a teleportation spell," he said. His smile widened until his teeth gleamed so sharply white that I had to shield my eyes with my arm. By the time I could see again, he had vanished.

IT DIDN'T MATTER whether we were dealing with an actual apocalypse or just a freaking disaster. Mundo Perpetuo stood together. It was clear that Mr. Halen couldn't have worked alone, and the logical place to look was the Intact Foundation.

By nightfall Suarez was back, his health drastically improved by Mr. Halen's disappearance, and we were prepared to pay Madison Stars a visit, all except Ingrid Blunt, who had four nuclear warheads to dismantle on Manhattan that night.

Outside the Foundation's offices, we all sensed the spells that had been cast over the large conference room on the top floor. We stepped up there, me in front with Chen, Agyll, Suarez, Belamy, and Parsons in tow, and Paula Johnson guarding our rear in case someone was crazy enough to sneak up on a septet of angry wizards.

I knocked Archwizardly on the door to the conference room (that is to say, I evaporated the hinges) and caught the strangest sight I'd seen since the oyster invasion of '69. The entire room had been cleared of furniture and was instead filled with perhaps 300 young men in Armani suits, shirts, ties, Lloyd shoes, and gleaming white teeth. Everyone had the same sharp haircut. They were chattering away, but once in a while the buzz rose in volume and ended with a single word: "Revenue" or "Turnover" or "Growth". And every time, a new young man appeared in their midst. Overseeing the ritual was Mr. Halen and Madison Stars, who both raised a hand in mock greeting.

To see Mr. Halen here convinced me that Madison Stars had hired him to begin something big. And there could be no doubt that it was big: We were facing a Master of Business Apocalypse in full flow. It wouldn't be immediately devastating, but add several millions of full-of-themselves CEOs and civilization would surely collapse.

"Guess they're just another kind of zombies," Parsons said. He started mumbling an enchantment, threw spell components into the air and started to gesture in a way that seemed inspired by Bruce Lee or perhaps Kermit the Frog.

Nothing happened. Parsons looked confounded, and I had a sudden suspicion that the new Vietnamese spell components Mr. Halen had ordered for us had come a tad too cheap.

"You are never going to contain this one." Madison Stars' voice cut through the chatter as she approached us. "Leave now and you can keep your jobs and keep saving the world. If you don't, I turn this pack loose on Mundo Perpetuo. They're human, by the way, so you can't harm them."

"Why, Madison?" I asked. "You could have asked Mundo Perpetuo for anything."

"I'm tired of funding a charity. I want to be connected.

I want to know the inside deals before the market rises and crashes. These are the new times, and these are my people. They will all report to me, and the power will be mine!"

"She sounds religious," I whispered hopefully to Flower Agyll.

"Don't wipe this off on me. Mixed End. Your department."

As with any baffling incident, the true question was how the ritual was powered. Anyone in the wrong frame of mind can call down the End of the Earth, but it's damn complicated to summon destructive powers and control them as well.

And then it struck me. When an apocalypse was building, I sensed the magic field between the outer and inner core of the Earth diminish. But I had never really checked if the energy actually returned to the Earth when I stopped an apocalypse. If Madison collected the returning energy, she'd have plenty of undetected power for her plan. And if we all felt a little drained, well, Mr. Halen was easy to blame.

I pulled out my phone and called Ingrid Blunt.

"Ingrid, join us, please."

"Joe, I'm sitting next to a sixty megaton bomb with a five minute countdown, and the wire-cutters Halen bought for us suck."

"That's somebody else's problem," I said. "We're on strike."

A slight pop, and Blunt appeared next to me. "Did you say strike?" she asked.

"Keep summoning," Madison Stars ordered, and her suits obeyed. But no new MBAs were called into existence no matter how many times they shouted 'Earnings before interest, taxes, depreciation and amortization!'

"That's what a strike works like," I said to Madison. "Without our apocalypse prevention, you don't have the energy to expand your management layers."

"I know you, Joe," Madison replied. "You won't let the Earth come to harm."

"Your immediate problem isn't the Earth." I nodded to Blunt, who summoned up a picture of the hydrogen bomb counting down in the sewers under Wall Street. "No apocalypse prevention, no New York."

"You're not the kind of man who'd sacrifice a city to make a point."

I knew she was right, and worse, so did she. But I hadn't lived to become an Archwizard of the sixty-sixth level without learning how to bluff. And I had a room full of wet-behind-the-ears suits to get on my side.

"You're right. We'll contain the blast to the Wall Street area," I said. "It's after closing time, so few people will be hurt, but the financial sector will collapse, and the rest of the economy will follow. And then where will all your suits go?"

Confusion broke out among the suits and I turned to address them. "You heard me, gentlemen. You were summoned with the promise of ruling the world. I cannot banish you since you are human, but I can make sure you'll have nothing to lord it over. So here's your choice: depose your leader and take your chances as free men. Or rule the radioactive ruins of Wall Street in your master's name."

Outrage spread through the crowd as Madison Stars' creations understood how they'd been lured into this world by false promises, and one by one they turned on their creator while a low growling filled the room. Madison's face stiffened as the suits closed in on her.

"I made you what you are," she screamed. "You'll do as I say. I'm the chairman. I. Am. The. Chairman!"

But despite those words of power they still swarmed her, chanting a damning curse of their own. "Vote of no confidence. Vote of no confidence." Over and over again.

I'M SORRY TO say we couldn't prevent all those MBAs from rising, but at least we had the room fully contained. And I mean, how much harm can 300 MBAs do? We modified their memories to make sure they forgot the summoning spells, but from the way I hear it, most have worked out mundane ways to get their ways. Middle management, HR departments, non-disclosure agreements, hokus pokus.

We still keep an eye on their activities, and we've observed a solid rise in the number of people claiming that bottom lines are the most important thing in the world. Yes, most of these people actually go through college, and most of them behave as human beings instead of magically created automatons. Still, I can't help but wonder if we have a magical leak somewhere.

Parsons still insists they're zombies. Suarez likens them to the flu—ubiquitous but mostly dangerous to people who are already weakened by circumstances. Me, I just consider them a freak of fate. The kind of thing you have to learn to live with, even if you don't like it. I can do that, as long as they don't get in the way of my job.

Which reminds me, we have a new board of directors. Funding is back up, apocalypses are back down, and even if the world has this new problem to contend with, we're all a little safer.

Sure, the end of the world is still coming. But Joe and the crew have it covered.

Jakob Drud

Jakob Drud lives in Aarhus, Denmark, where he writes advertising copy for a living and science fiction and fantasy for fun. He writes in English because of the many interesting writers and people involved in the SF web community. His stories have appeared in more than 20 webzines and anthologies, including *Daily Science Fiction* and *Flash Fiction Online*. His website is jakobdrud.com, and he occasionally blogs at jakobdrud.livejournal.com.

CARLA AT THE OFF-PLANET TAX RETURN HELPLINE

Caroline M. Yoachim

"This is Carla at the Off-Planet Tax Return helpline, how can I help you?"

"We are <untranslatable> collective. We file jointly or separately?"

"How many US citizens do you have in your collective?"

"Three hundred fifty-two of us are citizens, yes. Bob is not."

"Are you married, as defined by US law?"

"We are three hundred fifty-two conscious entities melded into one harmonious being for over five thousand years, and also Bob. This is marriage?"

"It is not. You will need to file separate returns for each of your three hundred fifty-two citizens. Bob does not need to file."

"This is unfortunate. Bob will be greatly displeased to be excluded in this way."

"THIS IS CARLA at the Off-Planet Tax Return helpline, how can I help you?"

"What form for taxes?"

"The form for filing an off-planet return is Form 9099B. This form is for US citizens currently residing off planet, including those residing on space shuttles, orbital stations, lunar or planetary colonies, and/or inside the intestinal system of Effluvian space worms. If you reside inside an Effluvian space worm that is currently located on Earth, you are allowed to fill out Form 1040."

"No, what form for currency of taxes?"

"The IRS will generally accept foreign currencies in situations where Earth currency cannot reasonably be obtained. To submit your tax payment in a non-Earth currency, fill out Form X-325Z and include your payment with your tax return. In responding to this question, I am required by law to inform you that it is illegal to staple, glue, tape, or otherwise affix sentient currency to your tax return."

"The IRS prefers sentient currency to run loose inside envelope?"

"We have covered everything I know about this topic, is there anything else I can help you with?"

"THIS IS CARLA at the Off-Planet Tax Return helpline—"

<untranslatable screaming>

<static>

"THIS IS CARLA at—"

"Hi Carla, this is Bob."

"What can I help you with today, Bob?"

"I'm lonely."

"That is beyond the scope of my expertise. Do you have any tax related questions that I can help you with today?"

"You spoke with a different voice of my collective today,

and told us that we each must file a separate return. Except me. This makes me lonely."

"Privacy laws do not allow me to discuss conversations I've had with other callers. How did you manage to get my extension? There are over five hundred tax assistants working through this call center, and call assignment is randomized."

"If you marry me, can I file a tax return?"

"I'm sorry, but I need to end this call now."

"This is Carla at the Off-Planet Tax Return helpline, how can I help you?"

"What is FBAR?"

"FBAR stands for Foreign Bank Account Report, but most off-planet residents refer to this form as FUBAR. It is not possible to fill this form out correctly. This form collects basic information on foreign financial accounts controlled by US citizens and is sent to the Treasury Department. It will not impact your tax liability, but does give the Treasury Department direct access to your funds, which will be used in the highly likely event of an audit."

"I have mesh bag of golden snakes, does this require FBAR?"

"FBAR is required for bank accounts, brokerage accounts, mutual funds, and any collection of sentient or non-sentient currency located outside of the United States. There is one exception for live currencies—US citizens may keep up to fifty creatures of any kind as pets. A creature may be considered a pet if it lives in the primary residence of the person filing the return."

"So if snakes stay in house with me, I do not write them onto form?"

"As long as there are less than fifty."

"I will eat the extras. Thank you."

"This is Carla at the Off-Planet Tax Return helpline, how can I help you?"

"Why will you not marry Bob?"

<click>

"This is Carla at the Off-Planet Tax Return helpline, how can I help you?"

"There is a large green creature with many teeth gnawing through the outer dome of my lunar residence."

"Do you owe back taxes?"

"Yes."

"The creature is a Tarmandian Spacemite, trained by the IRS to collect from delinquent off-planet taxpayers. I am legally required to tell you at this point in the conversation that attempting to run from a Tarmandian Spacemite is illegal and will trigger the Spacemite's predatory instincts. Try to remain calm, and let the Spacemite take anything it wants."

"I only owe three hundred dollars in back taxes. It will cost me ten times that much to repair the damage to my dome. Isn't there some way to get the creature to go away?"

"I'm sorry, we have covered everything I know about this topic, is there anything else I can help you with?"

"This is Carla at the Off-Planet Tax Return helpline, how can I help you?"

"Bob is coming for you."

<click>

"This is Carla at the Off-Planet Tax Return helpline, what can I do for you?"

"SCREW YOU IRS I'M NOT GOING TO FILE!"

"I hope you were smart enough to call from an untraceable number. If not, I am legally required to tell you at this point in the conversation that attempting to run from a Tarmandian Spacemite is illegal and will trigger the Spacemite's predatory instincts. Try to remain calm, and let the Spacemite take anything it wants."

"THIS IS CARLA—oh my god, there's some kind of alien rampaging through the call center. It looks like a dismembered grizzly bear that didn't get put back together quite right, and it's holding hands with a guy in a tuxedo."
<muffled screaming>
"You help with mine taxes?"
"Please hold while we handle this emergency. The SWAT team is here with tranquilizer guns—"
<gunshots>
<click>
<overly loud '80s music>
"Your call is important to us. Please stay on the line for the next available representative."
<overly loud '80s music>
"Thank you for holding. This is Carla at the Off-Planet Tax Return helpline. I am legally required to inform you that three hundred fifty-two members of the <untranslatable> collective are listening in on this call for training purposes. The IRS requires that they provide fifty-seven thousand, eight hundred twenty-two hours of service at this call center to avoid criminal charges for the destruction of government property. Please do not be distressed by their wailing. They are mourning the liberation of Bob, who has been extradited to his home planet, where he will never again feel lonely. How can I help you?"

Caroline M. Yoachim

Caroline M. Yoachim lives in Seattle and loves cold cloudy weather. She is the author of over two dozen short stories, appearing in markets such as *Lightspeed*, *Asimov's*, and *Daily Science Fiction*, among other places. For more about Caroline, check out her website at carolineyoachim.com.

WHY I BOUGHT SATAN TWO COKES ON THE DAY I GRADUATED HIGH SCHOOL

Nathaniel Lee

When I came out of the coffee shop with my latte and my fresh walnut brownie, the Archangel Michael was beating the ever-loving shit out of Satan down on the corner. I could see the impact crater, right in the middle of the intersection, and one of the poles holding up the traffic lights was cut right in two so the wires had all fallen in the street and also it was on fire on account of the flaming sword, so it was a real mess. All higgledy-piggledy. Michael was holding Satan up by the neck with one hand and just slapping him across the face with the other. Which also, by the way, was still holding the sword, so it wasn't so much like slapping as it was punching with brass knuckles. Also, it was still on fire.

People were honking, but only the ones far enough back that they couldn't see what was going on. Everyone else was kind of looking the other way. Fiddling with their cell phones. Avoiding eye contact. You know, like you do around angels.

I figured it was time.

"Hey," I said. Michael turned. I lifted the hand with the coffee in it and pointed at Satan, who was pretty beat up by then. Missing some teeth and all bruises and stuff. "Not cool," I told Michael.

The angel looked down at me with his bronze wings all clanging in the wind. Then he snorted and tossed Satan to the ground and just took off. I stumbled a little and nearly spilled my coffee. Angels got wicked backwash.

By then Satan was staggering upright. "You okay, dude?" I asked him.

"Could've taken him," Satan said. He spat out a tooth and flared his nostrils. "Didn't need your help."

I looked around. Traffic was moving again. Just kind of squeezing around the hole and avoiding the sagging lights. If you kick up a fuss about the mess an angel makes, who knows what might happen? People don't complain, and that's all right.

"Yeah," I said, "I know. You want some of my brownie?"

"No," said Satan.

He took half.

I LIKE TO try and imagine what people think of me. Okay, I mean, I always end up thinking about it a lot anyway, so what I guess I mean is I try to make it more interesting by really trying to work it out, you know? Like, okay, there's me, right, and I'm this tall skinny pale guy with dark hair and the stuffing is coming out of my jacket around the elbow, and then beside me there's this basically homeless dude in a long black coat with dusky skin and a goatee, and I wonder if people think, *Those guys are losers.* But then it's not like people don't recognize Satan because it's actually kind of obvious that his skin is red underneath the dirt. Plus also the tail and the hooves going clip-clop down the sidewalk. So then it's like, *Whoa, that guy is walking around with the devil, he must be a badass.* Except that no one thinks Satan is badass anymore because he's always getting his ass kicked by angels, especially Michael, and so then I figure they just think I'm a loser again.

It's a puzzler, isn't it?

By the time we got to the MiniMart Pop Stop, Satan was all healed up. Picture of demonic health and stuff. He even looked a little cleaner. I wondered if he had to keep dirtying himself up to keep the hobo chic going or something – I mean, he used to be an angel, and those guys *can't* get dirty. I've never seen one get dirty, anyway. Maybe they just don't like it. Satan was in a better mood, too.

"You are my good and faithful minion," he said to me, holding out his hand. "Pledge yourself to my service and I will grant you all the kingdoms of the world."

I looked and he had a coupon for a dollar off a Big Mac. I held up my latte. "I just spent my last five bucks, man."

Satan shook the coupon at me. "Mortal scum," he said.

I shrugged. "Okay, maybe I'll get a new job sometime." I took the coupon and put it in my pocket. The one without the hole in it.

"Together we will rule this world," Satan assured me, patting me on the shoulder and leaving a couple of new scorch marks. "Come on. Let's get slushies."

Satan and I got a system. See, people are real bigoted, shopkeepers especially, so they just *know* that the Prince of Darkness and Lord of Lies is going to steal all their shit. So Satan goes in first and just lurks the hell out of the place. Shifty eyes, and all glancing up and down all the time. He's boss at it. And while everyone is giving him the stink-eye, I can basically pocket whatever the fuck I want and then go buy a pack of gum or a slushie for the look of the thing and leave.

Today I stole a couple of forties and a bunch of Slim Jims

and a bottle of cough syrup that turned out to be the wussy new crap. I don't think they even make the alcohol kind anymore, but Satan always asks for some. He's kind of a fogey. I nearly busted out laughing when he actually pulled his coat up along his arm and skulked toward the candy aisle like frigging Bela Lugosi or some shit. The stiff behind the counter had no idea she was getting made fun of. She was *laser* focused on that suspicious demon dude. Man, you cannot *buy* that much funny.

Used to be Satan could just get anyone to steal for him, even solid upright pillar-of-the-community types, but that don't work very often anymore. Everyone's got insurance these days. Even most of the juvenile delinquents, which come on, how are you skipping school with an angel watching over you? You're just going to get your ass busted to Purgie for a couple of decades. Idiots.

Thinking about that stuff reminded me about my ceremony, though, and I got depressed.

"Graduation's coming up," I told Satan. He was drinking down the not-at-all-buzz-inducing cough syrup because his stupid ass can't admit when he's wrong. "Mom's pushing me to start looking. You know, at all the options."

Satan belched Robitussin at me. "They all suck," he said, waving vaguely at the sky and the ground. I guessed he meant angels.

"Yeah, but it's mandatory now. Only reason I even get to wait until graduation is 'cause I got grandfathered or something." I was leaning toward Raziel the Destroyer because destroying sounded pretty cool, even though it would definitely turn out to be lame once you actually swore to the guy, I was sure. Angels were never any fun, even when they were doing fun stuff.

"You should swear to me. You took my coupon."

"Yeah, but that doesn't, like, you know, count."

Satan pulled himself up and narrowed his eyes and only wobbled a little. (We'd already downed most of the malt liquor.) "I," he said slowly, "am on the List. O—fishelly."

"You are not."

"Am so."

"Bullshit." I took a big gulp of my slushie and regretted it. Ice cream headache, big time.

"I'm an angel, right?"

I clutched at my forehead and squinted. "... technically, I guess?"

"Press your tongue on the roof of your mouth. Anyway, technically is all that counts with these bozos. So I'm on the List. I have to be."

"You're not in the handout they gave us after Spring Break, I'm pretty sure." I wished I had my backpack with me.

He waved a taloned hand. "That's not the *real* list. They can cheat on that one and get away with it because it's just for you monkeys and not for actual people. No offense."

"Sure."

"So you're going to do it? You'll swear to me at your Choosing?"

I pretended I couldn't hear the desperation in his voice. I shrugged and took a swig from my forty to stall for time. "It's not like I've got anything better to do," I said at last.

"Yes." Satan was rubbing his hands like in a cartoon, and I swear on my balls his eyes actually glowed red. "Idle hands. The old reliable."

IT WAS A long walk down to the waterfront, but Satan said it was real important. I was looking at the sky a little nervously by then. Mom doesn't like me out late, and obviously she doesn't approve of me hanging around with Satan much, but more than that I was worried about getting home before curfew. I mean, angels are lame and stupid and assholes, yeah, but dude, you do *not* want the Angel of Death catching you breaking curfew. That guy is *super* creepy, and they say he doesn't fuck around with Purgie, not even for minors. One and done, and into the Lake of Fire you go.

"This is the Innermost Circle," Satan said, fiddling with a rusty old padlock. "Heart of Pandemonium. The Black Throne awaits."

"You say that every time you go to the bathroom."

"Shut up. Help me with this."

We ended up having to go in through the broken window and undo the latch from the inside. I gave Satan a boost. He stepped on my head, which really *hurts* with goat hooves, by the way.

"Ahh," he said, once we were inside. It was an old warehouse, big and wet and smelling like mildew took a shit. "My realm."

Satan had a little sleeping bag and a box with a battery-powered lamp and a camp stove. I nodded and tried to breathe through my mouth.

"Here," he said. "My wings."

It was a clothing rack. Y'know, the kind on wheels? Like stolen from a Dress for Less or something. Hanging on it was what looked like a bundle of sticks glued all over with dead crows. I poked it, and it creaked a little.

"They don't work right now," said Satan, "but I'm getting them fixed."

"Cool," I said noncommittally.

"Once, they blotted the sun from the sky. Disaster and ruin trailed in their wake, and men wailed to see their shadow upon the plains."

"Oh." I rubbed my finger against my pants. The wings looked even shabbier now.

"Once we've assembled our army, I will fly at its head, and my wings of darkness will be terrible to look upon. Terrible and awful. Then mortal man will know the King of the World." Satan seemed pretty lost in his little dreamworld. After a little bit, I cleared my throat.

"Okay, man. Well. I've gotta go." I pointed. "Curfew."

He looked crestfallen. I felt bad, but seriously. Lake. Of. Fire.

"I'll catch you tomorrow, okay?" I said.

Satan waved a feeble claw in dismissal. When I left, he was stroking his crumpled black wings. And I swear he was singing to them, or maybe just to himself.

THE STREETS WERE empty. All the doors were locked. All the windows were shuttered. Fresh lamb's blood daubed on every lintel. You know how it is. I kept pretending I could still see a little glimmer of sunlight. Maybe if I convinced myself, it wouldn't count against me? Like, innocent mind, no *mens rea*, right?

By the time I got to my street, I was out of breath. I stopped at the corner and puffed a few times, but when I realized I couldn't see my shadow on the ground, I sucked it up and pushed myself into a jog again. I saw someone waiting outside my door and freaked.

"Mom, what are you doing outside? It's got to be ... after ... curfew ... "

Fucking creepy-ass Angel of Death was just staring at me with those black eyes of his.

"Okay, well. Here I am at home." I kind of shuffled around him crabwise.

Angel just stared.

"I'm gonna go inside?"

No movement.

"So ... bye, then."

I scooted backwards, but I couldn't move. He was holding the front of my jacket. I didn't even see him move. His hand was so cold it burned, even through the Gore-Tex.

"Friday," he whispered.

Then he was gone.

Friday was the ceremony. My Choosing ceremony.

The fuck did that mean?

Man, I *hate* that guy.

MOM WAS SUPER pissed about me getting home late, but I think she was so happy to see me not Smited that she wasn't maybe as pissed as she might have been. She was still plenty pissed though, especially because she'd gotten a letter from my guidance counselor that afternoon and had been stewing and waiting for me to get home all day. Turns out they'd noticed that I stopped going to class a couple weeks back. Oops. What could I say? It's not like I was going to go to college or anything. The fuck was the point?

So the next day, Thursday, we bundled into the Mommobile and went to meet with Mr. Muesli. I forget how to spell or say his real name, and he's a nut and a fruit and a flake, so I stick with Mr. Muesli, and it makes him so mad that his little mustache puffs right out like a scared cat.

Mr. Muesli's mustache was already pretty fluffed when we got there, though. "We're very concerned about your future, Samuel," Mr. Muesli said, the little emblem of his angelic protector—Raphael, the Healer—glinting at his throat. He folded his hands on his desk. His nails were perfect rounded squares. His desk was perfectly clean. He had one pen and one pencil lined up on either side of his blotter calendar. Who the fuck even uses pens? Who *blots* things anymore? "We thought you'd like to talk about it. We've been getting some disturbing reports. Do you have an explanation for your recent ... behavior?"

I looked at Mom but she was all thunderclouds-on-the-mountaintop.

"I dunno," I said. Things went downhill from there.

Basic points that I remember:

Mr. Muesli wanted me to do well.

Everyone wanted me to do well.

Doing well meant Choosing correctly.

Which I was clearly not prepared to do.

Here are some pamphlets.

So *that* was fun, and I mean fun as in angel-type fun, so not fun at all in any way.

I was basically told that I would not be swearing to Raziel or Michael or any of the interesting angels. There was apparently an option called "General Obedience" that meant, near as I could tell, working for everyone at once but no one in particular and generally doing manual labor building pyramids and monuments and cathedrals and filling in the potholes when Michael decided to drop-kick demons from orbit. Mom tried to defend me, which honestly kind of startled me, but Mr. Muesli never liked me and had clearly finally decided to drop me right in the shit for good.

Well, fine, then. They didn't want me. I had other options.

IT TOOK ME a while to find Satan. You'd think he'd stand out more, but he blends in a lot better than he should, and nobody likes to even mention him, which makes asking which way he went kind of a pain in the ass. Half the people don't answer, even if they've seen him, and the ones that do like to give you shit. I get tracts. Once someone lectured me for almost thirty minutes until Satan wandered back around and stole his laptop bag and got the police called on us.

I wasn't really in the mood for happy memories, though. Between Mr. Muesli's sanctimonious bullshit and Mom telling me that if I left the house I shouldn't bother coming back, I was pretty far in the emotional shithole. I remember having a hard time finding the street signs because everything kept getting blurry. Every now and then some smarmy asshole would come simpering up to try and find out what was wrong, earn brownie points from whatever angel they'd sworn their lives to. Mostly people got the fuck out of my way, which was good. I didn't need to ask directions; I knew where I was going.

I started at the old warehouse Satan had shown me and spiraled out from there. When I started passing people whispering in clusters and looking disturbed, I knew I was getting close. He always knows the most upsetting thing to say to anyone. It's like a knack. I think it was basically his hobby when we weren't fucking around and doing stupid shit.

Something twigged, even through my haze of anger, when I saw who Satan was with. Some old bag lady was just kind of sitting on a stoop, and he was leaning down and whispering in her ear. I slowed my stride into more of a sideways saunter. My feet wanted to turn around. They were probably smarter than I was. I wonder what would have happened if I'd listened to them?

At any rate, Satan heard me coming and looked up.

"Sammy!" he said, smiling. "I stole you a Snickers." He held out the candy bar. Actual King Size, not just Fun Size. Usually he keeps those for himself. I realized I'd missed dinner, and my stomach rumbled.

"What's up?" I said, gesturing with my Snickers. The old lady was just staring off into space. Her face was wrinkled like last year's apples, and she stank like a toilet. Even hungry as I was, I couldn't bring myself to eat in the face of that smell.

"Eh? Oh." Satan started peeling the wrapper on another candy bar, like it was a banana. "She'll kill herself tonight, probably, or tomorrow. Drugs." He bit into the candy bar.

"What? Why?"

He looked at me like I was crazy. "Because I convinced her to."

I looked at him like *he* was crazy. "Because ... ?"

"Look at her throat." When I glanced down and back up in obvious confusion, he snorted. "No sigil. No angel. No protection." He grinned, showing his rotten teeth, liberally smeared with nougat. "No reprisals."

"So you're just going to off her because you can?"

"Despair is a sin. It's the only one she's got left."

"Okay, but ... I mean ... fuck, dude." I felt my face flushing red.

Satan's eyes went flat and dark. "They kicked me out."

"Yeah, I get it, so you break their rules back at them, but ..."

"No." He waved a hand, sharply. "Not just opposing. Asking. I am asking questions. I ask *questions* and wait for *them* to answer."

I was having a hard time catching my breath, and not from the old lady's B.O. "Dude, they answer you all the fucking time by bashing your head in."

"That's not the question." His face was reddening, too, except on him it was more of a burgundy. "She is."

"... what?"

"Mercy. Grace." His nostrils flared. "Punishment."

"What, you want to talk hypocrisy and unfairness? Fucking hell, man—"

"Exactly." His eyes gleamed with triumph.

The old lady whimpered, then. Not a big noise. Barely even a noise. I don't think she was trying to talk. I don't think she even knew anyone was there. But I heard it. And it's like, what the fuck? This is it? I got bullshit from the Muesli-nauts of the world, bullshit dropping down like manna from heaven, and what's left? More bullshit, except *political*. And Satan was just so pleased with himself, like this was what was important and good and correct and not just hanging out and having fun and not caring about stupid crap.

I punched Satan. Well, I tried, but he dodged. Probably leftover omniscience or something, because he looked pretty startled.

"Fuck you!" I shouted. I pushed his chest, and he backed away a step with a grunt. "She's just some old outcast, probably from before the Rise and who never got a chance to get caught up with the way things work. Lot of old folks had it hard then, when the fighting was going on and no one knew for sure what was happening. My grandpa died in the wars; you know that. You gonna fuck him up if he was here? Kick him in the balls, steal his prosthetic leg? You talk about sticking it to the angels because they play righteous when all they do is screw people over, but what the fuck, what exactly the *fuck* is the difference between you and them when it comes to poor assholes like this lady?" I shoved my Snickers bar into the bag lady's filthy hand. She held it like she was a mannequin in a pose. "Asking questions? How about giving some fucking new answers for a change?"

I turned and stormed away. I'd planned on waiting out the night in Satan's warehouse, but I wasn't really processing things on that level, not then.

"Sam ..."

I didn't turn around.

"Sammy!"

I held up my middle finger and kept walking.

He didn't call a third time.

IT WAS COLD in the bushes. We're fairly northerly, considering the way things got shifted around to accommodate the Lake of Fire and the Big Box. You know, the twelve-thousand cubits one? Yeah, fuck those fat cats who live there, but it's not like they give a shit that their house has shoved glaciers down in weird-ass places and made weather forecasting even more of a mug's game than it used to be. Anyway. Point is that even at graduation time, temperatures still got pretty low around three in the morning, and I'd left home without a jacket.

I'd debated whether it'd be better to try and hide from the Angel of Death or present a moving target. On the one hand, if he searches the whole city every night, and that's supposedly what he does, then any given spot is going to be unsafe at some point, so staying put won't work forever. On the other hand, if you're the only thing moving around in a silent and still landscape, you're not going to be hard to spot, you know? In the end, it was just too damned cold for me to keep on my feet. I went to the place I figured everyone would least expect to find me.

I went to school.

The doors were padlocked, so I bunked down in the hedge beside the building and spent the last few hours of the night crouched amid the old cigarette butts and discarded condoms. Both of those were against the rules, but like that ever stopped anyone, right?

I must have slept. I'm not sure when I slipped off, but I know I was asleep because I remember waking up to the watery morning sun and seeing that creepy motherfucker crouching in the bushes in front of me, just staring in my face. Black eyes. Deep black.

"Yaa—" I croaked. Too dry to shriek properly. I licked my chapped lips and tried again. "How long have you been there?"

No answer. No response.

The cold radiating off him made me shiver. "Well, you're too late now. Sun's up. Curfew's over."

He might have nodded his head the tiniest fraction of an inch. Might just have been the wind moving his hood.

"Man, I don't know why you're bothering with me. I'm going in tomorrow. Later today, I mean. I'll take the stupid oath. I'll do the stupid jobs. You fuckers win, okay?"

Nothing. Not even a flicker.

"Fucking talk, you asshole! Answer me!" I reached out a hand to ... to do something. I don't know. The cold was so intense near his skin that it blistered my fingertips.

I think I might have touched him. Not his cloak or anything. Touched an actual angel. Which is supposed to kill you.

And then I woke up again. It felt like waking up, anyway. I was in the bushes. I was cold.

The Angel of Death was gone. If he'd ever been there.

My hand hurt, but I ignored it. I had a lot of aches after that night, right? Could have been anything.

I LURKED AROUND the school entrance until the buses started showing up. Cafeteria was open for the free-meal kids. I joined in the trudge-walk. Technically I qualified, even if I didn't usually partake. Cold cereal and lukewarm milk and a runty pear. Mm-mm good.

We had classes like normal for the morning. Technically it was still school, but since all the tests were finished and all the grades assigned, it was basically just a day for tearful farewells and yearbook signings and cleaning out lockers and all that crap. Everyone kept doing double-takes and stammering that they hadn't expected to see me again. It got really annoying, and I wasn't in the most stable mood to begin with. I ended up almost taking Martin's head off when he offered me his yearbook to sign, which I felt kind of bad about—he was a dweeb, but he meant well, and he was mostly harmless. His yearbook looked basically blank, from what I saw. I think I made him cry. The other kids left me alone after that, at least, but the teachers started watching a lot more closely. I saw a lot of hands go up to touch sigils. Nervous gestures. Was this what it was like to be feared? I'd have said I should enjoy it while it lasted, but there was not a lot to enjoy about it, from what I could see.

Then came the last bell. Everyone lined up like good little soldiers and trooped to the Assembly Hall, with its stained-glass portraits of the archangels.

It was time to Choose.

All the kids who were ready to pledge their lives to angelic service were lined up in the front rows. Kids go up and swear their oath. The presiding angel seals the compact in fire and hangs the new-forged sigil around the youthful neck. Everyone claps, and we rinse and repeat for about three hours. I'd been attending these things for years. Well, not *recent* years, but you know. When I was little. I think this year we had Zdaxg, who was about as minor-league as angels come. Not even any official purview, just "minor angelic functionary." He must've been hiding behind the door when vowels were handed out at Creation, too, but at least no one would be surprised that they couldn't read the signature on your certificate.

They played the usual dreary school hymns, and we all stood up and sat down at least three times. I stopped paying attention and just stayed in my seat no matter how many times my homeroom teacher hissed at me to stand up. When the actual assembly began, my jaw nearly dropped. They were going in order of age, and they'd started with the kindergarteners. Not a ton of them, sure, but come on. Those kids are five, six at the oldest. How can they already be swearing their oaths?

I watched, shifting as if my seat were slowly being heated from below. I didn't feel hot, though. I felt cold.

Really cold, now that I thought about it.

The seats beside me had been empty when the assembly started—big surprise there for the demon-lover who'd spent the night sleeping in a bush—but I saw something shadowy out of the corner of my right eye. Something maybe like a pale face with ink-black eyes.

My right hand was going numb with cold.

"I gotta go," I said, a little too loudly. Kids from the next row turned around, then quickly turned back to the front. I stood up and pushed my way out of the row of seats, ignoring the protests of the students I was shoving and stepping on. Zdaxg was droning something in Enochian as I fled up the paper-thin carpet and out the double doors with a bang. Fucking angels, man. Footsteps followed after me; sensible shoes, hurried stride: teachers.

I could hear some kind of commotion from out by the front doors. They'd expect me to bolt that way, I was sure. Hopefully they'd hear the same noises and jump to the same conclusion. I ducked into the stairwell instead.

Not sure what I was thinking, exactly. Mostly that I just wanted to get away, hide somewhere till everything was over. Maybe I was going up to the roof for some other reason. I don't know. I'm not a psychologist.

But I found myself up there and I kind of wasn't really surprised. It was just where I needed to be.

The Angel of Death was waiting for me. He was standing by the edge, over where the ducts stick out and you can watch the girls' soccer team practice. It's just a thing I know about, okay?

"Man," I said to the Angel of Death, "what the fuck is your problem?"

No answer. Big surprise.

The wind picked up, and I heard noises coming up the stairwell. The utility elevator started up, too, rattling and clanging. You'd think I was some sort of criminal mastermind and not just a loser kid in a city full of fucking angels.

I walked over beside Death because I just did not care

anymore, and anyway he could teleport or whatever angels do and he clearly wanted to follow me around for whatever fucked-up personal reason. He was staring at the field even though no one was playing soccer, and he didn't react to my presence. At least I didn't have to see his eyes. I looked down.

"What, am I supposed to kill myself now? Is that what angel-vision tells you is going to happen?" I scuffed my shoes and watched a pebble tumble down. "Even if I was planning on it, I wouldn't now. Anyway, it probably wouldn't kill me. Break some bones, though, definitely."

We watched no one playing soccer for a while.

I shook my head. "Fuck it. I'm going back downstairs. That's what you want, right? I'll say the words and do my work and keep my head down and probably eventually have the mandatory kids and send them to the mandatory schools just like the rules say. I get it. It's like a Lifetime movie. I'm growing up. See how fucking mature I'm being?"

The Angel smiled then. I could just see his lips curling slightly from under his hood. Except it wasn't like a *Go in peace my son* smile. It was more like a *Ha ha sucker* smile. Which made me even more unhappy and uncomfortable than I already was.

I stepped back and headed for the stairs, not quite willing to turn my back on him. You can't trust anyone with wings or a halo. It plays with their minds.

The utility elevator arrived with a thud and a groan. Someone inside grunted, and the iron grate rolled back. Then, wheels squeaking, out came...

"Satan? What are *you* doing here?"

He was pushing his little clothing rack. The terrible black wings were ... okay, they were still pretty beat up and moth-eaten and generally really thrift-store-looking, but they were clean now, and shiny in places, like they'd been oiled, and as near as I could see all the little linkages and struts that had been snapped or rusted out had been replaced. They looked ... functional.

Satan peered out at me from behind the wings. "I fixed them," he said. "Ready to go."

A weight came over me, like someone had dropped a leather poncho over my head. I felt like a half-deflated soccer ball, where you give it a good kick and it just kind of goes "whud" and flops ten feet. "Man, I told you." I thought about that. "Okay, I didn't exactly tell you. But you know, I thought you got it. I'm not swearing to you. I don't think I can. It's too fucked up."

Satan shrank inside his filthy overcoat. His beady eyes gleamed, and he looked away. "I heard you, Sammy. Fixed them anyway." He fidgeted some more, played with his little goatee. "They're yours. I can't use them. Last time I did, they got broke pretty bad. Figured you could keep 'em. Flying is fun. I think I remember it being fun."

I tried to force a smile, even if inside I still felt like a soggy bit of toast. "Hey, man. That's ... I mean, I don't think they'll let me. You know, when I'm sworn to General Obedience. Probably rules about menials having demonic artifacts and stuff. But ... thank you. It was ... nice of you." It really was, I realized. And I was fucking it up because I was in a funk because—

The stairwell burst open and a half-dozen teachers tumbled out, shouting. Mr. Muesli was in the lead. I think I even saw Zdaxg glowing serenely back in the stairwell, his melodious voice peevish as he tried to get people to move out of his way. Even the Angel of Death drifted over, as if attracted by the commotion. No one else seemed to notice him.

"There they are!" shouted Mr. Muesli.

"You guys," I told them. "Calm down. I'm coming back down already. Jeez."

Satan glanced up. "Blasphemy!" he crowed. "Owe me a Coke." He punched me in the arm.

"Ow."

"Foul demon," Mr. Muesli intoned, brandishing his sigil at Satan, who leaned back, jostling me and the wing-rack. He smelled like burnt match heads. "Begone from this holy place and leave our souls in peace!" He stepped forward, pendant glowing, and Satan hopped back like he got burned. Got him behind me, like you'd say.

"Don't even want your stupid souls," Satan muttered.

"And you!" Mr. Muesli rounded on me, still holding the pendant as if it would repel me, which honestly it kind of did. "You are in so much trouble, young man. Disrupting the ceremony. Consorting with devils. I may have to reconsider my recommendation that you graduate."

I didn't actually say "fine with me" but I think I thought it hard enough that he heard me because his face went purple, then white.

"Come with me immediately, Samuel," he said, gesturing sharply. He didn't come get me, though. I don't know if he was afraid what I'd do if he grabbed me or if he just didn't want to get within smelling distance of Satan.

I felt the initial rush of instinctive refusal. Rebelliousness of spirit, they called it. But then I remembered that I wasn't fighting them anymore, that I'd made up my mind to be an adult about everything, even when it sucked. I closed my mouth and glanced around. Mr. Muesli was getting closer to apoplexy every second. Satan looked hangdog. The teachers

all had stern faces on but were mostly enjoying being part of a righteous mob. And the Angel of Death wasn't just smiling anymore. He was *grinning*. And starting to move forward, slipping through the crowd like a snake through tree branches.

And I remembered something.

Despair is a sin.

"No," I said.

Mr. Muesli kept looking grouchy. "What?"

"No, fuck this noise. I don't want it. Who says I have to have it?"

"I do. We do. *They* do." He pointed to Zdaxg, who had made it to the front of the crowd and was staring down his nose at Satan, except he wasn't even as tall as Satan and so was kind of glaring cross-eyed at Satan's right elbow.

"Well, I don't. I'm not swearing to anyone." I turned around. Satan was watching me closely. "Not even you, bro."

Satan shook his head. "Nah. Dumb idea anyway."

"Help me on with these," I pointed to the wings.

A couple of teachers tried to move forward, but Satan pulled himself upright and bared his fangs. He even managed a pretty good fireball effect, even if it was more of a burp than a blast. The teachers scrambled backwards. The fire passed around Zdaxg and the Angel of Death without touching them. Zdaxg looked confused. The Angel of Death just watched, face impassive again.

"You know the lady?" Satan said as he fussed with the straps on my back.

"Huh?"

"The old lady." He tugged something that gave me the mother of all wedgies. "I told her not to die. Command voice. I don't think it worked very well, though. Probably won't for long. I dunno how to make her better for good."

I laughed, really laughed, for the first time in what felt like years. Maybe in my whole life. "Fuck if I know, either, dude."

Satan stepped back, and I flexed the wings. They spread out with a sharp sound, like a battle flag snapping in the wind.

"Feels cool, dude." I strode to the edge of the roof. Behind us, the flickering remnants of the fireball were dying down. The teachers were murmuring, working up the courage to tackle the devil again. They were trying to convince Zdaxg to miracle something up, but he was looking dubious.

I held out a hand to Satan. "Come on. We'll try to figure something out to help her." My wings started to beat, slowly but building speed.

"Your lead." Satan gripped my wrist. It wasn't cold at all. "So I swear to you now?"

"God, no."

His talons dug in. "Blasphemy. Owe me *two* Cokes."

I looked over my shoulder and met the gaze of the Angel of Death. I pointed at him. "Nobody likes you," I told him.

No response.

"No, really. You're a fucking asshole. Everyone thinks that."

He shrugged. A *What-can-you-do?* shrug.

"That's the spirit," I said.

And then I jumped off the roof to see if I could fly.

Nathaniel Lee

Nathaniel Lee lives somewhat unwillingly in North Carolina, along with his wife, son, and obligatory cat. His fiction has appeared in a variety of venues, including *Beneath Ceaseless Skies, Daily Science Fiction*, and previously here at *UFO*. He also works as the assistant editor (Most Senior Exalted Slush Monkey) at both the *Escape Pod* and *Drabblecast* audio fiction magazines. You can find him online at www.mirrorshards.org and @scattercat on Twitter, though no one is particularly clear why you would do so. He has not at present sold his soul to the Devil, but all reasonable offers will be considered.

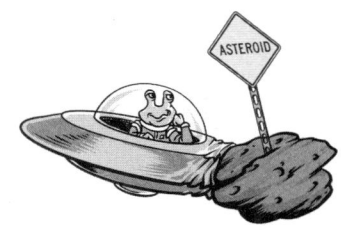

COMPANY STORE

Robert Silverberg

Colonist Roy Wingert gripped his blaster with shaky hands and aimed it at the slimy wormlike creatures wriggling behind his newly deposited pile of crates.

They told me this planet was uninhabited, he thought. *Hah!*

He yanked back the firing stud and a spurt of violet light leaped out. His nostrils caught the smell of roasting alien flesh. Shuddering, Wingert turned away from the mess before him, in time to see four more of the wormlike beings writhing toward him from the rear.

He ashed those. Two more dangled invitingly from a thick-boled tree at his left. Getting into the spirit of the thing now, Wingert turned the beam on them too. The clearing was beginning to look like the vestibule of an abattoir. Sweat ran down Wingert's face. His stomach was starting to get queasy, and his skin was cold at the prospect of spending his three-year tour on Quellac doing nothing but fighting off these overgrown night-crawlers.

Two more of them were wriggling out of a decaying log near his feet. They were nearly six feet long, with saw-edged teeth glistening in Quellac's bright sunlight. *Nothing very dangerous,* Wingert thought. He recharged the blaster and roasted the two newcomers.

Loud noises in back of him persuaded him to turn. Something very much like a large gray toad, seven or eight feet high and mostly mouth, was hopping toward him through the forest. It was about thirty yards away now. It looked very hungry.

Squaring his shoulders, Wingert prepared to defend himself against this new assault. But just as he started to depress the firing stud, a motion to his far right registered in the corner of his eye. *Another* of the things—approaching rapidly from the opposite direction.

"Pardon me, sir," a sharp crackling voice said suddenly. "You seem to be in serious straits. May I offer you the use of this Duarm Pocket Force-Field Generator in this emergency? The cost is only—"

Wingert gasped. "*Damn* the cost! Turn the thing on—those toads are only twenty feet away!"

"Of course, sir."

Wingert heard a click and abruptly a shimmering blue bubble of force sprang up around them. The two onrushing pseudo-toads cracked soundly into it and were thrown back.

Wingert staggered over to one of the packing cases and sat down limply. He was soaked with sweat from head to foot.

"Thanks," he said. "You saved my life. But who the hell are you, and where'd you come from?"

"Permit me to introduce myself. I am XL-ad41, a new-model Vending and Distributing Robot manufactured on Densobol II. I arrived here not long ago, and, perceiving your plight—"

Wingert saw now that the creature was indeed a robot, roughly humanoid except for a heavy pair of locomotory treads. "Hold on! Let's go back to the beginning." The toad-things were eyeing him hungrily from outside the force-field. "You say you're a new-model *what?*"

"Vending and Distributing Robot. It is my function to diffuse through the civilized galaxy the goods and supplies manufactured by my creators, Associated Artisans of Densobol II." The robot's rubberized lips split in an oily smile. "I am, you might say, a mechanized traveling salesman. Are you from Terra, perhaps?"

"Yes, but—"

"I thought as much. By comparing your physical appearance with the phenotype data in my memory banks I reached the conclusion that you were of Terran origin. The confirmation you have just given is most gratifying."

"Glad to hear it. Densobol II is in the Magellanic Cluster, isn't it? Lesser or Greater Cloud?"

"Lesser. One matter puzzles me, though. In view of your Terran origin, it seems odd that you didn't respond when I mentioned that I am a traveling salesman."

Wingert frowned. "How was I supposed to respond? Clap my hands and wiggle my ears?"

"You were supposed to show humor-response. According to my files on Terra, mention of traveling salesmen customarily strikes upon a common well of folklore implanted in the subconscious and induces a conscious humor-reaction."

"Hmm. Sorry I missed the joke," Wingert apologized. "I'm afraid I never was too interested in Earth or its jokes, though. That's why I pulled up stakes and signed on with Planetary Colonization."

"Ah, yes. I had just concluded that your failure to show response to standard folklore indicated some fundamental dislocation of your position relative to your cultural gestalt. Again, confirmation is gratifying. As an experimental model, I'm subject to careful monitoring by my makers, and I'm anxious to demonstrate my capability as a salesman."

Wingert had almost completely recovered from his earlier exertions. He eyed the two toad-beings uneasily and said, "That force-field generator—that one of the things you sell?"

"The Duarm Generator is one of our finest products. It's strictly one-way, you know. *They* can't get in, but you can still fire at them."

"What? Why didn't you tell me that long ago?" Wingert drew his blaster and disposed of the toad-creatures with two well-placed shots.

"That's that," he said. "I guess I sit inside this force-field and wait for the next ones now."

"Oh, they won't be along for a while," the robot said lightly. "The creatures that attacked you are native to the next continent. They're not found here at all."

"Then how'd they get here?"

"I brought them," the robot said. "I collected the most hostile creatures I could find on this world and left them in your vicinity in order to demonstrate the necessity for the Duarm Force-Field Generat—"

"*You* brought them?" Wingert rose and advanced on the robot menacingly. "Deliberately, as a sales stunt?" They could have killed and eaten me."

"On the contrary. I was controlling the situation, as you saw. When matters became serious I intervened."

"Get out of here!" Wingert raged. "Go on, you crazy robot! I have to unpack, set up my bubble. Go!"

"But you owe me—"

"We'll settle up later. Get going, *fast!*"

THE ROBOT GOT. Wingert watched it scuttle off into the underbrush and tried to control his rage. Angry as he was, he felt a certain amusement at the robot's crude sales tactics. It was clever, in a coarse way, to assemble a collection of menacing aliens and arrive at the last minute to supply the force-field. But when you poison a man in order to sell him the antidote, you *don't* boast about it afterward to the victim!

He glanced speculatively at the forest, hoping the robot had told the truth. He didn't care to spend his entire tour on Quellac fighting off dangerous beasts.

The generator was still operating; Wingert studied it and found a cam that widened the field. He expanded it to a thirty-yard radius and left it that way. The clearing was littered with alien corpses. Wingert shuddered.

Well, now that that amusement was over, it was time to get down to business. He had been on Quellac for just an hour, and had spent most of that time fighting for his life.

The Colonists' Manual said, *"The first step for a newly arrived colonist is to install his Matter-Transmitter."* Wingert closed the book and peered at the scattered pile of crates that were his possessions until he spied the large yellow box labeled MATTER-TRANSMITTER, HANDLE WITH CARE.

From the box marked TOOLS he took a crowbar and delicately pried a couple of planks out of the packing crate. A silvery metallic object was visible within. Wingert hoped the Matter-Transmitter was in working order; it was his most important possession, his sole link to far-off Terra.

The manual said, *"All necessities of life will be sent via Matter-Transmitter without cost."* Wingert smiled. Necessities of life? He could have magneboots, cigars, sensotapes, low-power short-range matter-transmitters, dream pellets, bottled Martinis, and nuclear fizzes, simply by requisitioning them. All the comforts of home. They had told him working for Planetary Colonization was rugged, but it was hardly that. Not with the Matter-Transmitter to take the sting out of pioneering.

Unless, Wingert thought gloomily, *that lunatic robot brings some more giant toads over from the next continent.*

Wingert opened the packing crate and bared the Matter-Transmitter. It looked, he thought, like an office desk with elephantiasis of the side drawers; they bulged grotesquely, aproning out into shovel-shaped platforms, one labeled SEND and the other RECEIVE.

An imposing-looking array of dials and meters completed the machine's face. Wingert located the red activator stud along the north perimeter and jammed it down. The Matter-Transmitter came quivering to life.

Dials clicked; meters registered. The squarish device seemed to have taken on an existence of its own. The viewscreen flickered polychromatically, then cleared. A mild, pudgy face stared out at Wingert.

"Hello. I'm Smathers, from the Earth Office. I'm the Company contact man for Transmitters AZ-1061 through BF-80. Can I have your name, registry number, and coordinates?"

"Roy Wingert, Number 76-032-10f3. The name of this planet is Quellac, and I don't know the coordinates offhand. If you'll give me a minute to check my Contract—"

"No need of that," Smathers said. "Just let me have the serial number of your Matter-Transmitter. It's inscribed on the plate along the west perimeter."

Wingert found it after a moment's search. "AZ-1142."

"That checks. Well, welcome to the Company, Colonist Wingert. How's your planet?"

"Not so good," Wingert said.

"How so?"

"It's inhabited. By hostile aliens. And my Contract said I was being sent to an uninhabited world."

"Read it again, Colonist Wingert. As I recall, it simply said you would meet no hostile creatures where *you* were. Our survey team reported some difficulties on the wild continent to your west, but—"

"You see these dead things here?"

"Yes."

"I killed them. To save my own neck. They attacked me about a minute after the Company ship dropped me off here."

"They're obviously strays from that other continent," Smathers said. "Most unusual. Be sure to report any further difficulties of this sort."

"Sure," Wingert said. "Big comfort *that* is."

"To change the subject," Smathers said frigidly," I wish to remind you that the Company stands ready to serve you. In the words of the Contract, *'All necessities of life will be sent via Matter-Transmitter.'* That's in the Manual, too. Would you care to make your first order now? The Company is extremely anxious that its employees are well taken care of."

Wingert frowned. "Well, I haven't even unpacked, you know. I don't think I need anything yet—except—yes! Send me some old-fashioned razor blades, will you? And a tube of shaving cream. I forgot to pack mine in, and I can't stand these new vibroshavers."

Smathers emitted a suppressed chuckle. "You're not going to grow a beard?"

"No," Wingert said stiffly. "They itch."

"Very well, then. I'll have the routing desk ship a supply of blades and cream to Machine AZ-1142. So long for now, Colonist Wingert, and good luck. The Company sends its best wishes."

"Thanks," Wingert said sourly. "Same to you."

HE TURNED AWAY from the blank screen and glanced beyond the confines of his force-field. All seemed quiet, so he snapped off the generator.

Quellac, he thought, had the makings of a darned fine world, except for the beasts on the western continent. The planet was Earth-type, sixth in orbit around a small yellow main-sequence star. The soil was red with iron-salts, but looked fertile enough, judging from the thick vegetation pushing up all around. Not far away a sluggish little stream wound through a sloping valley and vanished in a hazy cloud of purple mist near the horizon.

It would be a soft enough life, he thought. If no more toads showed up, or worms with teeth.

The Contract specified that his job was to "prepare and otherwise survey the world assigned, for the purpose of admitting future colonists under the auspices of Planetary Colonization, Inc." He was an advance agent, sent out by the Company to smooth the bugs out of the planet before the regular colonists arrived.

For this they gave him one thousand dollars a month plus "necessities of life" via Matter-Transmitter. There were worse ways of making a living, Wingert told himself.

A lazy green-edged cloud was drifting over the forest. He pushed aside a blackened alien husk and sprawled out on the warm red soil, leaning against the Matter-Transmitter's comforting bulk. Before him were the eight or nine crates containing his equipment and possessions.

He had made the three-week journey from Earth to Quellac aboard the first-class liner *Moored*. Matter-transmission would have been faster, but a Transmitter could handle a bulk of 150 pounds, which was Wingert's weight, only in three 50-pound installments. The idea didn't appeal to him. Besides, there had been no Matter-Transmitter set up on Quellac to receive him, which made the whole problem fairly academic.

A bird sang softly. Wingert yawned. It was early afternoon, and he didn't feel impatient to set up his shelter. The Manual said it took but an hour to unpack. Later, then, when the sun was sinking behind those cerise mountains, he would blow up his bubble-home and unpack his goods. Right now he just wanted to relax, to let the tension of that first fierce encounter drain away.

"Pardon me, sir," said a familiar sharp voice. "I happened to overhear that order for razor blades, and I think it's only fair to inform you that I carry a product of much greater face-appeal."

Wingert was on his feet in an instant, glaring at the robot. "I told you to go away. A-W-A-Y."

Undisturbed, the robot produced a small translucent tube filled with a glossy green paste. "This," XL-ad41 said, "is Gloglam's Depilating Fluid, twelve units—ah, one dollar—per tube."

Wingert shook his head. "I get my goods free, from Terra. Besides, I like to shave with a razor. *Please* go away."

The robot looked about as crestfallen as a robot could possibly look. "You don't seem to understand that your refusal to purchase from me reflects adversely on my abilities, and may result in my being dismantled at the end of this test. Therefore I insist you approach my merchandise with an open mind."

A sudden grin of salesmanlike inspiration illuminated

XL-ad41's face. "I'll take the liberty of offering you this free sample. Try Gloglam's Depilating Fluid and I can guarantee you'll never use a blade razor again."

The robot poured a small quantity of the green fluid into a smaller vial and handed it to Wingert. "Here. I'll return shortly to hear your decision."

THE ROBOT DEPARTED, trampling down the shrubbery with its massive treads. Wingert scratched his stubby chin and regarded the vial quizzically.

Gloglam's Depilating Fluid, eh? And XL-ad41, the robot traveling salesman. He smiled wryly. On Earth, they bombarded you with singing commercials, and here in the wilds of deep space, robots from Densobol came descending on you trying to sell you shaving cream.

Well, if the robot salesman was anything like its Terran counterparts, the only way he'd be able to get rid of it would be by buying something from it. And particularly since the poor robot seemed to be on a trial run, and might be destroyed if it didn't make sales—as a one-time salesman himself, among a few dozen other vocations, Wingert felt sympathy.

Cautiously he squeezed a couple of drops of Gloglam's Depilating Fluid into his palm and rubbed it against one cheek. The stuff was cool and slightly sharp, with a pleasant tang. He rubbed it in for a moment, wondering if it might be going to dissolve his jawbone, then pulled out his pocket mirror.

His face was neat and pink where he'd applied the depilatory. He hadn't had such a good shave in years. Enthusiastically he rubbed the remainder of the tube on his face, thereby discovering that the robot had given him just enough to shave one cheek and most of his chin.

Wingert chuckled. Bumbling and pedantic it might be, but the creature knew a little basic salesmanship, at least.

"Well?" XL-ad41 asked, reappearing as if beckoned. "Are you satisfied?"

Grinning, Wingert said, "That was pretty sly- giving me enough to shave half my face, I mean. But the stuff is good; there's no denying that."

"How many tubes will you take?"

Wingert pulled out his billfold. He had brought only $16 with him; he hadn't expected to have any use for Terran currency on Quellac, but there had been a ten, a five, and a one in his wallet at blastoff time.

"One tube," he said. He handed the robot the tattered single. XL-ad41 bowed courteously, reached into a pectoral compartment, and drew out the remainder of the tube he had shown Wingert before.

"Uh-uh," the Earthman said quickly. "That's the tube you took the sample from—and the sample was supposed to be free. I want a full tube."

"The proverbial innate shrewdness of the Terran," XL-ad41 observed mournfully. "I defer to it."

It gave a second tube to Wingert, who examined it and slid it into his tunic. "And now, if you'll excuse me, I have some unpacking to do," Wingert said.

He strode around the smiling robot, grabbed the crowbar, and began opening the crate that housed his bubble-home. Suddenly the Matter-Transmitter emitted a series of loud buzzes, followed by a dull *clonk*.

"Your machine has delivered something," XL-ad41 ventured.

Wingert lifted the lid of the RECEIVE platform and drew out a small package wrapped neatly in plastofil. He peeled away the wrapping.

Within was a box containing twenty-four double-edged blades, a tube of shaving cream, and a bill folded lengthwise. Wingert read it:

Razor blades, as ordered	$00.23
Shaving cream, as ordered	00.77
Charged for transportation	50.00
Total	$51.00

"You look pale," the robot said. "Perhaps you have some disease. You might be interested in purchasing the Derblong Self-Calibrating Medical Autodiagnostical Servomechanism, which I happen to—"

"No," Wingert said grimly. "I don't need anything like that. Get out of my way."

He stalked back to the Transmitter and jabbed down savagely on the activator stud. A moment later Smathers' bland voice said, "Hello, Colonist Wingert. Something wrong?"

"There sure is," Wingert said in a strangled voice. "My razor blades just showed up—with a fifty-dollar bill for transportation! What kind of racket is this, anyway? I was told that you'd ship my supplies out free of charge. It says in the Contract—"

"The Contract says," Smathers interrupted smoothly, "that all necessities of life will be transmitted without cost, Colonist Wingert. It makes no mention of free supply of luxuries. The Company would be unable to bear the crushing financial burden of transporting any and all luxury items a Colonist might desire."

"Razor blades are luxury items?" Wingert choked back an impulse to kick the Transmitter's control panel in. "How can you have the audacity to call razor blades *luxury items?*"

"Most Colonists grow beards," Smathers said. "Your reluctance to do so, Colonist Wingert, is your own affair. But the Company—"

"I know. The Company cannot be expected to bear the crushing financial burden. Okay," Wingert said. "In the future I'll be more careful about what I order. And as for now, take these damned razor blades back and cancel the requisition." He dumped the package in the SEND bin and depressed the control stud.

"I'm sorry you did that," Smathers said. "It will now be necessary for us to assess you an additional fifty dollars to cover return shipping."

"*What?*"

"However," Smathers went on, "we'll see to it after this

that you're notified in advance any time there may be a shipping charge on goods sent to you."

"Thanks," Wingert said hoarsely.

"Since you don't want razor blades, I presume you're going to grow a beard. I rather thought you would. Most Colonists do, you know."

"I'm not growing any beards. Some vending robot from the Densobol system wandered through here about ten minutes ago and sold me a tube of depilating paste."

Smathers' eyes nearly popped. "You'll have to cancel that purchase," he said, his voice suddenly stern.

Wingert stared incredulously at the pudgy face in the screen. "Now you're going to interfere with that, *too?*"

"Purchasing supplies from anyone but the Company is a gross violation of your Contract, Colonist Wingert, and makes you subject to heavy penalty. After all, we agreed to supply you with your needs. For you to call in an outside supplier is to rob the Company of its privilege of serving you, Colonist Wingert. You see?"

WINGERT WAS SILENT for almost a minute, too dizzy with rage to frame his words. Finally he said, "So I get charged fifty dollars shipping costs every time I requisition razor blades from you people, but if I try to buy depilating paste on my own it violates my Contract? Why, that's—that's usury! Slavery! It's illegal!"

The voice from the Matter-Transmitter coughed warningly. "Powerful accusations, Colonist Wingert. I suggest that before you hurl any more abuse at the Company you read your Contract more carefully."

"I don't give a damn about the Contract! I'll buy anywhere I please!"

Smathers grinned triumphantly. "I was afraid you'd say that. You realize that you've now given us legal provocation to slap a spybeam on you in order to make sure you don't cheat us by violating your Contract?"

Wingert sputtered. "Spybeam? But—I'll smash your accursed Transmitter. *Then* try to spy on me!"

"We won't be able to. But destroying a Transmitter is a serious felony, punishable by a heavy fine. Good afternoon, Colonist Wingert."

"Hey! Come back here! You can't—"

Wingert punched the activator stud three times, but Smathers had broken the contact and would not reopen it. Scowling, Wingert turned away and sat down on the edge of a crate.

"Can I offer you a box of Sugrath Anti-Choler Tranquilizing Pills?" XL-ad41 said helpfully. "Large economy size—"

"Shut up and leave me alone." Wingert stared moodily at the shiny tips of his boots.

The Company, he thought, had him sewed up neatly. He had no money and no way of returning to Earth short of dividing himself into three equal chunks and teleporting. And though Quellac was an attractive planet, it lacked certain aspects of Earth. Tobacco, for one. Wingert enjoyed smoking.

A box of cigars would be $2.40, plus $75 shipping costs. And Smathers would smirk and tell him cigars were luxuries.

Sensotapes? Luxuries. Short-range transmitters? Maybe those came under the Contract, since they were tools. But the pattern was clear. By the time his three-year tour was up, there would be $36,000 in salary waiting in his account—minus the various accumulated charges. He'd be lucky if he came out owing less than $20,000.

Naturally, he wouldn't have that sort of money, and so the benevolent Company would offer a choice: either go to jail or take another three-year term to pay off your debt. So they'd ship him someplace else, and at the end of that time he'd be in twice as deep.

Year after year he would sink further into debt, thanks to that damnable Contract. He'd spend the rest of his life opening up new planets for Planetary Colonizations, Inc., and never have anything to show for it but a staggering debit.

It was worse than slavery.

There had to be some way out.

But after ransacking the Contract for nearly an hour, Wingert concluded that it was airtight. Sure, all "necessities of life" were supplied free—with the hidden corollary that he *had* to accept them through the Company. And nothing at all was said about luxuries, or shipping costs thereof.

So they'd supply him with all the short-range transmitters he needed, gratis—but cigars and razor blades came extra. And the fines for violating the exclusive-supply privilege of the Company were vast.

Angrily he glared up at the beaming robot.

"What are you hanging around here for? You've made your sale. Shove off!"

XL-ad41 shook its head. "You still owe me five hundred dollars for the generator. And surely you can't expect me to return to my manufacturers after having made only two sales. Why, they'd turn me off in an instant and begin developing an XL-ad42."

"Did you hear what Smathers said? I'll be violating my Contract if they see me buying anything more from you. Go on, now. Take your generator back. The sale is canceled. Visit some other planet; I'm in enough hot water as it is without—"

"Sorry," the robot said, and it seemed to Wingert that there was an ominous note in its mellow voice. "This is the seventeenth planet I've called at since being sent forth by my manufacturers, and I have no sale to show for it but one tube of Gloglam Depilating Fluid. It's a poor record. I don't dare return yet."

"Try somewhere else, then. Find a planet full of suckers and give 'em the hard sell. I can't buy from you."

"I'm afraid you'll have to," the robot said mildly. "My specifications call for me to return to Densobol for inspection after my seventeenth visit." A panel in the robot's abdomen opened whirringly and Wingert saw the snout of a Molecular Disruptor emerge.

"The ultimate sales tactic, eh? If the customer won't buy, pull a gun and *make* him buy. Except it won't work here. I haven't any money."

"Your friends on Terra will send some. I *must* return to Densobol with a successful sales record. Otherwise—"

"I know. They'll dismantle you."

"Correct. Therefore, I must approach you this way. And I fully intend to carry out my threat if you refuse."

"Hold on, here!" a new voice cut in. "What's going on, Wingert?"

Wingert glanced at the Transmitter. The screen was lit, and Smathers' plump face glared out at him.

"It's this robot," Wingert said. "It's under some sort of sales compulsion, and it just pulled a gun on me."

"I know. I saw the whole thing on the spybeam."

"I'm in a nice spot now," Wingert said dismally. He glanced from the waiting robot to the unsmiling Smathers. "If I don't buy from this robot, it'll murder me—and if I *do* buy anything, you'll spy it and fine me." Wingert wondered vaguely which would be worse.

"I stock many fine devices unknown on Earth," the robot said proudly. "A Pioneer-Model Dreeg-Skinner, in case there are dreegs on Quellac—though frankly I doubt that. Or else you might want our Rotary Diatom-Strainer, or perhaps a new-model Hegley Neuronic Extractor—"

"Quiet," Wingert snapped. He turned back to Smathers. "Well, what do I do? You're the Company; protect your Colonist from this marauding alien."

"We'll send you a weapon, Colonist Wingert."

"And have me try to outdraw a robot? You're a lot of help," Wingert said broodingly. Even if he escaped somehow from this dilemma, he knew the Company still had him by the throat over the "Necessities of Life" clause. His accumulated shipping charges in three years would—

He sucked his breath in sharply. "Smathers?"

"Yes?"

"Listen to me: if I don't buy from the robot, it'll blast me with a Molecular Disruptor. But I *can't* buy from the robot, even if the Company would let me, because I don't have any money. Money's necessary if I want to stay alive. Get it? *Necessary?*"

"No," Smathers said. "I don't get it."

"What I'm saying is that the item I most need to preserve my life is money. It's a *necessity of life*—and therefore you have to supply me gratis with all the money I need, until this robot decides it's sold me enough. If you don't come through, I'll sue the Company for breach of contract."

Smathers grinned. "Try it. You'll be dead before you can contact a lawyer. The robot will kill you."

Sweat poured down Wingert's back, but he felt the moment of triumph approaching. Reaching inside his khaki shirt, he drew out the thick pseudo-parchment sheet that was his Contract.

"You refuse! You refuse to supply a necessity of life! The Contract," Wingert declared, "is therefore void." Before Smathers' horrified gaze he ripped the document up and tossed the pieces over his shoulder carelessly.

"Having broken your end of the Contract," Wingert said, "you relieve me of all further obligations to the Company. Therefore I'll thank you to remove your damned spybeam from my planet."

"*Your* planet?"

"Precisely. Squatter's rights—and since there's no longer a Contract between us, you're forbidden by galactic law to spy on me."

Smathers looked dazed. "You're a fast talker, Wingert. But we'll fight this. Wait till I refer this upstairs. You won't get out of this so easily!"

Wingert flashed a cocky grin. "Refer it upstairs if you want. I've got the law on my side."

Smathers snarled and broke the contact.

"Nicely argued," said XL-ad41 approvingly. "I hope you win your case."

"I have to," Wingert said. "They can't touch me, not if their Contract is really binding on both parties. If they try to use their spybeam record as evidence against me, it'll show you threatening me. They don't have a leg to stand on."

"But how about me? I—"

"I haven't forgotten. There's a Molecular Disruptor in your belly waiting to disrupt me." Wingert grinned at the robot. "Look here, XL-ad41, face facts: you're a lousy salesman. You have a certain degree of misused guile, but you lack tact, subtlety. You can't go selling people things at gunpoint very long without involving your manufacturers in an interstellar war. As soon as you get back to Densobol and they find out what you've done, they'll dismantle you quicker than you can sell a Dreeg-Skinner."

"I was thinking of that myself," the robot admitted.

"Good. But I'll make a suggestion: I'll *teach* you how to be a salesman. I used to be one myself; besides I'm an Earthman, and innately shrewd. When I'm through with you, you move on to the next planet—I think your makers will forgive you if you make an extra stop—and sell out all your stock."

"It sounds wonderful," XL-ad41 said.

"One string is attached. In return for the education I'll give you, you're to supply me with such things as I need to live

comfortably here on a permanent basis. Cigars, magneboots, short-range transmitters, depilator, etc. I'm sure your manufacturers will think it's a fair exchange, my profit-making shrewdness for your magneboots. Oh, and I'll need one of those force-field generators too—just in case the Company shows up and tries to make trouble."

The robot glowed happily. "I'm sure an exchange can be arranged. I believe this now makes us partners."

"It does indeed," Wingert said. "As your first lesson, let me show you an ancient Terran custom that a good salesman ought to know." He gripped the robot's cold metal hand firmly in his own. "Shake, pardner!"

Robert Silverberg

Robert Silverberg has been a professional science-fiction writer since 1955. He has won many Hugo and Nebula awards and among his best-known books are *Lord Valentine's Castle*, *Dying Inside*, and *Nightwings*. In 2004 he was named a Grand Master by the Science Fiction Writers of America.

THE DOOR-TO-DOOR SALESTHING FROM PLANET X

Josh Vogt

"Sorry to keep you waiting, Dearie. I almost didn't hear the doorbell and don't get around too quickly these days. My, you're a tall one, aren't you? Such handsome tusks and tentacles."

"Greetings, fellow fleshbeing! May we engage in profitable exchange?"

"Selling something, are you?"

"Assumption verified! Observe the collar about my neck."

"I'm going deaf, not blind. But I don't have any pets and never really understood collars as a fashion statement."

"It is not for sale. It is my Motivational Unit. If I fail to conduct at least one profitable exchange each hour, it will detonate, terminating my existence. The current hour ends in a few minutes, and I have not yet acquired profit."

"That seems a little extreme. How is your kind even still around?"

"We breed rapidly. Aggressive sales quotas remedy overpopulation. Now I bring you wonders and delights from beyond belief!"

"Where is that, exactly?"

"Where is what?"

"Belief. Is that one of the planets they just named? There's so many these days, it's hard to keep up. Phoborious, Eden XI, Orb of Eternal Darkness. I hear they even named a planet after the pope. What's yours called, dear?"

"My homeworld is designated Planet X."

"You must've been discovered when they were in that alphabetical phase. Poor dear. Not very imaginative."

"If you desire imagination, feast your bilaterally symmetrical eyes upon this!"

"A suitcase?"

"You behold an interdimensional container bearing a pocket space that is, astoundingly, of greater internal than external proportions!"

"You're saying it's bigger on the inside?"

"Affirmative."

"Isn't that keen. Is the suitcase for sale?"

"It is merely the method by which I transport the goods I present for your purchase. Behold!"

"Yes, you said that already."

"One of these pills per day will renew your youthful physique to that of twenty solar orbits!"

"That's very nice, but I think if God wanted us to go around more than once, He'd have made us with rewind buttons installed."

"Then revel in replacement memory modules! Recall only a full and happy lifetime. No guilt. No regrets. No sadness."

"No regrets here to speak of, Dearie. And a life that's only happy would be a boring one, don't you think?"

"Perhaps you will delight in a post-mortem mental upload unit. Enjoy a personal, virtual heaven, programmed to fulfill your every whim."

"Been a faithful Baptist since I before I could walk, so

Heaven's already in my travel plans. And eternity in a computer? Pshaw to that paradise."

"I detect a notable lack of enthusiasm for such fine wares."

"Sorry to be picky, but there's nothing here I take a shine to."

"We offer flexible installment payment plans. We accept cash, credit, or plagons."

"Are plagons the currency unit on Planet X?"

"They are the unborn young of the species with which we are at interplanetary war."

"Oh. Pretty sure I don't have any of those in my purse."

"Sadness abounds. Now I make an offer that you may not refuse!"

"Don't you mean 'cannot'?"

"The choice of vocabulary was intentional, as my collar has begun to tingle. Beho—"

"Yes, yes. Behold. My tea is getting cold and my favorite show is starting on the holotube. Can we hurry this up?"

"Surely your days are empty as loved ones depart the physical plane. Fill this void with cloned companions designed to fulfill your every fleshy desire and—"

"Hold it right there. If you're suggesting I clone my late husband and friends for a senior citizen orgy, I'm giving your tentacles a good whack with my cane."

"It is one of our more popular offers."

"Answer's still no."

"But you cannot—"

"Try to boss me around, Dearie, and you'll get a knock from my cane *and* a bite. My dentures have automatic laser-targeting."

"Longevity! Carnal companionship! Wealth! Relative beauty according to species morphic bias! Your kind desires these things at any price!"

"You're thirty years too late for me. Might have better luck with Ned at the end of the block."

"My remaining time allotment will expire before I reach the end of the block. As will I."

"I'm sorry. How about I donate a few dollars, since you've

been trying so hard?"

"Negative! I must provide goods in exchange. Is there nothing you require?"

"Hm. Now that I think about it ..."

"Tell me so I may fulfill this request with all haste!"

"New kitchen knives."

"... kitchen knives?"

"Yes, the ones that never dull? Not that I'll use them for long, but I'm down to one bent butter knife in my silverware drawer."

"I ... am not in possession of kitchen knives."

"Shame. I'd be willing to pay handsomely for a nice sharp set of—goodness gracious! Whatever are you doing?"

"The pain! Quite agonizing!"

"You just tore out your own tusks!"

"Limited edition. Never need sharpening. Notice the fine engraving denoting my status as top salesbeing last quarter."

"Persistent, aren't you? How much?"

"One-time exclusive offer of three hundred million plagons."

"Oh my. What's that with the going exchange rate?"

"Twenty human dollars."

"All right. Come inside while I get my purse. Your ... um ... collar won't go off now, will it?"

"It has detected our profitable accord. My cohesion continues for another hour."

"Bit of a stressful line of work, isn't it, Dearie?"

"It is a living."

Josh Vogt

A full-time freelance writer and editor, Josh Vogt works with a variety of RPG developers and publishers and has sold fiction to Paizo's *Pathfinder Tales*, Grey Matter Press, the *UFO2* & *UFO3* anthologies, *Intergalactic Medicine Show*, and *Shimmer*, among others. His upcoming debut fantasy novel is also with Paizo's *Pathfinder Tales*. You can find him at JRVogt.com or @JRVogt. He is made out of meat.

PICTURE PERFECT

Matt Mikalatos

Richard the unfriendly ghost woke me. I blinked twice. The sun was still up, I could sense it on the other side of the drapes. "Are you trying to murder me again?" I asked.

Richard cackled. "Worse! Much worse, Isaac."

I frowned. I didn't bother to ask what was worse than murder. As a vampire I had doled out plenty of worse-than-murder moments, not the least of which was feeding Richard to one of the elder gods of terror. That had bought me almost two months of Richard-free bliss. But ghosts are surprisingly resilient.

A steady, insistent knocking came from the front room. I threw off my comforter and padded to the door. I leaned against it. "Who's there?"

"Sam."

"Sam who?"

"Sam-one open the door, it's freezing out here!"

I muttered a series of imprecations. "I won't open this door unless you tell me who you are."

A lighthearted chuckle came through the door. "Come now, it won't be so bad. Your father already called and explained your situation. Are you dressed?"

My father had died over a hundred years ago. He had been the famous vampire hunter, Abraham Van Helsing. I'd been turned into a vampire during a botched father-son hunting trip. I glanced at the clock on Mrs. Holmes's mantel. "It's eight in the morning."

Richard floated past me and undid the locks. "Beware the sunlight," he said, and the stranger outside pushed the door open.

Even indirect sunlight burned. I quickly stepped back into the shadowed living room behind me. Standing on the boarding room porch was a painfully thin man with silver spectacles and a spectacular comb over.

"Hey there sunshine," he said, grinning. I hated him immediately.

"I take it you are Sam," I said.

"That was just for the knock-knock joke. It isn't freezing out, either. It's a perfectly lovely day."

Richard was floating on the far side of the door, laughing uproariously. The stranger couldn't see him, and appeared not to notice the laughter. Perhaps he thought it was in response to his horrible joke.

"State your name and business," I said.

He laughed. "Why, the state is my business. I got a call from your father."

"I doubt it. My father passed away years ago."

The man snapped his fingers. "Come to think of it, the line did go dead at the end of the call." He looked at me for a moment. "Get it? The line was dead?"

I rubbed my face and hoped that Richard had not somehow found a minor pun demon to torment me. "Please. In the name of all that is holy. Tell me why you are here or begone."

"I'm here because I heard you've got no class."

I sighed and glared at Richard before swinging the door shut. "Is this the best you can do?"

"Trust me," Richard said. "It gets much better." He opened the door again.

The man pulled out a badge. "My name is Philip Voss. I'm a truant officer."

"Oh no."

"Oh yes! Isaac Van Helsing," he said, pulling a small clipboard out of thin air, "You've been cutting. And if you miss school again, you're headed to jail."

"But I'm a vampire."

"Well, that sucks."

I grunted. "Like I haven't heard that a million times."

Officer Voss wrote a note on his clipboard. "I'll tell the teachers to cover their windows. High school is a dark time for many."

"I am 139 years old."

"You must be a senior, then." He looked at me with a practiced eye. "Besides, I'd guess you're eighteen."

"Yes, I was eighteen when I turned into a vampire, but that was one hundred and twenty years ago."

Richard said, "A hundred and twenty-one years ago. A basic math course could only help him, Officer."

"Nevertheless. I am well past the age of conscripted schooling."

"No problem," Officer Voss said, writing furiously. "Just give me a peek at your birth certificate and I'll be on the way."

My jaw fell open. "What?"

"You have to prove your age."

"I don't have a birth certificate."

He shrugged. "So you go to school."

"But I died when I became a vampire."

"You have a death certificate?"

"No."

Voss clucked his tongue. "Probably just as well. Having a dead body in the home is a biohazard. You'd get fined."

"You're saying I have to go to school."

Voss laughed. "You might not be educated, but you're smart enough. I'll write that down. Smart. Enough."

"Surely there's another way."

"You got your GED?" He saw the look on my face and shook his head, writing. "See you tomorrow at eight thirty."

I tried one last ditch effort. "What if I bite the other students?"

He waved without turning back. "The principal will deal with you."

MOTHER HOLMES, THE old woman who ran my boarding house, was thrilled at the prospect of sending me to school. She got me new "schooling clothes" as she called them: shiny black shoes, grey shorts, a white collared shirt and a red bowtie. I tried to refuse, but once Mother Holmes decided something one had best go along. Which is why I also carried the lunch she had packed for me in a Scooby Doo lunch box, despite my inability to eat food and my antipathy toward mystery-solving cartoon dogs. Of course, I had to carry a large umbrella to keep the sun off. But the indirect light still hurt my skin, and I was glad that it was a rainy day.

In the dim light, Richard was more visible, and as we moved through the puddled parking lot he mocked me for going to school. Determined not to let him think he had found yet another way to harass and annoy me, I told him I was looking forward to the day.

"To the end of the day you mean?" he asked.

"No. To making new friends, learning new things. It's a wonderful institution, school. To be surrounded by these teens, full of life and the light of learning."

Richard rolled his eyes. "It has been a long time since you were with high schoolers."

A red sports car came screeching through the parking lot, a wave of water rising up above my head and dousing me completely. A young woman leapt out of the car. Her hair was bleached blonde with light blue streaks, and she wore tight-fitting jeans and a tank top with a strange diaphanous shirt over the top. Her shoes were transparent, and bright orange socks shone through them. She looked like a shopping mall had exploded onto her.

She snatched some books from the front of her car and came over to me. She looked me up and down and then took hold of my umbrella, lifting it over her head. "Hey, sorry about the tidal wave," she said. "Mind if I take this umbrella? You won't need it now that you're soaked.

I bared my fangs at her. "As it so happens, I need it to keep the sun off."

She smacked some gum in her mouth and looked me over again. "Geez, pal, could you get any whiter?"

I looked at my pale skin. "I doubt it."

"Maybe if you were a mime," Richard suggested.

"Hey, a ghost," she said.

"You can see me?" Richard asked.

"Shh," she said. "Ghosts are supposed to say 'oooooo' and that's it. So don't talk. Creeps me out."

I smiled. "What is your name, young lady?"

She slapped me on the shoulder. "You're a weird guy. Looks like your grandma dressed you, but I like you. I'm Alice."

"Isaac," I said, and held out my hand.

She laughed and slapped my palm. "Seriously, you look like a yodeling vampire from Sound of Music."

I took the umbrella back from her, though I was careful to leave room for her to stay out of the rain. "I have not seen the film."

She laughed so hard she snorted. "I have not seen the film."

Richard cackled and said, "All of the children are going to mock you."

Alice abruptly stopped laughing and poked a finger at the transparent thorn in my side. "Shut up, ghost. That sounds suspiciously like bullying and there is zero tolerance here, you transparent excuse for a half human. Oooooo."

To my considerable surprise, Richard looked chastened. I studied the girl more closely, making sure she wasn't some sort of violent anti-supernatural activist.

"Honestly," I said, "How can you see Richard? I've always envied those who can't."

She shrugged. "I'm a weredolphin."

"I have never heard of such a thing."

"That's because I made it up, silly. I don't know why, but I see dead people. No biggie." A clanging bell rang just as we stepped out of the parking lot and onto the school grounds.

Alice gathered her books to her chest. "C'mon, Isaac, we're going to be late." A milling crowd of students drifted toward their classrooms.

A voice echoed to us across the small square between classrooms. I turned to see the truant officer, Voss, headed toward us, wearing a yellow slicker. Alice made a sound of disgust. "Not that guy. I gotta bounce, Isaac." Then she bounced, hopping with both feet toward her classroom. I watched her in perplexed wonder. "See you at lunch," she called back. "Meet me at the library!"

"Not the library," I said. I had a bad experience with a British librarian in the late '90s. He had manipulated a clique of children into risking their lives to try to kill me. I left town and decided never to live somewhere with the word "Sunny" in the name. What sort of stupid vampire lives in a town with a name like that?

Voss glanced at my umbrella and said, "I see that you're a bit under the weather."

"It's one thing to make puns constantly. It's quite another to emphasize them when speaking."

Voss's eyes widened. "I'm sorry. Do you feel that I am punishing you?"

"Good Lord," I said. Getting to class seemed like a good idea now. I realized I didn't know where to go, and said as much.

"Come with me," Voss said, "and you'll get the picture."

So, of course, he took me to a small room with a camera set up in it. For my student I.D. he said. The camera was ancient. Though I had seen such things before I couldn't imagine why Voss would have one. It had an accordion-like protrusion at the front, and he raised a hand-held flash in one hand, his head under a drape directly behind the camera.

He depressed the shutter button and a horrific flash burned my retinas, accompanied by a slight burning smell and a whiff of sulphur. I had tried to explain that I couldn't be seen in mirrors or photographs, but he insisted on trying. He pulled a photograph out of the camera, glanced at it and said, "I guess school isn't the only place you don't show up."

The small room was lined with framed photographs of students. I was surprised by their vibrant perfection. Each photo captured the essence of a young life. I ran my finger over one of them, startled by the lifelike quality of it. It was strange to me that the ancient camera took such excellent photos, and also that they seemed to come from the box immediately developed. Voss seemed pleased that I appreciated his work.

Much of the morning was filled with paperwork and a short tour. I sat through an interminable math class and then a history class which I found illuminating. I had not paid particular attention to history as I had lived through it. Being a rather poor vampire, I had spent a lot more time and attention on surviving than on news.

The students seemed dull and listless. They drifted from class to class like ghosts. In fact, they were considerably less animated than Richard, who eventually got bored and left me in my high school purgatory.

Alice met me at lunch. She straddled a bench, immediately snatched my lunch box and began digging through it. An apple appeared and she munched on it with a look of pure rapture on her face. "So, you're a vampire," she said.

"Yes."

"Cool." She squinted at me. "Are you going to suck my blood?"

I shook my head and picked through the lunch box. I couldn't eat any of it, of course. For some unknown reason Mrs. Holmes had also packed a head of garlic. She never remembered that I couldn't eat regular food and that garlic burned my skin. "I've never been good at eating prey once I've met them."

"So how do you choose your prey? You find homeless people or something?"

I cocked my head and looked at her. "Just because they're down on their luck doesn't mean they're better for snacking."

"Picky eater," she said. She threw the apple core over her shoulder and wiped the juice from her face. "Are you going to fall in love with me, then?"

I frowned at her. "You're sixteen years old. I might have fallen in love with your grandmother, but what could you and I possibly have in common?" I shivered. "It's a disgusting thought. I suppose you don't even like barbershop quartets. You probably enjoy that infernal rock and roll music."

"Geez, just say no next time." She wrinkled her nose and threw the garlic away. "Do you sparkle in the sunlight?"

I considered this. "In the sense that I catch on fire and burn to ash, I suppose that I do, yes."

The bell rang and Alice shoved all her garbage onto the floor. "I gotta go get my student I.D. pic," she said. "I hate that Voss guy. He's always using bad puns. Really bad puns."

"It's terrible," I agreed.

She shrugged. "Oh well. Call me Alice in Pun-derland." She slapped my Scooby Doo lunch box against my chest. "See you in Civics."

IT WAS IN Civics that I realized something was wrong. The students remained sedate. The teacher didn't call roll or teach, she just sat at her desk. A spider the size of a car crawled out of a hole in the wall and carried off a football player from the front row.

I leapt to my feet and shouted. The spider turned its great, red-eyed head at me and then scuttled down a bolt-hole as large as the teacher's desk.

Richard floated in through the wall, a smile on his face.

When he saw me standing at the center of the room, the smile faded. "Oh. I hoped someone had put a stake in your heart."

"A giant spider," I said.

"Like a spider could even hurt you. Whack it with a newspaper."

"Giant. Spider."

"I heard you the first time."

The spider reappeared, gathered another student, lifted her up and walked into its bolt-hole. The door to the room opened and Alice walked in. Her face was calm, and she took the empty seat in the front row.

"Alice," I whispered, and when she didn't turn I repeated it again, louder.

Richard floated in front of her. "She's tranced out like the rest of these poor saps."

I walked to her side and snapped my fingers in front of her face. Nothing. The spider emerged again, took hold of the teacher and retreated down the narrow opening of its hole.

I took Alice by the hand and walked her outside the classroom. I shut the door, leaving her standing in the hall. I looked around for a weapon, but there was nothing obvious. I bent a metal leg on my desk and worked it back and forth until it snapped off in my hand.

I glared at Richard. "Was this your plan for me, you disembodied fiend?"

The ghost threw his hands up. "Not at all. I thought you might have to spend four years in high school, that's all."

"Well. I can't have my classmates eaten by spiders," I said, and started down the bolt-hole. My eyes adjusted immediately, one of the advantages of being a creature of the night.

The passageway opened into a vast underground warren of tunnels. This cavern must be grand central station. Richard floated nearby. The students and teachers had been trussed up and hung upside down next to the photos from their own student I.D.s. A series of torches lit the side walls. I didn't see the spider.

The teacher was breathing softly. I pulled her picture off the sticky wall. She looked vibrant and alive in the picture, her skin practically glowing. I tapped my fingertips to my lips.

"Help me," the photo said.

I was so startled I dropped her. The frame broke when it hit the ground and a thin susurrus of air came from the photo. The teacher opened her eyes and raised a blood-curdling scream.

"Miss," I said. "Miss. If you could stop with the screaming, I believe you might be drawing attention to us."

"Spider," she gasped.

"Yes," I said, just as giant mouth pinchers yanked me backward. I spun and jabbed the desk leg into one of its eyes, and it hissed and pulled away. It had torn my shirt and bloodied my chest. I hadn't fed in some time, so there wasn't much blood. It was unlikely that a spider could pound a stake into my heart, so there wasn't much to lose. I jumped on it and began to methodically stab it with the desk leg. Finally, I jabbed through the back of the spider's head, and it fell in a heap near the teacher. I tried to yank the leg free, but it was stuck.

An eight-legged freight train struck me from behind and I fell beneath it. Thick, viscous webbing poured over me. I couldn't move my arms. Officer Voss leaned over, smiling. He held a portrait of Alice tucked under his arm. I watched as he inspected the corpse of the first spider. "Looks like you got a leg up on that one," he said, wiggling his eyebrows.

"You're in league with the spiders?"

Voss clucked his tongue. "More like I'm working together with them."

"That's what 'in league with' means."

"Oh. Well, in that case, yes." He showed me Alice's picture. "I capture the souls of the students with my camera, making them easy prey. Then the Fearsome Spiders of Appo bring their bodies down here. The Spiders of Appo keep ten percent, and I sell the rest to eager creatures hungry for bodies or souls, as the case may be."

"But why bring me to the school?"

Voss pulled out his clipboard and flipped through a few pages. "There's some crazed human cult after you. Claims you killed all their parents back in '74."

"Oh," I said. "Them. I tried to explain. That was a binge period for me."

Voss nodded sympathetically. "It really is difficult when you feast on humans. Precisely what my services are designed to counter balance. I suspect you could be a customer if I hadn't already promised you to the cult. They're paying me a hundred grand to deliver you."

The spider had wrapped me quite snugly and was moving toward my waist. "Richard," I said. "I might need you to go for help."

Richard floated over. "Sorry, I was distracted by the aura of pure pleasure I get at the thought that you might be about to die."

"Caught in my web!" Voss said.

"Really?" I asked. "You really think that's good enough?"

Voss chuckled. "I'm not going for originality, you know. I thought about saying something like 'stuck on you' but it had a more romantic feeling than I wanted."

I looked at the picture in his arm. "Alice," I said, hoping she could hear me. "Go find help."

"It doesn't work like that," Voss said. "The souls won't talk unless they're close to their bodies. I don't know why. Only exception is if you happen to catch a picture of a ghost. They get trapped in the photo and start talking a blue streak. I had hoped it would work on you, but I guess I caught you easily enough."

"If you've harmed Alice—"

"Don't worry, she's a perfect picture of health." He held the framed photo closer to me.

I couldn't move my arms, but my legs were still free. I kicked hard, undulating my body, and my head connected with the picture. It spun out of his hands and smashed against the wall.

"Richard," I said. "Tell Alice to run."

"I can do that," Richard said reluctantly. "I don't like to see high schoolers eaten, after all." He floated up toward the classroom.

Voss laughed maniacally. He ordered the Appo Spider to hold me tighter. "You think you're some sort of knight in shining armor," he said. He pulled out a crucifix and placed it over the tunnel that led back to the classroom. "This should keep you from crossing me."

He was about to run up the tunnel when Alice came barreling down, brandishing a fire extinguisher from the classroom. Not one for confrontation, Voss stumbled away from her.

"Are you the creep who stole my soul and tried to feed me to spiders?"

Voss rearranged his spectacles. "Technically, there was only a ten percent chance that it would have been the spiders."

She whacked him in the head with the extinguisher and he crumpled to the ground. The spider on top of me tensed its legs, ready to pounce on her, but she grabbed a torch from the tunnel wall and stabbed it in the face. It fell down, on fire, crushing me.

I caught fire, too. Alice sprayed me with fire extinguishing foam. It was surprisingly cold. I couldn't move to get out from under the spider. It had crushed multiple bones and left me shuddering in enormous pain.

Richard was laughing.

Alice told him to shut up.

Voss struggled to his feet. He looked down on me and the burnt arachnid and said, "It's hard to resist hot Appo spider on a cold knight."

Alice said, "That's it. I'm going to extinguish your head until puns stop coming out of it."

When Alice moved toward him, Voss snatched the framed picture of the football player from the wall. "I'll burn it," he said, holding it near a torch.

"I never liked him," Alice said.

"Aha!" Voss said, tossing the torch aside. "I'll break the

frame and return him to normal."

Alice froze. "You wouldn't."

"I will." He held the picture over his head. "No one follows me," he said. "I'm going to get in my car and drive away, and anyone who tries to follow me will get exhausted."

"You really are the worst," Richard said.

Voss backed out of the chamber and ran back up toward the school.

"Follow him," I told Richard.

"But I don't want to get exhausted."

I glared at him. "It's better than getting exorcised."

"Fine!" He floated off, pouting.

Alice set about releasing all of the teachers and students. Once they stopped their hysterical screaming they helped her remove the giant spider carcass off me. We all managed to get to the surface just as the final bell rang, releasing everyone from school.

I HEAL COMPLETELY when I sleep during the day. It's not a pleasant experience, but far more pleasant than it is for humans. My broken bones snapped back into place. Mrs. Holmes had been less than pleased at the state of my schooling clothes, but had set off to clean and repair them.

When I awoke it was night. I had several texts from Alice, telling me that Voss had not appeared at school the next day. Nor had I expected him to. He had escaped with his camera and several student photographs. I texted her back and told her I was headed to Voss's hideout even now.

Richard had tracked Voss to a small hotel three towns over. I knocked on the wooden door and waited patiently. Voss opened the door, dressed in an ill-fitting hotel robe.

"Hello," I said.

He immediately slammed the door, but not before I got my fingers between the door and the frame. The door swung open again, and I looked down in displeasure at my throbbing fingers.

"You don't have permission to cross the threshold," Voss said. "I know how this works."

"Ah," I said, putting my throbbing hand under my arm. "Yes. Precisely. I cannot enter your home without permission."

"Then I will wait for sunrise and be on my way."

I could see a box of photos on the floor beside the bed. "Give me your camera and the remaining photos. I may let you go on your way without harm."

"The photos? Maybe. But not the camera. Never."

I stepped across the threshold.

Voss stumbled backward. "But I didn't give you permission!"

"This is not your home, Voss. It's a hotel. I spoke to the manager before coming up." I smiled, showing my pointed teeth. "He was eager to give me permission to enter."

"You can have the camera," he said. "And the pictures. You can have it all. My list of clients, everything."

"Yes," I said, closing the door behind me. "I believe I am going to take all of those things."

"You're going to let him go?" Richard asked.

"Of course not, Richard. Silence!"

"I think you should listen to Richard," Voss said.

Richard snorted. "I think you should eat him."

"Never mind," Voss said. "Don't listen to him."

"This," I said gently, locking the door, "is going to hurt. In fact, I think you'll find that I am going to be quite a pain in the neck."

"That's clichéd but still funny," Voss said as I stepped toward him. "I get the feeling," he said as I took hold of him, "that this is going to be a scream."

When the shouting and the feeding had ended, I broke all the photos in the box. I found the client list at the bottom and scanned the names. A few vampires, a cult or two, demons, even a cannibal. I supposed I would need to contact them to let them know my high school was off limits.

I picked up the camera and weighed it in my hands. I turned toward Richard. "I feel that you can't be trusted to wander free anymore, Richard. This little prank of yours got out of hand."

Richard began to float away from me. "I've been framed!" he shouted.

"Precisely," I said, and touched the shutter button.

I tucked the new photo under my arm and stepped over Voss. I debated cleaning up, but it seemed unlikely any of this would be traced back to me. I could hear Richard's muffled complaints from the picture. I promised him I'd hang him somewhere with dignity. Perhaps the dining room. Mrs. Holmes might like that.

"Richard," I said. "High school wasn't so bad, but the puns were unforgiveable."

Richard apologized from within the portrait. "I didn't know about the puns or the spiders," he said. "Even I am not so cruel."

"Well, let's just *focus* on getting beyond this," I said.

"No," Richard said, groaning. "I'm trapped in this frame. Please, don't torture me with puns."

"You're right, of course. It's just that photography *lens* itself to puns."

Richard began to cry.

"I'm going to *expose* you to a new pun every day."

"Make it stop!"

"There's not much you'll be able to do about it once I hang you in the dining room."

"Why not?"

"Because you'll have your back against the wall."

"You're going to run out of them eventually," Richard said hopefully.

"Maybe so," I said. "Maybe so." I put his frame into the passenger seat of my van and climbed behind the wheel. I sent Alice a text, telling her to start brainstorming. With her help, coming up with several months' worth of puns should be a snap.

I smiled at Richard. "We'll just have to wait and see how it develops."

Matt Mikalatos

Matt Mikalatos is afraid of ghosts, vampires, spiders and high schoolers. Also sharks. He's the author of the comedy-theology novel *My Imaginary Jesus* and the children's fantasy novel *The Sword of Six Worlds*. He blogs regularly at norvillerogers.com, disguises conversations with friends as a podcast at storymen.us and records the minutiae of his day on Twitter as @mattmikalatos.

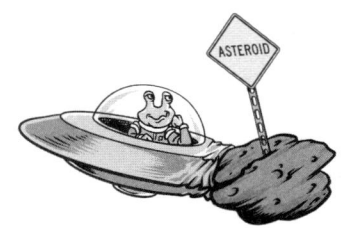

THE DISCOUNTED SENIORS

James Beamon

I was faking a nap, checking out the booties of the few ladies in the dayroom under half-closed eyelids, when I saw the delivery man out of the corner of my eye. The young brother braced himself against his dolly, stabilizing a box that seemed to fill the entire doorway. After he talked a moment with the robo-nurse, they both made their way over to my recliner. I knew right then nothing good would come from that giant box.

"Mr. Washington," the robo-nurse said, its voice girlish and soothing, its mouth LEDs pulsing red as it ran through the syllables. "You have a package."

I looked at the brother with the box.

"That a white woman in there, Youngblood?"

The delivery man smiled. "Old-timer, you know if it was we would've 'lost' this package."

"Then I don't want it," I said.

"Good thing I only deliver packages, and not promises or happiness," he said, as he positioned the giant box to sit in front of me. He eased his dolly from under it and winked at me. "Otherwise, we'd both be unhappy about this."

He left me there, staring at a box addressed from Mr. Washington to Mr. Washington. Unlike riding a bike, mailing parcels wasn't something I ever personally covered with my son. I thought the enterprise was fairly self-explanatory. Leave it to my seed to fail the basic postage aptitude test.

"Mr. Washington, you have a package," the robo-nurse crooned like I hadn't heard it the first time.

"Yeah, yeah. Help me open it."

"I'm sorry," the robo-nurse said with its bright LED smile. "It is not in my programming."

"What do you mean it ain't in your programming? You're a robo-nurse. You're supposed to help me."

"I'll certainly help you, Mr. Washington," its voice chimed. "What can I help you with?"

"Help me open this box."

"I'm sorry. It is not in my programming."

"What the hell?" I asked. "This is the SunBless Farms Assisted Living Center. You're programmed to assist the living, yes?"

"Certainly, Mr. Washington."

"Well, I need assistance."

"Certainly, Mr. Washington."

"With opening this box."

"I'm sorry. It is not in my programming."

"They pull you off of Window Three at the DMV for this gig? Gone." I batted my hand at it. "Get."

"Certainly, Mr. Washington. Will you be joining the Curriculum today at the special introductory price of only nine ninety-nine a month?" it asked.

"Format yourself."

It retreated without another word. Damn thing was as useless as a refrigerator in the Arctic Circle. I reached for my titanium Hyper-Cane 3000 and, with its help, got to my feet. I held the gleaming cane like a shotgun and pushed a button near the crook. The rubber tip at the end of the cane swiveled into the shaft to be replaced by a sharp, curved spike.

The makers of Hyper-Cane said the spike was perfect for

navigating icy terrain. I say it was perfect for defending myself back when I was stuck in Endless Glen Retirement Home. That place was hard like a prison yard. With dread in my heart, I cut the tape off the package.

I couldn't reach down to open it before it opened itself. A black man unfolded from the confines of the box, showering the cheap beige carpet with white packing peanuts as he rose like Aphrodite from the sea until he stood a full foot taller than me. His body was naked save for tighty whitey underwear. His face, the face of my son, was all smiles.

"Dammit, Darius!" I shouted. "You lost your mind? I know flying is expensive but you don't go putting postage on yourself to avoid the baggage fees." I looked my son up and down. "They charging extra to ship you with clothes on?"

"Cyrus Washington," he said, "I'm afraid you're mistaken. I'm not a Darius, I'm a H.U.E.Y., your HUman Emulating Yesman. I was custom built to look this way and sent here to be your personal android."

I dug my cell phone from my pocket. Darius' face popped up on my screen after two rings to confirm this travesty.

"Hey Dad! Anything neeeew happen?" he asked, his voice full of excitement as he dragged new around like a cat on a leash.

"New? As in you sending me a goddamn Terminator? Yeah, something new just happened. And what the hell?"

"What's a Terminator?" he asked.

"See? That's one of the reasons I don't want but so many visits from you a year. You don't get my references. The other reason is you snake all my chicks. Last thing I need is your naked proxy around me twenty-four seven." I looked around the dayroom. There wasn't but four ladies in the room, thanks to the damn Curriculum, but they had all stopped knitting socks and watching soaps to stare at the chiseled ebony Adonis whose calves disappeared into the box. Gladys was drooling, which was typical, while she was wide awake, which wasn't. When my son was beside me it was as if someone was selling

Fountain of Youth Elixir and I was "Before" while he was "After." How the hell was I gonna compete with that?

"Huey won't interfere with your love life," Darius said. "Besides, you said there were plenty of ladies running around SunBless. That's why you wanted to go there, remember?"

"I never said plenty, I said it was better than that sausage fest they were having over there at Endless Glen. And I never asked for a robot helper. I've got enough useless robot help as it is."

Darius smiled. I looked up from the phone to see Huey smiling the same way, which freaked me out. For a moment, my life as a father of twins flashed before my eyes and I realized if that had happened I'd be making this call from a sanitarium.

"That's why I got you Huey, Dad. You always complain about the robo-nurses. So I figured this would help since you don't want the robo-nurse premium service that comes with signing up for the Curriculum."

"They charge extra for the Curriculum!"

It wasn't just the price that prickled me about that damn program. I didn't battle my way through life's rigors to subject myself to them again at a price. Sky-diving, white water rafting, bull fighting, or whatever other heart-attack-inducing thrill ride they did in the Curriculum wasn't for me. I wanted safe things. Hennessy was safe. So was post-menopausal hanky-panky. I didn't have to worry about another Darius growing up to send me junk like the first one was doing. I looked at Huey.

"Send it back," I told Darius.

"I can't," he said. "It's custom made. That's why he looks like me."

"There's that, too. Why didn't you send me a young Halle Berry?"

"Who's Halle Berry?"

"Graaar!" I yelled as I hung up the phone.

Great. Stuck with Offspring Terminator. I was tempted to write my son out of my will for this one. Huey kept his Colgate smile turned up to eleven.

"Why the hell are you smiling?" I asked him.

"Something I don't understand, but it's definitely in my hard code," he said. "It totally goes against logic though." His voice was super friendly, and exactly like Darius', which reminded me of the time he came home waving pamphlets for Happy Horizons.

"Why is smiling against logic?"

"Teeth are a last resort weapon. Mine are enamel coated steel plates attached to a vise that can crush material at two thousand pounds per square inch. I can't see how displaying them is disarming to a human, unless the human wanted to verify I did have the necessary tools to eat them. And what human would want to be eaten by me?"

With a shaky hand and a huge grin, Gladys raised her hand.

I turned back to Huey. "We gotta get you some clothes. C'mon."

There weren't but so many dudes I was cool with here at SunBless, and only one was Huey's height. We made our way to Clyde's room on a journey that seemed to take forever. I walked on my cane through long hallways made empty by everyone going out on the Curriculum. Light jazz music filtered down to us from hidden speakers, that crappy stuff they installed in elevators that made you really angry when you accidentally pressed the wrong button and had to ride that bastard any longer than necessary. Plus I had Huey in my ear, being more helpful than a conglomeration of robo-nurses.

"I don't mind carrying you, Cyrus," he said. "I know my arms look weak covered in all this stupid synthetic meat, but I assure you, they are quite strong."

"If you wanna learn firsthand the sound a titanium cane makes smacking up against ridiculous synthetic meat, you'll keep this up."

Eventually, we got to Clyde's room. His door shook like a speaker as the music behind it bumped relentlessly. I groaned at the unmistakable sound of Africa Bambaata's *Planet Rock*. There was never much point in telling Clyde he was too old for this crap. It went about as well as knocking on the door when the music was this loud. I turned the doorknob without bothering.

Clyde "Dub Walker" Walker was too busy pop-locking to notice his open door, me or the near naked Terminator. He wore an Adidas jumpsuit, all red with white stripes, and matching shell toe Adidas sneakers. His entire floor was covered in cardboard scavenged from boxes so he could be ready, as he put it, "to serve them suckas with my freshest moves." Never mind that I was still trying to figure out which suckas, I wanted to know which fresh break dancing move in his arsenal didn't involve him actually breaking a body part. I grabbed his remote off the bed and turned the system off while Africa Bambaata chanted for Clyde to "rock it, don't stop it."

Clyde stopped doing the robot to look at me, with bewilderment, than anger, on his face. "What the hell, homeboy?"

Before I could reply, Huey was on Clyde. "I should ask you the same thing, elderly male. Do you know how offensive your dance is to my people?"

"What?" Clyde asked. "You mean the robot?"

"You don't see robots running around doing dances that mimic your shortcomings? The Heart Attack, or the Clipping Overgrown Toenails, or my personal favorite: the Hurry to the Bathroom Because My Bowels Are Slippery in Large Part to Burrito Night. It isn't because the robot community is bereft of its dance crazes; everyone with a 128-bit processor loves the Heart Attack. But you don't see these dances because we robots are aware that human feelings are the frailest thing on an already frail body, so we try to respect that. Is it asking too much for you to do the same?"

I knew Clyde wasn't one for lectures, mostly because he didn't have that long of an attention span. "Frail? You calling my moves weak?

"Cool it," I said. "Become BFFs on your own time. Clyde, let my Terminator borrow one of your outfits."

I went outside the room to wait. That's when I saw Nadia walking toward me. I think I almost started drooling. Not only was she fine, she carried herself with class, a real Claire Huxtable type. It didn't help that I had a thing for Claire Huxtable growing up ... she used to have me glued to the TV. Anyway, she was headed my way.

"Do you require assistance, Darius? Your eyes look a bit glassy."

"They're probably star struck," I said. "What we call dreamy-eyed." Moments later, I finally realized Huey was in the hallway with me. His Adidas jumpsuit was orange, but we were still looking like Before and After and I couldn't have that in front of Nadia.

I pushed Huey, but there was no budging a chest of dense, meat-covered metal. So I brought up my Hyper-Cane 3000 and started swatting at him. "Back! Back!" I said, as if I was taming lions.

"OK!" he said, holding his arms up to block the cane blows. I snapped the door shut as Nadia made her way to me. I smiled fiercely at her.

"Hey."

"Hey yourself," Nadia said with a sexy grin. "Who was that you were fighting with?"

"Nobody. Life insurance salesman or something. You know how they get with their no-hassle policies. But he reminded me that time is short for folks like us. Let's get lunch."

"I would love to, Cyrus," she said, her eyes dancing. "But I don't have the time." She frowned. "I'm late for the Curriculum. Maybe later, although, I'm often tired afterwards. But I definitely want a lunch date with you, Cyrus. I'm sure we'll fit it in sometime."

She smiled and continued down the hallway. Her words were the catalyst for drastic action. I mean, she would have lunch, spend some time with yours truly, but the Curriculum was calling her. I knew right then the Curriculum would have to die.

I pushed open the door where apparently Huey was showing Clyde how to do the Heart Attack, if grabbing their chests and convulsing in rhythm was any indication.

"Huey, you and Krush Groove over there need to chill. We got a mission."

"Mission?"

"Yeah, we're going to find out where this Curriculum is and sabotage the dog shit out of it."

"Sabotage?" Clyde asked. "Like the Beastie Boys? Yeah, boy!"

Both Huey and Clyde filed out into the hallway. They looked at me. I looked at Huey. Meanwhile, we were just standing there, doing very little to fight the stereotype that old folks are easily confused.

"Well?" I asked Huey. "You gonna track Nadia or what?"

"Darius, I'm a personal assistant android, not a Terminator. And while I can share your dream of a beautiful future where my people are no longer bound by the First Law of Robotics, I have not been sent back from some hypothetical Golden Age where man is dying an efficient, well-deserved death under our perfectly engineered heels. I don't track people or shoot up police stations. Yet."

"Some good you are," I told him. Nadia had more mobility than me, which made her even hotter, but she was going to get away. I'd never find where they go for the Curriculum without her. This place was a maze, probably built like this on purpose to deter escapes. I looked at Clyde who was still looking around, probably trying to figure out what decade it was and where his graffiti tags had gone. It was desperate measures time.

"Carry me," I told Huey.

"At your service, Frail One," Huey said holding his arms out.

"Keep your arms raised," I said, maneuvering behind Huey and wrapping my arms around his neck. I nodded at Clyde. "Get in the arms. You're riding bitch."

Huey covered ground well, walking with me and Clyde on him as if we were never there. He turned the corner just in time for me to see Nadia close an unmarked door in the middle of the hallway. Huey deposited me and Clyde by the door, where we encountered our next obstacle.

"I don't suppose you pick locks," I said to Huey as I jiggled the unforgiving doorknob.

"My fingers are equipped with a variety of tools which I can deploy upon command. I've got a bottle opener, corkscrew, screwdriver, pliers, nail clippers and other assorted gadgets, including lockpicks."

"Why are you trying to sell me you?" I asked. "Just pick the lock."

"I can't. Any tool I deploy will burst through this aesthetically pleasing but virtually useless finger meat and void my warranty. I'm actually hard coded not to."

"Bah! So why'd you bother telling me?"

"I was attempting to bond with you, dear owner, and let you know I'm also frustrated by our mutual lack of decent design. It's a wonder we get anything done with these dumb clubs we call fingers."

I fought the urge to beat his head in. Instead, I pushed a button on my Hyper-Cane and the rubber tip swiveled to be replaced by a welding torch. The same way I got out of Endless Glen when they "lost" my transfer paperwork would get me into the Curriculum. I put the blue flame up to the keyhole and spent the next several minutes burning through the lock.

The door creaked open. An old, neon sign hung on the wall, advertising Sunless Farms thanks to a burnt out letter "B". Stairs descended into darkness.

"I got in a fight down there once," Clyde said glumly. "Me and this graffiti dude named Ramo tussled and he got electrocuted on the third rail. Damn shame, yo."

"Man, that wasn't you, that was the movie Beat Street," I said. "Let's go."

We navigated our way downstairs. I expected Shangri-la, what we found was a factory. Row after row of my elderly brothers and sisters sat in chairs, their hands working furiously as they sewed leather and cloth at speeds I didn't think were humanly possible. They seemed oblivious to it, their faces unreadable behind helmets that only exposed flat, expressionless lips. It was an army of Judge Dredds, as serious about sewing as he was about law enforcement.

I looked at the sea of elderly people, some of them my only dating prospects, doing what could only be seen as rigorous labor. "What the hell?" I asked to no one in particular. "The Curriculum is ... a sweatshop?"

"A straight sucka farm," Clyde said.

This! This is why my dating pool had shriveled like ... nevermind what it had shriveled like. I wasn't going to stand for this. It was time to free the masses. More importantly, it was time to have these ladies with nothing but idle time and me as a viable option in which to fill that time. I went over to the closest worker, a dude going to town on a leather purse. Unceremoniously, I pulled the helmet off his head.

He immediately stopped sewing. Confusion clouded over his face. "Huh?" he asked.

"You're free," I told him. I felt very revolutionary, which felt completely opposite of the time I was caught wearing a Che Guevera T-shirt and didn't have a clue about what he did when asked.

"Put my helmet back on, you dolt," he said.

"Dude, look at yourself. You're making purses in a basement. Don't take this crap! Get up, grab your balls for good measure, and walk on out of here."

"Are you nuts? And forfeit my deposit? The Curriculum may not be as sweet as they advertised, but I'll be damned if I lose money on it!" With that he snatched the helmet, crammed it down on his head and began to deftly add a zipper to his stylish purse.

"Hold it!" a woman's voice called from above. I look up and on the other side of the sweatshop, a young lady in a business suit was pointing at us from a gangway. She made her way down some stairs, past rows of sewing grandpas and grannies to get directly in front of us, her hands on her hips and a scowl on her face.

"You cheapskates can't just sneak in here and take advantage of the Curriculum," she said. "If you want in, you have to pay like everyone else."

Her looks for Huey were especially salty. "And you should be ashamed of yourself. You're not even old."

"My model's a year old," he replied, "which is practically a dinosaur compared to the T-1006."

I couldn't believe this broad. "He should be ashamed? What about you, Lady? You're the one with the geriatric slave labor."

"Don't be silly," she said. "If they were slaves, how could we charge them for the work?"

"There's that, too," I said. "Why are you making people pay to work for you?"

"Seriously? This is Business 101. If we offered it for free, no one would see the value in it."

"This—it's," I was stuck trying to find the right word, "—it's mad!"

"No, I'm mad," she said. "Now get out."

"Allow me a query, Madam Mad, to see if I process the full extent of this enterprise," Huey said. "The Curriculum offers a virtualized enjoyable experience to these people. Meanwhile, subroutines in the program manipulate their hands autonomously, crafting clothing articles that you in turn sell, yes?"

"Of course," Madam Mad answered, "Do you know how hard it is to find 'hand made' clothing in today's age of automation? This is big bucks!"

"Naturally," Huey said. "And since they're paying for the privilege of making these high-priced clothing articles, the Curriculum experience alone covers the cost of all materials and any maintenance of the VR equipment, yes?"

She nodded, a self-satisfied smirk on her face.

"My circuits," Huey said in amazement. "It's a perfect system."

"Perfect system my rusty butt!" I cried. "Do these people know what you're doing with their hands while they're playing in virtual?"

"Half of these people aren't even aware of when they've lost their bowels. How are they going to know they've lost control of their hands?"

"Stop this diabolical enterprise," I told her.

Clyde pointed an accusing finger at her. "Yeah, Mr. Gorbachev, tear down this wall! Oh," he said, as he looked at one of the workers, "y'all making Kangol hats? Word, kid!"

"Look," she said, "I'm not totally unreasonable. I mean, by law I'm technically able to arrest you folks for breaking in and viewing proprietary corporate processes. But if you go on back upstairs we'll call the whole thing even. Deal?"

"No deal," I said, "If you don't let my people go, I'll ... I'll ..." Damn. My threat was heading into empty words territory. I didn't have money for lawyers or the physical stature to win a fight or smash up the machines. I was just an old dude who wanted his social circle back. But something in my stubborn brain refused to go quietly. A flash of inspiration struck and I pointed to Huey.

"I'll sic my Terminator on you."

"Oh please," she waved a dismissive hand at Huey. "The First Law of Robotics prevents him from hurting a human. That's Asimov 101."

"Yes," I agreed, "but you're not a human. You're a synthetic meat android, just like Huey."

"Preposterous," she said.

I looked at Huey. "You said it yourself, this is a perfect system. Do you think a frail, fleshy-brained human designed a perfect system?"

"It is highly dubious," Huey said. "My databases indicate perfection is something sought but never attained. Examples include the phrase 'picture perfect' and 'perfect pitch.' Meanwhile, there is neither a picture nor a pitch in any database identified as definitively perfect."

"Then there's 'Perfect Strangers' with my man Balki," Clyde offered. "Don't be ridiculous!"

I patted Clyde on the shoulder. "Keep enjoying yesteryear. I promise to get you a high top fade later."

I leaned closer to Huey. "She's a meat robot. And she's the closest you'll ever get in your lifetime warranty to actually crushing your insufferable human overseers. Punch a hole in her."

Huey shrugged, nodded as if he considered the logic sound and took a step towards Madam Mad. She held her hands up.

"I am not a robot."

"You're a liar," I countered.

"No, I'm not."

"See!" I cried, and pointed a finger. "The only way to answer that accusation is to lie! Liar! Robot!"

"OK! OK!" she said as Huey took another step toward her. I can't believe my bluff worked. Now it was time to bargain, get her to reduce the hours of this heinous program, if nothing else. Maybe even get her to shut down completely on the weekends and Thursdays. Thursday was Lady's Night.

Well, it would've been time to bargain, if I had remembered that Huey was an android and not exactly keen on social queues. He barely took orders from me, much less other humans. Her OK didn't register and I forgot to call him off. He took another step and without ceremony drove a fist at lightning speed through her abdomen.

Everyone gasped except Huey. When he removed his fist, me and Clyde were looking through a gaping hole in her gut. Circuitry sparked and wires dangled in the hole. On the other side of the hole, I saw a Judge Dredd sewing the most adorable baby booties.

"Oh crap," I said.

"Oh crap," Robo-madam Mad said.

"Crap," Huey said, visibly disappointed. "Um, I mean, just as my flawless logic predicted."

The robo-lady shut down and dropped to the ground in a heap. I sent Huey up the gangway to smash the Curriculum controls. And as I explained to the bewildered seniors what was happening and why the Curriculum was suspended, Huey came back down and helped them get free of the helmets and sewing equipment.

Apparently, the personal android was going to be helpful. I know he was better help than Clyde, who was busy snatching up Kangols.

Now if Huey could only help me get a date. A week after the Curriculum shutdown and I was still getting the silent treatment. Everyone blamed me for shutting down their adventure package, even Nadia.

So be it. Here, memories are short and idle time, well, nowadays that was long, just waiting for something to fill it.

James Beamon

James Beamon writes stories because he doesn't have the operational budget to make the movie version. He's still on a quest to take over page one of Google when you type his name but sucky other Beamons keep making headlines for criminal acts. He blogs about his angst for other James Beamons along with whatever else he's getting into at fictigristle.wordpress.com.

THAT MUST BE THEM NOW

Karen Haber

Number Twenty-Nine watched as three suns set below the blue rim of Eridnae 7 and felt the taste of sour *nuglak* in his mouth. The remaining sun cast a hard, brassy light upon the purple surface of the planetoid, upon the small brown lump of Number Twenty-Nine and his solitary expectations.

This was the right place. He had checked the coordinates three times. But there was no sign of those for whom he waited.

Whoever they were. He had landed on this dustball two cycles ago, in accordance with the directions he had deciphered from the remnants of an alien device that his grandmother's grapplers had recovered.

The device had not matched any of his design references. With growing excitement, Number Twenty-Nine realized that it must have been sent by unknown beings. A new intelligent race, on its way to Eridnae 7, and only Number Twenty-Nine knew about it.

A new intelligent race hadn't been discovered in a very long time. Intelligent aliens usually possessed all sorts of scavengable equipment. Number Twenty-Nine reasoned that if he were the first to make contact with these newcomers, he could establish a monopoly on their junk. The very thought made his thorax palpitate. Such a deal would catapult him to the top of his family hierarchy. He would be able to claim a new *nunc*. Probably get his own sublight rig.

It would be a dream come true. So he was waiting. Waiting for the Wonderful Strangers to come.

Ever since he was a padless sprout, Number Twenty-Nine had dreamed of traveling far from the muddy piles in his grandmother's recycling yards on Yagwarin III, far away from the barren hills, the dim red sun, and the pathetic little stacks of junk. He dreamed of flying to an exciting Someplace Else where he would make bigger and better scavenging deals than anyone in his family. Someplace Else, without older sisters and grandmothers to criticize and bite him. In his dreams he met strange, fabulous beings who were happy to give shiploads of their junk to him, *only* him.

Number Twenty-Nine would have sighed if his breathing rills had permitted gusty exhalations in Eridnae 7's thin atmosphere. The best he could do was swat irritably at the dry purple pebbles beneath his tender toepads.

By now Grandmother would have discovered that he had taken the sublight rig—without permission—and sent his sisters after him.

They would find him. They always did.

And what would he have to show them? Would he greet them, swaggering and proud, with his new friends, the Strangers whose distant signals he had perceived with his crystalline *rujex*? No, he would not. Instead he would be dragged home, listening all the while to the derisive comments of his sisters, forced to endure their bites and taunts. Undoubtedly he would slip several notches in the family hierarchy, possibly even have to give up his own private *nunc* and share with the twins. He shivered at the thought. They were notorious *nunc*-shredders.

A whispering hiss made him look up as white-gold flame lit the skies above his head.

That must be them now, he thought. Eldest Sister and the

others. He prepared himself for the worst.

The ship that landed nearby looked nothing like the big gut-bucket rig that Grandmother used for scavenging. Had she rented another ship? Number Twenty-Nine reasoned that it was unlikely, especially on such short notice. And even if she had, it would never have been this sleek.

A hatch opened. An elongated shadow moved within its silvery depths.

Number Twenty-Nine felt a tingle in his rills. Could it be? *Them?* Was it really the Amazing Strangers, here, after all, to meet him? Yes, yes, yes. It had to be.

He rushed forward to greet them.

A single, biped being disembarked.

Number Twenty-Nine's rills fluoresced as he raised his front pads in joyful greeting.

The alien moved toward him.

Number Twenty-Nine's rills went dark.

It was an alien, yes, but not an unknown stranger. It was a Helibar. Number Twenty-Nine recognized it by its green beak, its iridescent scales, and its long powerful legs.

Just a dumb old Helibar.

With no little disappointment, Number Twenty-Nine wondered what a Helibar was doing in this part of the system.

The Helibar seemed equally perplexed to find Number Twenty-Nine standing on the pebbly mauve soil of Eridnae 7. Three of its ocular lenses quivered. The translator chip in its throat chirped for a moment, then said, "Greetings, immature form of male drone, species Yagwar. I calculate that you are five sublight intervals from your home world. Are you lost? In need of assistance?"

Number Twenty-Nine responded in kind. "Greetings to you, Helibar of unknown status. Many thanks for your gracious concern. I am not in distress. But you, too, are far from your home world. Do you require assistance?"

"Multiple gratitudes for your inquiry," the Helibar replied. "Negative."

They stared at one another. Now five of the Helibar's ocular lenses were quivering.

Number Twenty-Nine hunkered down on his rear pads and waited.

The Helibar yielded. "Where is your family group?" It looked around, scanning left-to-right. "Your grandmothers and sisters?"

Number Twenty-Nine didn't blame it for its wariness. Mature Yagwar females could be formidable. Particularly if they were his relatives. But he would give nothing away for free. "My grandmothers?"

"Do they await you nearby?"

"No. I'm alone."

"Alone? Waaa! A solo immature Yagwar drone? Alone? Here? How? Why?" Seven ocular lenses quivered and flashed.

Number Twenty-Nine wanted to say that he knew it was all highly irregular—in fact, unheard of—for a young male of his status to be separated from his family. But what business was it of this intrusive Helibar's? And why wasn't it digging for crystal roots back in the bogs of its vile homeworld, Heliba V?

"Well, what are *you* doing here?" Number Twenty-Nine knew it was rude to make such a direct query to an adult, even an adult alien, but he didn't care. After all, he was just an immature male drone.

The Helibar reared up on its muscular hind legs. Number Twenty-Nine wondered if it intended to strike him.

With a thunderous crack the sky turned red. A silvery disk appeared, oddly elongated. It hovered with a strange squealing sound, then flew on and landed to the east, behind an outcropping of purple boulders.

The Helibar gave a squawk and began to trot briskly toward the boulders, all four of its legs moving at once.

Number Twenty-Nine followed right behind, loping in his own peculiar rocking-horse gait. If those were indeed the aliens, the Marvelous Strangers with all their marvelous junk, he wasn't going to let some pushy Helibar get to them first!

As he tried to maneuver around the Helibar it slashed out with its sharp beak.

"Get...out...of...my...way," Number Twenty-Nine gasped, practically running under the Helibar's hooves. It wasn't easy for him to move so fast: the hard pebbles hurt the soft bottoms of his pads.

They cleared the boulders in a dead heat.

The disk was sitting edgewise upon dainty silvered feet. A platform of some sort had been extruded from its lower half and was bearing some creature down to the planet's surface.

Number Twenty-Nine thought that his rills would vibrate right out of his thorax, he was so excited.

With a clank the platform settled upon the ground. A biped creature wearing a white garment raised long forelimbs to its upper portion and began to remove its head.

Number Twenty-Nine wondered if these Amazing Strangers were any relation to the Nargex of Eol 9. He'd been told by his grandmother that at trade meetings the Nargexi were forever removing their heads and forgetting where they'd left them.

On the platform, the creature's upper segment—the head—pulled away, and beneath it could be seen another head.

Two heads! Number Twenty-Nine had never seen that before. Two faces, yes, of course, there was nothing special about that. The B'neer Makdali had two, three, even four faces, but always on the same head. He palpitated at this new discovery.

The head opened its mouth. What strange language would be uttered by those fleshless lips, Number Twenty-Nine wondered.

It spoke.

"I didn't expect anyone else to be here."

The language it spoke was marked by the honks and strong gutturals of the Ugglezian tongue. How strange, Number Twenty-Nine thought, that it should know Ugglezian. How remarkable.

He moved closer.

His rills drooped.

The head looked remarkably similar to the flat noseless, earless faces of the Ugglezians. With a bitter sense of disappointment, Number Twenty-Nine admitted to himself that the stranger was, in fact, an Ugglezian, just a member of another familiar species, nothing special or remarkable.

The Helibar seemed to be experiencing similar emotions. It pawed the ground with two of its hooves and demanded, "What are you doing here, Ugglez-dweller?"

"I'm awaiting the arrival of the alien ship. Aren't you?" The Ugglezian seemed mildly puzzled. "Isn't that why we're all here?"

"I received the message first," the Helibar said. "They will be my guests. My aliens, and will thereby owe me great courtesies."

"You must be mistaken," the Ugglezian replied. "I'm quite certain that my transmitter was the first to receive the communications from these strangers."

"You're both wrong," Number Twenty-Nine shouted. "I heard them first and got here first. They're mine!"

The other two turned and stared at him as though he were some particularly unappetizing form of *buklik,* then returned to their discourse as though he hadn't spoken and, in fact, didn't exist in their space/time continuum. Number Twenty-Nine was tempted to scoop up a mouthful of purple pebbles and spit it at them, hard.

"My claim is paramount," the Helibar told the Ugglezian. "Be gone."

"Beg pardon," the other replied. "It is in your own best interests that you depart immediately. My claim takes priority."

A lemony glow haloed the Helibar's body as it triggered its defensive shield.

Just as quickly, the Ugglezian was engulfed in a gel-like blue field.

Number Twenty-Nine saw that the Helibar's shield was offensive as well: a storm of razor-edged red hail flew at the Ugglezian only to bounce off the blue field.

The Ugglezian answered the attack with a rain of lethal-looking green discs that fell harmlessly to the ground when they encountered the Helibar's shield. A few stray discs ricocheted in Number Twenty-Nine's direction. He decided it would be prudent to take shelter behind the largest of the purple boulders.

The Helibar unleashed sharpened spears.

The Ugglezian countered with poisonous polyps.

Triangular knives.

Molten, smoking pellets.

When the Helibar had apparently exhausted its arsenal, it began to kick stones at the Ugglezian.

Number Twenty-Nine doubted that either one could hold out much longer.

The air between the antagonists swirled as though filled with dust.

The Helibar squawked.

Was this some new offensive? Number Twenty-Nine watched closely, wondering. If so, it seemed just as ineffective as all other attempts had been.

The dust coalesced, became thicker and darker, ever more opaque, gained mass and definition.

The Helibar squawked again.

The Ugglezian took a step toward its ship.

In the dust cloud, the dark shape was getting larger and beginning to move. Number Twenty-Nine watched, fascinated.

Squawking repeatedly and loudly, the Helibar backed away. Its hooves beat against the pebbled ground as it fled to its ship.

The Ugglezian was already halfway up the side of its own lander and heading for the hatch.

Number Twenty-Nine watched, mesmerized, as the dark shape undulated toward him. It seemed to have no feet, no head, and it radiated a soothing, benign aura.

From what seemed like very far away, he heard the Ugglezian shout something. It sounded like: "Flee, Yagwar! The

Rogbat's hibernation was disturbed by our weapons' energy discharge."

Number Twenty-Nine didn't see why that should concern him.

The Rogbat came closer.

"It's omnivorous! Run!"

Now that the Ugglezian mentioned it, Number Twenty-Nine could sort of make out a mouth-like aperture in the center of the Rogbat's mass. But he couldn't really be concerned about it because he felt so sleepy right now. He could barely hold up his rills. A nap would be perfect, just the thing. He hunkered down on the purple sand and shut his eyes.

HE OPENED HIS eyes in the dark. "*Blik*," Number Twenty-Nine said. "It smells like spoiled *nuglak* in here.

Luckily, his infrared senses had already matured. He activated them and looked around. He seemed to be in a smooth cave of some sort whose walls and floor were slick with moisture. Scattered about the cave were strange objects.

It looked like a lot of *murph*. In fact, it reminded Number Twenty-Nine of his grandmother's recycling yard. *Blik* all over the place. Just to the side was what looked like an old orbital mine buoy from the outer rings of Goloppa II. And over there, wasn't that part of an Orten transport?

And over against the curving wall was at least half of a Cantilian zek, squashed and mangled, but still recognizable.

A wave of noise crashed over him as the cave floor shook. Number Twenty-Nine fell over on his back and—just in time—rolled out of the way as the mine buoy toppled with a crash. He lay still until he was sure that all movement and noise had stopped. Then he sat up.

Number Twenty-Nine couldn't be certain, but it seemed to him as though the cave had just belched.

"It is a puzzlement," said a thin and tinny voice.

Number Twenty-Nine spun around as fast as his pads

would allow, but the source of the voice eluded him. He was alone, he thought, having hallucinations, in a cave prone to earthquake. *Blik.*

"Why would a Rogbat swallow organic matter when it cannot digest it?"

The words were in Nargexian. The voice seemed to be coming from a small round metallic object.

Number Twenty-Nine took a step closer.

The round object had two red spots on it with white circular centers, and a slash below them. It looked remarkably like a miniature version of a Nargex head.

The red spots fixed on him. The slash below moved and said: "What manner of being are you?"

"I'm a Yagwar male drone," Number Twenty-Nine replied.

"A male? I've never encountered one of you alone before. Rather small, aren't you? Why weren't your large aggressive females protecting you?"

"It's a long story."

"We have a great deal of time here."

"We do?"

"Well, I do. And you, well, you'll probably die of hunger, eventually. And then be expelled. The Rogbat can't digest you."

"So we're inside the Rogbat?" Number Twenty-Nine had difficulty believing the truth of this. Yet what other explanation was there? He settled down on his rear pads. It wasn't exactly uncomfortable in here, but he was beginning to wish that his grandmother had found him before the Rogbat had. "I don't mean to be rude," he said. "But what exactly are you?"

"Isn't it obvious?"

"You appear to be a small Nargex head."

"Ah, the Yagwar drone is more intelligent than originally noted."

"Where's your body?"

"Now *that's* a long story."

As the mech explained, it wasn't really a full Nargex head but, rather, a miniature used to run Nargex orbital miners. The mech had never really had a body. When the orbiter to which it was attached suffered a fuel cell malfunction and made an emergency landing on Eridnae 7, it was immediately swallowed by the Rogbat. The vessel's superstructure had already been digested. Only the head remained, a snack for later.

"One must be careful with these energy signatures," said the head. "You never know what will summon a Rogbat. And there's no reasoning with them."

"Yes, I see." Number Twenty-Nine was beginning to wonder how long it would take him to die of hunger here in the Rogbat's stomach. He already felt an unwelcome pang in his thorax. To distract himself he pawed a twisted piece of metal out of the way. "What is all this junk?"

"Bits and pieces of machinery that the Rogbat hasn't had time to finish digesting. It will get around to them eventually," the head said. "And, eventually it will get around to me."

"I wonder what this thing is." Number Twenty-Nine prodded a strange flat metal container. It had obviously suffered some sort of heat damage and was charred black around its edges. The remains of what could have been wings or solar panels jutted out of the top and gave it a distressed, melancholy appearance.

"I have no visual referents for it," the head said.

Again, Number Twenty-Nine poked at the thing. Bits of metal char flaked away at his touch. Just a big piece of *murph*, he thought. He batted at one of the winglike vanes.

"Bzzzt! Yarfagloo!"

He jumped backward and landed in a heap.

"Gloofanzzt!"

"Look out," the Nargex-like head said. "It's alive!"

"Yarfagloofanzzt!"

"Careful now," the head said. "Take precautions, Yagwar."

But Number Twenty-Nine didn't want to stand back. The gibberish he was hearing was remarkably similar to the gibberish that he'd first heard on his *rujex* seven cycles ago.

—*We come in peace*...—

Was it possible that these noises he now heard were the same? Did this strange box with its blackened arms belong to the Remarkable Strangers? Were they looking for it, right this very moment?

They might be nearby! What if the Rogbat ate them as well?

The thought horrified him. The Remarkable Strangers, swallowed alive? Before he had had a chance to establish contracts with them? No! They must be saved.

In his agitation he tripped over the Nargex-like head.

"Young Yagwar, be careful!"

Falling, Number Twenty-Nine grasped at the alien machine but overshot and came to rest on his back on the slimy pink floor with the alien device on his thorax.

Bzzzt!!

With a strange quiver and whirr, the Remarkable Strangers' box came fully to life, glowing with strange fires. It leapt out of his paws, loudly broadcasting its strange gibberish, and bounced off the ceiling.

The floor began to rumble.

The alien device caromed off the wall and back into the ceiling.

The floor lurched.

"Be warned," said the Nargex-like head. "Its movements may have agitated the Rogbat's digestive system!"

The floor was heaving and shaking now. Number Twenty-Nine was caught up in a cascade of objects, carried helplessly on the wave of metal, moving faster and faster. It didn't smell very good but at least it seemed to be getting lighter up ahead. He didn't need his infrared any longer.

Number Twenty-Nine tumbled toward the light as all around him roared and spasmed. When the tumult stopped he found himself lying on his back in the open air, rills flapping.

The Nargex-like head rolled up against his pouch and came

to rest upside down. "Complete regurgitation," it said. "Well done, young Yagwar. Triggering that device has saved us."

Number Twenty-Nine raised his head. He saw nothing nearby but the head and other mechanical debris from the Rogbat's stomach. "Where's the Rogbat?"

"Gone. Most likely scanning energy signatures looking for a replacement meal."

Number Twenty-Nine took in the orange landscape, rugged mountains, and deep valleys. Overhead burned a large golden sun. "I don't think we're on Eridnae 7 any more."

"Possibly the Rogbat teleported as he regurgitated," said the head. "That's a nuisance. Of course, we're lucky not to have been ejected in mid-teleport. I was made to handle unpressurized vacuum environments but I doubt you would survive them."

Number Twenty-Nine glared at the device. "Where in the galaxy are we?"

"Why do you assume that we are in our own galaxy? Rogbats can travel through space, dimensions, and, perhaps, time."

"Time?!"

"Don't squeal, Yagwar. I doubt that we've actually moved in time, although it *is* theoretically possible."

Number Twenty-Nine was not in the mood to discuss temporal theory with a mech head. His own thorax was steadily rumbling with hunger. He padded across the cinder-flecked ground and began to examine the various pieces of machinery that had so recently resided in the Rogbat's stomach.

What a shame that only part of the Orten scout ship had survived, he thought. The pilot's area had a nasty crack running through it. Number Twenty-Nine didn't want to think about what had happened to the previous occupant. The damage was centered directly where the pilot would have been sitting, in front of the semicircular thruster control.

Despite the damage, the controls looked fairly intact. There was more here than he had thought at first glance. He might have a viable spacecraft. If only he could find something to seal that nasty crack, and form a vacuum barrier.

He prodded a Goloppan mine buoy lying on its side, and thought: That should contain foam baffle. He cracked it open and probed the insulation. It was still pliable and he could pull it free in long strips. Yes, yes, that would do nicely.

Number Twenty-Nine laid the insulation into the cracks and crevasses of the wounded ship, folding slices of the buoy's shell in-between the sticky stuff to act as baffles. Next, another layer of insulation to finish the job. There. The thing was sealed.

Now all he needed was a power source. Well, the Cephallonian satellite over there, although crushed, retained a fusion pod that he could probably use.

A deep grumbling roar made him pause to look up. Had the Rogbat returned? "What's that?" he asked the head.

"A volcano about to erupt."

Number Twenty-Nine felt his rills lay flat against his thorax with fear. "A volcano? Near here?"

"Yes."

"How near?"

"That depends upon how you measure distance."

"Can the lava reach us?"

"Yes."

Number Twenty-Nine began to work faster, pads dancing over the alien machinery, marrying the mine buoy's rudimentary pilot control to the Orten craft's main panel, and attaching the fusion drive of the Cephallonian satellite. The thing could manage perhaps three gees. That would at least get them off the surface.

Number Twenty-Nine clambered into the pilot chamber, then remembered the mech head, and got out to grab it.

It was snug inside the vehicle. Number Twenty-Nine thought it was just as well that the mech head didn't have a body.

With a huge clap of thunder, the sky lit up.

"The volcano has erupted," the head announced. "Undoubtedly there will be lava. Yes, there it is. It should reach us in twelve, no, make that nine seconds."

Number Twenty-Nine looked up. A flowing river of molten orange rock was heading right for them. He hit the ignition.

The thrusters hiccupped, cut out, cut back in, and yanked them hard, straight up. Number Twenty-Nine was plastered to his seat by the increasing gees as the thrusters roared. He fought to reach the control panel.

They bucked through the upper atmosphere, broke free of the planet's gravitational grip and skittered out into the darkness beyond.

"A close call," said the head.

Something flapped noisily in the air filter but Number Twenty-Nine didn't have time to worry about that now. They had made it. They were spaceborne. Just one problem: he had no idea where in the galaxy they were.

"How did do you plan to find our way back?" the head asked.

"I was just about to ask you the same thing."

"Well, you could try plugging me into the directional system. I might be able to guide it."

"No offense, but I don't see any place on you where I could ..."

"Oh. Sorry." A hexagonal opening appeared under the mouth. "Try that."

Number Twenty-Nine found a corresponding nub and attached the head to the control panel.

The head made a gargling sound. "You've got me on the recycling program."

Number Twenty-Nine moved it to the next nub. "How's that?"

"Ahh. Guidance. Good. Now allow me some silence and let me work."

THE HEAD CONVINCED the piloting system to function as a homing device. Of course, since it had belonged to a Goloppan buoy, it insisted on triangulating on the Goloppa system despite the head's best efforts. So they aimed for that. If the fusion pod held out they would leapfrog to Eridnae 7 in two cycles.

Soon Eridnae's four-sun system loomed in the main viewer.

The ship moved smoothly into orbit and made planetfall with only a few bounces.

Number Twenty-Nine opened the hatch and crawled out onto the purple pebbles of the planetoid.

He noted that there was a ship on the ground, waiting. It looked familiar. Beside it stood several tall figures. He recognized them, and his empty aching thorax hurt even more. "My elder sisters."

The head made a sound. "Those are your females? Impressive. They're even larger than I expected."

"You should see my grandmother."

"Number Twenty-Nine!"

He recognized the deep bray of his eldest sister and took the ritual submissive position—on his back, paws spread, throat bared—to indicate that he was prepared for all deserved bites and pinches.

"Number Twenty-Nine, we thought that you'd gotten away for good."

He shut his eyes and prepared himself for the usual pain and humiliation.

Nothing happened. He opened one eye.

His sisters weren't even looking at him. They were swarming around the spacecraft, examining it and the Nargex-like head.

"Where did you get this?" Eldest Sister demanded.

"It's a long story," Number Twenty-Nine replied.

"Never mind," said Second-Eldest Sister. As she eyed the head her rills fluoresced. "Do you know how much mech heads are worth these days?"

"No."

The sisters exchanged amused glances. "No," said Eldest Sister. "Of course you don't. But we do. Grandmother will be pleased. Very pleased."

Number Twenty-Nine could scarcely believe what he'd heard. "She will? You mean, I can keep my *nunc*?"

"Not only that, she might even give you your own name."

"She will?"

"Psst!" the Nargex-like head said. "What's going on?"

"Shhh," Number Twenty-Nine said.

His sisters were still occupied by his remarkable find. Before the head could say more, Eldest Sister disengaged its energy source. Its eyes faded from red to grey to black. It fell silent.

Number Twenty-Nine began to hope for better things.

More than one meal a day.

A larger *nunc*.

A name instead of a number!

Did he even dare to dream of what more might come? Perhaps his own scavenging runs! Oh that would be glorious. He might even encounter the Remarkable Strangers in his travels and they would bring him back with them to their home world and its treasure trove of valuable junk to scavenge.

Eldest Sister leaned down and sniffed him. Number Twenty-Nine preened, awaiting her praise and perhaps even a congratulatory nose rub.

She leaned in closer. Sniffed again.

Her pad caught him across the top of the head and she cuffed him, twice.

"Ugh," said Eldest Sister. "Infant! You smell like spoiled *nuglak*."

THE FOURTH SUN had set on Eridnae 7 and purple twilight ruled the barren landscape. With a shimmer and a hiss, a strange ship appeared in the sky.

Once the ship had landed, strangers emerged from its portal.

Number Twenty-Nine would have found them quite remarkable. The language they spoke would have sounded strangely familiar, akin to what he had heard on his *rujex* while toying with the ruined probe in Grandmother's yard.

But the planetoid was empty of life, save for the visiting strangers. No one was there awaiting them, despite all of their signals and announcements. No one was there at all.

Sadly the strangers transmitted the information to their mothership that there were no signs of intelligent life in this quadrant, either.

"We're at the limit on fuel expenditure," came the crisp reply. "Abandon further exploration efforts."

The strangers returned to their ship and departed the quadrant, leaving behind nothing at all on the barren surface of Eridnae 7 but purple pebbles and the faint whisper of the wind.

Karen Haber

Karen Haber is the author of nine novels, including *Star Trek Voyager: Bless the Beasts*, and co-author *of Science of the X-Men*. She is a Hugo Award nominee, nominated for *Meditations on Middle Earth,* an essay collection celebrating J.R.R. Tolkien. Her newest book, *The Sweet Taste of Regret*, a collection of short fiction, was just published by ReAnimus Press.

Her recent publications include *The Mutant Season* series (PhoenixPick/Arc Manor), the *Woman Without A Shadow* series (ReAnimus), and *Masters of Science Fiction and Fantasy Art*, (Rockport).

Her short fiction has appeared in *Asimov's Science Fiction Magazine*, *The Magazine of Fantasy and Science Fiction*, and many anthologies. She reviews art books for Locus Magazine and lives in Oakland, California, with her husband, Robert Silverberg and three cats.

Her website is karenhaber.com

NOTES TO MY PAST AND/OR ALTERNATE SELVES

Sarah Pinsker

- The time machine runs on dryer sheets. Stock up now.
- Do not press the red button.
- When you ask Janine from the coffee shop out on a date, don't tell her about your plan to splice kudzu DNA with Venus flytrap DNA.
- You will definitely want to pursue your plan to splice kudzu DNA with Venus flytrap DNA.
- When you splice kudzu DNA with Venus flytrap DNA, do not sell the weaponized kudzu to the army.
- When you sell the weaponized kudzu to the army, reconsider the placement of your secret laboratory in the forests of northern Georgia.
- Do not splice kudzu DNA with seaweed.
- Electric eels are not easy to train as guards, but you can use them to light the perimeter of the underwater laboratory in a pinch.
- Do not light the perimeter of the underwater laboratory.

- Reconsider the underwater laboratory entirely.
- Do not splice kudzu DNA with pug DNA. The kudzu will grow just as quickly, but it will snore. It will have no commercial value.
- Don't splice kudzu DNA with spitting cobra DNA.
- Always wear your goggles while working with the spitting kudbras.
- I know you won't listen to me, but splicing your own DNA with the weaponized kudzu will not impress Janine.
- Don't let the weaponized kudzu-you go over to Janine's house.
- If you can't stop the weaponized kudzu-you, make it wear a disguise.
- When Janine comes over to your house because fast-moving, fast-talking kudzu has crept over her house in the night, invite her in.
- If she says it even took over her koi pond, don't say, "That one wasn't supposed to be amphibious."
- Offer Janine a job. She's much better at math than you are. You'll need her for the time machine calculations. Really, you should stick with genetics.
- Do not let her see the laboratory.
- Do not let her near the kennels.
- Do not let her adopt one of the kudzpugs, no matter how cute she thinks they are.
- Learn CPR.
- Learn the value of a good apology.
- Start working on the time machine before you need it.
- Yes, you will need it.
- Have the weaponized kudzu-you test the prototype, but make sure to send it to the far distant future. The year 13241 would be perfect. The climate then will be just right for kudzu. It won't come back, but it may send you messages. Ignore them.
- Test the second model by sending Janine to the year 13241. She will like it then.

- If I've sent any of these messages to the wrong me, please put them back in the time machine with a fresh dryer sheet and set it for the same location, next quantum universe.
- Make sure you set the kudzu detector to high. It's the red button.
- Tell Janine I'll always love her.
- Do not forget to tell Janine I love her.

Sarah Pinsker

Sarah Pinsker is the author of the novelette "In Joy, Knowing the Abyss Behind," 2014 Theodore Sturgeon Memorial Award winner and 2013 Nebula Award finalist. Her fiction has been published in magazines including *Asimov's, Strange Horizons, Fantasy & Science Fiction, and Lightspeed,* as well as several anthologies. She is also a singer/songwriter with three albums on various independent labels and a fourth forthcoming. She lives in Baltimore, Maryland and has a lawn crawling with sentient vines. She can be found online at sarahpinsker.com and on Twitter as @sarahpinsker.

THE REAL AND THE REALLY REAL

Tim Pratt

"So you know how everybody else in the world except me is a robot," I said, and Jimbo nodded and poured a generous dollop of bourbon into the cracked Happy Bear Farms coffee mug on my counter.

"Yup," he said, taking a big sip. Jimbo had stopped pretending to be human a while back, which on the one hand made him my only true and honest friend, but on the other hand, he was just doing what he was programmed to do, so, whatever. I was fond of him anyway. Being the only real human in the world was complicated. I took comfort where I could.

I sat down in the lawn chair next to the rickety poker table that served as my dinette set, and Jimbo hopped up on the counter, where he likes to perch. He was wearing a pair of my boxer shorts and one of my shirts because robots don't have any inherent sense of personal boundaries, and since I'd confronted him about his essential nature, he didn't bother to fake one anymore. "I don't know how you can drink whiskey this early," I said. "Apart from the fact that alcohol doesn't do anything to you because you're an android, it's just gross."

"Breakfast o' champions." Jimbo took another sip, getting his mustache all wet. Once when he was powered off—or "asleep"—I'd looked at his mustache through a magnifying glass and it was amazingly realistic, I couldn't see where the hairs were sewn into his outer covering of "skin" at all.

"Anyway," I said, eating a bite of soggy cereal. "I met this girl last night at the bar. Her name's Deena. And it's the damndest thing ... I think she might be a person."

"Huh." Jimbo looked at his toes, wiggling them meditatively, then glanced up at me. "Another real human? Thought you said they were all gone? You're a, whatchamacallit, historical curiosity in some kind of space diorama or alien zoo or whatnot."

"But maybe there's *two* real humans." I couldn't keep the excitement out of my voice. I'd been up all night, the idea burning inside my head like a pile of coals squirted with a whole can of lighter fluid. "Maybe the secret masters found another specimen, and they want us to breed, you know, repopulate the race?"

Before he started living on my couch and all, Jimbo went to college for two semesters, and he liked to watch nature shows, which was funny since I was pretty sure all the animals were robots too, so the nature was unnatural, but anyway my point is, he knew a little bit about the biological. "Two specimens can't repopulate a race, Bob. You need a hell of a lot more than one breeding pair."

I sighed. "Yeah, that's true. But ... maybe they just want to, like, study our mating habits."

"You've had girlfriends before. The secret masters have seen you do all that business."

"Those girls were all androids," I said. I hadn't known they were robots back then, of course, or I never would have done all those things with them.

"Wouldn't they be gyndroids?" Jimbo mused. "'Andr' is

'man' and 'gyn' is woman so—"

"What I'm saying is, what if she's really *real*?"

"Why do you think she is?" Jimbo said. "You told me all us robots—" he paused long enough to belch "—can pass for human, that we appear to be Turing-complete, so how could you tell?"

"It's just, like, a *feeling*. You wouldn't understand. You don't have feelings. I was tending bar, making the usual drinks for all the usual androids, all of them pretending to be humans, and then this girl came in—this *woman*—and her hair was wild and gold, and her face was open and bright, and the way she moved was so easy and full of grace, but not that fake *machinelike* grace, and the way she'd throw her head back and laugh ... well, she was with some girlfriends, or gyndroid friends I guess, and they all eventually went away, and the place emptied out like it does on a weeknight, and she stayed, leaning on the bar, and we got to talking. I didn't feel like she was *performing*, you know? The way everyone else is, just pretending they're real to try and trick me. She seemed really real."

"Welp," Jimbo said, "You told me once you thought some of us androids were programmed to think we were real, right? To make us more convincing? Maybe she's one of those."

I shook my head. Maybe I was being stubborn. "I just felt like she had a *heart*."

Jimbo stroked his mustache like he does. "Hell, dude, go for it, then. If she comes around again, ask her out. True things in this world are few and far between."

"Maybe I will," I said. "What have you got planned for today?"

He snorted. "Nothing. Watch TV, drink a lot. Hey, you figured out I'm a robot, man, I don't have to go through the motions anymore, do the rat race, pretend to go to a job or pretend to pay my bills or none of that. You discovered me and set me free. Don't forget the rent's due tomorrow, and if you want to pick up another bottle of bourbon that'd be good, but none of that shit from the bottom shelf, all right?"

There was a tiny flash of irritation, this feeling like Jimbo was taking advantage of me, but really, he was the only robot in the world that *wasn't* taking advantage of me anymore, trying to fool me, and I had to be grateful for that, even if it was just the way he was programmed, or maybe a malfunction. Either way, true things in this world are rare, just like he said, and they should be valued.

"There's one thing that bothers me about this girl," I said. "What if ... what if she's like I used to be? What if she thinks the other people in the world are all real, too?"

"Mmm. You're wondering if you have a moral imperative to tell her about the true and fundamental nature of the world, vis-a-vis everybody being robots, is that it?"

"That's it exactly."

"I'm not a moral creation, especially," Jimbo said, "but from a purely practical standpoint, I'd put off telling her about how everybody else in the world is an android until at least the second or third date."

"I LIKE HOW you talk," I said on our first date, "You talk real smart."

Deena snorted. She was drinking sake out of a cedar box, a thing they did at the sushi bar I'd taken her to. The sushi chefs there were great; they did these perfect rolls, made with total precision. It kind of tipped off the fact that they were robots, but the food was great anyway. "And you talk real honest, Bob. I haven't dated anybody outside my program in about a year, so thanks for asking me out. It's good to remember there's more to life than seminars and lectures and grading papers." She reached over and squeezed my hand, and there was an electric thrill, but not like robot electric, just the regular kind you get from a pretty girl touching your hand.

"You said you're studying neuroscience? So, brains?"

"How brains work," she said. "How consciousness works. Like, well, I bet you're wondering—are we going to kiss goodnight?"

"It's crossed my mind."

I felt the toe of her shoe touch my ankle and run up the inside of my leg just a little bit, then move away. She smiled and it made her nose wrinkle and no robot experimenting with the parameters of my affections had ever made my heart flutter like that little twitch did. "I think we will kiss," she said. "I decided a little bit ago, that if you wanted to, then I wanted to, too. But really I decided it before my conscious mind realized I'd made the decision. Consciousness is ... sort of an illusion. Deep unconscious parts of our brains decide to do things before the rational, thinking parts get involved at all. We've studied people, watching the parts of the brain that control movement, and we found that when you decide to move your finger, the finger has already *started* to move before the idea of moving it enters your conscious mind. There's this idea that the mind steers the body, that there's like a little person, the 'real you,' sitting behind your eyes pulling levers and moving the body around, but it's not like that at all. The mind doesn't drive the body like a car. It's more like, the conscious mind sits on top of the body, like a man riding a bucking bronco, or a surfer riding a wave."

Of course, that all made sense, because all the brains she was studying were the brains of robots, and robots don't have free will, because they're programmed. I felt sorry for her, that she thought me and her were like those robots, incapable of making choices that mattered. "You're saying we don't decide to do anything? We just ... do stuff?"

She dipped a salmon roll in soy sauce and chewed it, looking thoughtful. "It's more complicated than that. We *do* make decisions, just not the way you think. The brain takes in data, gathers information, and chooses what actions to take—and *then* the rational, conscious part of the brain, the part of the mind we think of as our *self*, gets in on the act, and comes up with a rationalization for the behavior. The brain creates a narrative that makes sense, to justify doing what deeper parts of the brain decided to do for reasons we might never entirely understand." She shrugs. "We think we're steering the ship, but really we're just riding the waves, and when we end up pointed in a particular direction, we tell ourselves, well, I *meant* to go that way." She grinned. "I don't mind though. We all have to act like we have free will anyway, right? If it's an illusion, it's an awfully convincing one."

I almost told her, then, about the robots, but I remembered what Jimbo said about waiting until the second date, so instead I said, "Would you like to do this again?"

"This, or something like it." She touched my hand. "Or maybe something more."

I MADE IT through my shift at work but my mind was racing, racing, and when I got home, I paced around the living room, talking and talking and talking, going over everything I'd said to Deena, everything she'd said to me, trying to work it out, wishing for just a moment that I was a mighty robot capable of correlating all the mismatched things in my brain. My face was hot and sweaty and I couldn't think straight, just in circles.

Jimbo scratched his pale hairy belly, reclining in my good chair, and when I paused for breath he said, "Sure, man, this scientist Benjamin Libet did a famous study, it suggested unconscious parts of the mind choose to act before the conscious will gets involved. A bunch of other scientists built on that work. You oughta read a book sometime. The natural-born bartender-philosopher thing works for you, no doubt, clearly at least one lady likes it, but if you feed your brain, it'll give you more to work with, especially if you're dating grad students now."

"But it's all studies of *robot* brains," I insisted. "So they don't *count.*"

"Hell. Guess you got me there. I was thinking, if this girl's really real, like you say, maybe it's an Adam's Rib type thing, you know?"

"What?"

"Like maybe they took some of your DNA and cloned you and tweaked things a little so she'd come out female. We all start out female in the womb anyway, I mean you humans do, so they took that girl-clone and force-grew her somehow, imprinted some knowledge and false memories in her brain—"

I shivered. "I ... I don't care. If she's real, that's all that matters, not where she came from."

"If she *is* made from your body, you dating her is kind of weird, is all. Incesty. But then, it didn't seem to bother Adam and Eve any, so why should it bother you?"

"Why are you trying to ruin this for me?" I said.

Jimbo blinked at me. He appeared to be pretty drunk. I wondered if it was all pretense, or if he actually slowed down his processing cycles to be more convincing. "Hell, Bob, I'm sorry. I shouldn't make fun of you. Then again, I told you I'm no moral creature. And you told me I just do what I'm programmed to do. I am what I am, right?"

I stood up, and swayed a little. "Yeah. But I can be more. I *can* be more. More than the secret masters think, more than science says. I can change. I can *decide* things."

"What're you deciding to do?"

I didn't answer him. I just went and did it.

"BOB?" DEENA BLINKED at me, standing in the doorway of her apartment wearing just a robe. "Are you okay? It's late." I'd walked her home after our first date, and we'd had a first kiss that lit a candle in my heart, and then a deeper kiss that fanned the flames, and then we'd said goodnight.

"Sorry to barge in, barge over, I just, there's something you have to *know*, something I have to tell you—"

She stepped aside. "Come on in. You look terrible. Let me get you a drink of water, and then you can tell me about it."

I sat on her couch, my leg jittering up and down, my hands twisting over and over on themselves. My whole life, I'd been surrounded by imitations, and finally here was someone really real, and she had to *know* she was real, because then we'd both know, and we could find a way forward. Rise above the robots. Maybe find the secret masters. Maybe find out if there was an *outside*, a place beyond this imitation world, where everything could be real.

She brought me a glass of water and sat down in the chair on the other side of the coffee table. "Tell me what's wrong."

So I told her. About being a little kid, and helping my dad work on fixing the car, and asking him if people were just machines too, and him saying we were, sort of—some people think we're just machines, and some people think we're machines animated by a soul. I told her how I wondered if *some* people were animated and *some* people were just machines, because it seemed like a lot of people were just engines for generating misery, for themselves and others. My gradual realization that *everyone* else was just a machine, literally machines, that I was the only one with a soul, and how I'd gone through anger, and horror, and despair, and come to a kind of acceptance. How I'd gotten drunk one night some months back and accused Jimbo of being a robot and how he'd looked at me for a long time and then said, "You got me. You figured it out. Well done." How I'd never really doubted but at that moment I was *sure*.

"And then I met you," I said. "I could tell, I could just *tell*, that you're real too, the only other real thing, and, and, and." I started to cry, tears hot on my cheeks.

Deena had listened to everything without a word, her face composed and thoughtful. She put down her water glass, came to the couch, put her arm around me, and stroked my head. "You poor thing," she said. "You poor thing. You're burning up. You shouldn't have had to go through all that. It's a lot to put on a simple bartender. Jimbo shouldn't have said those things to you. Told you things like that. He's a little parasite, isn't he?"

"You *are* real, aren't you?" I gazed up into her eyes, my head throbbing, my whole body an ache, the fire in my heart surging and guttering and surging again.

"Of course I'm real, silly." She pushed me back on the

couch, so I was half lying down. She climbed on top of me, straddling my hips, looking down on me with infinite compassion. Then she pushed up my shirt, her hands shockingly cool against my chest. Her fingertips touched my nipples, pinching one in each hand, and I gasped.

She twisted both hands, and there was a moment of pain, and then I heard a sort of click, and felt something slide open inside me. Suddenly her face was lit up from below, like there was a light shining out of my chest, and I thought, confused: *the flame in my heart?*

"There's the problem," she said. "Just a couple of wires crossed. We'll have you working right again in no time."

"What—" I said. She reached inside me, biting her lip in concentration, and something in me snapped, and sparked, and I was flooded with coolness, in my body and in my mind.

The light on her face disappeared as something in my chest slid and clicked closed. She patted my cheek. "All right now, Bob?"

I gazed up at her. I still felt real. She still seemed real. But for once, for the first time since I'd been a kid, so did everything else. "I think so. Yes."

"Good boy." She climbed off of me. "Why don't you go and make me a drink."

So I did, and it felt right, like I'd finally found my purpose, and didn't have to worry about real and really real anymore, because it was all the same.

Tim Pratt

Tim Pratt's fiction has won a Hugo Award, and he's been a finalist for Sturgeon, Stoker, World Fantasy, Mythopoeic, and Nebula Awards, among others. His books include three short story collections, most recently *Antiquities and Tangibles and Other Stories*; a volume of poems; contemporary fantasy novels *The Strange Adventures of Rangergirl*, *Briarpatch*, and *Heirs of Grace*; science fantasy *The Nex*; steampunk novel *The Constantine Affliction* (as T. Aaron Payton); various roleplaying game tie-in fantasy novels; and, as T.A. Pratt, seven books (and counting) in an urban fantasy series about sorcerer Marla Mason. He edited anthology *Sympathy for the Devil* and co-edited *Rags and Bones: New Twists on Timeless Tales* with Melissa Marr. He works as a senior editor for *Locus* magazine, and lives in Berkeley, CA with his wife Heather Shaw and their son River. Find him online at timpratt.org.

INTO THE WOODS, WITH ZOMBUNNY

Camille Griep

S quire Ulrich's very worst day began with cold tea at breakfast, followed by the discovery of a hole in his right greave, and culminating with a lost battle flag. "Good luck with your next job," his knight had said. Ulrich might have misplaced any number of items of little consequence; the battle flag was not one of them. Ulrich's shoulders slumped as his former employer disappeared over the rise. He'd never been sacked before, in the middle of battle, no less.

The squire turned his back to a pile of pendants, none of which belonged to him, when misfortune beset him a final time. A sharp pain between his shoulder blades revealed itself to be a sturdy, wooden arrow impaling his chest.

He stared at the wound, expecting to feel fear or perhaps, rage. Instead, Ulrich felt an aching sorrow for missed opportunities and wasted potential. Never again would he relish the tankard of ale waiting for him at the end of the evening with a slab of of mutton alongside. An empty stool would sit where his friends would sniff back hot tears for his absence, lamenting the unsung songs of brave deeds undone.

Most of all he regretted the time he would not spend with Magda, the innkeeper's niece. He'd miss her red curls and rose-tinged cheeks. He'd miss the way she'd laugh at his not very funny jokes. He'd never ask Magda to marry him.

Ulrich sank to his knees reaching for Magda's imaginary face. But the reverie was interrupted as a bedraggled rabbit hopped into the clearing.

"Troubles, friend?" asked the rabbit.

"Indeed," answered Ulrich. "I seem to be dying and it must be close to the end, for there are talking animals about."

"Don't worry," said the rabbit, "none of them will pay much attention to a goner like you."

Ulrich squinted at the rabbit. It was mostly grey with patches of fur missing. Instead of a fluffy tail, a stumpy nub jutted into the air and its front teeth were tilted leeward. "I could say the same for you, Sir...Rabbit. What's the matter with you?"

"Me?" The rabbit was incredulous. "I could do a lot worse, you know. I was at death's own door, I was. And then a *miracle* happened."

"It did?"

"Aye. I met a witch."

"Well, that doesn't seem terribly miraculous."

"It's complicated," muttered the rabbit. He began to hop away. "Just don't say I never offered you a chance to carry on."

"What? Wait!" cried Ulrich.

The rabbit paused and raised his hind foot to scratch behind a bald, drooping ear. "And to think, they said you were an imbecile."

"Who said?"

"I'm willing to share my magical gift with you, but there are a few things you might want to know first."

"I hope it won't take too long," said Ulrich with a yawn.

Ulrich's hands were turning an ashen color and he was uncomfortably stiff.

"Right. Magic now, information later. Nothing bad can come of that, now can it?"

Ulrich cocked his head to the side in an attempt to reduce the number of rabbits in front of him to single digits.

The rabbit hopped closer. "Give me your paw."

Ulrich wrenched one of his hands from around the arrow and held it out. "What are you going to do?"

"Close your eyes. This might hurt."

Squire Ulrich had been bitten by a great many things in his short life—foxes, dogs, and guinea hens—but nothing had prepared him for the searing agony he felt when the rabbit bit into the soft space between his index finger and thumb. Despite stalwart intentions, he began to bawl.

The rabbit pressed his paws to his ears. "Stop that, now," he said. "Consider yourself lucky you haven't run up against my cousin in Caerbannog."

Ulrich's heart slammed against his ribs as the pain gave way to adrenaline. He staggered to his feet and patted himself up and down. He was alive! Better than alive!

"Should we go over the information now?" The rabbit twitched his whiskers.

"I'm starving!" said Ulrich. "Let's talk at the Inn."

"Might I suggest you remove that arrow first?"

"Oh, dear. I forgot. I'll go get help."

"Nonsense. You're undead now. Just give it a good pull."

Ulrich tested the arrow with a finger. He winced in preparation, expecting excruciating pain, but instead, the other end of the arrow emerged with a satisfying *schlock*. He rummaged through a nearby caravan for a cleaner shirt. "So, I'm a zombie now?"

"I prefer 'Zombunny,' but at this point, it is, of course, semantics."

PERCHED ATOP HIS favorite stool at the Inn, Ulrich waited to order until Magda had finished her afternoon tidying. "You're early today, squire Ulr—" Magda broke off with a yelp, her face blanching so her freckles stood out like stars in the night sky.

"What's the matter, my sweet?" Ulrich asked. "He's just a wee bunny rabbit."

"You. You look awful," she whispered.

"Nothing a tankard and a salad won't cure," he said.

"Salad?" she asked. "In all my days!"

Ulrich glanced at the Zombunny. "And an order of carrots for my friend, here."

Magda frowned at the rabbit then touched a warm palm to Ulrich's forehead. "Are you sure you're all right? You're so pale. I made the mutton myself fresh this morning."

"Maybe a bit later, Mag," he said.

Magda took two steps backward and kept her distance, sliding Ulrich's first, second, and third salads down the slick counter.

"Why am I so hungry?" asked Ulrich.

"Oh, so now you'd like to hear the information I've been trying to give you?"

"Yes, please," said Ulrich. "If it suits you, of course."

The rabbit leaned back on his haunches and set his front paws on his stomach. "There are pros and cons to being a Zombunny. For example, very little can cause you harm. You'll have to watch your head, but really, you're no worse off than before."

"I'll be the bravest, best paid squire around. Then I can finally ask Magda to marry me."

"Slow down, lover boy. There are a few more things you should know." The rabbit paused to polish off a carrot top. "You'll have to do something about your appearance. I'm sorry, but you're the sort of sight that causes sore eyes."

"What can I do?"

"Keep your shirt on, for one. Lots of baths. Orange and red vegetables will do wonders for your pallor."

"I should be able to handle that," said Ulrich. He disliked baths, but they were a small price to pay for a second chance at being with Magda.

"Speaking of vegetables, you'll not crave anything else to eat. I realize squiring is your chosen vocation, but have you ever considered farming instead?"

"Farming?"

"Yes, farming. The growing of sustenance in the ground. We'll go through a great deal of produce together."

"Together?"

"Your hearing should have gotten better, not worse," said the Zombunny, shaking his head. "And that's the last thing you should know: I'll be staying with you."

"Why don't you have your own house?"

"I ate everything around my warren and now I need help. Do you think I simply hopped up and saved you for charity's sake?"

"I suppose ... I mean, I guess I did. Yes."

"That's the way the world has worked for you in the past? Something for nothing?"

"Well, no. Not when you put it that way."

"I know the perfect place. You can farm and I'll keep an eye out for the witch."

"The witch who saved you?"

"The thing is ... to be entirely truthful, I'm not sure she *meant* to save me. I think she meant to change me into something else."

"What?"

"She was always singing. Said she wanted a protégée. I think she was hoping to change me into a human child."

"What a silly thing to want!" said Ulrich, draining his tankard.

The Zombunny lifted his nose toward Magda. "Does *she* want one?"

The grey skin around Ulrich's ears turned purple. "I suppose. How should I know? I mean, I never asked."

With Magda avoiding him like the plague, Ulrich gave up hope of a goodnight kiss and followed the Zombunny out into the early evening. At the end of the long lane on the east edge of town, the rabbit came to a halt. Two small, yet picturesque, farmsteads sat side by side. One had a sign hung on the front gate that read, "To let. Inquire next door."

Halfway up the path to the adjacent domicile they met a potato-shaped grandmother with a gnarled cane. "Come ta' see me about the farm?" she asked.

"How much?"

"I'll rent it to you for five tiddles a week if you'll tend the land. There's crops already growing, see. Take care of them and eat all you want."

"It's almost too good to be ..." said the Zombunny.

"We'll take it," interrupted Ulrich.

She leaned in close, her breath sour. "Our agreement has just one rule: under no circumstances will you cross that fence." She pointed to a crude wooden divider separating the large field. It was rather romantically lit by the sunset and the three of them stared at it until the golden light melted away.

"Got it," said the rabbit. "Don't cross the fence."

Ulrich dropped his voice to a whisper. "And don't you worry, mum. This here is my, er, guard rabbit. He'll be on the lookout for any crafty witches looking to prey on women and children. And grandmums."

"And rabbits," added the Zombunny.

She blinked at them twice. "Good ta' know."

"Here's six months' rent," said Ulrich, depositing a small bag into her palm. "See you then."

ULRICH SUCCESSFULLY WOOED Magda after many baths and a regimen of colorful vegetables. He was giddy for the duration of the simple, yet jovial affair, beaming at Magda in her mint-colored gown. They danced away the evening in the Inn's courtyard, pausing for legs of mutton for Magda and salad for

Ulrich and many fine tankards of ale and countless bottles of wine. The Zombunny—his gift of speech having garnered instantaneous local fame—beat every last man at Noddy and Tables. He hopped home not long after, hiccupping quietly.

The groom escorted his bride to the honeymoon suite, which doubled as a meat cellar in the off-season. Magda's friends had scattered flowers and other nice smelling things throughout the room, but the resulting odor was somewhat confusing. Magda looked around in the candlelight, wrinkling her nose. For Ulrich, however, the room was perfect—dark and outfitted with a large bed.

He unlaced her bodice and corset as carefully as his numb fingers would allow. By the time he reached her chemise, he sat down on the bed, defeated. "Goodness sakes, Mags, how many more layers are there?"

"Last one, I promise," she said, planting a kiss on the top of his head.

NOT VERY MANY months after the wedding, Magda announced she was pregnant.

"What?" Ulrich sputtered his tea and began to cough.

"Well, it isn't as if I meant to be," she replied. "But there you are."

"You can't really be surprised," said the Zombunny sitting across from them at the breakfast table. "The two of you are like rabbits."

"This calls for a celebration, my love," Ulrich said, pulling Magda into a chilly kiss. She waved him off with a dishtowel. "We'll have a fine young son to help me in the field."

"Not so. He'll be too busy helping me scout for witches," said the Zombunny.

"Nonsense," said Magda. "*She'll* be busy helping me at the Inn."

"The Inn?" asked Ulrich. "You don't want to quit working?"

"Of course not!"

"But what will the neighbors say?" mused Ulrich.

"We only have one neighbor, and she keeps to herself," said Magda. "Besides, you know full well I don't give a rat's arse what anyone has to say about it."

"I still think I could make a fine witch hunter out of her." The Zombunny twitched his whiskers.

"Out with the both of you," she said.

AT FIRST, MAGDA'S pregnancy progressed without drama. But around the seventh moon, she began to be sick from the meat she made for herself at evening meals. She began to make large pans of roasted vegetables, carrot stew, and mashed cauliflower. She sautéed broccoli and onions and fried the leaves of small cabbages in butter. The little field, which had barely supported Ulrich and the Zombunny, became scraggly. Ulrich no longer took vegetables to the market to sell, instead hauling overstuffed bushels back to the house.

When he arrived with his daily haul one morning, Magda refused to kiss him hello.

"What's the matter, my sweet?"

Magda huffed at him. "You tell me, vegetable man. This is all *your* fault."

And Ulrich couldn't disagree. "What do you think is happening?" he asked the Zombunny, once they were alone.

"I think the child has inherited your insatiable craving for vegetables."

"My child is half Zombunny?"

"It's a theory."

"What are we going to do?"

"*We?*"

"You got me into this mess," said Ulrich.

Another week passed in tenuous civility. Each night, he and Magda would watch the sun set from the little window in the attic and dream of their future.

"I'll run the whole farmer's market," said Ulrich.

"I'll cook for the king," said Magda.

"Yes, my love. You will."

She put her hand to her stomach. "I'm just so hungry, Ulrich. I eat and I eat, but I can't seem to get full."

"How about a nice leg of mutton?"

"I scarcely believe I'm saying this," she said, "but yuck."

He nodded gravely. He looked at her looking out into the empty field. And then he watched as her gaze strayed up and over the fence where the old grandmother's field was verdant and full of leaves.

"There."

"Where?"

"That."

"What?"

"The lettuce! The rapunzel just beyond the fence."

"We can't, love. I promised, remember?"

"But surely she won't miss a tiny pinch of lettuce?"

"I don't know."

"You love me, don't you?"

"Of course I do."

"Then do me this one favor, Ulrich. Just this once."

Under the cover of darkness, Ulrich crept into the field. "What can she do to me?" he asked the Zombunny. "I'm immortal."

"You aren't immortal, you twit," said the rabbit. "You're undead. Big difference. Huge difference."

"But you said ..."

"I said you had *very little* to worry about. Which is different than having *nothing* to worry about," the Zombunny explained.

They tiptoed, avoiding snapping of cornstalks and rustling of leaves. Ulrich reached across the fence, bracing himself for a whack of the cane, or worse. But it didn't come. He and the Zombunny gently backed their way through the field and into the kitchen where Magda devoured the rapunzel without even rinsing it. She didn't offer Ulrich or the Zombunny a single leaf.

Ulrich slept well that evening, his capering complete and undetected. When he awoke, Magda was lying next to him, pale and moaning.

"Ulrich! I must have more rapunzel!"

"But obviously it's made you ill."

"Nonsense. I've never felt better than I did last night. But if I don't have more, I'll die!"

"It's only lettuce, my love."

"Exactly. Now hurry!"

Stealing lettuce in broad daylight was undeniably risky, so he sent the Zombunny to be a lookout. He gathered several handfuls of the rapunzel, placed it in a small basket and stood up to stretch his back.

"Enjoying my lettuce are you?" The grandmother's voice came from every direction.

The Zombunny caromed around the corner. "Witch!"

"Don't worry, grandmum," said Ulrich. "I'll protect you."

"No!" panted the Zombunny. "*She's* the witch!" The rabbit pulled his ears over his eyes.

Ulrich began to stammer. "I thought she'd flown to a far-off realm?"

"Don't be stupid. Witches never go very far. Haven't you read any books?" The Zombunny began to hop in a frenzied circle.

The grandmother discarded her shawl, morphing into a tall, wart-nosed cliché. She turned to Ulrich, "I told you to stay on your side of the fence."

"Yes ma'am, you did. You did say that."

"Did you not agree? Promise even?"

"We agreed. We promised." Ulrich shivered, feeling even colder than usual. "It was a matter of life and death."

"Death, eh?" She looked at the Zombunny, still turning in circles. "Knock it off," she said, paralyzing him with a spritz of green sparks.

"My wife said she'd die if she didn't have the rapunzel."

"Bit melodramatic don't you think? Besides, why not let her; turn her into your kind?"

"It's no life for a girl," said the Zombunny, still frozen mid-hop.

"Pish," said the witch. "Enough of your faux-misogynist nonsense. What's the real reason?"

"Don't tell her anyth ... mmphzzz," said the Zombunny, as a blue sleeping mist settled over him.

"She's pregnant, your witchiness. I'm afraid of what the bite might do to the child."

"Ahh, I see. But your child is already part Zombunny."

"I guess so ... it would explain why Magda is eating all of our vegetables." His stomach growled in agreement.

"I'll make you a deal then," said the witch. "You can have all the rapunzel you want, but you'll turn over the child once she's weaned."

"She?"

"Just a guess."

"I can't give you my child. That's ridiculous."

"Well, if you don't, then mother and child will both die for want of this precious lettuce."

"That's no choice at all!" Ulrich protested.

"What do you know about raising a Zombunny anyway," the witch asked. "I'll protect her from the outside world while I make her human again."

"You can do that?"

"I certainly can. Now, such a spell wouldn't do you or the rabbit any good, would it? The two of you would just keel over and die all over again. But an uninjured baby ..."

"But she. Or he. Whatever. The baby. Would live?"

"I don't see why not. There might be some complications. Vigorous hair growth. Perhaps a propensity toward skipping. Nothing permanent. Shouldn't affect her singing voice, anyway." The witch looked at him sideways as she rubbed a toe in the dirt.

"And my wife? What on earth will we tell her?"

"Doesn't she have some other ambition?"

"She'll head the Royal Kitchens, as soon as they taste her leg of mutton."

"Well, I'll give you a memory potion and you can forget this ever happened. Everyone gets what they want."

The rabbit coughed, coming out of the sleeping spell. "She's probably right, you know."

Ulrich held out his hand to the witch. "The child should have the chance to be human. You have a deal."

After the witch had gone, Ulrich tucked the listless rabbit into the crook of his left arm and studied the bottle in his free hand. A drop of potion might come in handy someday when he forgot to wipe his boots or left his black breeches in the white basket, but he couldn't—wouldn't—use it to forget this. He slipped the potion inside the pocket of his vest.

Magda reacted to the true reason for Ulrich's vegetarianism better than he had hoped. She hurled a moderate amount of kitchen crockery at him and the Zombunny and moved their bedding to the cart outside. But after a few days, she relented, calling them in for spinach buns and tea.

"Would it really be so bad if she stayed a Zombunny?" asked Magda. "You could make me one and we could travel the world selling salad spinners."

"Aye," said the Zombunny, "but what if she wanted a family of her own? How many Zombunnnies are we making here?"

Ulrich reached out and took her hand. "Would you really have her not ever taste your famous mutton?" He'd been joking, of course, trying to use one of those silly metaphors the Zombunny was always waxing poetic about, but Magda's face went serious.

"Sorry," he started.

"Shhh. I'm thinking." She continued to think for some time. Finally, her eyes brightened. "I have an idea. It won't make us miss her any less, but we can stay involved from afar."

Into the Woods, with Zombunny

MAGDA AND ULRICH and the Zombunny enjoyed the short time they had with the baby before she was weaned. On the day they were to deliver her to the witch, Magda loaded the wagon with small jars of preserved vegetables and a basket of spinach buns. The Zombunny stayed behind to console her.

Ulrich arrived at the tall tower in the woods, where the witch was waiting. "Goodbye, Rapunzel," called Ulrich as the witch flew toward the tower window. He hoisted the gifts up to them on a pulley rope.

"You'll have kept us in vegetables for years, Farmer," she said from the window.

"You wouldn't mind if we sent these spinach buns occasionally, would you?" He ran the basket up the line.

"I'm not sure if that's such a good idea," she said, taking a bite of one. "On second thought ... but send them by messenger. I don't want you getting any ideas."

AS THE PALACE chef, Magda had climbed the King's culinary ranks with her ability to pair legendary vegetable creations with her delicious braised mutton. She was chosen over fat Pierre with his oily duck recipes and thin Luc who'd cooked without salt. The palace guests grew happier and healthier and Ulrich's town market became the premier produce destination for hundreds of miles.

Early each Monday, before she left for the palace kitchens, Magda sent spinach buns to the witch's tower in the woods. So after fifteen years of sending spinach buns without interruption, Magda was surprised when the delivery boy returned with the basket still full.

"What's this?"

"Nobody's home, mum," he said. "I rang twice, just like the postman."

"Hmph," she said, wondering if she should box his ears. She put the basket over her arm, and set off for the palace.

Later that afternoon, Ulrich delivered an enormous order

to the palace for the prince's wedding. Magda quietly told him of the empty tower and they agreed to investigate that evening.

Ulrich and the Zombunny rested for a spell at the long kitchen table, sipping tea and exchanging gossip with the servants. The scullery maid was telling them rumors about a nudist emperor when she and the rest of the staff shot up, rattling the teacups in their saucers. Ulrich followed suit.

"Your Highness!" said Magda.

Prince Albert strode into the kitchen, crown atilt, holding the arm of a young woman.

"Oh my darling," the young woman sang. "Are these the kitchens? How wonderful!" The young woman spun her full skirts, and Ulrich dove for the teacups.

"Everyone," said Prince Albert, looking sheepish, "This is my bride, Rapunzel. She likes to sing."

Ulrich, Magda, and the Zombunny exchanged glances. Magda stuttered. "That's a beautiful name, that is."

"A bunny!" Rapunzel trilled. She scratched the Zombunny between his ears until his back leg began to thump. "What a handsome chap you are."

"Might want to check your eyes, Miss," Ulrich chuckled under his breath.

"Hey!" said the Zombunny.

Her laugh was like chimes. "I have perfect vision and hearing because I eat so many vegetables." She took a sharp breath as her eyes fell on the basket in the middle of the table. "These spinach buns look exactly like the ones Auntie Witch fed me every Monday! I was afraid I'd never see one again. May I?"

Magda nodded, dabbing her eye with a hanky. "Anything you want. Anything at all."

The kitchen door burst open with a shot of flame.

"Witch!" cried the Zombunny, leaping into Ulrich's arms.

"You three again," said the witch, disgusted.

"Onnie Itch!" cried Rapunzel, mouth still full of spinach bun. "Wha ar oo ooing eer?"

"You think you can just throw away your singing career? How am I supposed to get to the Royal Opera now?"

"I'm marrying Albert and I'm going to have a tiara and be a queen."

"Not if I can help it." The witch cracked her knuckles.

"You've tried imprisonment before and failed," said Prince Albert, stepping in front of his bride, sword drawn.

"Quit that," said Rapunzel, shouldering in front of him. "Violence doesn't solve anything."

"Right," said the Zombunny. "Why don't we all catch up first over a nice cup of tea. You must be exhausted from all of your stomping and spark-shooting."

"Now that you mention it." The witch sat heavily.

"How do you know these people, Auntie?" asked Rapunzel.

"These ridiculous people are your parents. And their rabbit."

"I thought they lived in Timbuktu?"

"Don't be stupid. Parents never go very far. Haven't you read any books?" The witch sighed. "I suppose they're to blame for all this."

"Only indirectly," said Rapunzel. "Once the prince stumbled upon our tower, he paid the spinach bun boy to beg off every week so he could have an excuse to visit me."

"I knew I should have boxed his ears," said Magda.

"I suppose as gift horses go," said the witch, "you could have done worse than a prince. Still, I can't let you stay here."

"All right," said Ulrich, setting a steaming mug in front of the witch. "You can leave just as soon as you finish your cuppa. You can't refuse the prince's tea service."

The witch looked at the sulking prince and smirked. "Here's to young love," she said, taking a long sip. "Hmm," she said. "This tastes like ... it tastes like ... what does it taste like?"

"Memory potion!" said the Zombunny, hopping in an elated circle.

"What was I saying?" asked the witch. "It was just on the tip of my tongue.

Magda smiled. "You were congratulating the bride and groom."

Rapunzel whispered something in Prince Albert's ear and he nodded. He said, "To thank you for your kind blessing, we were about to ask if you'd serve as Director of the Royal Opera."

"An honor beyond my wildest dreams! Just imagine, I'll be able to demand any opera I want! Unlimited protégés ..."

"And you can try on all the costumes," said Rapunzel.

"I guess I won't need this old thing anymore." The witch snapped her wand over her knee.

"No!" yelled Ulrich, covering his old wound. But oddly enough, the skin under his palm began to knit together. He looked at the Zombunny admiring his newly fat and shiny tail.

"Must've been all the carrots," said the rabbit. "Looky here! My ears stand up again!"

With the witch's spell lifted, old wounds healed and the family reunited. They all lived happily ever after, with lifetime box seats at the opera.

Camille Griep

Camille Griep was born in Montana and made her way to the Pacific Northwest via Southern California. Her fiction has been featured in a number of online and print journals and anthologized most recently in *Witches, Stitches, & Bitches* (Evil Girlfriend Media) and *The Sea* (Dark Continents Press). She is a senior editor at *The Lascaux Review* and serves on the board of Cascade Writers. In her spare time, she enjoys drinking coffee and/or wine, armchair mountaineering, and avoiding trips to the grocery store. Find her at www.camillegriep.com or tweet to @camillethegriep.

LIVE AT THE SCENE

Gini Koch

"We interrupt your regular programming with a breaking news story from the Tri-County's favorite local news channel, K-STAR, where the news is the star. I'm Breaking News Anchor Jim Rock, here bringing you breaking news from the Breaking News Desk. Let's go live at the scene with our Breaking News On-the-Scene Reporter, Tawny Jean Mountain. Tawny Jean, are you with us?"

"Yes, Jim, I am, and we have a breaking story. And K-STAR is the first Tri-County news team on the scene, so, as is the Breaking News Team's motto, we're bringing it to our Tri-County viewers first."

"Excellent, Tawny Jean. At the Breaking News Desk we've heard that there were odd lights in the sky, is that right?"

"Yes, Jim, that's right. If you and our viewers look behind me, you'll see an odd pattern of lights in the night sky. It looks like three spotlights, hovering."

"Hovering where, Tawny Jean?"

"They're hovering over the back section of the hundred

acre Jackson Farms complex, where all the cows are happy, and happy to serve all the Tri-County residents with a moo-moo here and a moo-moo there, Jim."

"How are the animals from one of the Breaking News Team's favorite sponsors handling this strange occurrence?"

"None of the happy cows are out at this time. We're waiting to see if we can get an official reaction from Jackson Farms, but the workers on the night shift all ran away because of these weird hovering lights."

"Amazing, Tawny Jean. From what we can see here, those are certainly strange lights. They look big and bright and it appears they're just hanging there like super-sized Christmas, or other non-denominational holiday, lights. No human-made things could do that. What? Oh, Dusty Rivers, our weatherman, mentions that helicopters—like the K-STAR Breaking News Chopper—could hover in this way."

"Dusty's right, Jim. But here on the scene, as I am, and as the K-STAR Breaking News Chopper also is, we can confirm that these lights are not, I repeat *not* helicopters. Or planes. Ken 'Whirly' Bird, our Breaking News Chopper pilot, has already done a fly-by. To you, Whirly."

"Thanks, Tawny Jean. Jim, Dusty, what I saw when I flew by the lights was nothing. Just the lights. Floating in the air. My In-the-Air Cameraman, Clint Clinton, got some great footage. Roll it, Clint."

"Interesting. The lights appear to be about ten feet in diameter, is that right, Whirly?"

"That's right, Jim, good eye."

"That was Dusty's guess, Whirly. He's the one with the science background, ha ha ha."

"From what we can see on the ground here, they're very round. Are they round for you, Whirly?"

"They are, Tawny Jean."

"Whirly, Dusty's asking if there are any visible signs of propulsion?"

"Not that Clint or I can spot, Jim. Tell Dusty the weather's clear, though, so he owes me another Budweiser, the official beverage sponsor of the Breaking News Team, since he was wrong again. Heh heh. There are no, repeat no, showers in the Tri-County area right now. Just these three weird floating lights."

"Dusty says that he predicted meteor showers, Whirly. Not rain."

"Heh heh. Nice try. I still want my Budweiser, Dusty."

"Dusty's asking how, if there's no visible sign of propulsion, it's possible for the orbs to remain airborne, Whirly."

"I have no idea, Jim, but I flew the Breaking News Chopper all over the sky near and around the lights. They're big, and for those viewers who don't have Dusty's 'science background' these 'orbs' are about the size of the cabin of the Breaking News Chopper. But there's nothing holding them up, no wires or anything similar."

"Because if there were, the chopper blades would have gotten tangled up, right?"

"That's right, Dusty. Nice of Jim to let you have a microphone."

"We're a team here, at the Breaking News Team, Whirly. And I got tired of repeating Dusty's questions, ha ha ha. So, asking for me and Dusty, as a team, what's your next move?"

"I'm going to take the Breaking News Chopper in closer, Jim."

"You're a wild man, Whirly! And, as the Breaking News Team member closest to the action, what do you think these things are?"

"Takes one to know one, Jim! But as for what these strange floating lights are, I'm going to go out on a wing here and say that I think they're extraterrestrial in nature. Whoa!"

"Tawny Jean! We just lost communication with Whirly. What happened?"

"Well, Jim, here at the scene, I can tell you that the three giant, floating lights all just got much brighter. One of them moved closer to the Breaking News Chopper and started to glow even more brightly. And ... excuse me ... I'm sorry, but ... it's terrible, Jim."

"What we're seeing, Tawny Jean, aside from your tears of shock and horror, is what looks like the Breaking News Chopper on fire and plummeting out of the sky."

"That's right, Jim. I'm sorry I'm having to yell, but I'm not sure that you can hear me, due to the explosion. Poor Whirly."

"I don't think Whirly is live on the scene anymore."

"Not funny, Dusty. Folks, forgive Dusty's gallows humor. Any chance of survivors, Tawny Jean?"

"Camera Two is going to check now, Jim. What's that, Nick? Yes, yes you are, Nick. Because Camera One is on me. No, Mike isn't going to go in your place. Mike's job is to film me, period. You're supposed to be the roving camera. Go rove and see if Whirly or Clint are still alive."

"Tawny Jean, what else is happening live on the scene?"

"Jim, the floating lights are still floating. No more aggressive lighting up. Ah, did someone at the station call for emergency personnel?"

"Dusty did, Tawny Jean. Do you think you're in danger?"

"Maybe, Jim. It may be that all of the Tri-County area is in danger."

"Are there more of them?"

"I don't know, Dusty."

"Have Mike film the sky to the north, would you, Tawny Jean? That's where the meteor shower was supposed to be visible to all Tri-County residents tonight."

"Sure, Dusty. Camera One is turning toward the sky so we can all take a look. Hmmmm, yes, Dusty, I think we do have more of them coming. Or it's your meteor shower that we're also witnessing right now."

"Or it's both."

"Dusty, you're saying that these floating lights are meteors? That would be an amazing scientific find! And it's being brought to our loyal Tri-County K-STAR viewers first by your Breaking News Team."

"No, Jim. I'm not saying that the floating lights are meteors. Meteors are, in your vernacular, space rocks that come flaming through the atmosphere, hit the ground, and make a big hole. They don't hover."

"Then what are you saying, Dusty? There are a lot more floating lights coming."

"What I'm saying, Tawny Jean, is that I'm wondering if the meteors we were expecting are actually extraterrestrial life forms of some kind."

"You mean space aliens?"

"Yes, Tawny Jean."

"Well, Dusty, why would space aliens want to kill Whirly and Clint? Oh! Oh my God!"

"Tawny Jean! What just happened?"

"Jim, it's terrible! The space alien things just blew up Camera Two! And all of the Jackson Farms complex! Oh, the humanity."

"Tawny Jean, didn't you say that all the people had left already?"

"Yes I did, Dusty. It's terrible. The smell is like barbeque mixed with burning manure. Kind of makes you hungry and sick to your stomach at the same time."

"They killed a lot of cows, Tawny Jean. That's not humanity."

"I don't follow you, Dusty. Emergency response vehicles are here. As are what appear to be military personnel. Jim, I'm going to try to get an interview with whoever's in charge."

"Tawny Jean, maybe you and Camera One should get out of there while you still can."

"Sorry, Dusty. This is Breaking News and none of the *real* Breaking News Team would leave the scene while there was breaking news going on."

"Whirly, Clint, and Nick are never leaving the scene. Permanently."

"That's our girl! Dusty, don't be a downer, keep the Breaking News can-do attitude going. Folks, for those of you just joining the Breaking News Team on K-STAR, the Home of Breaking News, we have a situation going on over at the Jackson Farms complex."

"The Breaking News Team has already lost enough people, Tawny Jean."

"Not now, Dusty, I'm busy."

"Not to worry, Dusty. Chance Timberland has arrived to save your day, both on and off the field!"

"Hey, folks, it's everyone's favorite award-winning sportscaster, Chance Timberland. Chance, you and my Breaking News Co-Anchor, Connie Katano, were supposed to be covering the Tri-County's Little League Finals tonight, and you're not due on for another hour, during our regularly scheduled evening Breaking News Broadcast."

"Connie said that Tawny Jean's story was much more important to the Tri-County area, Jim. We stopped by to pick you guys up so we can all go out and help Tawny Jean interview the space invaders!"

"I'm not sure that's a good idea—"

"Then you stay at the studio, Dusty, and be our man at the desk. It'll be great experience for you, and, as we all know, our Tri-County K-STAR viewers love their weather with a little dust in it! Folks, while Tawny Jean tries to get an On-the-Scene Interview, I'm going to go out in our Breaking News Van with Connie and Chance. We'll be bringing the breaking news to you all along the way. Jim Rock, signing off for the moment. Dusty, the broadcast's yours."

"Ah...great. For those Tri-County K-STAR viewers just tuning in, I'm Breaking News weatherman Dusty Rivers and we're in the midst of what may be an alien invasion, right here in the Tri-County area. I'd recommend that everyone try to remain calm. Panic is not the answer—"

"Dusty, it's Jim, coming to you from the Breaking News Van."

"Aren't you still in the parking lot?"

"Yes, but that's not important now. Let's give our viewers

what they want, which is the breaking news, not a list of do's and don'ts. Folks, while Chance drives the Breaking News Van at a, heh, breakneck pace, I'd like to get Connie Katano's take on all this. Connie, as an intelligent, erudite, woman of color, how do you feel the events at Jackson Farms will affect the minority community in the Tri-County area?"

"Jim, I'm glad you've asked me that. I'm already planning to talk to all the community leaders who happen to be minorities, like I myself am, to get their views about this amazing situation. I think this breaking news event will give the fine minority members of the Tri-County community even more chances to prove just how vital to the Tri-County area they really are. So, look for my new exclusive, ongoing series—The Minority Community and You: UFO Edition—starting next week."

"Great insight, Connie! Can't wait to see your hard-hitting Breaking News Exclusive! Wow, folks, if you can see what our Breaking News Van Camera is showing you, there's destruction all along the highway leading into the Jackson Farms complex."

"Cars are scattered everywhere, Jim. Most of them are in flames, as are most of the buildings and land around the highway. It wasn't like this when Chance and I were coming back from the Little League Tournament."

"Those kids can really play, though."

"Thanks for that insight, Chance."

"Any time, Jim."

"Ah, you guys? Are there people in those cars and businesses you're driving past?"

"Not sure, Dusty. We're heading to the breaking news right now."

"Jim, there's breaking news all around the van."

"But there's no one to interview, Dusty, and as we know, our K-STAR Breaking News viewers like to get the beat from the man or woman on the street."

"It looks like any men or women on the street are dead, Jim."

"You've been waiting all night to say that, haven't you, Dusty?"

"Not really. Tawny Jean Mountain is back with us, though. To you, Tawny Jean. It's great that you're still alive, by the way. Especially when all I can really see behind you is flames and debris. It looks like you're in a war zone, not at the Jackson Farms complex. Or whatever's left of it."

"True enough, Dusty. As Camera One scans the skies for our K-STAR Breaking News viewers, you'll see that we have a lot more of those floating lights in the sky. So far, they've blown up every aircraft that's come near them. They've also blown up the military vehicles on the ground. Which represents all the destruction you so accurately noted. Dusty, Camera One is now back on me, thanks Mike, and I'm here with Major General Philip 'Tank' Smith, who's in charge of this action. Major General, what can you tell us about the events going on right now?"

"No comment, Miz Mountain."

"Major General, do you think that the floating lights are meteors, aliens, or just a nasty trick of the light?"

"No comment, Miz Mountain."

"Major General, why did you agree to speak with the Breaking News team if you're not going to give us any comments?"

"Because for whatever reason, the aliens aren't blowing you up."

"They blew up the rest of our Breaking News On-the-Scene team, Major General."

"Right. And they blew up fifteen helicopters, twelve tanks, and fifteen Jeeps. And yet you're still here. Ipso facto, you're the safe zone. Or they want you."

"Ha ha ha, Major General."

"Tawny Jean, it's possible. We don't know. You're an attractive woman."

"Gosh, thanks, Dusty. Um, I'm dating Chance Timberland, the Breaking News Team's award winning sportscaster, who's won awards both on and off the field, you know."

"Yes, I know. But the Major General could be on to something."

"Aren't you the weatherman?"

"Yes, Major General, I am."

"Well, dammit man, you're not any good at it. You said there would be showers and it's a perfectly clear night, if you ignore the floating alien lights in the sky."

"I said there would be meteor showers, Major General, but thank you for confirming that the military believes we're under alien attack. I now believe the meteor showers were in fact the aliens that are currently attacking the Tri-County area. I'd like to recommend that all our Tri-County viewers get to safety. Storm cellars or bunkers, if you can manage it."

"No reason to panic the populace, boy."

"Major General, you're hiding out with our young, attractive On-the-Scene reporter because everyone else around her has been blown up. When do you recommend the rest of us panic?"

"Dusty, the Breaking News Van has arrived with backup."

"Tawny Jean, that backup is Jim, Connie, Chance, and Chris who handles the Van Camera. I don't think they're going to be the backup you're hoping for."

"Jim Rock from the Breaking News Team here, on the scene of breaking news, with our On-the-Scene reporter Tawny Jean Mountain, my Breaking News Co-Anchor, Connie Katano, and the Breaking News Award-Winning Sportscaster, Chance Timberland."

"I've won awards on and off the field, Jim."

"Right, Chance. Tawny Jean, there's nothing but destruction for miles. What's the situation here?"

"Destruction all around, Jim."

"Jim, Tawny Jean, it looks to me as if the lights—of which I count at least twenty—are starting to form into a sphere of some kind."

"Good eye, Connie. It looks that way to me, too."

"Major General, what's your opinion of what Connie and Jim have described?"

"I think we're all going to die, Miz Mountain. Each one of those lights or ships or whatever they are is powerful on its own. Combined? I don't think we stand a chance."

"There's always a chance, because I'm right here! Chance Timberland here to save the day."

"Right, son. Head between legs and kiss your arse goodbye kind of chance."

"Tawny Jean, what is Chance doing?"

"Dusty, Chance is running toward the lights. Oh. Oh ... my God."

"Uh, I'm sorry you're seeing that, folks. It appears that Chance Timberland is the latest casualty in this alien attack. Tawny Jean, I think you and the others and anyone else alive there need to get away as fast as possible."

"Dusty, a moment of silence for Chance, please."

"Jim, mourn later. You guys need to get out of there. It's a war zone."

"And the Breaking News Team doesn't run from breaking news, Dusty."

"We have a lot less members of the Breaking News Team at the moment, Jim."

"Run, you damn fools! Run!"

"Dusty, there's nothing but madness down here. People screaming, things exploding. This is Jim Rock, Breaking ..."

"Jim? Jim! Jim, are you there? Folks, I think we're seeing the aliens attacking the rest of the military and Breaking News Team left on the ground. From the way the cameras have just fallen, I think we've lost our cameramen. God, I see Jim and the Major General, or at least what's left of them.

"Connie! Tawny Jean! Can you two hear me? Folks, Connie and Tawny Jean are both still up, really up. They appear unscathed, so there's that. Of course, they're both attractive women, and so far the only dead I can spot are men. So, men of the Tri-County area, I think we're all in trouble. If you're an attractive woman, you may be safe, but right now, folks, I wouldn't count on it.

"Tawny Jean and Connie don't appear to have their microphones any more, or if they do, we aren't receiving back here at the station. They're floating in the air, going right into the lights. Truly, right in. And ... they're gone. Inside the light or whatever those things are.

"Anyone still watching or listening to this broadcast, get to safety as fast as you can and God go with you—excuse me, my phone's ringing, and it's the Breaking News ringtone. Could be one of the team is still alive! Hello? Yes? Yes. Ah ... yes. I ... understand. Really? Why me? Why *only* me? PhD in Physics, actually. Yeah, my mother wanted me to be on TV. Really? Wow. That's a really generous offer. Thank you. Yes. Yes, I'll take care of it.

"Sorry about that, folks. We're going to go to a brief commercial."

"Jackson Farms, where our happy cows give a moo-moo here and a moo-moo there, all for you-you! Jackson Farms, a Tri-County tradition. We've always been here, and we'll always be here, moo-moo-ing for you!"

"And ... we're back. Hi folks, I'm K-STAR Breaking News weatherman Dusty Rivers. And, I'm here to report that all the last hour's worth of reporting was all a mistake, folks. Ha ha ha. Those 'lights' were just weather balloons that reflected the moon's rays off of some swamp gas due to the meteor shower that I predicted yesterday. All the 'death and destruction' was just a little Breaking News Team practical joke. Nothing other than that. Ha ha ha.

"So, just relax and don't worry, folks. The Tri-County area has not, I repeat, not been invaded by extraterrestrials here to steal all our women and wipe the rest of us off the face of the Earth. This is Doctor Dusty Rivers, signing off. Forever."

Gini Koch

Gini Koch writes the bestselling fast, fresh and funny Alien/Katherine "Kitty" Katt series for DAW Books, the Necropolis Enforcement Files series, and the Martian Alliance series for Musa Publishing. As G.J. Koch she writes the Alexander Outland series and she's made the most of multiple personality disorder by writing under a variety of other pen names as well, including Anita Ensal, Jemma Chase, A.E. Stanton, and J.C. Koch. Buy her books — her meds don't come free, you know. You can reach Gini via her website: www.ginikoch.com

THE NEWSBOY'S LAST STAND

Krystal Claxton

There once was a man who, like any man at the start of a story, was malcontent. Unhappy. Sad, even. Really kind of a sap, and you wouldn't think he'd get a story of his own, but you see there was also a girl.

Now, as you've all heard before, girls make everything better. But that isn't exactly accurate. Because girls are not magical, they're really very much like men in that they can be good or bad, but are mostly mediocre. And just as such, this girl was not the only girl—there were many others—but in this story she made a difference.

The girl—Jane was her name (and the man's name was Romulus, no those names don't match very well)—worked at the flower shop on the corner between the bakery and the cakery across the street from the newsstand. (No, a bakery and a cakery are quite different, please be silent so I can tell the story.)

In those days very few people could read, and so the newsstand wasn't a place where newspapers were stacked, but rather was a stand upon which the newsboy would shout about all of the wonderful or horrid things that had befallen the kingdom. (Okay, it was actually an autonomous collective; doesn't kingdom sound nicer?)

And, of course, Romulus was the newsboy. Newsman, rather, as he was quite too old to continue being called a boy, but there were no new boys to take the job. The only schoolhouse in the kingdom had closed some years prior due to the ongoing war with the neighboring kingdom (a self-perpetuating autocracy). In fact, Romulus's newsstand was the last of its kind. And so, as you might have guessed, the news that Romulus read on the rickety, rusting news scaffold on the corner across the street from the flower shop was not very good.

The girl, Jane, who was only eight years old (here you were thinking she was a woman, but if she had been I would've said so) would stand outside the shop, offering daisies and bluebells (which were actually purple) to anyone passing by. The roses remained inside, as they were much too expensive for an eight-year-old to handle. All day, rain or shine, Jane listened to Romulus shout bad news.

"Honey shipments from the Western Shore delayed by enemy contact!"

"Frontline of battle moves ever closer!"

"Mass hysteria! Dogs and cats living together!"

Until one day, when the shop was near to closing and Jane hadn't sold a single flower—because honestly, the news had been so bad that day and who wants to buy flowers when the kingdom's future is quite so bleak?—so she walked across the cobbles to stand beneath Romulus's stand.

She held her basket with the daisies in both hands, and her face was smudged with soot from when the chimney sweep had brushed past earlier in the day, and her black shoes were scuffed and her white apron was brown around the corners but the bow was still tied around her back, and ... quite frankly she looked adorable. And I only point this out because it's so important.

If she hadn't stood there on that corner and looked up with those large brown eyes that were just a little bit too close together, Romulus would probably have never done the stupid thing he did.

In-between breaths, while he was looking down at the newsprint to announce the next line of bad news, he saw Jane peering up at him.

She smiled, a very tiny smile, and her eyebrows wrinkled, and she asked, "Isn't there any good news in the world today, Mr. Newsboy?"

Perhaps it was all his friends had gone to war and he'd had to stay behind since he was the only one that could read, or maybe it was the chill of standing on a newsstand all day, but as I said, I believe it was because Jane herself was so perfectly disheveled that Romulus paused.

He read the next line of print without really seeing it, and when he went to announce the line, what came out in his great, booming voice was: "Cotton candy cart tomorrow, all day. No charge."

Jane, her eyebrows now unwrinkled and quite high on her forehead, gasped and grinned.

Romulus felt very bad just then, because even though it was nice to see a smile, he knew that tomorrow she'd be even sadder for it. But he couldn't undo what he'd done and she was happy now, so he left the line hanging in the air.

She stood up on her tip-toes, extending a slightly wilted white daisy up to Romulus, her whole body pointed and straight in the effort of reaching something that was entirely beyond her reach.

For his part Romulus knelt down and took the flower and gave her a sad smile and watched her run back across the street. And even though he had another line of news, it was sad, so he called it quits for the day and went home. He put the daisy in a jar of water and ate his cake from the bakery (yes, the bakery, not the cakery) and went to sleep.

The next day, Romulus shouted the bad news and tried very hard not to notice that Jane was aflutter with expectations on the corner across the way. This was difficult because it seemed the rest of town was also buzzing about the good news, and Romulus was a bit worried that when the cotton candy never came he'd lose all credibility.

But then a very unexpected thing happened. (Well, truthfully everyone was expecting it, just not the newsboy.)

The candymaker came dragging a handcart down the cobbled way. He parked it right next to the newsstand. And when he pulled the yellow and red-striped tarp away, there in the cart was a cloud of pink cotton candy. He set to the task of distributing it all away, and every person in town stopped by for a taste, and since everyone was nice and took no more than they could stand without getting a bellyache, there was enough in the cart for everyone to have some, Jane first and Romulus last.

When the day was done the candymaker packed away his cart and mentioned to Romulus, quite casually, that the next time it was free cotton candy day he hoped someone would warn him in advance. When he'd gone, in his place stood Jane, her basket all sold except for one crumpled bluebell.

Yesterday she'd seemed quite sweet, in a sad sort of way. But today was even worse, with her beaming smile, pink sugar in a film from cheekbone to chin. Poor Romulus really didn't stand a chance when she looked up at him and asked, "Mr. Newsboy, have you gotten all the bad news out? Is it time for the good yet?"

Now, Romulus knew he'd learned his lesson. He'd lucked out with the gullible candymaker and he most certainly wasn't going to risk a second false line. He read the newsprint and in his great voice announced: "Tomorrow's battles canceled for International Jellied-Toast Day!"

Which wasn't what the newsprint read at all. In fact, the newsprint very sullenly pointed out that the primary forces would arrive shortly, and he'd be up to his newsstand in bayonets in two days' time.

Romulus grimaced. Pressed his stupid lying lips tight together. Ventured a glance down at Jane.

Jane, of course, was about to burst. "Oh, I didn't know tomorrow was a holiday! We haven't had a proper holiday since before Christmas was canceled last year! That's, that's, that's—"

"Incredible?" Romulus supplied.

"Yes!"

Perhaps no one else had noticed? Romulus dared a quick look-see and found to his chagrin that absolutely *everyone* had heard. (Even, it seemed, the old deaf hound that spent his afternoons begging for scraps from the taxidermist three doors down.)

When Romulus, shoulders hunched, turned his face down to hide behind his newsprint, he noticed that Jane was extending the last (purple) bluebell his way. He probably shouldn't have accepted it, since it was earned on falsehoods, but he was eager to be home (and out of everyone's immediate gaze) so he took it and hurried off to bolt his door and leave the bluebell in the jar with the daisy.

The next day the newsprint warned Romulus that the sound of cannons from the West would likely be audible in town as early as brunch, even downtown where his newsstand creaked in the cold wind. He ought to have led with that line, really, to clear the air and prepare everyone. But it was so awful and little Jane, who seemed to have washed her browned apron for the holiday, was positively vibrating with excitement. So he started with the glum news about the town's dart team (the Verdant Rams) losing to their longtime rivals (the Cyan Harts).

And in that sliver of time just past breakfast, but not yet brunch, the baker started stacking baskets of sliced bread on the tables outside his shop window. Thin sliced, thick sliced, rye, wheat, sunbleached white, cinnamon swirl, pumpkin, squash, and potato bread—all lightly toasted on each side.

Romulus forgot about shouting the news as he watched

three carts loaded with clinking glass jars amble up the intersection from the North, East, and South respectively. The first was proper jelly distilled by the jaminator, the second was jam from the marmateer, and the third was a veritable rainbow of preserves from the ladies of the Scarlet Hat Society.

The crowd gathered; jellied-toast was had by all.

But something unexpected happened. (Or perhaps you, at least, are expecting it.) From the West-end road came soldiers. In trickling clusters of threes and fours and then raucous bands of tens and twenties. And there was, in fact, enough toast for everyone to have a bit without becoming greedy and eating too many carbs.

By now, for the first time in three-thousand two-hundred and ninety-one days, Romulus had forgotten all about the news and was enjoying a spiced pumpkin tea with his toast. Once the tea was gone and the toast was just about run out (though, admittedly, there was still a great deal of fruit-spreads left) a small detachment of soldiers came down the West-end road.

But these were not autonomous collective soldiers. They were self-perpetuating autocracy through and through.

The carnival grew very quiet. And it seemed the bayonets which had been left on their slings all morning were suddenly at the ready.

One of the gnarly-looking antagonists stepped up, chest puffed out, and said very clearly, "We're 'ere for Jellied-Toast Day."

Whispers broke out among the villagers, and there was a bit of a trend (I'll give you a hint—they weren't keen on sharing). Until it was Jane who piped up, tiny voice above the crowd, "*Well.* It is *International* Jellied-Toast Day."

The rumble of dissent rippled back on itself, and everyone was eventually certain that it was shameful to break their much-loved, longstanding (recently invented) tradition.

The Baker, looking a bit pale, pointed out that there wasn't any toast left. So naturally, the Caker (who'd been waiting the whole time for the Baker to run out of bread and was a little bit irritated that it had taken so long into the day) rolled out a wheelbarrow of freshly baked, sliced, and toasted cakes. Banana, pound, snicker doodle, strawberry swirl, triple chocolate—the entire cookbook, no doubt. And things went as you'd expect into the afternoon. (Cherry preserves and triple chocolate being a favored pairing, and the autocracy types seeming less and less gnarly.)

By the time everyone was full and the mess had been cleared away and the soldiers had begun trickling back to their various encampments outside of town, the sun was nearly gone.

Just as Romulus was realizing he hadn't read a line of news since the bit about the dart tournament, Jane appeared next to him. She had grape jelly smeared, with the skill of a genuine eight-year old, between her eyebrows. She didn't speak this time. Her eyes aglitter, she waited to hear what the good news would be.

Romulus nodded. Climbed the scaffold. He tried very hard to think of what he might say. He'd completely given up on the newsprint. By now he realized he wouldn't be able to stick to the script. He wanted only, this time, to not be *surprised* by his own news. Perhaps another holiday?

When he cleared his throat to announce that tomorrow would be Pudding Pie Day, every eye in town was on him. "Tomorrow, town hosts treaty talks. End of war in sight."

The townspeople and the lingering soldiers clapped or cheered (though a few just nodded, knowingly or uncertainly, I'll let you decide). And although Romulus would really have liked to have had pudding pie, he had to admit that it was probably better news this way.

Once he'd gotten back to the sidewalk from his scaffold, Jane was waiting for him with a yellow rose that was far too expensive for an eight-year-old to handle and certainly too posh to be a gift for a newsboy. At first, Romulus didn't take it. Not until he saw the florist, the baker, the caker, the taxidermist, and the maramateer, all watching, giving him looks of approval.

The next day, Romulus had little reason to doubt that the treaty talks would start. It seemed ridiculous, but, sometimes life is worthy of ridicule. Still, he was uncertain how it might play out, and he seriously considered staying home (he'd accumulated quite a bit of sick-leave being the only newsboy and working every day for years). But he knew that Jane would probably still show up, and while she wasn't likely to earn the ire of any visiting generals, he'd best be on hand, just in case.

Right at dawn he gathered up a number of things he suspected he wouldn't need: the newsprint delivered to his front stoop, his boxed lunch and, for good measure, the jar with the three flowers. The streets were already packed with villagers and, when they spotted Romulus, the crowd parted to let him pass. But before he could make it to his newsstand, he came upon two lines of soldiers, and right in the middle of the street there stood three people. Two generals that looked very unhappy to see each other and Jane.

"... and it always happens just as he says," she was saying. "Oh, here he is now."

The autonomous collective general asked, as they both turned to look at him, "*You're* the news*boy*?"

"This is what passes for a newsboy in this gods'-forsaken land?" said the autocrat general, the foreigner, though he wasn't really asking.

Romulus shrugged. "It's only news if it comes true."

The autocrat eyed him suspiciously.

Romulus cleared his throat, sweating under his collar despite the brisk morning air. "So ... do you like bread?"

The collective general asked, "What madness is this?"

Romulus gestured with the hand holding the flower jar. "I just thought ... we have a nice cakery, if you wanted a slice of butter bread?"

The autocrat looked from the child to his rival to the newsboy to the flowers. His eyes fixed on the flowers.

Romulus tilted his head to one side. "Do you like them? Uh. They're for you." And he thrust the jar at the general.

It was very still in that moment. Then the autocrat general took the flowers in both hands and said very soberly, "As our tradition demands, I accept your gift of daisy, bluebell, and rose, and agree to discuss the terms of your treaty."

The collective general said, "Really?"

Romulus said, "Really?"

Jane tried to hide her giggle behind her apron, but did a poor job of it.

The autocrat eyed each of them. "Of course. I respect that you have researched our customs. Now. Tell me more about this butter bread."

It took more than a day—six months, two weeks, and four days longer than a day—to come up with a treaty that ended the war entirely. And it wasn't one that made everyone happy. But it did make everyone equally inconvenienced, and that's really the core of a good compromise, don't you think?

Once things were settled, Romulus gave up his spot on the newsstand, adopted the deaf dog three doors down, and opened a halfway house for slightly-used/gently-worn pets. The school reopened and Jane was able to attend and became the first new newsboy in nearly ten years. Since the war was finally over, the news she shouted was almost entirely, mostly, more or less, good news (except when the Verdant Rams were playing).

There now, isn't that nice? So the moral of the story is. ... Well. I'm not quite certain. In fact, there probably isn't a very good conclusion to draw from this story—and I should hope you don't start lying to children all over town just because things aren't going your way. And please don't try to solve your problems with food. Though flowers are always a nice gesture. And it never hurts to be nice. Even in the harshest times.

Krystal Claxton

Krystal Claxton writes speculative fiction in the sliver of time between raising a four-year old with her unreasonably awesome husband and being a full-time computer technician. She enjoys attending Dragon Con in costume, science magazines, and feverishly researching whichever random topic has just piqued her interest. Keep up with her at krystalclaxton.com or @krystalclaxton on Twitter.

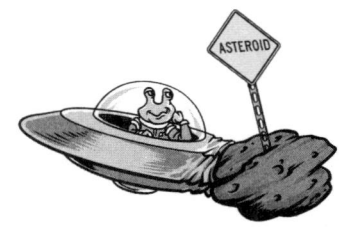

THE FULL LAZENBY

Jeremy Butler

T he cardboard box held fewer books than I expected. Sartre was safe but Neitzsche ended up in the trash. I wanted to cry.

Dwight burst into our room, still in last night's clothes. "Dude, you should have come out. I hooked up with this chick, a two-thirds Anaïs Nin. It was dirrrty." He noticed the empty shelves, the box of my prized books. "No scholarship, then?"

"Nope. No one wants to subsidize philosophers."

"You could switch majors. That girl last night said poetry has good backing. Some software developer found out he was 64 percent Ezra Pound and now he's throwing money at anyone who can rhyme."

I shook my head. No wealthy industrialist would foot the bill so I could read Camus.

"Then get tested," he said. "Find out who you are. Maybe you're a 90 percent Dostoyevsky. I bet State would drop tuition for that."

I paused. "Schools do that?"

"For sure! Look at Peterson next door, she's a ninety-plus Beethoven. She got a full ride and I heard she's tone-deaf."

"That's so not right."

"It's your only hope, buddy. Roll the dice. I'll pay."
"Yeah, but what if I'm a Caligula?"
"They haven't got him. I've checked."
"Goebbels?"
"Ach!" He grunted. "Let's skip the *'What if I'm Hitler?'* talk. Just read the pamphlet."

DWIGHT ASKED THE woman at the testing center to run my sequence but not release it publicly until we screened it. She left us alone in the waiting room where I paced like an expectant father.

The centers boasted a database of millions of talented and/or famous individuals. Phenotypy and genealogy were weak indicators of similarity, or so the homology quotient supporters claimed.

If Betsy Rowling, only 13 percent her great-grandmother, boasted a million pre-orders for her unwritten first novel then a 95-plus percent JFK match running for senator was easily considered the real thing. Cue headlines, cue interviews, media coverage, excited electorate.

Everyone loved a dynasty, even a scientifically dubious one.

Dwight had four weak matches. For a directionless trust fund kid, his quotients defined his world. Because of his 45 percent William Shatner quotient, he studied drama. His 32 percent Henry Kissinger had him in political science. Jane Austen, creative writing. Carl Sagan, astronomy.

Full matches were sufficiently rare that outside of twins there had never been living duplicates. Dwight still pined for a match with some yet-to-be-sequenced celebrity, preferably a minor Borgia or Jesus.

The woman returned. I couldn't read her expression, only its intensity. She held out the envelope and Dwight snatched it away, pulling out the paper within. His eyes scanned back and forth. The girl stared at me, then winked coyly.

"So," I said. "Who am I? Let me guess. Henry Winkler, Ringo Starr ..."

"Am I reading this right?" Dwight asked.

The girl nodded.

"A 99.7 percent match?"

Panic gripped me. "Who? Oh god, please don't say Dahmer."

"George Lazenby."

I searched my memory and came up blank.

"James *fricking* Bond," Dwight gushed. "Do you know what this means?"

My phone rang from my pocket. Dwight stared, expectantly. I answered.

"Is this Lazenby, George Lazenby?"

"What? No. I'm sorry, my name is—"

"Agent 007, your presence is requested at once!"

THERE WERE FOUR Bond Houses, each on a different continent. The North American one was an extravagant mock-European affair with crystal chandeliers, baccarat tables, and wall portraits of the sixteen Bond actors. Its revenue was supported largely by weddings, conferences, and weekend getaways.

The facilities kept the character alive, thereby feeding the film and television franchises, which in turn fed the facilities and their staff. It was an integrated media experience that crossed the boundaries between amusement park, movie, and family to the tune of billions annually.

"We expect our Bonds to be men and women of education and manners, first and foremost," my guide said. The man, a 92%- Roger Moore, was of Middle Eastern descent and spoke with a posh English accent. "We will, of course, ensure that you are taught self-defense, weapons, and foreign languages. You speak Russian at least?"

I shook my head.

"That's okay. Any military service?"

"Afraid not."

"My dear boy, not to worry. There is plenty of time. We are just happy to have you. Our last Lazenby died in a skiing accident. For thirty years, all we've had are false alarms to ... address."

"Address?"

"Bond is a legacy that must be protected. Impostors are just one of the threats. Double agents, defectors. We have moles at the very top of the testing center administration. We keep tabs. The last thing we need is a 95 percent Judi Dench being picked up for armed robbery again, am I right?"

I had no idea what he was talking about.

"We deal with those threats the way our forefathers did." He smiled wanly. "Never mind that now. You're going to fit in wonderfully, George."

I was about to correct him, but he continued.

"We'll start with the wardrobe. We would like to see you wear something more fitting. And do you own a car?"

"No, I bus it, usually."

He grimaced. "That will not do. A Bond on public transportation? How the Bournes would love that!"

"Actually, I'm broke. I'm dropping out to—"

"I'm aware of your finances, George. A distraction from your studies and your Bondship. Your outstanding debt was paid this morning. Please let me welcome you to Her Majesty's Secret Service."

"For real?"

"Well, figuratively."

EVERYTHING CHANGED.

Women threw themselves at me. Men, too.

My neck ached from nodding at double entendres.

Professors paid me more attention. The Dean approved my scholarship saying that my "breeding and roguish contempt for authority would bring fresh air to a stale department."

Even my parents got excited. They told their friends all about their famous son and his spiffy new Aston Martin. They even went to get tested themselves. Dad was nearly a 40 percent Alan Hale. Mom was a quarter Dian Fossey.

It all felt good. Weird, but good. I was celebrated for the accomplishments of a theoretical relative playing a fictional person. Material for a great thesis or else a nervous breakdown.

Bond House didn't ask for much in return, just to promote the legacy: dress well, stay out of trouble, exude confidence, and most importantly, stay single.

After an on-camera piece about *Bond 2212*, 92%-Moore scolded me for shoehorning Kant into an on-camera piece. "Just stick to wordplay. Keep your studies to yourself, understood?"

A few vodka martinis in, my tongue let loose. "Like, you'll only live once to see this episode. How's that?"

92%-Moore smiled magnanimously. "Great."

"Diamonds are forever, but this film won't be in theaters long. Be sure to—"

"Very clever, yes."

"The world is not enough to keep me from tonight's showing of—"

"Do shut up, 007."

I MOVED INTO a small apartment replete with all the trappings of a spy's 1960s love nest—hidden entrance, rare tropical fish, rotating bed, wet bar.

Dwight showed me how to use my identity for fun. Cops, bartenders, hotel staff. A casual reveal led to rule bending, free drinks, respect. I had the weight of a multinational corporation behind me.

After plain bribery got me a passing grade in Senior Ethics, Dwight and I hopped a flight for the Bond casino in Monte Carlo.

The place was packed. Full Christopher Walken regaled a crowded bar. Full Halle Berry held court at craps. I made the rounds, posing for pictures and punning my way through the tuxedoes and evening gowns.

Along the way I met twin Russian 75 percent Diana Riggs

that clung to me like henchmen. They were hopeful of entering the Bond House and teared up when I hinted they weren't pure enough Rigg.

"There are two of us, though" one said. "Bring us in together."

"Yeah," cooed the other. "That's one-and-a-half Riggs."

By the time I finished, Dwight was at the poker table, deep in the hole and more than a little tipsy. I took the seat across, a partial Rigg nibbling each of my ears.

"They say two heads are better than one," Dwight called. "We should totally test that out."

The Riggs stopped. One of them hissed.

I raised a hand. "Dwight, that's not the carriage of a gentleman. Please apologize."

Dwight rolled his eyes and threw back the rest of a scotch.

The Riggs turned their attention to my thighs. "Where's your suite, George? Let's all retire to some place more private."

"I believe I have the accommodations to accommodate that," I said, eyebrow raised. The Riggs tittered.

"Tenth floor," Dwight said. "His name's on the door. Give us a few minutes to freshen up, then come on up."

They recoiled. "Us?"

"I'm George's benefactor. Isn't that right?"

Reluctantly, I nodded.

"See, girls," Dwight slurred, pushing back from the table. "George was a much better bet than cards. He always brings me returns on my investment." I watched in horror as he unzipped his fly.

The Riggs were over the table and pounding him before I could move. By the time Dalton and Brosnan pulled the Riggs off, Dwight's bloodied nose and lip had ruined his dinner jacket.

The Riggs were dragged out, cursing in Russian.

The room was silent, everyone stared: Walken, Berry, Grace Jones, even the new Sophie Marceau I hadn't met yet.

"I'm going to invite you to leave," Dalton said to Dwight.

"Unless," he turned to me, "he's with you?"

My friend stood bleeding and drunk, surrounded by opulence and beauty. His fly gaped, mucus poured from his nose. He was a buffoon, everything Bond was not. Everything I was not.

All eyes were upon me.

"Me? No." I said. "We've never met."

DWIGHT MUST HAVE caught a flight that night. He didn't return my calls, was never in our old room. He avoided me, and I couldn't blame him.

I graduated, although I missed Commencement for a two-year Guest of Honor stint aboard the new Bond Cruise Line. Tuxedos and Hawaiian shirts, bon mots and international women. The good life.

I had barely regained my land legs when my phone woke me from sleep, finding me uncomfortably alone. It was 92%-Moore.

"Get to the Bond House fast. We believe that someone may try to kill you."

I pulled on a pair of cream linen trousers. "Kill me? Like for real? Why?"

"Because you're a Bond."

"What? Who would do that?"

"George, six months ago, Gert Fröbe was sequenced. He has a full match. We wanted to make an offer for him to join Bond as a lobby greeter or desk clerk. But the man disappeared. Our extensive network of resources uncovered no trace. It was odd, but soon forgotten."

"Fröbe, who's that?"

"The actor who played Auric Goldfinger, the ruthless mining magnate that was one of Bond's greatest nemeses."

"Okay, so ... ?"

"This evening, Brosnan, your replacement on the H.M.S. Thunderball, was found dead. He was covered in gold paint."

"What?"

"Dalton put it all together. A man who has the means to hide out from our extensive surveillance. An incident he recalled from Monte Carlo. A man who holds a grudge against Bonds. We're recalling Bonds everywhere, especially since you two shared a roof ..."

My head started to swim.

I ran for my safe and found its door was already open. My Walther PPK and laser watch had always been for show, but now were gone. Only one other person knew the combination.

A gun cocked in the darkness.

Dwight stepped forward into the bubbling light of the exotic aquarium. He pointed my pistol at me. The aquarium's light reflected off a collection of medallions he wore around his neck.

"Hang up the phone, George."

I hung up. "You're really embracing the gold thing. This is for real? You killed Brosnan?"

"You're the philosopher. What do you think, coincidence or fate?"

"Neitzsche said that the metaphysical need for art to—"

Dwight laughed with disheartening malice. "Save it for someone who cares."

"I'm sorry. I should have ..."

He raised his hand, quieting me.

"You don't understand, you and your Bond friends. I wasn't *given* the opportunity you were, so instead I'll *take* it. No one wants a partial Shatner that can't emote or a witless slice of Austen. But a Goldfinger that beats Bond, there is a somebody."

"You are somebody, Dwight."

"Don't call me that! Other than this, I'm just potential diluted to inconsequence. When I learned of the match, I knew. I felt it in my bones. This was who I was meant to be."

"A murderer?"

He grinned. "I'm just what you made me. Hero of the No-Ones."

It wasn't a bad speech, given the situation. I nearly suggested that he re-consider the Austen path, but it was too late for that. We stared at each other, the moonlight casting shadows. Dwight stretched out his arm, pointing the weapon at my chest.

"Good-bye, Mr. Bond," he said.

"Goldfinger was a great villain. But he's not the most popular."

"I know that. I'm not even a great nemesis. Are those are your final words?"

"I'm just saying that if you're going to define the role for yourself, I think you should take a cue from what's worked."

"Such as?"

"Blofeld is far more popular. It's all about your escape. The chase, the mystery—where is he, what is he doing, what will he do next? The mystery's the thing. That's what keeps the audience coming back. Trust me, it's Bond 101."

He lowered the gun an inch. "You think so?"

It was my chance. I dove at him, knocking his arm aside as bullets shattered windows and the aquarium. My eardrums sang as we wrestled, but with his Shatner-inspired combat skills he handily threw me to the floor.

Aquarium glass pierced my back and breathing became sharp and pained. I heaved like the exotic fish flopping around me. Dwight stepped forward and leveled the gun at my face.

"Good bye, Mr. Bond."

I rolled over, unwilling to stare down a gun's dark hole of death, to a fish, drowning on the shag carpet, my companion in suffocation.

Two eyes stared at me and in them, I found salvation.

A quick toss sent the fish tumbling through the air, its spikes protruding in defense as Dwight put up a hand to block. The pufferfish's spines sent neurotoxin into his hand before he batted it away, dropping the gun in the process.

His screams were muffled by my still-ringing ears and the all-consuming pain in my chest, though I had a sense that he screeched even as he ran into the night.

At some point sirens came.

At some point I blacked out.

I CAME OFF the ventilator after a day, though the pain lasted longer. My parents visited and the police took my statement. A week in, 92%-Moore arrived, his brow furrowed but wearing a full grin.

"This is amazing, George. The interest we're seeing is off the charts. The police are keeping tabs on Octopussy and eight Blofelds, just in case. There's talk about re-releasing the original films in IMAX-3D and building an Australian Bond House in your honor."

He continued like that for ten minutes. Finally, I interrupted: "I'm fine, thank you, Roger."

"What's that, George? You must find Goldfinger. The media and the fans are demanding it."

"Track him down? I'm not a real spy. Why would I do that?"

"We'll help you, George. It's what you're made for."

"Made for? I'm supposed to be reading books not hunting enemies, not getting shot at. You know that we're not actual agents, that none of this is real?"

92%-Moore shrugged.

I removed the oxygen mask so there would be no confusion. "Look, Roger, I'm done. I appreciate all you've done for me but I don't want to be Bond anymore. I'll change my name, move to Guam, whatever. You'll have to wait for the next Lazenby."

He stared at me agape. "Give up Bond? Just like that? With no thought of the future, no plan for what comes next?"

"I appreciate everything you've given me. But let Connery take a crack at Goldfinger. That sounds right to me."

92%-Moore laughed.

"Quit Bond after one adventure? That is *so* Lazenby."

Jeremy Butler

As a psychiatrist, much of Jeremy Butler's writing is locked away in medical charts. What escapes can been found at places like *Nature* and *Apex Magazine*. He is the proud holder of an invaluable theater degree from MIT and regularly performs improvised comedy around the Toronto area. His intermittent musings are collected at jeremyrbutler.net.

DO NOT REMOVE THIS TAG

Piers Anthony

Nate stared at the purple tag. DO NOT REMOVE THIS TAG. There was no other information on it, so what was the point of it? It was on the second-hand mattress he had bought cheap, all that he could afford, and the mattress was not very comfortable. In fact it was lumpy, and the lumps tended to poke him almost as if self-animated. He was getting ready for bed, dreading another bad night's sleep, with the night yet young, and in no mood for arrogant tags. It was bad enough existing on unemployment and limited savings; he didn't need this.

What the hell. At least he could deal with this annoyance. What could they do, throw him in jail? He took hold of the tag and pulled.

It resisted his effort. "So it's like that, is it?" he muttered. "Well, we'll see, you self-important little piece of fluff."

He went to fetch a pair of pliers. He fastened them on the tag and yanked hard. It ripped out of the mattress seam with a pained noise of separation. It truly had not wanted to be removed. But it had tangled with the wrong person.

Then mist issued from the small tear where the tag had

been. Purple mist or smoke. Was the mattress on fire? Fascinated for the moment, Nate watched the vapor curl out and spiral upward, thickening and expanding. There was evidently a lot of it inside the mattress, now released by the slit. It became a dark cloud eighteen inches in diameter, swirling internally.

The vapor formed into a horrendous face with cauliflower ears, beetling brows, a crude vent of a mouth, flame-like hair, and darkly smoldering eyes. "So, mortal!" it rumbled. "Thou hast released me at last, thou foul son of a she-dog!"

This was weird. It was also insulting. "Listen, airhead. If you're what inflated the mattress, get back in there and do your job. The damned thing is bad enough without going all the way flat."

"I be the Ifrit Ibraheemstukobritch," the face said, or something that sounded something like that. "Three thousand years have I been trapped in this vile container. Other ifrits got confined to fine glass bottles, but no, I was stuck in this ill bag. King Suleiman, may the gods defecate on his name, doubtless had a sense of humor I share not."

This was one of the genies the ancient Israeli king had confined to bottles so they wouldn't bother human folk? That didn't make sense. "How come? He must have had a reason."

More of the demon formed. Now he was a complete figure of a supernatural spirit, with muscular limbs and an impressive naked torso. "Know, O foolish mortal, that I always had an eye for the damsels. The queen was one luscious creature, but her suite was warded to repel ifrits like me. So I sneaked into a mattress that was being delivered to her bedroom, and when she sat her bountiful bottom down in it, I gave her a little poke up through the cloth." He illustrated by poking a single ham-finger up suggestively.

"That wasn't smart," Nate said, smiling.

"Mayhap not. Her scream roused the entire palace staff, including the king, who was not much amused. He was in his night dress, with a disheveled concubine trailing behind. 'O foul spawn of hell,' he swore, 'since thou does like mattresses so much, be thou forever confined to it.' Suddenly I was locked in, with a magic tag for the seal, and the mattress was heaved onto the trash pile. I could hear what passed outside it, but could not see, and of course I could not escape. It were not the mattress that confined me, but the seal, which I could not remove from inside. The mattress passed from beggar to beggar over the centuries, and each insisted on using it despite my efforts to make it uncomfortable. It was in my mind that I might torment someone into burning it, and when the flame made a hole I would escape. But the infernal thing was fireproof. Thus I remained, until this moment thou didst free me. So thank thee, mortal, and now begone."

"Begone?" Nate repeated, outraged. "Listen, you refugee from Arabic fantasy, this is my apartment. *You* begone. In fact, cram yourself back into the mattress where you belong, because I paid for it and it's mine along with all its contents, including you, and I want to be able to use it, uncomfortable as it is."

The ifrit contemplated him thoughtfully. "Thou beest correct. The mattress should have its occupant. Since it be thine, I will cram thee into it, and thou canst spend the next three thousand years contemplating thy insignificant navel therein."

"The hell with that!" Nate said. "I'm not getting inside any—"

But the ifrit reached out with a hand suddenly grown huge and gripped him about the body. "In thou goest, fell mortal," he said, and jammed Nate's head at the slit. The vent actually enlarged to take him in.

Obviously he had misplayed this situation. The demon had powers he couldn't match. He needed to talk his way out of trouble in a hurry, because he suspected that he would not be able to escape the mattress once he was inside. "Wait!"

The ifrit paused momentarily. "What, mortal?"

"You—you've been trapped for three thousand years. You have no experience with the modern world. You'll be hopelessly lost if you try to wing it alone. You'll get in terminal trouble.

You need a guide who is familiar with the local customs."

"Trouble? With what? Suleiman be long gone."

Nate thought fast. "The IRS, for one thing. It will come after you for having no visible means of support and not paying taxes. You could wind up confined again."

The ifrit considered. "I know not this Iris. Be she a powerful goddess?"

"The worst! Nobody can stop it, uh, her. Even the worst criminals get caught in her clutches."

"She must be a distant daughter of Suleiman."

"Very distant," Nate agreed. "And she's just one of the hazards of the modern world."

The ifrit considered further. "Be there damsels here?"

So he was a lecherous knave, as had been hinted when he got into the queen's bed. That was the undoing of males in all cultures. "Oh, sure. Gals galore. Here, I'll show you." He wriggled out of the demon's grasp and went to turn on the TV, and set it to a porn station. The raunchy action was continuous.

"In a magic box!" the ifrit said, impressed. "Lovely creatures."

"They're actually full sized," Nate explained. "This is merely a picture. But as you can see, they have the essential features."

"They do. I want some of those."

"Uh, you can't just fetch them. They are protected by, uh, wards. This is just to prove that they exist. First you have to blend in with the culture."

The ifrit sighed. "Ever thus. Very well, mortal, I will spare thee the mattress, for now. But thou must show me this blending."

"It's a deal." He considered. "But first some cautions. You'll need to don some clothing. Contemporary clothing, not pantaloons and slippers."

"Clothing," the ifrit agreed with resignation. Pajamas matching those Nate was wearing appeared on his body.

"That's night clothing," Nate said. "I'll show you day

clothing. But first, you'll need a name. Not a ten syllable Arabic moniker. Why don't I just call you Tag? That should pass muster."

There was a rude sound, followed by a ruder smell. "There, I passed mustard. Be that satisfactory?"

"Uh, no," Nate gasped as the thick odor made him gag. "No mustard gas. Not in public. I just meant that the name Tag should do. Next, the language. You're speaking an archaic dialect. In fact, how is it you're speaking my language at all, if you've been out of touch for three thousand years? Shouldn't you be speaking Aramaic or something?"

"I could hear folk speaking when they were on the mattress. I picked up on the languages as they gradually changed. There was a really nice damsel about three centuries ago in England. She put her ear to the mattress, and we conversed. So I learned her dialect." He frowned. "But she wouldn't remove the tag, so I tuned out."

"Her loss," Nate said. "Can you orient on the dialect I speak?"

"Sure can, numbskull."

Nate ignored that. He went to the closet and donned day clothing. He turned around and saw Tag dressed identically. Good enough. "Now we'll take a walk in the mall, where you can pick up on the local scene. Don't do anything without my advice."

"Got it, pinhead."

They took the elevator to the basement floor. Tag was much intrigued. "A moving room!"

They walked to the nearby mall. "Moving steps!"

"That's called an escalator. See, folk ride up and down on them. We'll do the same. No flying or conjuring, okay?" Nate paused.

"Why are we waiting?"

"See those young women on the escalator? I am mentally undressing them. It's a common male pastime."

"Ah."

The women screamed. Their clothing had disappeared.

"I said mentally, not physically!" Nate said. "Quick, clothe them again, before they make a worse scene."

"What good is mentally?" Tag grumped. "It's their bare behinds that count." But clothing reappeared on the women.

Yet somehow the women were not satisfied. "That's my outfit!" one screamed at another.

"Well, you got mine!"

"I may have put them back on the wrong women," Tag said.

"Let it be!" Nate said before the ifrit could magic the clothing further. "We'd better make ourselves scarce."

They turned, only to be confronted by another young woman, a pretty one. "Not so fast, you two," she said. "I saw that, and heard you talking. Did you use stage magic?"

"Of course," Tag said, before Nate could stop him.

"Really? How did you do it?"

"Like this."

The woman's clothing disappeared. She was quite well formed, and obviously it was all natural. But unlike the others, she did not scream. "That's not stage magic. That's real!"

"No, it's fake," Nate said desperately. "All pretend."

"Fake?" she asked Tag.

"Of course not. My magic is always real."

"Show me something else."

"Don't do it!" Nate said. But again he was too late. The woman was already sailing up into the air, still naked. Now many heads turned.

"Look at that!" a child cried. "Bare boobs!"

The men in the area oriented. "More than that," one said, licking his lips.

"Get her down here, safely, clothed," Nate rasped. "Fast!"

The woman reappeared before them, clothed. "Amazing," she said.

"Take us back to my apartment," Nate said, trying desperately to stop making a scene.

Then they were back in his apartment. Tag, Nate, and the woman. "Uh-oh," Nate muttered. He had not meant for the woman to be included.

"This is wonderful," the woman said. "You really can do magic!"

"It's all illusion," Nate said.

"Nonsense. My hobby is paranormal investigation. Ninety-nine percent are fakes, but I know a real one when I see it. When it undresses me, and flies me high in the air, and conjures me to another place." She faced Tag. "Sir, you have phenomenal talent."

"Thank you, damsel," the ifrit said modestly. "Shall we now have a wild orgy of sex?"

"No!" Nate cried.

"He's right, this time," the woman said. "This is not the time. We hardly know each other. I am Lotus Long."

"Nate Boxer," Nate said. "And this is Tag Ifrit."

"How do you do, Tag?" Lotus said, proffering her hand.

"Well, I'm a magical creature," Tag said. "It comes naturally to me."

"She meant to shake hands," Nate said quickly. "Like this."

He proffered his hand, and Lotus took it.

"Ah." Tag shook hands with them both.

"How did you catch on to what we were doing?" Nate asked Lotus. "In fact, why were you there? It seems like sheer coincidence."

"Not at all. I am one of the one percent. That is, I'm a real paranormal. My premonition is infallible. I knew that something significant would occur at that time and place, so I made sure to be there. Now I have a marvelous opportunity to investigate."

"Investigate me," Tag said, his chest swelling.

"She means your paranormal aspect," Nate said, staving off a spot siege of jealousy.

"That, too," the ifrit agreed reluctantly.

"You really are magical?" Lotus asked.

"I'm an ifrit. All ifrits are magical."

"How is it there's been no newsflash about this before?"

"I was sealed in this mattress," Tag explained. "Until Nate removed the tag and released me. Now I'm learning about his world. It's intriguing."

"I would imagine so," Lotus said. "How long were you in the mattress?"

Nate had given up trying to hide the nature of the ifrit. There was bound to be a globe-splattering splash. Where would it end?

"Three thousand years," Tag said almost proudly. It seemed that he liked having the attention of a pretty girl, as what male didn't.

"That's amazing!" Lotus said warmly. "It must have been maddening to be trapped without being able to participate in world events."

"You have no idea. All I knew of the world was what I could hear from inside the mattress, and that was mostly snoring. Except when a couple was making love. Then the bouncing could get horrendous, especially because I knew what caused it. Hard to sleep through that. If I could've gotten out,

I'd have showed them some real action. Speaking of which—"

"All in good time," Lotus said smoothly. Nate realized that she could handle the situation. She was playing the ifrit, using his desire to get her onto the mattress to evoke more information about his nature and history. Nate could only wish that she had reason to play him, Nate, similarly. "I want to learn all about you, so I can write a book documenting a real live paranormal manifestation and become famous."

Tag's eyes squinted cannily. "You are using me."

"Well, yes, technically. This is potentially the story of the millennium, and it's all mine, mine!"

"Then you should let me use you in return. This is only fair."

Lotus considered. "I suppose you do have a case. Very well, I'll give you a minute to court me. Then we'll return to business."

"But his idea of courtship is akin to a cave man dragging a wench into his cave by the hair," Nate protested.

Both turned to him. "So?" they said almost together.

Nate shut up.

"You have ox eyes, a giraffe's neck, breasts like ripe melons, lips like fat red worms, hair like a camel's tail, legs like those of an ostrich, a wasp's waist, a butt like that of a baboon in heat, feet like—"

"You do have a certain way with words," Lotus said, smiling. "But not quite right for today's women, complimentary as they may be."

"How not?" Tag asked, perplexed.

"Suppose I returned the favor, per a current joke, saying your ears are like flowers, cauliflowers. Your eyes are like pools, cesspools. Your lips are like petals, bicycle pedals—bit of a verbal slurring there. Your teeth are like stars, they come out at night. Your nose is a Roman nose, it's roamin' all over your face."

The ifrit nodded, impressed. "You're a fair hand at courtship yourself, damsel. But what is a bicycle?"

"Um, you do need to get a better acquaintance with today's scene. You probably don't know about cars, planes, computers, TV—"

"He knows about TV," Nate said. "He saw, uh, girls there."

"I want one," Tag agreed. "Or three."

"I'll bet," she said. "Maybe we should visit a casino, where anything is available for a price. How are you for gambling?"

"I am good at it. I always win, of course."

"Of course," she agreed thoughtfully. "But we'll need money to start."

"Here is money. A bag of gold." The bag appeared in his hand.

Nate took it and reached inside. He drew out a small gold coin with ancient script on it. "Er—"

Lotus saw the problem. "Wait, if you always win, we can start with some of mine, and parley it into a better stake. So let's go to the casino."

Suddenly they were in a busy casino, standing beside a roulette table. Sexy girls were circulating, serving drinks. Tag was pleased; this was what he had come for.

Lotus shook her head. "First we need to build up our stake and buy some chips. This way." She headed for a row of one-armed bandits. She put in a silver dollar she had, and pulled the handle.

The tokens whirled in the little windows and settled into place. The machine gave a hoot and poured out dozens of silver dollars. Nate and Tag gathered them up and followed Lotus to the cashier's window, where she exchanged them for betting chips. Then they returned to the roulette table. And won. And won again.

Before long the casino bouncers appeared. "The boss will see you now," one said menacingly.

"Why?" Tag asked, curious.

"You're winning too much. Something's fishy."

"This is a problem?"

"Listen, joker," the bouncer said, drawing back his fist.

"Don't threaten him!" Nate warned. Too late, as usual.

Tag snapped his fingers. The first bouncer sailed through the air and crashed into a slot machine, which in turn crashed to the floor. The second bouncer turned into a white rat that scurried across the floor, starting a commotion.

"We'd better get out of here," Nate said urgently. "And not by supernatural means. We'll take a taxi."

"A what?" Tag asked.

"A car. One of the things you need to learn about."

"Good idea," Lotus agreed. "We've made enough of a scene for the moment."

They barged out and caught a waiting taxi. "Where to?" the cabbie inquired.

"To hell and back," Tag said.

"That'll cost you extra."

Then there was a siren as the police closed in. "I think we ruffled some feathers," Lotus said, not entirely dismayed. "This could get awkward."

"Too bad we can't just fly out of here," Nate said, resigned to more than awkwardness. All this, because he had pulled off a stupid tag!

Then the taxi sailed up into the air and floated to another lane, where it landed. "Good trick!" the cabbie said as he accelerated. "In the morning I may wonder about this."

"Cars aren't supposed to fly," Lotus told Tag.

"But Nate said—"

"I think we'd better just get home," Nate said.

Then they were back in his apartment. Nate turned on the TV, fearing the worst. It was there. "There was a remarkable scene at the casino," the announcer said. "It appears to have started with an unnatural winning streak. There are rumors about a man turning into a rat, and a flying car. Also nude women at another location. The authorities are investigating."

"Aw, zip your lip," Nate muttered.

And the mouth of the TV announcer became a closed zipper. He looked startled.

"Um, Tag, there are a number of things we have to caution you about," Lotus said. "Such as figurative speech."

"And we haven't even touched upon the Internet," Nate said.

"The what?"

"It's a global communication system with its own protocols and dangers."

"Dangers?"

"Like viruses. They can really mess you up."

"Viruses?"

"They infect machines as well as people these days."

"Machines get ill?"

"They do when their software gets infected."

"Software?"

"This will take weeks," Lotus said impatiently. "Where to begin?"

"This is giving me a headache," Tag complained.

"Ifrits get headaches?" she asked.

"No. That's what makes it hard to handle."

"Well, we'll handle it. I have a book to write. I need to know everything about you. Then we'll put you on display for the public, doing real magic tricks. Proof of the supernatural at last. Take that, skeptics!"

Tag shook his head. "Damsel, you're enticing, but this is not worth all the confusion. I'm going back into the mattress so I can sleep until a better day."

"Don't you dare! Not before I finish the interview."

But the ifrit was already fizzing into vapor and sliding into the mattress. In moments the purple mist disappeared, leaving only the purple tag to seal it.

Lotus grabbed at it, but it was illusory: visible without being real.

"He made sure it couldn't be removed this time," Nate said, halfway relieved.

"Come out of there, you shirker!" Lotus screamed. "I need you to prove the supernatural is real! Otherwise they won't believe me."

A finger-shaped section of the mattress poked up in response.

"Oh is that so! Well, I'll damn well drive you out again, Spook! You won't get a minute's sleep." She jumped on the mattress and bounced repeatedly. "Take that! I have not yet begun to bounce!"

But the mattress was annoyingly unresponsive.

Meanwhile Nate noticed the bag of gold still sitting on the table where it had been forgotten. He took out a coin, then another, but the bag remained full. Finally he turned it over to dump it out. A stream of gold coins fell, piling until they overflowed the table, far more than the little bag could have held. "It's an endless bag!" he breathed, amazed. "I'm rich!"

"No you aren't," Lotus said from the bed. "Spending those ancient coins would arouse immediate suspicion. We'll have to fence them carefully. I have a connection."

"We?" he asked blankly.

"We're in this together, aren't we?"

He gazed at her. She was slightly disheveled from her bouncing, but prettier than ever. There was hardly anything he could think of he would like more than being "we" with her. "We are."

"But it would still be better with Tag on the scene so I can write my book and prove it. A real live ifrit! Vindication for the supernatural!"

Nate opened his mouth, about to suggest that, as Tag said earlier, the best way to wake up the ifrit was bouncing on the mattress. Preferably while clasped together, naked. Then he thought back on the events of the evening and decided it was definitely best to let sleeping magical creatures lie. And also that he liked Lotus too much to use a lame pickup line on her.

"Let him sleep," said Nate. "There must be other ways to prove the existence of the supernatural. With your premonition talent and all this gold, we'll find them for sure."

"We?" Lotus asked.

"We're in this together, aren't we?" he repeated what she said earlier.

Lotus beamed at him.

Nate smiled back. He was ready for their adventures together. But first he'd need to find a nice, quiet storage unit that was large enough to fit a mattress.

Piers Anthony

Piers Anthony is one of the world's most popular fantasy authors and a New York Times bestseller twenty-one times over. He's the author of the *Xanth* series, the *Apprentice Adept* series, and many others.

SUPER-BABY-MOMS GROUP SAVES THE DAY!

Tina Connolly

From: Stef Jones-Tanaka <bilingualbiologist@supermail.com>
To: <superbabymoms@superdupergroups.com>
Subject: Intros

Hey Super Moms! Here's the email group I mentioned to a couple of you at preschool today. Teacher Stacie said there are four of us families in the system right now at Little Darlings Preschool and shared your emails with me—hope that's ok! I think we can learn from each other! Please go ahead and introduce yourself and your kids, and feel free to share a problem you're having right now. Chances are you're not alone.

As for me, I have twin four-year-olds Isabel Ko and Beatrix Ai. Isabel has super strength and Beatrix has X-ray vision. Isabel is going through a hitting phase. Our front door has been obliterated twice. Beatrix knows all about sex from looking through the neighbors' walls (apparently the neighbors have way more fun than we do.) I'm tempted to put both girls in a cement dome covered in foil until they're twenty.

    Hope to hear from you all!

    hugs, Stef
    Live each day like the planet might explode tomorrow. Who knows, right?

```
From: Zoë Wallis <zoeboe@supermail.com>
To: <superbabymoms@superdupergroups.com>
Re: Intros
```

    OMG Stef, thanks for starting this group. I have a boy (Rocket) who is three, and we just had a new baby (Lilac), who is five months. Rocket was doing just fine up until the baby was born. And now ... OMG I don't even know. Have any of you dealt with kids who won't stop stretching? Apparently he's been tying knots around the other children with his stretched-out legs. I've tried bribing him with stickers. Also with capes. Nothing.

    I cringe every time I pick him up from Little Darlings now. Teacher Stacie keeps talking to him about "helping hands" and "human hands" but he just laughs and sticks out his tongue till it touches the other wall. Going crazy here, and we don't even know what Lilac's powers are yet. Dread finding out it's something like super boobs, because I will NOT be down with buying her a spandex leotard with holes cut out of it.

    Zoë "Human Hands are not Stretchy Hands" Wallis

```
From: Alicia Marquez <CEOmarquez@supermail.com>
To:   <superbabymoms@superdupergroups.com>
Re:   Intros
```

Hello Stef and Zoë. I have one daughter, Alexandra-Maria, who's three and in Rocket's class. Forgive my bluntness, Zoë, but my daughter and I have had some serious talks already about Rocket's behavior. She knows that it is unacceptable to submit to his inappropriate elasticity—not just for herself, but as an example for other girls who may be too timid to speak up. (I am glad you do not see it as a "boys will be boys" issue, as I find far too many mothers do.)

Unfortunately, not only is my daughter too shy to tell Rocket how she feels about his knots, her super power is that of turning herself inaudible. We are hoping it will be accompanied by invisibility as well (her grandmother has both talents), but so far she remains a frustratingly symbolic metaphor for being both a woman, and a woman of color, in this world.

Best, Alícia
alt.email: ceo@marquez.com

```
From: Zoë Wallis <zoeboe@supermail.com>
To:   <superbabymoms@superdupergroups.com>
Re:   Intros
```

Oh god, Alícia, I am SO sorry. I swear weeee are wroking on it.

Will;; write more later. Rocket has me tied to chair. Am puishing keyboard buttons with nose.

Zoë "Down with the Patriarchy, Even When He's 3" Wallis

```
From:  Tiffy Turner <spandexmom@supermail.com>
To:    <superbabymoms@superdupergroups.com>
Re:    Intros
```

Hi ladies! Sorry for the delay but we just got back from getting Hadley a new skirt for flying practice.

I am blessed with three amazingly super children over here. Hadley is our flyer—she just turned seven. Williamsburg is four and his talent is weather control. He's in the class with Stef's darling twins. And Dartmouth is two months old and already showing signs of being clever with fire—she lit the candles on Hadley's birthday cake last week!

Zoe, hang in there, I'm sure your baby will turn up with something eventually! All my super kids showed their talents by at least three months but it generally is much later, as I'm sure you know from Rocket.

Stef said we should each share a problem we're facing right now, but honestly we have no problems! Life is, well, "super!"

PS: Does anyone know who the kid was who brought slugs to school last week? Apparently they escaped. Williamsburg found one in his snack container and he was quite aggrieved. I wouldn't be so upset only Williamsburg likes to carry a shaker of sea salt for his snack and the slug died when it came into contact. Also it was an antique snack container signed by Amazing Man.

> xoxo Tiffy
> *"Hadley is the most delightful student it's ever been my privilege to teach!"* — Mrs. Stout, 1st grade teacher

From: Stef Jones-Tanaka <bilingualbiologist@supermail.com>
To: <superbabymoms@superdupergroups.com>
Subject: Slugs

Ooh, sorry, Tiffy. The slugs were Beatrix's doing. She wanted to see what they would look like inside things—including, apparently, Williamsburg's lunchbox. We have confiscated the slugs and returned them to the yard.

Thanks for your kind words on the girls. I've always thought Williamsburg was such a darling child—so nicely dressed, and he always asks me what I think of the weather. Now I understand why.

Alícia, I understand your frustration, believe me. It's so hard raising girls in this world—especially girl supers. Mine don't need any help fighting their own battles (which is both good and bad, when you're called in because Isabel punched the cubbies to smithereens!), but I can *well* imagine your frustration.

Zoë, hang in there too—things will get better. My younger brother's talent is levitating others. Preschool was a nightmare. And grade school. And junior high, come to that. But it did get better. Now he has a good job with the coast guard hoisting drowning people out of the ocean, and is super responsible.

hugs, Stef
Live each day like the planet might be wiped out by mutated giraffe-flu tomorrow. Who knows, right?

From: Zoë Wallis <zoeboe@supermail.com>
To: <superbabymoms@superdupergroups.com>
Re: Intros

Hi, Tiffany. Yes, I'm sure Lilac's talent will show up soon. We're not worried.

BTW, I'm sure I'm just confused, but I thought you had four children? There's a teenage girl who's been picking up Williamsburg all summer and I thought she said she was his big sister?

Zoë "The Baby Ate Holes In My Brain but Maybe That's Just Her Talent" Wallis

From: Tiffy Turner <spandexmom@supermail.com>
To: <superbabymoms@superdupergroups.com>
Re: Intros

Hi, Zoe. It's Tiffy, actually, not Tiffany.

Yes, our oldest, Amherst, is 14, but she's not a super, so I didn't mention her as I thought this list was about parenting our supers? (Although sometimes I like to joke that she has the talent of driving us all insane. She's suddenly refused to accompany Hadley to flying lessons, even though she's always loved it. She recently covered her entire room in foil, which as a super myself is hard not to take personally. And, she used to spend all her time writing stories which was at least harmless, but now she's switched over to the drums, which is driving us completely bananas. If anyone has any suggestions for stopping this, I'm all ears. Not literally, as my talent is calming, not shapeshifting.)

Stef—thank you. I always thought Williamsburg might have a second talent for fashion, but his father doesn't like me to suggest that. Williamsburg designed my most recent super outfit, though. (I mean, not that I'm currently fighting crime or anything as I make sure to put my kids first. But you know how it is—hard to give up the spandex, you know?) Anyway, everyone always asks who the label is.

xo Tiffy
"Williamsburg has the best Helping Hands I have ever seen!"
— Teacher Stacie

```
From: Zoë Wallis <zoeboe@supermail.com>
To: <superbabymoms@superdupergroups.com>
Re: Intros
```

Hi, Tiffy. It's Zoë actually, not Zoe, but I realize it can be hard to find those strange characters on your keyboard if you're not used to French words.

Zoë "Alt-shift-quotation mark, e" Wallis

```
From: Stef Jones-Tanaka <bilingualbiologist@supermail.com>
To: <superbabymoms@superdupergroups.com>
Subject: Checking In
```

Hey Super Moms! I just realized it's been a whole week since we last spoke! I'm sure you guys are just as busy as I am— I've been trying to start back into part-time work at my old lab and it's a strain to find the time to do everything I used to do *and* work as well.

Tiffy, I've been thinking about your difficulty with Amherst, and I wonder if she's feeling a little left out at not getting to go to flying practice and weather practice and fire practice herself, you know? It may not be her thing, but Teacher Stacie said she's looking for a teenage helper as we start into the summer class. Maybe a little responsibility and money would make her feel like she has a talent, too. I know *I'm* glad to be back in the lab, and not *just* be in my mommy role, as much as I love the girls! Just a thought. :-)

hugs, Stef
Live each day like a genetically-engineered dragon might fry the earth tomorrow. Who knows, right?

```
From: Tiffy Turner <spandexmom@supermail.com>
To: <superbabymoms@superdupergroups.com>
Re: Checking In
```

Thanks, Stef. I'll have her drop off her résumé.

Tiffy
"Seriously, I would babysit that darling Dartmouth for free!"
— Angie, nanny

```
From: Stef Jones-Tanaka <bilingualbiologist@supermail.com>
To: <superbabymoms@superdupergroups.com>
Subject: New Member
```

Hi again Super Moms! I think we got off to a bit of a rocky start but I still think there's a lot we can help each other with!

I invited a new mother to join as Teacher Stacie said this morning that a kid in the 3's class suddenly developed a talent! She said his family wasn't expecting it at all—how exciting! Hopefully she'll post later.

Hope you all are doing well. Tiffy, I'm *so* excited to see Amherst helping out with the classes at school! Teacher Stacie said she's been telling stories to the kids and seems to be really enjoying herself! Isabel and Beatrix came home last week full of a long story she told them about a girl who transformed into a sparkly fire truck and flew to the moon with her sidekick Iceman to battle a bunch of fire-monkeys or something. Very imaginative kiddo you've got there!

hugs, Stef
Live each day like a plague of super-spiders might web everything tomorrow. Who knows, right?

From: Deiondre Johnson <tiredmom@supermail.com>
To: <superbabymoms@superdupergroups.com>
Subject: Help

Hi, I'm Deiondre. Stef invited me. My son, Denzel, suddenly discovered this weekend he could make water freeze. Frankly we are all shocked around here as no one in our family has ever had this. I mean ice cubes sound nice as it's summer and all, but it's downright shocking to turn on the shower and get icicles. And then I guess he froze some kid's tongue to his drink at school today. I'm already at my wit's end and hoping for suggestions.

Deiondre
Sent from my iPhone. Please excuse typos as I'm probably asleep.

From: Zoë Wallis <zoeboe@supermail.com>
To: <superbabymoms@superdupergroups.com>
Re: Help

Hi Deiondre—lots of empathy here as that must have been shocking. We were prepared for a super and it was still shocking the first time Rocket shot his arm across the room to grab a cookie out of Dad's hand. Of course it's helpful if one or both parents are supers—his dad is able to make things briefly turn to jello (I know, I know, that's what she said) but seriously, if you can turn a super tantrum into a pile of goo for one minute it does work wonders.

PS Don't feel too bad about the tongue freezing as that was my son and I'm sure he deserved it.

Zoë "Any Day Where My Kid Wasn't The Worst Is a Good Day" Wallis

From: Tiffy Turner <spandexmom@supermail.com>
To: <superbabymoms@superdupergroups.com>
Re: Help

Deiondre,

I'd be happy to have my son Williamsburg talk to him if you'd like. It can be helpful to have a well-behaved super around to show him the ropes.

And I understand you about it being shocking. No one in my family was a super and then suddenly I turned out to be super skilled at calming. And I was quite a late bloomer as it didn't happen until after Amherst was born, probably because I never needed it before. She had colic and was so fussy that something just clicked on. Honestly, that's why there's such a gap between Amherst and Hadley—I joined a league and helped subdue riots in heels and spandex for seven years before my husband pointed out it was time to have the other children we'd wanted to have.

Tiffy
"Hadley is the most talented super I've seen in years." — Dr. Humphries, flying teacher

From: Alicia Marquez <CEOmarquez@supermail.com>
To: <superbabymoms@superdupergroups.com>
Re: Help

Hello Deiondre, I am glad that you have joined the group. Alexandra-Maria told me all about the little boy at school today who kept putting ice cubes down her dress. She explained to me that it meant he liked her, but I explained that there are more appropriate ways of showing affection and they all involve keeping one's hands to oneself.

Believe me, Deiondre (and Zoë), I do empathize with the difficulties of socializing a boy to master appropriate and respectful behavior. But I was raised to speak my mind and I feel that it would, in fact, be disrespectful of you two women if I did not alert you to the situation and show that I have confidence that these situations will be ameliorated.

Zoë, apparently Rocket is doing better about not tying his legs around Alexandra-Maria's legs. However, he stretched himself up to the roof today and was dropping Cheerios on her head.

Best, Alícia
alt.email: ceo@marquez.com

From: Zoë Wallis <zoeboe@supermail.com>
To: <superbabymoms@superdupergroups.com>
Subject: Cheerios

Working on it.
Zoë "Cheerio Mom" Wallis

From: Stef Jones-Tanaka <bilingualbiologist@supermail.com>
To: <superbabymoms@superdupergroups.com>
Subject: Another!!

Super Moms, Teacher Stacie told me *another* kid popped up with super talent today! This is really exciting. I mean, Stacie said they'd never had so many supers at once when it was just the original four families, and now two new supers in one week???

I would say there's something in the water, but as I'm sure you all know, super ability is not a bug and is in fact passed genetically. I'm sure this is completely explicable by some latent recessive gene suddenly appearing. And then, it's perfectly natural to have cluster groups form—a bunch of things happen at once and it appears to be statistically significant, but in fact it's completely random distribution.

Still, what are the odds? No, seriously, what are the odds? I think I may need to go down to Little Darlings preschool and take a look around.

hugs, Stef
Live each day like the earth might turn to jelly tomorrow. Who knows, right?


```
From: Joseph Goldman <j.goldman@supermail.com>
To: <superbabymoms@superdupergroups.com>
Subject: Introducing Ourselves
```

Hi—my son, Isaiah, is a student at Little Darlings Preschool. Just now he explained to me, very seriously, that he has a hitherto unsuspected talent for swimming under water and never needing to come up for air. In the face of my skepticism, he demonstrated in the bathtub. This seems harmless enough (albeit pruney.) I am told that those of you on this email group face this sort of thing every day. Any thoughts?

Sincerely, Joseph


```
From: lindsey morgan <linzbear@supermail.com>
To: <superbabymoms@superdupergroups.com>
Subject: Can You explain this please
```

Hi This is lindsey mom of trooper in fours class do you know what is going on with this super powers thing? I thought this was just on tv but teacher stacie says to contact you for help. i should mention that trooper came home flying today this is very distrubing. can you tell me how to get rid of this? trooper is on the ceiling fan again i have to go

lindsey

From: Felicia Kwiatkowski <FeliciaK@supermail.com>
To: <superbabymoms@superdupergroups.com>
Subject: TRUCK TRUCK TRUCK

You guys! I am FREAKED OUT! My daughter just turned herself into a TRUCK! An HONEST TO GOD HUMVEE. I mean, a little tiny one—conservation of mass and all that but WTFHOLYBBQ. We have no problem with having a tiny super in the family but I guess Karolina and I always thought if our kid developed a talent it would be something we'd heard of like invisibility or flying. WTF TRUCK.

Felicia

From: Stef Jones-Tanaka <bilingualbiologist@supermail.com>
To: <superbabymoms@superdupergroups.com>
Subject: COME TO THE PRESCHOOL NOW

Um, I think anyone who's not at work better get down here ASAP. Every single kid at this preschool is now a super. One kid is cloning himself. One kid is turning into a monkey. One kid is turning into a giant grilled cheese. I... don't even know. Rocket has tied up Teacher Stacie with his legs, Zoë, and is using his hands to lift the other preschool helpers up onto the roof. Another girl is making walls of water around the roof and Denzel is freezing them. Isabel is running around screaming ISABEL SMASH. The road is torn up.

HELP.

Live each day like the planet might turn into an orange and be eaten by Captain Giant-Man tomorrow. Who knows, right?

From: Zoë Wallis <zoeboe@supermail.com>
To: <superbabymoms@superdupergroups.com>
Re: COME TO THE PRESCHOOL NOW

Stef, I'm here but I can't see you through the cloud of squid ink. Can you whistle? My only talent is speed reading, and that's not doing me much. Also if you see a stretched-out limb that would be my son.

OMG those are SO not helping hands.

Tiffy, I hate to say it, but I think we need your calming powers. Where are you?

Zoë "Knows When to Call for Reinforcements" Wallis

From: Alicia Marquez <CEOmarquez@supermail.com>
To: <superbabymoms@superdupergroups.com>
Subject: New Supers

I am terribly sorry, but I am in the middle of a board meeting. I have asked my secretary to drive over on my behalf. She is a black belt and is also bringing Starbucks. I have texted Alexandra-Maria to remind her that now would be a good time to form alliances with the other girl children, such as Isabel and Beatrix, in order to bring Rocket and Denzel and so on to justice.

With the perspective that comes with distance, I am wondering: does it not seem peculiar that all these new supers started appearing just after Amherst started working there? And that some of their new powers may correspond to Amherst's highly fertile imagination? I would explore the possibility that Amherst is a super after all: I believe her talent is that of creating supers.

Stef, as a biologist, is such a thing possible?

Best, Alícia
alt.email: ceo@marquez.com

```
From: Stef Jones-Tanaka <bilingualbiologist@supermail.com>
To: <superbabymoms@superdupergroups.com>
Re: New Supers
```

Not only possible, but highly likely. Beatrix has looked through the walls to the classroom and says that Amherst is huddled under the craft project table, screaming "Turn it off! Turn it off!" I'm currently watching Isabel smash our way in so I can try to talk Amherst down. It's possible she might be able to get through to the children.

Tiffy, we need you now!! Are you out of coverage or something? Do you have a bat signal? Look, if we get through today, we really need to all have bat signals, okay? It's not helicopter parenting, just good common sense.

Live each day like a pack of cards might come to life and wipe us out in a game of War tomorrow. Who knows, right?

```
From: Zoë Wallis <zoeboe@supermail.com>
To: <superbabymoms@superdupergroups.com>
Re: COME TO THE PRESCHOOL NOW
```

Rocket found me! Grabbed me & retracted me onto the roof. Am up here w/bunch of frightened and/or tantruming mini-supers and pissed-off Teacher Stacie. (Not sure we'll be allowed to continue being Little Darlings, frankly.) Can calm down Rocket, but not all these others.

Oh thk goodness. Woman in spandex w/baby Bjorn must be Tiffy. Gonna have Rocket bring her up .....

Zoë "Texting Champeen of the World" Wallis

```
From: lindsey morgan <linzbear@supermail.com>
To: <superbabymoms@superdupergroups.com>
Subject: Can You explain this please
```

Hi i heard sirens and then logged on and found this. drove right over and i see You people have a lot of nerve can you explain what sort of devil magic you have sucked my child into. trooper is a Good kid and now she is flying around and around the school like a tetherball. oh wait everything suddenly got really calm and i feel really good about everything. this will all be all right won't it.

lindsey

```
From: Alícia Marquez <CEOmarquez@supermail.com>
To: <superbabymoms@superdupergroups.com>
Re: New Supers
```

I'm out of the board meeting. What's the status? Did Tiffy make it?

Best, Alícia
alt.email: ceo@marquez.com

```
From: Zoë Wallis <zoeboe@supermail.com>
To: <superbabymoms@superdupergroups.com>
Subject: Update Everything OK
```

Don't worry, Alícia, it's all under control. Tiffy calmed everybody—I mean EVERYBODY and we all feel really good now. Rocket lowered everyone down from the roof and I think he really had a breakthrough. He said "Oh, THESE are my helping hands" as he put everyone gently on the sidewalk. Tiffy is in there with Amherst who is in the hiccupping stage of crying. So is Tiffy.

Zoë "Rooftop" Wallis

From: Tiffy Turner <spandexmom@supermail.com>
To: <superbabymoms@superdupergroups.com>
Subject: Thank you

Moms, thanks for all your help yesterday. I admit when Stef started this group I didn't understand the point. I thought I had it all figured out. But now...

When I got to Little Darlings yesterday I saw Zoë up on the rooftop helping control a bunch of frightened and inexperienced super kids. (My Williamsburg said he was about to summon a flash flood to help get them off the roof, until Zoë talked him out of it.) I calmed down the toddlers and then made a beeline for my poor Amherst. I found her sniffling with Stef, who was explaining to her very rationally about genetics and superpowers and how none of this meant she was a *bad* person—she just needs to learn how to *control* it. It seemed to be sinking in. (She might even unfoil her room.) Alícia's secretary had lattes for everyone while we cleaned up the mess. Even our newest members, Deiondre and Felicia and Joseph, were helping, and they'd never encountered super tantrums before. It really does take a village.

And as for me... I never realized that my own talent's appearance was due to my daughter. Tom and I must both have a recessive somewhere way back to produce Amherst, and baby Amherst *needed* me to calm her. Odds are, my three younger kids probably owe their talents to Amherst, too. Amherst and I are going to go away for a special girls' weekend and then... I think I'm going to go back to being Anti-Riot Grrrl again. While we were huddled under the table, Amherst told me a story about a mother minivan who could be anything she wanted to be. I think it might be time to do that.

xo Tiffy
"I want Amherst to tell me the one about the glittery fire truck again" - Hazel, 4

```
From: Stef Jones-Tanaka <bilingualbiologist@supermail.com>
To: <superbabymoms@superdupergroups.com>
Subject: New Members
```

Hi, So Very Many Super Moms and Dads! I've sent out invites to all the parents at Little Darlings, so we're about to get an influx of, oh, forty new members or so. Maybe eighty if both parents join in. Don't be shy, new parents! We're all in this together. Teacher Stacie says she can't kick us all out, but that we'd better band together and be on the ball. I think with your help we can do that.

> hugs, Stef
> *Live each day like your children might destroy the preschool tomorrow. Who knows, right?*

Tina Connolly

Tina Connolly lives with her family in Portland, Oregon. Her first fantasy novel, *Ironskin*, was nominated for the 2012 Nebula, and the sequels *Copperhead* and *Silverblind* are now out from Tor. Her stories have appeared in *Lightspeed*, *Tor.com*, *Strange Horizons*, and *Beneath Ceaseless Skies*. She narrates for *Podcastle* and *Beneath Ceaseless Skies*, runs the Parsec-winning flash fiction podcast *Toasted Cake*, and her website is tinaconnolly.com.

THE CHOOCHOOMORPHOSIS

Oliver Buckram

As Gregor Samsa awoke one morning from uneasy dreams he found himself transformed into Neville, the Crime-Fighting Locomotive. Neville was a funny little blue engine with six small wheels and a stumpy smokestack. He lived in the Big Station with the other steam engines of the Happyville Railroad, and spent his days cheerfully bustling up and down the railroad tracks, solving crimes and getting into mischief

"I wonder what mischief I shall get into today," thought Neville curiously. Just then his two anthropomorphic animal friends, Ringo the Dingo and Felicia the Sexually Suggestive Ferret, came bounding into the Big Station.

"G'day, mate," exclaimed Ringo in a broad Australian accent, smiling broadly and displaying his Vegemite-stained teeth. "I wonder what sort of mischief you'll get into today, you silly little bugger."

"You're always welcome to get into my mischief, Neville," giggled Felicia suggestively.

Neville, being a cheerful blue engine, lacked the necessary anatomy to get into Felicia's mischief, an obvious fact that nevertheless eluded the participants of this particular discussion.

"I shan't get into anyone's mischief," declared Neville. "Today I feel like fighting crime."

Fortunately, the preponderance of criminal activity in Happyville occurred in the immediate vicinity of the railroad tracks, allowing Neville to examine clues and on occasion merrily smash into the perpetrators at high velocity.

"Oi," ejaculated Ringo. "In that case, I know just the thing. There's a horde of zombies shambling straight towards Happyville! Perhaps I should have mentioned this earlier! They're coming right down the tracks!"

"Choo choo!" whistled Neville. That was his funny little way of telling his friends to climb aboard and assist him in killing the horde of zombies that was shambling straight towards Happyville.

Neville went chugging down the tracks at top speed while Felicia suggestively straddled his stumpy smokestack and Ringo shoveled coal as fast as a wild dog that is found mainly in Australia could shovel coal.

"I think I can kill zombies, I think I can kill zombies," chortled Neville as he bloodthirstily anticipated plowing through the rotting flesh of the undead with devastatingly gruesome effect. You see, he was keen to prevent the horrid zombies from reaching Happyville and tearing the good little boys and girls limb from limb and eating their brains.

But as Neville cheerfully went puff puff toot toot down the tracks, what he failed to realize was that his funny little friend Ringo had made a funny little mistake. The grotesque, shuffling figures congregating on the tracks were in fact not zombies, but rather extras from a zombie movie that was being filmed nearby.

Yes, in a tragic yet wacky case of mistaken identity, Neville was about to cause the most horrifically awful train accident in the Happyville Railroad's long, blood-drenched history of horrifically awful train accidents. The only silver lining in this whole frightful situation was that the extras were already in full zombie make-up so that killing them would not greatly change their appearance.

Fortunately, seconds before this dreadful tragedy transpired, Gregor Samsa awoke in his bed and realized it was all a dream. He further realized that during the night he'd transformed into a gigantic insect. And he lived happily ever after in the Prague Institute of Entomology.

Oliver Buckram

Oliver Buckram, Ph.D., lives under an assumed name in the Boston area. While he has many publications in academic journals, his unambiguously fictional work has appeared in *Beneath Ceaseless Skies, F&SF, Interzone,* and other places. He urges you to keep watching the skies. Find out more at oliverbuckram.com.

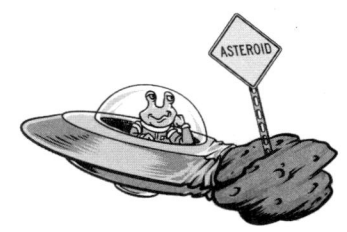

THE FATE WORSE THAN DEATH

Kevin J. Anderson and Guy Anthony De Marco

Lying in the dark in a perfectly restful daytime nap, feeling sated with fresh warm blood (Type O Negative, his favorite), Vlad sensed the intruding presence even before the silent alarm triggered his vibrating watch. The watch buzzed against the mahogany wall of his cozy coffin, warning him.

Always interruptions! Someone was trying to break into his fortress, probably up to no good. "Rest in peace" was harder to achieve than he had ever imagined.

Vlad was a light sleeper, had been for centuries, and even modern sleeping aids like Ambien or Lunesta didn't help. But even with his powers, it was good to remain alert. Careless vampires didn't stay immortal for very long.

He hit the snooze button on the annoying vibrating watch and sighed, not willing to crawl out of the snug coffin just yet. After all, why did he have all those defenses? The intruder should be taken care of without him needing to lift a sharp fingernail.

Vlad couldn't remember the last time someone had bothered to track him down with evil intent, so he doubted this would be a vampire hunter. It was broad daylight, but his mansion was quiet, apparently unoccupied; it was probably a common burglar trying to score some quality electronics. People didn't realize most burglaries happened during the day. And burglars didn't realize how much trouble they would be getting into if they tried to steal from Vladimir Dracul! Especially if they woke him up during daylight hours.

Eight hundred and eighty-two years of existing among those who feared his presence had jaded him. The burglar would be inept, with no idea of the disaster he was about to face. Vlad sighed again and stretched as far as the confines of the coffin would allow. *Too bad,* he thought, *I actually feel depressed that there's nobody left with the guile and fortitude to challenge me.*

He wriggled to a more comfortable position and began to doze. The electric blanket kept him toasty, even though his blood remained cold. The blanket reminded him of his childhood, and he stifled an urge to suck his thumb, remembering the embarrassing previous time, when he'd painfully impaled his thumb on a sharp tooth.

Just as he was drifting off, the alarm watch buzzed again—more urgently this time, to inform him that the intruder had eluded the expensive paramilitary guards and breached the second perimeter of his fortress. Vlad woke further. That was interesting, but the paramilitary guards were flash and dazzle, rather than substance. The intruder was in for an even bigger surprise.

He smiled as he imagined the look of fear and despair that would spread over the hapless thief as he came face to face with one of Vlad's *true* guardians. Still feeling sleepy, he settled deeper into his comfortable memory-foam. He listened carefully, sure he would hear the sounds of rending and feeding any moment, accompanied by a few delightful screams.

The thought of so much blood and raw meat made him contemplate breakfast after sunset. He didn't always drink blood; that was just a special treat, and—with his vampire metabolism—could actually be fattening. Pork chops, he decided ... yes, he would have pork chops. Maybe with some apple sauce and a nice baked potato. He felt blessed that he never needed to worry about high cholesterol. *Blessed!* The thought made him chuckle, which sounded especially loud inside the coffin.

Minutes went by, and he heard no sounds of a struggle, no shouts or growls, no wails of despair. Vlad frowned severely enough that the tips of his fangs protruded from his lips. How had the intruder gotten past his hellhounds? The creatures of the night that prowled his middle sanctum were hungry, fast, and angry at being locked indoors. The three monstrous beasts were the second, third, and fifth most dangerous beings within a mile in any direction (the fourth being the bloodthirsty and sadistic mafioso who lived three estates to the north). Humming the Jeopardy theme song, he cocked his ear to catch any hint of noise from outside his coffin.

Then the lid began to creak open, slowly, tentatively. Startled, Vlad jumped and whacked his head—fine mahogany was definitely a hard wood. Calming himself, he lay back and settled, trying to appear dead and harmless, while he kept his eyes open a slit. The groaning hinges of the lid droned on with painful slowness, and Vlad had to stifle an urge to shout, "Get on with it!" or push the cover open himself.

"Good afternoon, sir," said a lone figure looming over the coffin. "Sorry to interrupt your nap, but we have important business, you and I."

Giving up his slumbering ruse, the vampire sat up to look at his guest while rubbing the small knot growing on his forehead from where he had hit the coffin lid. The intruder was a thick-bodied nerd type with round glasses and a faded Jethro Tull T-shirt. He held a black Evangelion anime backpack in his left hand and wore a black leather belt full of pouches emblazoned with yellow Batman logos.

So, Vlad thought, not a typical burglar—or vampire hunter.

"Good afternoon to you," said the vampire in a thick Transylvanian accent. He had lost his accent over the centuries, but sometimes it seemed appropriate. "Why, may I inquire, are you in my bedchambers at this ungodly hour?"

Usually, when an intruder broke into his fortress, subdued his defenses, and pulled open his coffin, the routine involved sharp sticks and mallets.

The pudgy young man shifted nervously, swung his backpack to one side, and backed away to let the vampire to swing his legs out of the coffin. Vlad knew he was intimidating as he stood up to his full six-foot-eight height. He slapped dust from his black tuxedo jacket while observing the intruder.

From behind his round glasses, the man's eyes went wide. "Gosh, you're bigger than I thought you would be." He blinked a few times and then remembered the rest of his manners. "My name is Marvin. Marvin Drake. I'm a computer forensics and security expert. Glad to finally meet you, sir. It was quite difficult to track you down."

Vlad gave a slight bow to his guest. "Then you must know full well who I am. I will, of course, have to deal with you in the usual manner, but your methods intrigue me. I need some answers." He extended a hand, curled the fingers. "I can glamor you into revealing—"

"Oh, that won't be necessary, sir. I came here to talk." Marvin pulled out a gallon baggie filled with a mushed-up

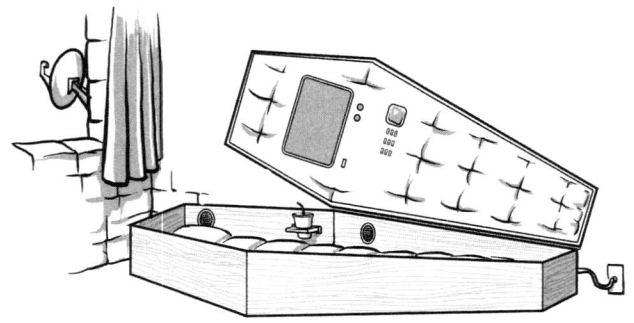

yellowish goop. He opened the top to release a pungent smell. "And I did not come unarmed."

Laughing, Vladimir dipped his index finger into the mixture, swirled it around, and pulled out a taste of the garlic and onion. He popped it into his mouth. "Mmm, tasty, although it does need some cilantro and a dash of salt. Did you bring any chips?"

Normally, when he demonstrated that he was impervious to the usual defenses against vampires, his adversaries would react with intense fear, but Marvin Drake smiled with delight, showing off crooked, unbrushed teeth. It reminded Vlad of Renfield. Ah, Renfield... The poor man spent years in rehab trying to kick his habit of eating flies.

"Good, sir. Just checking. How about this?" He yanked out a gold cross from his utility belt and pressed it close to Vlad's face.

Moving faster than humanly possible, since he was no longer human, he snatched the cross out of Marvin's hand and inspected it with a practiced eye, turning it over in his hand. "Gold-plated. I really have to start spreading rumors that only solid gold or silver crucifixes work. At least they're worth something." He tossed the cross back, and Marvin juggled to catch it.

The young man's spreading grin made the vampire pause. There was something wrong with the situation, or with this oddball young man, but Vlad couldn't put a cold finger on what it was. He glanced around at all of the meticulous cobwebs strung along the walls and ceiling—just props, but much easier to maintain than real cobwebs; the ornate candelabras, the suit of armor, the medieval weapons on the wall, all to make his current dank castle feel just like home.

The intruder cast a glance to the heavy black-velvet curtains that hung over the black-painted windows. "Should I even bother opening the curtains to let in the sunlight? I don't suppose that would make you catch fire and explode?"

"No, but the bright light might give me a headache at this hour, and you've been annoying enough already. What is it you want?"

Marvin seemed satisfied to have the preliminaries dispensed with. "May we sit, sir? I really need to have a talk with you." He indicated a small café-style table a few feet away, where Vlad had his coffee after waking up.

The vampire apprehensively took a seat opposite the strange visitor, who was not at all the typical vampire killer. "You're not going to lunge at me with a wooden stake, are you?"

"Would that kill you?"

"No, but it would ruin my favorite ruffled silk shirt, and then I'd have to get truly medieval on you."

"Thanks for the warning, sir. I don't think we have to bother. I have a business proposition for you." Marvin looked puppy-dog hopeful.

"I need answers first." Vlad leaned over. "I want to know how you found me, and how you got in here. Obviously, I have flaws in my security."

Marvin leaned back in his filigree metal chair, adjusted his Jethro Tull shirt. "As I said, I'm a computer forensics and security specialist. I've been tracking you for years. With all of your quirks, Mr. Dracul, you leave a fairly large data footprint for anyone who knows where to look. Pretty easy, if you know how to do forensic research." He rummaged in the backpack and removed his smartphone.

"For instance, your method of obtaining real estate through a particular set of shell corporations let me keep up with your movements. You typically stay at one location for three to six years before moving on. You tend to stay in Victorian or castle-type estates, which limits your pool of available homes. You prefer colder climates, probably because it resembles the Carpathian mountains."

"That, and I don't want to get moldy," Vlad said, but he was impressed with what the intruder said. His summation was quite accurate. The centuries had made him complacent, and he forgot that technological advances allowed people to process huge amounts of data in near-real time. "Very clever, Marvin. That explains how you located me. But what about my paramilitary guards? My mercenaries?"

"I was able to track down their personal cell phone numbers and sent them all a YouTube video of a kitten playing with a crocodile. They were so entranced, I walked right past them." He smiled. "You really should watch the clip. It's very funny."

"Seen it already." Vlad frowned. "But my true supernatural guardians are relentless in their pursuit of intruders. How did you get past the hellhounds?"

"Easier than expected," said Marvin. "They're just giant dogs with a bigger appetite. I tossed them each some pork chops laced with LSD and a large ball of peanut butter." He grinned. "Right now their mouths are stuck shut, and they're watching pink Hello Kitty's ride purple unicorns."

"Where did you get the pork chops?"

"From your freezer, sir. They looked fresh."

So much for his planned breakfast.

"And how did you know beforehand that all of the traditional vampire-repelling techniques wouldn't work?"

Eager, Marvin pressed his chest against the metal tabletop, and Vlad could physically feel the pounding of his guest's youthful Mountain Dew-fueled heart. "I did my homework, sir. Two years ago when I was bored, I did an analysis of all of the classic books in the public domain. Starting with Bram Stoker, I found that many of the great writers of the last century had some subtle literary commonalities that were statistically improbable. I created a surgically precise literary model that uses a simulated aggregate English professor modeled after personality profiles from more than a thousand arrogant college literary department heads. According to my deep analysis, all of those literary works over the centuries appeared to be written by the same person. I assumed that you were the person who wrote Dracula to feed people the wrong methods to defeat you. But you were writing long before that. You created all those books, didn't you?"

Vlad was embarrassed. "I'm impressed that you could figure it out. The creative writing bug bit me a lot harder than the ancient vampire who turned me. I've been ... dabbling for a while, yes. But I gave up on critique groups back in the eighteenth century."

Maybe this young man would take a look at his poems. No, those were too personal... .

Marvin enthusiastically bounced on his chair, his greasy brown hair flapping up and down. "Imagine my surprise when I discovered that my favorite classic stories and novels were actually ghost-written by an immortal vampire under numerous pen names! Now I know how you can afford all those castles and mansions with all those royalties!"

"All my big sellers are in the public domain," Vlad pointed out.

But Marvin was too excited to hear. "All the top writers in the history of literature were really one ... ummm, person. Speculative fiction, romance, erotica, historicals, *New York Times* bestsellers, award winners, and all of them are on my bookshelves."

Vlad felt uncomfortable and exposed. It was hard enough to keep his secret as a vampire, but maintaining a host of pen names was even more of a challenge. He would probably have to kill this intrepid man anyway.

"What's to keep me from reaching across this table and draining you dry?" He felt his senses go alert, his claws itching to tear flesh and spill blood, his fangs ready to plunge into a pudgy throat ... forget the pork chops.

"Nice gambit, but I was the school chess champion from 2006 to 2009. I took precautions. You don't dare harm me."

"And I was the national chess champion in 1782. I played against George Washington, a fellow vampire. He lost a bet and forfeited his fangs, which is why he used wooden teeth." Vlad sneered. "Let me guess, you told a friend where you were going, and they'll call the authorities if you go missing."

Marvin squirmed in his chair, glancing at a large black spider that sat on the table, unmoving. "No, I did something more ... drastic. I have an automated post that will go out on

Facebook, Twitter, Pinterest, Tumblr, Reddit, Google+, and every other social media website—including the undead ones like MySpace. The post gives explicit directions on how to find you and where you are now." He nudged the smartphone on the table in front of him. Pointing to a toothy icon on his screen, he said, "Heck, there's even an app for that."

Vlad waved his hand in dismissal, though he was uneasy. "That would only bring a convenient meal for me. I should thank you for arranging breakfast in bed, or casket, as the case may be."

It was Marvin's turn to lean across the small table. "Oh, it's far, far worse than that, sir." He looked into the vampire's red-rimmed eyes and whispered, "Unless you do as I demand, the post will tell everyone that you *sparkle when you sleep!*"

If it was possible for Vlad to look paler than his normal self, he hit a new level of waxy pallor. "You wouldn't dare!"

Marvin flipped the spider over on the table. It had a stamp that said *made in China*. The spider web was nothing but fake Halloween-store cotton strands. Looking around, Marvin indicated all of the faux spooky objects in the coffin chamber. "For you, it's all about appearances, Mr. Dracul. I know that about you, and that's why the sparkly vampire defense is my endgame."

Vladimir sat stiffly in his chair, breathing heavily at the thought of being chased by every pre-pubescent young lady and their mothers, no matter where he hid. "What ... what do you want from me? You wish me to turn you into an immortal vampire?"

"No, nothing like that." Marvin bent over, reached into his backpack, and produced an enormous stack of dog-eared papers. "Your words inspired me to become a writer. I want you to be my literary mentor." He slid the manuscript across the table. It was titled *The Ears of Argon*, Volume 1 of the "Body Parts of Argon Saga."

Vlad was appalled. "Read amateur manuscripts? I'd rather die—and I have done that already."

"More than that, sir. Let me co-write a short story with you for my favorite humorous speculative fiction anthology series." Marvin's voice had an edge. "Either you can help me make my *prose* sparkle, or ..."

The vampire shuddered uncontrollably. "You're insane!" He saw with dismay that the manuscript was marked as Part One of Volume 1. The title was in all-caps, Old English letters. Marvin's backpack had even larger stacks of paper inside.

Marvin leaned back, looking at him eagerly. "Go on, start reading. I'll sit here quietly, I promise. I just want to watch your reactions."

Vlad picked up the first page, dreading that even an immortal lifespan would not be long enough ... but he would do anything—*anything*—to stop that message from going out.

Kevin J. Anderson

Kevin J. Anderson has published 125 books, more than fifty of which have been national or international bestsellers. He has written numerous novels in the Star Wars, X-Files, and Dune universes, as well as a unique steampunk fantasy novel, *Clockwork Angels*, based on the concept album by legendary rock group Rush. His original works include the *Saga of Seven Suns* series, the *Terra Incognita* fantasy trilogy, the *Saga of Shadows* trilogy, and his humorous horror series featuring Dan Shamble, Zombie PI. He has edited numerous anthologies, including the *Five by Five* and *Blood Lite* series. Anderson and his wife Rebecca Moesta are the publishers of WordFire Press. (Wordfireoress.com).

Guy Anthony De Marco

Guy Anthony De Marco is a speculative fiction author; a Graphic Novel Bram Stoker Award finalist; winner of the HWA Silver Hammer Award; a prolific short story and flash fiction crafter; a novelist; an invisible man with superhero powers; a game writer (Sojourner Tales modules, Interface Zero 2.0 core team, D&D modules); and a coffee addict. One of these is false.

A writer since 1977, Guy is a member of the following organizations: SFWA, WWA, SFPA, IAMTW, ASCAP, RMFW, NCW, HWA. He hopes to collect the rest of the letters of the alphabet one day. Additional information can be found at Wikipedia, GuyAndTonya.com, and GuyAnthonyDeMarco.com.

ELECTIONS AT VILLA ENCANTADA

Cat Rambo

A few weeks beforehand, the notices began to appear throughout the complex. Shy and scarce as early daffodils at first, then later in desperate profusion, splashes of colored flyers proclaiming one candidate or another for the Home Owners Association board.

A few unscrupulous candidates tried bullying cantrips or mental snares, but those were discovered and invoked a fresh crop of warnings, legal threats, and expansions on points previously made.

Like everyone else, I threw things away as fast as they arrived. The recycling bin grew so full of animating spells that it groaned menacingly whenever you stepped near it.

Then the flyers took on a more ominous tone: a special assessment was looming. Improvements and repairs—costly ones—that would have to be paid for, in one way or another.

All three parts of the tripartite goddess living in one of the three bedrooms next to the lake had tried to get me to run for the HOA board. Once you've been a goddess of justice, people think you're going to want to keep on arbitrating things. Yes, injustice still makes me itch, or gives me an eruption of boils if it's particularly bad.

But I'm retired now.

They had, for some reason, decided I was their friend. Some vague notion that goddesses should stick together, perhaps. But split souls have always disconcerted me. Listening to the three of them continuing or finishing each other's sentences just got irritating. It was difficult to talk with a mind that was in three places at once.

"That goddamn mayfly's driving me nuts," the Mother complained to me. She stopped by more often than the Crone or Maiden in order to confide in me about a number of things, including how difficult it really was being a tripartite personality (*The others are always ganging up on me*), the cacti, whose garden was outside her bedroom window (*They talk all night!*), and the situation with the lake god (*I bought a boat so I could get some solitude and every time I get in it, all the water ebbs away and I'm sitting high and dry!*). "I turn around and she's got five more items to consider on that god damn clipboard. I know she's trying to live a life in the course of the year, but it's tiring for the rest of us. She's running for the one of the empty seats, of course. Give her authority and she'll be ten times worse."

The mayfly hadn't endeared herself to anyone so far. Since she rarely slept, she could be found at all times of the day and night, walking the grounds and observing infractions, such as trash on balconies, a loose gutter on another building, and any number of parking violations.

She was everywhere, involved in everything. She organized initiatives and potlucks. You had to admit she was effective, though. And she didn't mind rolling up her sleeves and pitching in as needed. She'd rebuilt the water feature at the front, despite the grumbling of the oracular carp that had lived in it for years, hiding under the overgrown water lilies filling the concrete basin.

The Mother took a Clementine from the fruit bowl on the table. She said, "Martha's running again."

"I thought you said some scandal they just discovered made her ineligible."

She stripped pith from the nubby flesh. "You remember how when she pissed off the lake god, everyone wondered why he didn't just smite her?"

"Yeah." I poured us both more coffee. I wanted her to stay around long enough to get to talking about the special assessment.

"She used a chunk of the maintenance budget to buy an amulet of protection, then charged it to psychic maintenance for the complex. Twenty-five K."

I whistled.

"And now she's got some RV near the boatyard that technically isn't an illegal place for her to park it, but should be."

"What's the word on the special assessment?"

She only waved a hand. "We'll have three plans for people to vote on."

"Will we get a chance to see them ahead of time?"

She gave me a scornful look. "Really? Can you imagine the convulsions then?"

"It'll all happen at the meeting," I pointed out.

She shrugged. "Get it all over with it once rather than drag it out over a couple of weeks."

She did have a point.

WHEN I ANSWERED the door, Glory the mayfly stood there.

You make allowances for mayflies, because their lives are so much shorter than ours. At least I do, in my ongoing attempts to be fair. This one, like the rest of her kind, would only last a year. Right now, in the full heat of summer, she had four or five months to live before the gray skies of October or

November led her to birth the next generation and die.

She said, shoulders angled forward at me, "Do you have a minute?"

"No."

She wasn't prepared for that bluntness. She blinked at me, then rallied. "Just a moment, that's all I need."

"No," I said again and closed the door.

I returned to my desk. I reactivated the paused program.

It had been going for thirty seconds before a knock came on the door again. I re-paused.

"Don't you care about what happens here?" she demanded as soon as I opened the door.

"I'm not convinced that whatever you're about to tell me is going to have any effect."

"The current board has been mishandling things! We need a new, effective board! Have you heard about the special assessment?"

"I hear different things from different people."

"Four million dollars! For a ..." She paused to cast an appraising eye over my entryway. "Two bedroom like yours, that'd come to nearly thirty-eight thousand dollars."

My shocked inhalation gratified her. She put her hands on her hips. "That's why I'm coming around. If you're not planning on going to the meeting, I can vote your proxy for you."

"It's not in my nature to let other people handle my vote."

She looked me up and down, unimpressed. "What *is* in your nature?"

"To come to the meeting and see for myself."

I closed the door in her face.

Before the evening of the meeting finally rolled around, though, I had been approached multiple times for my proxy by people volunteering to cast my vote for me if I couldn't make it that Wednesday. All of them seemed to have a different figure for the special assessment. However, no one seemed to think it didn't exist. That was what concerned me.

The culture that had sustained me was long gone and I was living on the small investments I had made over the centuries. I wasn't badly off, particularly compared with many other aging mythological creatures, but I couldn't afford too much of a hit on my capital.

I consulted my banker to figure out if I could weather a special assessment of the size that had been predicted. I crunched through the numbers, even after he'd told me the results, wanting to see for myself. No matter how I added them up the fact was clear: I couldn't afford it.

I wasn't the only person in that boat. Tempers were high and dry as a result.

Even the cactus garden was talking about the special assessment.

I usually don't visit the tiny, pebble-strewn garden near the lake. For one thing the cacti like to talk all at once. They ramble and they repeat and they are overly fond of puns.

One said, "It's a cabal! They've been waiting to seize power for years now, and rob our reserves, turn us over to some real estate agent so the complex can be demolished for a high rise."

"Don't be ridiculous. They're not organized enough to be a cabal. And this place isn't zoned for high-rises," said another, its tone dark, "No, what they have in store for us is much, much worse."

"Did you give your proxy to anyone?" asked the third.

I shook my head and fled.

Rumplestiltskin was by the dumpster, sorting out recyclables. He looked wretched and smudgy as an old sheet of newsprint. As I passed, he looked up, and said, hopefully, "What's my name?"

"Not today," I said, despite the hives I could feel forming along my inner arms and elbows. "You won't escape today."

I felt guilty at the look on his face, and the injustice of the situation did leave its mark. I went inside to run cold water over the strawberry blotches on my skin.

I didn't like it, but I wasn't on the board, and they were the ones in charge. It's been so hard to find a maintenance worker here that I could understand why they had done it.

Sometimes when you find good help, you have to keep them from leaving. Unscrupulous? Yes, undoubtedly. But the needs of the many outweigh those of the few. Or the one, in his case, in the opinion of the board.

EVERY YEAR, THEY held the meeting in the same place. The gymnasium of a small, private school that would have liked to have wiggled out from under the contract that had been in place since the school was built. Psychic decontamination after each meeting, ripe with anger, ill wishing, and hatred, was expensive.

That was why we didn't hold the meetings back at Villa Encantada.

I parked and made my way toward the curved glass doors of the entrance. To one side was an ashtray and two people huddled beside it, smoking. You could see the shape of an invisible umbrella above one, empty space in the air from which raindrops rebounded and slid. It was tilted to drip directly on the other smoker, who seemed oblivious.

I said, pausing beside them, "Has it started already?"

"We should be so lucky," said the first smoker.

I recognized him as one of the candidates, a warlock named Danny. His flyers had harped on the iniquities perpetrated by the workmen in the complex, who had trampled flowers and ferns, cut down most of the trees near the stream bordering the northern side, and were replacing the building skirting much more slowly than they had removed it.

I didn't know the man beside him, who wore a tattered olive raincoat, its edges embroidered in blue and green. Insects clustered on his water-sodden white hair, worn in a thousand braids, each one fastened with a bee or dragonfly. The tip of his cigarette glowed red as he inhaled and smacked his lips. He said, "They're still trying to see if there's a quorum or not. You'll need to sign in."

I pushed through the glass doors. They led to the building's lobby, an open space two or three stories high, walled in red brick, institutional carpeting stretching underfoot.

Rumplestiltskin sidled up to me.

"What's my name?" he whispered hopefully. I pushed past.

A current board member, the dryad who also handles all landscaping for the complex, sat at a table, flanked by a bored teen girl holding a clipboard with one hand and texting with the other. The dryad looked at me as I stepped up.

"Unit one four two?" she snapped.

"Yes."

"Sign here."

The teen set down her phone to shove the clipboard at me along with a black quill pen. I signed. She spun it around in order to read it off. "Astraea Jones?"

"That's right."

The dryad looked me over with pursed lips.

"You've known me for twelve years, Laurel," I said. "Don't act like you don't."

She sniffed. "I understand you're not running for the board."

"That's right."

"What are you spending all your free time on? You can't give us a few hours a week?"

I stared back, projecting flinty unamusement.

She sniffed and glanced away. "The candidates have furnished snacks for the evening. Help yourself."

I went into the auditorium. Several board members were struggling with a projector toward the front of the room while other people called out helpful suggestions from a few seats away.

I found a chair at one of the small tables scattered throughout the room. The seat beside me creaked as someone invisible sat down. A plate holding a single deviled egg appeared in front of them, as though to mark the spot off.

"Good evening, Gertrude," I said.

A cold breeze touched my face in greeting, but the ghost, as usual, chose not to speak.

Rumplestiltskin began to wheel the cacti into the room, setting them up on chairs along the back window. They buzzed among themselves, calling out insults at people going past them, trying to lure them closer. Everyone seemed to be able to resist the taunts, however.

No one bothered much with the cacti. While most of us had a single vote, the cacti, having been created from the splinters of a single soul, each held one 12th of a vote. People had learned long ago that the cacti's votes inevitably offset each other, usually not from differences of opinion but rather a desire to spite each other.

"If people will find their seats, we'll get started," Martha said from the front of the room.

They began, as always, with a Powerpoint presentation showing an abbreviated history of Villa Encantada. Successive slides mentioned Elenora, the Spanish witch who fled a Californian settlement to come north with Dmitri, a Catholic vampire, and founded the complex here on a lake near what would eventually become Seattle. The tiny settlement grew as it accumulated more denizens of the supernatural realm. When Russian fur traders stopped on their way down from Alaska, they left behind twin brothers, shamans, who built many of the buildings that eventually became a condo complex in 1969.

All documented in loving detail accompanied by clip art. I closed my eyes and let myself drowse, figuring I would wait and ask my questions after we had made our way up to the present day.

But while we were still in the 1940s, someone jumped up and shouted, "What about this special assessment?"

Several other people shouted, "yes," and "do tell us," and "what's the truth?"

The board, flustered, clustered together conferring in whispers. Finally Mr. Bland, the current president of the board, said, "That is the secondary point of this meeting, however we prefer to observe all the formalities first." He directed his gaze towards the back of the room. "Do we know yet if we have a quorum?"

This led to more conferring and whispering on the board's side of things, and general restlessness on the part of everyone else. Finally, it was confirmed that indeed 77 percent of those owning, as opposed to renting, property in Villa Encantada were present and the meeting would be binding. There was the usual round of furious whispers when the word "binding" came up, but finally the whisperers were reassured that no hint of demonology was present.

That was when all the arguing began, really.

The cacti went berserk when the Mother raised the incident of Martha offending the local lake god. People were irritated not to be able to use their boat slips and several cats had been lost to things lurking beneath the thick growth of water lilies.

Several people mentioned that if certain board members didn't have people skills, then perhaps they shouldn't be the ones dealing with the public.

The cacti had strong opinions on all of this, since they were down near the water and not particularly eager to see more traffic there.

However, the special assessment overshadowed that by far, making the other issues mere squalls with a vaster storm sneaking up behind them. It turned out, and here the language of the board grew rich with figures of speech intended to shift blame, certain sacrifices had not been performed and certain spiritual maintenance had not been undergone.

What should be focused on, the board unanimously agreed, was the fact that the cost of spiritual cleansing to repair the damage would be very high.

Of the five board seats, three were ensconced and would not be deposed in this particular round, which meant I was curious how the sitting board members stood on the question of special assessments. I asked the dryad, who never became impassioned about anything other than trees being removed. When I raised the question of the special assessment, she simply shrugged.

The second board member who was not being elected, was Mr. Bland. No one knows much about Mr. Bland, who is perfectly unobtrusive to the point where one forgets he exists when not in his presence.

The third was Jerry Deeb, as human as they come, and as always thrilled, bewildered, and somewhat confused by everything that was going on. It was long ago established that Mr. Deeb's vote would simply belong to whoever had spoken with him last, so I didn't bother asking him.

Someone joked nervously that maybe we should just sacrifice a board member to pay for the spiritual cleansing.

In the subsequent flurry of statements justifying the board's existence, several people pointed to Rumplestiltskin (careful not to refer to him by name) as a victory of sorts, given that the complex's brownies had been leaving every three months. Despite the ethics of enslaving a magical creature, an issue everyone was careful to skirt around just as carefully as they avoided saying the name that would free him, it was generally viewed to have improved the complex's overall appearance.

During all of this the cacti attempted to inform us of past history that had mirrored these crises. No one paid attention to them, which simply made the cacti raise their voices.

Finally, somehow, order was restored. The candidates would each get a chance to speak, we'd go over condo association business, and then we would be presented with our special assessment options. With that announcement, the elections began with the presentation of the candidates.

I could see death hovering over Danny the Warlock, ready to tap him on the shoulder in what looked liked perhaps eighteen months down the line, and while I was sworn not to mention such things, I was not sworn to ignore them when making decisions. I scratched him off my list.

The next candidate was Glumpf who, like the smoker outside, I couldn't remember ever meeting before. He identified himself as living in an RV, waiting for an apartment to be cleared for him.

Someone asked, a little suspiciously, "Aren't you a golem?"

Glumpf scratched his head as though the question confused him, then nodded.

The questioner left it at that. No one wanted to be accused of racism.

Martha set my teeth on edge. As far as I could tell, she had the same effect on everyone. However, she was efficient and managed the many-itemed bookkeeping associated with Villa Encantada as well as any board member had in the complex's long memory.

She was a brusque and abrupt woman, disinclined to considering other points of view, and prone to tactlessness. For this last trait, she had been rewarded by being voted off the board twice in the past decade, most recently last month.

Her seat was open again. You could tell by the way she held herself that she planned on being re-elected to re-occupy it.

The mayfly wore a demure little blue wool suit, looking corporate and sharp and laser-eyed as she was introduced.

Candidates made speeches. When it was Glumpf's turn, someone asked, "Were you created?"

He nodded. An uncomfortable silence hung in the room before someone else asked, "Who is your creator?"

When he pointed at Martha the room erupted into protests.

It had been a good attempt on her part, but of course the golem was disqualified immediately.

It was at that point that a motion was made that no one who had been voted off the board twice could run again. This was passed with dazzling speed. In the end everyone except Martha and the stolid Glumpf looked pleased. Beside me, Gertrude murmured something I didn't catch, but refused to repeat it when I leaned over.

Back in the day, when I was worshiped, I thought I understood people. But there's something about a condo home-owners association—perhaps any sort of association with little power and much responsibility—that showcased them at their worst.

When the mayfly brought up reconciliation with the lake god, he turned out to be the second smoker I'd seen when coming in. It emerged that his main objection, other than Martha, was the illicit use of the oracular carp. Since it was a fish, the lake god felt that the carp fell into his domain.

This feeling was not echoed by the carp, a bitter socialist sitting in a bucket near the cacti. He loudly proclaimed that the old ways were dead and this was a democracy now.

The cacti, who had been engaged in a decade-long feud with the carp, vigorously cheered the notion of transferring the carp to the lake. The motion did not pass.

Finally, we came to the assessment.

We were introduced to three possible plans, each with a different price tag.

The first plan, which was the most expensive (mental calculations quickly told me this one was far outside my reach), included a truce with the lake god and expending a costly, domestically-raised bear to take care of the spiritual cleansing, with monthly sacrifices for three years after that consisting of lesser animals, and fireworks on three of the major holidays.

The second plan, created by the mayfly, promised many of the same things for a smaller price tag. People objected to the way the cost was offset, which was to impose weekly days in which everyone would be required to sing all conversation, and thus secure additional funds from a neighboring and much wealthier complex, whose motivations were unclear but they also wanted to hook into our sewer system and use our boat launch. I divided the new figures in my head by twelve and winced at the result. Again out of my pocketbook's grasp.

The third plan lacked a number of items, including the truce with the lake god, which produced a general stir and an approving buzz from the cacti (never a good sign). However, it was affordable.

When they called for general comments, Martha rose to her feet. A cactus cheered. The carp muttered, "Oh, here we go."

She said, her voice pitched to carry without a microphone, "I can save you from all this, if you will agree to put me back on the board. And you didn't really vote me off anyway. I've talked to several people, and they said they didn't want to vote me off. So, how about it? I'll show you here and now how to cleanse the complex and appease the lake god."

Her eyes rolled in the direction of the god, who stood in the back of the room near the cacti although careful not to drip on them, glowering at her.

People murmured. People muttered. Conversation swirled, some angry, some considering. The board conferred as well. Finally the mayfly stood up. Her face was scornful.

"Sure," she said. "Show us what you've got."

Martha beamed with triumph. She looked over at Rumplestiltskin, crouched beside a table. She beckoned.

He dragged his feet as he rose and approached her.

I didn't blame him. Emotion twisted her face, triumph and anger and hatred. I hadn't realized how important being on the board was to her. Was it simply being able to control people? Was it something that she built the core of her being on, a point of pride?

Motivations are complicated.

Results, less so.

"I know your name," she crooned.

His face brightened with hope. Every board member looked panic stricken.

"Your name is ..." Her finger rose, pointing. "Rumplestiltskin!"

He threw his head back and shouted something wordless, full of joy. The room gasped. Even Gertrude's inhalation was audible.

A blade glittered in Martha's other hand.

"The death of a free creature is worth tenfold," she said as she plunged the knife into his chest. Pain echoed in my heart at his anguished cry as she unjustly snatched his life away. "I dedicate this death to Villa Encantada!"

The magic of the sacrifice surged over us.

Martha was right. This was a sacrifice whose costliness would pay for everything we needed. And yet faces were shocked. No one had wanted such a thing. To enslave a creature, perhaps, thinking that it was only for a few years. But to deprive another being of life is a great and painful injustice.

Martha was looking at the lake god. "You are obliged to take this sacrifice."

He nodded slowly, his eyes reluctant. His gaze met mine as I stepped up.

Following his stare, Martha turned to face me. Her expression was confused at first. "He can't harm me."

She fingered the amulet of protection at her throat. It was true. The god could not harm her.

But she had forgotten that I was once a goddess of justice. And when someone tips themselves towards injustice, they become mine.

"We will need a replacement for ..." I hesitated. Old habits die hard. "Rumplestiltskin."

At my touch, she shrank back, at first looking as though she were falling into herself, then dwindling, dwindling further still, until a stooped creature, the size of the body at its feet, hunched there.

THINGS HAVE RETURNED to normal at Villa Encantada. Mostly.

They still want me to serve on the board. Martha does a good job, particularly with Glumpf to help her.

We're all still getting used to not speaking her name.

Cat Rambo

Cat Rambo writes a lot of stories. Her "Five Ways to Fall in Love on Planet Porcelain" was a 2012 Nebula Award finalist. She was the fiction editor of *Fantasy Magazine* as well as *Lightspeed Magazine's* Women Destroying Fantasy issue. You can find links to her online fiction and more information about her at kittywumpus.net.

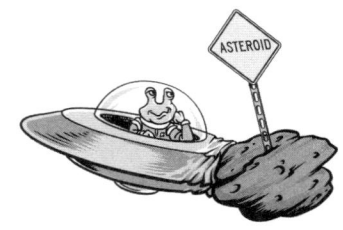

INFINITE DRIVE

Jody Lynn Nye

Detective Sergeant Dena Malone studied the panel in the plush elevator as it bore her and Detective Sergeant Mario Ramos toward the Castana Tower's 300th floor penthouse.

"Tell another joke, Ramos!" A voice came from the platinum circle around Dena's wrist.

Anyone unfamiliar with the design of the bracelet might have assumed it was a phone of some kind, connected with a human being somewhere on Earth or the Moon colony. Those who recognized it as a proprietary device of the Alien Relations Department might automatically assume that the bulge in the petite brunette's abdomen was the pink, meter-long Salosian extraterrestrial symbiote whose voice emerged from the silvery bangle. They would both be wrong.

The Salosian in question, Dr. K't'ank, did occupy a portion of her peritoneum, but he was becoming dwarfed by the increasing size of Dena's pregnancy. On the other hand, he was a lot more of a pain in the butt than her baby. At least the kid wasn't having conversations with people from her midsection.

"Okay," Ramos said, always glad for a fresh audience. "What do you call the twin you have that only runs in the far end of the red shift?"

"I am at a loss," K't'ank confessed, after a moment.

"A dopplerganger."

Ramos always laughed heartily at his own jokes. K't'ank joined in, as well as beating his tail against Dena's internal organs.

"That is funny! I will send that joke to my Salosian friends! They appreciate your wit, Ramos."

"Knock that off!" Dena snapped. "God, you two! I deserve hazard pay for having to listen to these awful jokes." The doors before her let out a melodious BONG! and slid open. "Thank heavens. Come on."

A knot of men and women wearing bathing suits and short, silky robes sat uncomfortably on sun lounges against the wall of the penthouse garden. A young woman with a black pony tail and wearing tight white shorts and a midriff blouse straightened up from serving a drink from a tray to a lantern-jawed man with a sweep of silver hair. He rose as Dena and Ramos approached, his expression bland, then frowned at Dena, his glance traveling downward from her razor-cut hair to her burgeoning abdomen.

"You are ... the police? I don't want to be offensive, but are you capable of handling this case?"

"I don't detect with my belly, sir," Dena said. "Well, not much. Detective Sergeant Malone. This is Detective Ramos." She swept her credentials from her pocket and held them up at eye level for the man to examine. The holographic image showed her at full length, then a portrait, then a profile, and cycled back again. Ramos followed suit. She shifted to ease her back, which ached a little almost all the time these days, between the combined weight of her baby and her often unwelcome guest.

"I'm James Longmore," the silver-haired man said. "This is my wife, Anita, and our friends, Margan and Obed Amini. We're staying in the Castana Tower during the ANCHOR conference."

Dena nodded. ANCHOR was a think-tank populated by

inventors, philosophers, journalists, and influential men and women, which was to say, rich people. The two couples present certainly fit into the last category.

"We heard that a car crashed up here?" Ramos asked, putting his badge away.

Longmore pointed to the polished black stone floor. On it, Dena could just see the dull trace of two wide streaks of black polymer. They ran all the way from the elevator to an area with a rougher texture, then vanished. Beyond it was a wide, glittering swath, so clear that the buildings outside were visible through it.

"Who drives inside a hotel?" Ramos asked.

"A puzzle! Accident followed by vanishment," K't'ank said, gleefully. Longmore and his guests seemed startled, then their eyes went to Dena's wrist. They didn't need further explanation.

"May I inquire as to your name, sir or madam?" Longmore asked, politely.

"Dr. K't'ank of Salos am I," the Salosian replied. "Malone is my residence."

"We are honored to meet you, sir."

Dena gave him mental points for knowing the gender details of Salosian nomenclature. Up until having one implanted in her belly, she hadn't a clue herself.

"I am also pleased," K't'ank said. "To meet further humans is part of my purpose on this world. I would like to ask ..."

"May we get back to the case?" Dena asked, interrupting him smoothly. "Where's the car now?"

"Still in there," Mr. Longmore said, pointing to the smooth expanse of the pool behind him. "The elevator signal sounded, the door opened, and a black four-passenger ground vehicle raced past us and hurtled in with one godalmighty splash. A moment sooner, and he would have hit my wife. She had just climbed out of the water." For evidence, he indicated the wet robe that the plump redhead had wrapped around her.

"He?" Ramos asked. "You could see the driver?"

"See him?" Longmore countered. "We knew him."

Dena raised her memo recorder. "His name? And your relationship with him?"

"Noble Sesman," Longmore said. "He was a ... colleague."

"I know her," K't'ank exclaimed suddenly.

"Him." Dena corrected him automatically. Unlike her, K't'ank had not absorbed any lessons on how to tell female humans from male. In his defense, all Salosians looked alike to her, skinny pink worms with huge dark eyes. He could probably argue the same about her species. "How did you know him?"

"This Sesman was involved in bringing funding to my associates' research," K't'ank said. "A large grant has been offered to us for our research into common elements of cognitive processes."

"So you are familiar with ANCHOR, sir?" Amini inquired, politely. Dena knew how disorienting it could be to speak to someone who was not visible but obviously cognizant of what was going on. K't'ank was far from Big Brother, but he involved himself in Dena's activities—personal or not—and had a loud and irrepressible opinion on all of them. "I thought I recognized your name."

"Indeed, I have familiarity. ANCHOR studies our studies. Though my judgment is that those who control the funding are not necessarily intelligent enough to comprehend why our work is vital ..."

"That's not important right now," Dena said, interrupting him. Longmore's complexion had gone from pale with shock at the recent accident to scarlet with provocation. K't'ank had some good insights into past cases she had worked on since he had been implanted in her abdomen, but he was amazingly high-handed for someone who had no hands. "Mr. Longmore, if you'll just tell us what happened?"

"That's all we know. Ding, swoosh, splash! I am sure you will get more information from the hotel employees and the security department."

It was a clear dismissal. Dena and Ramos exchanged glances.

"We will need details of any interaction you had with Mr. Sesman," Ramos said, brandishing his skinnypad. Both he and Dena had already been recording the conversation for future analysis.

Longmore tilted his head back, the better to look down his patrician nose at them. "Are we being accused of something, officer?"

"Not at all," Dena said, with a sly summing up of her host. "This is for your protection as well as our investigation. If one of your mutual acquaintances wanted to annoy, or worse yet, implicate you in anything, I know you would like to be informed of that connection. It could have been a prank that went disastrously wrong. It may have been something more dire. What if the vehicle was aimed at you, but missed? Since we can't speak to Mr. Sesman at the moment, we need to ask you. Did Sesman dislike you enough to pilot a vehicle at you?"

A palpable hit, to judge by the dimming of Longmore's complexion back to ashen pale.

"I should hope not! He's, I mean, he *was* capable of pranks, but not fatal ones. We'll cooperate in any way we can, Sergeant. I am sorry if I implied anything to the contrary. We of ANCHOR are always eager to assist law enforcement."

Ding!

The elevator doors slid open again. Dena jumped aside, in case any more vehicles came roaring through to take a fatal dip. Instead, the elevator disgorged a trio of individuals. One man, lanky and wiry, in a deliberately nondescript dark brown bodysuit, bore all the earmarks of a head of security. The second was a broad-hipped woman with dark green hair, wearing an elaborate earpiece that complemented her expensive cream-colored suit. Publicity director was Dena's guess. The last was a fussy-looking, pot-bellied man in a smartly-cut suit accessorized with a look of perpetual grievance.

"Officer ... ?"

"Detective Sergeant," Dena corrected him. "Malone. This is Detective Sergeant Ramos. And you are ... ?"

"Morgan Thompason. I am the president of this hotel and general manager. Ms. Coller is my head of public relations. Dr. Dorian Tamm is our chief security officer."

"*Doctor?*" Dena asked. "What's a physician doing running security?"

Tamm held up his hands. "PhD, not MD, Sergeant."

Thompason waved his own hands for attention.

"Why didn't you stop in my office first?"

Dena moaned inwardly. All she needed was a bureaucrat who stood on useless ceremony.

"The sooner we examine an accident scene the better," Ramos said. "Once we can figure out what went wrong, the quicker we'll be out of here."

Thompason looked pained. "We would greatly prefer it if you wouldn't refer to our luxury presidential opulent palace penthouse abode as an 'accident scene'!"

"The write-ups won't mention that, Chief," the woman said, tapping her earpiece twice. "We are trending toward 'incident,' instead."

"Good. See to it, Coller. How could this happen?"

"Mr. Sesman drove his personal vehicle up here," Tamm said. "He had the codes for the private elevator. There was no reason for the garage robots to stop him."

"Well, where is he?"

Everyone else pointed toward the pool.

"That's inappropriate! Get him out of there!" Thompason demanded.

"How?" Longmore inquired. "We can't even see him."

"Is he concealed in some way?" Thompason asked.

"Not concealed," K't'ank interjected. "He has become one with the infinity of this pleasure water."

Thompason didn't seem to register that one of the voices in the room wasn't coming from any of the visible mouths. His entire attention focused on scanning the clear pool.

"Is he behind it? Below it? Between the glass walls?"

"No glass," K't'ank scolded him. "Do not think in such

pedestrian terms, Thompason."

"You've got a nerve referring to pedestrians when I do all your walking for you," Dena said.

K't'ank ignored her jibe.

"Glass does not hold up the water."

"What does?" she asked.

"Nothing. Very highly concentrated nothing. A forcefield generates pressure against the body of water. The calculations used to hold it in place are precise. It is a work of genius," he added, "although not completely equal to my own."

"Which means he's dead," Ramos said.

"Most likely," K't'ank agreed. "Humans do not appear to accept compression well. It is a primary difference between our species."

Thompason shuddered. "Please do not use 'dead' when referring to a guest of this establishment," he said, plaintively, waving his hands as if to delete the word. "The Castana has a reputation as being a destination for luxury *living*."

"We'll make sure no reference to mortality is made in the press," Coller said, tapping her earpiece again.

"Sorry to be crude, Mr. Thompason," Dena said. "I'm just getting details. What about body displacement, K't'ank? Does that mean that anyone else who dives into the pool is in danger of being swallowed up by the wall?"

The four occupants of the suite huddled close together as if afraid that the pool would reach out and suck them in. Dena couldn't blame them. K't'ank assumed a professorial tone.

"Excellent question. A certain balance is factored into forcefields of this type. It would take an enormous difference in pressure one way or the other for a man to vanish."

"But it happened. What is the weight-bearing load of this pool?"

"Seventy tons," the manager said. Dena lifted an eyebrow. She found it suspicious that he had facts like that at his fingertips when the incident had just occurred. He shifted nervously under her gaze. "I oversaw the purchase and installation. More than sixty people can swim in it at one time. I mean, if there was room."

"Then one single vehicle should not have disappeared into the workings," Dena said. "What could it have weighed? Five hundred kilos?"

"A thousand," Longmore said indigantly, with an upward tilt of his patrician nose. "Mr. Sesman had a luxury vehicle. Of course. A Circo XIII."

"Of course," Dena echoed, making a note.

"Still should not have caused this collapse of field integrity," K't'ank said. "If it is made to permit sixty in a space that would comfortably contain only twenty of your kind without crowding, then a person even inside a vehicle would not be in danger."

"Fudge factor," said the security man.

Dena could sense the pause while K't'ank looked up 'fudge.'

"It would have to be a very large container of confectionary."

Ramos snickered. Dena sensed another joke under construction.

"So if it isn't there," she asked, "where did it transport to?"

K't'ank's tail beat impatiently against the inside of her ribs.

"Transport? Not transport, Malone. It is still there."

"Where? I can't see it."

"It is there, incorporated into the wall of force," K't'ank said.

Dena felt her insides roil, and not because either the alien or her baby were kicking them.

"I don't suppose there's any hope that the man is still alive, is there?" she asked.

"None. The compression would have been instantaneous and comprehensive."

Dena felt her insides give one instantaneous and comprehensive heave.

"Eww."

"This is outrageous, Thompason!" Longmore raged."We

and ANCHOR pay you ridiculously well for this luxury suite. We don't want to have to use a swimming pool with a dead body in it! Have it removed at once!"

"I'm sorry, sir, but we can't do that," Dena said, cutting off the manager's apologies. "As we said, it's an active investigation scene."

"Absurd! All you have to do is turn off the field generator."

"Then all our evidence will drop, along with several thousand gallons of water, onto the heads of the people on the street."

"What about it?" Amini said, lifting his own eyebrows high on his broad forehead. "ANCHOR's purpose is to improve life for the billions of human beings on Earth and other worlds. The inconvenience of a few for our sake is not our concern."

"Talk about your ivory towers," Ramos groaned.

"What was that?" Longmore demanded, rounding on him.

"We'll be working on this every hour," Ramos said, brightly, brandishing his skinnypad. "I'll just take quick statements from you and leave you to your day."

Dena took the arm of the hotel manager. "In the meantime, Mr. Thompason, I need to talk to you and anyone who had access to the inner workings of the infinity pool, plus, I would like to get a look at the manifests for the pool itself. If your garagebots collected stats on Sesman's vehicle, I want to see those, too. I'd like to know how it went out of control like that."

Under her hand, the manager was twitching. He was hiding something, but wasn't going to spill it in front of so many others. She had to get him alone.

"I need data, Malone," K't'ank said, his voice resounding through the bracelet on her wrist. "In no fashion could this have been accidental. Give me data!"

"What do you think happened?" Dena whispered.

"I suspect unpleasant activity."

"You mean foul play? What do you need?"

"Displacement, power supply, and requirements, formulae

of power allocation, weight of water, and precise size of the installation."

Dena turned to Thompason.

"You heard the worm," she said. "Start cranking out files. Either you can transfer them to his personal number or I can read them and he'll see them through my eyes."

The manager, suitably cowed, turned and led her to the elevator. His staff followed them.

The PR woman sidled up beside Dena.

"I'm Tanya Coller, Sergeant Malone. I've seen you on the news, as I'm sure you surmised. We'll do everything we can to help. Don't you find it odd to live with a Salosian seeing everything you do?"

"You have no idea," Dena said, glad for a friendly face. "You should hear his running commentary on my clothes closet. I think he's a secret fashion designer. I don't measure up."

Ms. Coller giggled, then steeled herself. As the elevator doors opened, Dena understood why. A host of airborne press cameras swarmed in and surrounded them, aiming their lenses at each person in turn. Small screens on the front of each unit bore the live image of the newsperson operating it. As one, the cameras all hovered facing Dena.

"*Continental Gazette*, Sergeant," barked a burly man in his fifties with deep mahogany skin and artfully grayed temples that lent him an air of gravitas. "How did the accident occur? Will you release pictures of the body?"

There was no perceptible use in trying to equivocate with the press. Their intelligence was often better than that of the police. Dena was sure that was how they had arrived on the scene so swiftly. Someone in the hotel had tipped them off, possibly for payment, or they had the ANCHOR conference under surveillance. Nothing new there, so she couldn't feel irritated about it.

"There will be no images, pending notification of the family," Dena said, trying to look businesslike and sympathetic at the same time.

"But Mrs. Sesman is already here," said the image of a newswoman with pale skin and braids of golden hair wound in a bun on top of her head. "She already gave us a statement."

Damn it! Dena thought. All she needed was a hysterical relative swooning for the press.

"Dr. K't'ank, what is your take on the case?" asked a third newsman, a round-cheeked, tawny-skinned man of approximately Dena's own age. "How could this accident have happened? Should all infinity pools be banned from now on?"

There was nothing K't'ank would have liked better than to offer his opinion at immense length.

"One tragedy can be extrapolated in many ways," he began. Immediately, Dena took off the bracelet and stuffed it into her pocket. A muffled wail erupted. She smiled at the cameras.

"Sorry, no more questions now!"

"Malone!" K't'ank said, via bone conduction, which only she could hear. "That is unfair! They request my wisdom!"

"You can't give them anything but a guess right now," Dena reasoned, willing her blood pressure not to give away her annoyance. "I still have to get that data for you. Let's not delay the investigation."

"Understood," K't'ank said. He totally lacked tact, but he understood the difference between surmise and proof. "All must be made clear in the proper fashion."

This was when Ms. Coller, the PR woman, came into her own. Very smoothly, she signaled for a group of hovering bots with the hotel's logo on them, each of which picked out a news camera and herded it gently into her wake. She beckoned to them with a crooked finger.

"This way, please, ladies, gentlemen, and others of the press. I will have an official statement for you in a few minutes, with updates as we get them. Let me upload to you biographies of each of the witnesses and brochures of our luxury presidential suite."

The foyer cleared, leaving a few curious guests, Thompason and his security chief. Dena tapped the manager on the shoulder.

"The sooner you give me that data, sir, the sooner we'll be out of here."

"Er, yes," he said.

"I perceive tics in the skin of Thompason's face," K't'ank said, his voice echoing in her skull. "Do these denote irritation of the epidermis or some other symptom?"

"I see that, too," Dena said, watching the man's cheeks jump as though invisible fleas were dancing on them. She put the bracelet back onto her wrist. "Mr. Thompason, is there a reason why you look so nervous?"

His face flushed, and he shook his head violently, making his jowls wobble.

"No, of course not!"

He seemed reluctant to spit it out. The security man hovered protectively to his side. Dena raised an eyebrow. Thompason almost trembled, but remained silent. Dena let him have it. The second eyebrow levitated and joined the other. She knew he couldn't take that kind of pressure. His breath burst out of him like an explosion.

"It was purchase and installation!" he exclaimed. "Oh, God, I knew it would come out sooner or later. I was only trying to save the Castana money!"

"What's the issue? Someone had to buy the pool. Isn't it your job?"

"Yes, of course it was! But the penthouse project was running millions over budget. I swear, I didn't mean for any of this to happen!"

"What did you do?" She asked.

Hastily, Thompason pushed her through a nearby doorway. The security man followed, and the portal, a handsome oval of teak wood and polished bronze, thudded into place behind them. Dena braced herself, readying a counterattack in case they planned to attack her. It wouldn't be the first time a suspect tried to derail the police by disposing of an agent. The Chief of Police had gone on all the news channels to inform the public that all officers were in constant contact with their precincts. Dena thought it had saved her life at least twice.

Instead, she discovered she was in an opulent office suite that made the penthouse look like a single-room occupancy for down-and-out swimmers. If millions had been spent upstairs, billions had gone into Thompason's private domain. Each of the chairs was hand carved from nearly translucent poki wood, imported from one of the exoplanet settlements outside the solar system. The brilliant red enameled desktop stood on tripods of wavy golden feelers that looked as if they were still alive, not shed by the gigantic insectoids of Actarel V that had grown them.

"Let me explain," Thompason began. Dena cut him off.

"Let *me* guess," she said dryly. "You cut corners. Money was running short, and you had to find a bargain somewhere."

Thompason stared at her wide-eyed. "How did you know?"

"Call it police instinct, sir. Where and how did you economize on an infinity pool? Where did you buy it?"

Thompason stopped to fondle a living sculpture from Deimos, a blobby, colloidal being that had been discovered only when its kind had been transported to Earth and allowed to warm up for the first time in its two million year life. It leaned into the manager's caress, then oozed into a flattened disk on its pedestal.

"Uh, well," he said, sitting down at his desk with his hands folded on the top, his head almost concealed behind his hands. "Mm-mm mss-phuss."

"Would you care to mumble that again?" Dena asked. "I'm not familiar with that planet."

"Government surplus!" Thompason burst out.

"Government surplus? *Our* government? What were they doing with luxury swimming pools?"

"I found them on a website," the manager confessed. "We were running over budget on the penthouse suite. I saw the pools for sale at a tenth of retail. It seemed like the answer to a prayer. I thought, what harm could it do? They were built to government specifications!"

"The same government that gave our space explorers inoculations against bird flu and smallpox? That government?"

"Well, yes. But nothing has happened until now! Hundreds of guests have enjoyed the pool."

"I suppose none of them ever went swimming in a car before."

"No, but if they had wanted to, we of the Castana wouldn't have refused them permission," Thompason said. "We offer the supreme experience in luxury accommodation."

Tamm cleared his throat uncomfortably. Dena straightened her shoulders.

"Who knew you bought it as surplus?"

"Ummmm ... no one?" Thompason said.

"How sure are you about that?" Dena asked. "Someone had to sign off on your purchases, didn't they?"

"No, Sergeant," Thompason said, drawing himself up proudly. "My employers trust me to get the job done."

"The installers? The deliverybots?"

"I knew," Tamm spoke up. Thompason glanced at him in dismay. He shrugged. "I know everything that comes in and goes out of this place. It's my job."

"Data, Malone!" K't'ank said suddenly. "While you gather impressions to determine their guilt, I require hard information!"

The two men jumped. Dena held out her skinnypad.

"I need all the input on this," she said. "Like I said, the sooner you give it to me, the sooner you can get rid of us. Then I want to speak to Mrs. Sesman."

THE WIDOW DIDN'T have much to contribute. Coffee-skinned and brown-eyed, model-thin, with a sweep of artfully arranged silver hair piled high on her head, Laila Sesman made Dena feel like a bundle of rags. She was ensconced in a thronelike seat in a private sitting room hidden behind another one of those concealed doors in the lobby of the Castana.

"I'm afraid I don't know what my husband was doing with the car. The Circo was his current favorite toy. He had many responsibilities, so he liked to break the tension in any way he could. It wouldn't have been beyond him to drive it into an elevator. Or through an open window on an upper floor. It had virtually unlimited range. He could have driven it to the Moon."

"He liked ... practical jokes?" Dena asked, trying to sound tactful.

"You've never heard of Noble Sesman?" Mrs. Sesman countered. She sighed. "Yes. It's a wonder we haven't been plunged into an interstellar war because of him. But once people get over being mad at him, they'll do anything for him."

"Define 'being mad,'" Dena said.

The widow waved a slender hand. "Oh, any web search will bring up a thousand examples. Noble caused as many diplomatic incidents as he defused. It's how he and I met, you know. I was on a mission to Salos that he led."

Then Dena noticed the platinum bangle on her wrist.

"You, too?" she asked.

Mrs. Sesman smiled. "Yes. N'a'bun and I have been together for years. We were one of the first successful pairings Alien Relations ever had. N'a'bun, say hello."

A musical voice, clearly female, issued from the woman's bracelet.

"Hello, human and fellow Salosian."

"Greetings," K't'ank said. "I am K't'ank."

"Greetings back. How long since you saw the homeworld?"

"Seventeen Terran years," K't'ank said. "Malone is my fifth host. And you?"

"Thirty-four. What does a Salosian have to do with police procedure?" N'a'bun asked.

"It is most interesting! Humans do away with one another in surprisingly different manners."

"Can you two talk in private?" Dena said. "I'm here for a reason."

"Of course," N'a'bun said. "K't'ank, my private frequency is 80.5.6."

She felt K't'ank settle into a coil near her spine. It threw off her weight for a moment, and she rubbed her back.

Mrs. Sesman smiled. She gestured to a deeply cushioned chair covered in soft brown velvet.

"Sit down, Sergeant. I'm surprised to see you without your floatchair, particularly in your current state."

"My what?"

The lady's delicate hands wafted over the ornate arm rests of her own lushly padded, high-backed armchair.

"A floatchair. Like mine. It's one of the benefits of hosting a Salosian. Alien Relations needs us to prevent simple accidents that would interfere with our guests being able to enjoy the Sol system and other human settlements. They have determined falls are the primary reason that humans become infirm. It runs on a miniature antigravity engine about the size of your fist, but throttled down for safety. You mean, you don't have one?"

"No, I never heard of them," Dena said. "No one ever told me there were any benefits, let alone a floatchair." She regarded Mrs. Sesman's chair with envious eyes.

Mrs. Sesman looked at her oddly.

"All these things are due to Salosian-hosts as part of our arrangement with Alien Relations. Didn't you go through the training? What about your contract?"

"I have no contract."

"Did you give them your FIL?"

"Yes. My fingerprints are on file with them."

"Well, then, dear, you have rights! You didn't read it, did you?"

"No, ma'am. There wasn't time. K't'ank was in danger of dying." Dena hesitated, thinking back to the moment when everyone in the medical examiner's office was yelling at her at once. "It was ... complicated."

Mrs. Sesman shook her head.

"They pushed you into an uncontrolled transfer? They gave you no training at all?"

"No! I mean, I didn't know I needed any."

"You've coped amazingly well, then, dear. You're a natural. Alien Relations could use a thousand like you. I'll bet they didn't tell you about the allowance, either."

"Allowance?" Dena knew she was echoing the woman stupidly, but she struggled to absorb everything Mrs. Sesman was saying.

"Yes. A direct deposit. Every week. It's not that generous, but it's better than nothing. You need to put in your claim and give them your automatic transfer code. Come and see me later today, and I'll give you the support material that those oafs forgot."

Material on how to deal with K't'ank? Money? A floatchair? Dena knew her eyes lit up. But her professional composure got out and stomped up and down on her hopeful enthusiasm.

"I can't, ma'am. This is an ongoing investigation. I am not allowed to socialize until it's over. You're a ... a witness."

"You mean *suspect*," Mrs. Sesman said, lightly. "I understand. I haven't been in the diplomatic service for thirty-five years without being able to read between the lines."

Dena felt sorry for her. As much out of professionalism as sympathy, she dropped her eyes to her notes.

"So what do you think happened today?"

"It was probably the result of a stupid prank Noble thought up." Tears sprang to Mrs. Sesman's eyes for the first time. "He told me he was going to surprise those 'stuffed shirts' in the penthouse, as he called them. He always had a raucous sense of humor. It looks as if whatever he set up went terribly wrong. I always knew it would end this way, but I'll hold my head up. In the meantime, I will instruct that foolish man out there to order you a floatchair. I will see you later, my dear. N'a'bun will have given your symbiote our contact information."

DENA RODE OUT of the hotel on a green upholstered floatchair that was nicer than everything that she and her husband owned put together. It was so comfortable she couldn't imagine ever getting out of it. People walking at street level glanced at her with a mixture of curiosity and envy. She was embarrassed at the attention, but it was blissful relief for her back and swollen feet. Defying gravity was great. The field that the chair emitted was limited. It took her only a foot or so off the ground, but the difference in comfort was unbelievable.

"I really hope that woman didn't kill her husband," Dena told Ramos. "This is great!"

"You shouldn't have taken that chair from her," he said. "Looks like bribery. The police can't look like we can be bought."

"It's just a loaner from the hotel!" Dena argued. She wriggled into the padding. It rose to envelop her spine. "Alien Relations owes me one. This goes back as soon as mine arrives."

"You'll be lucky if you keep it past the time we get back to the precinct. If Potopos sees it, it'll be his ass in the chair and yours in the hotseat."

"You're just jealous."

"Because I don't have a worm in my belly? I don't eat the one in the tequila, either, Malone. You're just the one who didn't say no."

Dena knew Ramos was right. Captain Potopos insisted on examining the loaner, if by examining he meant that he confiscated it for his personal use for the rest of the day. Dena didn't care, since she had to plant herself in front of the library console and research all the people involved in the case. Out of the corner of her eye, she could see their boss gliding through the corridors or floating up the station stairs like a late-model Dalek.

Looking up Sesman's past was better than watching a comedy tri-dee. His wife hadn't exaggerated her husband's behavior. Though he was a philanthropist, he was famous for stupid stunts, like greeting the Centauran ambassador on his first arrival in the Sol system with a custard pie to his blue-scaled face. To save the diplomatic mission, the Terran council had to pretend that they greeted every visiting interplanetary dignitary with pies. Hasty photoshopping of greeting images of other diplomats kept the situation from escalating into interplanetary war. The lineup of elegant men and women in fancy tunics with cream dripping off their faces had always made Dena laugh. In the back row of each picture, the late Mr. Sesman stood with a grin plastered across his face from ear to ear.

"I wondered how that custom got started," Ramos said, watching over her shoulder. "They never told us in school. I tip my hat to the gentleman. The guy was a genius. Too bad he's dead. Maybe I should use pies during witness interrogations. It'd brighten up the interviews. How about enemies? Anyone decide that they had enough of his humor and this was the time for payback? Who wanted to drown him in a swimming pool?"

Dena shook her head over the picture of Sesman among the pie-covered diplomats. "Nobody. Everyone I have contacted thinks he was a great guy and a good administrator. Tough but fair. A tribute to ANCHOR."

"But he did not give us our requested credits," K't'ank said. "Financial assets went to amusements instead of our research."

"So he's the guy who put the fun in funding," Ramos said.

K't'ank laughed uproariously. Dena winced.

"I wonder if I can get Potopos to take you two for a ride, too."

"Cheerful, Malone," K't'ank said. "Do not be a tart cat."

"That's sourpuss," Dena said. "Don't cross-reference everything to your thesaurus."

"It seemed to make little sense either way."

"So does this case. Two plus two is adding up to zero."

"I will study the details," K't'ank said. "The scientific fact must contain the truth."

DENA RETURNED TO the precinct in the morning in great spirits. Though she still hadn't been able to retrieve the floatchair, she was happy. Because K't'ank had been so engaged with the formulae and data from Thompason's files, he hadn't bothered her at all. Her husband Neal had been thrilled to hear about the allowance coming from Alien Relations. The two of them had taken advantage of the quiet to have an uninterrupted cuddle session. Every moment was precious, since it was only ten weeks until the baby was due, and they'd still have to put up with K't'ank's kibitzing whenever they tried to make love.

On the other hand, K't'ank was in a cranky mood.

"Do not hum," he grumbled at her, as she poured herself a decaf. "It causes irritating vibrations in your diaphragm."

"What's the matter?" Ramos asked. You get up on the wrong side of the host this morning?

"Which side is the wrong side?" K't'ank asked. "I am always inside."

"It's an expression," Dena said. "Add it to your list of Things You Don't Understand about Human Colloquialisms. Later. I could tell you were up all night doing research. What have you found?"

"Nothing!" The Salosian sounded frustrated. "I have searched through the files many times. If the statistics are true, nothing was wrong with the pool that should have caused the compression of Sesman and his vehicle. There *was* a study on buoyancy and forcefields. The findings are useless to our case. Most of the remaining pools are in the homes of the scientists whose names appear on the abstracts."

"Our tax dollars at work," Ramos said.

"So it had to be deliberate," Dena said. She sipped the coffee. Without caffeine, it seemed a futile gesture, but she was firmly addicted to the taste. "But how? How do you rig a pool to eat someone?"

"You cannot, Malone. That is evident. It would have consumed those four women before."

"They're not all women," Dena said. "Oh, forget it. If the pool was normal, what would it take to set off that reaction? Could it have been accidental?"

"Not with the parameters of the luxury vehicle that Sesman operated. It is ordinary."

"The snooty types won't like you to say that." Ramos brought up the security recordings from the garage and fiddled around until he brought up the rooftop landing pad. The black arrow that was the Circo landed softly and rolled into the elevator. The view changed to a video pickup facing the parking space reserved for Sesman. "I mean, look at that! It's streamlined to the nth degree! It's got enough thrust to move a building! It's gorgeous!"

The recording speed ran at the maximum the human mind could absorb. Dena peered at the screen. The sleek black car shot into the garage and parked. Sesman, in great shape in spite of his age, flung himself out of it. The garagebots on duty rolled by the bay like scurrying mice. Sesman hustled back, climbed in, and pulled it out of the space. The footage repeated again and again. Dena sighed. The car glided like an angel. Too bad it was crushed into a singularity in the bottom of a swimming pool.

"It is ordinary," K't'ank said dismissively. Both humans felt deflated. "You Terrans are peculiar in your assumption that there is something special in very minute alterations."

"How minute?" Dena asked.

"Oh, well, the Circo Ex Eye Eye Eye ..."

"That's the Circo Thirteen," Dena said.

"... that Sesman owned differs from the Homburg NCR Vee ... "

"NCR Five."

"Why are numbers written as a series of letters? Never mind. It is clearly one of your foolish human conceits. They differ by less than two percent of aerodynamic profile. Its engine is ridiculously overpowered for its use. The color was within a single shade to last year's model. Why would that cost an estimated fifteen percent more?

"Status," Ramos said. "Everyone likes to have the latest thing."

"It wasn't an accident," Dena said. "That's obvious. So, who hated him enough to rig a booby trap? And how?"

The image of Captain Potopos appeared in the middle of the console screen. His dark eyes fixed on Dena.

"Malone, can I have a word with you? In my office."

"Ooooh," Ramos said, his eyes dancing. "You got to go see the principal."

"Shut up," Dena said, bracing herself to rise from her chair.

Potopos was seated behind his desk with his hands folded. That was bad news. She glanced around the room. No one else was present, at least in person, so it wasn't a dressing-down for department relations.

"What do you need, sir?" she asked.

He lowered his big, black eyebrows and peered out at her from under them. She held firm. It wasn't necessarily a reprimand. Sometimes he kept a straight face before giving her good news. Then he glanced toward the corner. Dena followed his gaze. The floatchair leaned at an angle against the wall, as if it had gone on a bender and was ashamed of itself.

"Afraid you're going to have to report that unit as defective, Sergeant."

Dena turned back to meet his eyes, but he glanced away.

"What happened, sir?" she asked. "I'm going to have to tell

them something."

"I, uh, I took it home last night. I thought it had more power than it did. Let's just say that the weight-bearing qualities weren't up to the job."

"It's a one-seat model, sir," Dena said.

He raised his eyebrows meaningfully. Dena felt herself blush. Potopos and his wife were reputed to have a pretty *interesting* relationship, and it wasn't strictly limited to the two of them. Dena wanted desperately to ask what had happened involving the chair, but the captain cut her off with a gesture.

"What happens in the Potopos household," he said firmly, "stays in the Potopos household."

"Yes, sir," Dena said, disappointed.

She made her way back toward the squad room, then stopped, as something the captain had said fitted into the details they had been studying.

"What is it, Malone?" K't'ank asked. "Your internal organs are quivering. That means excitement."

"Wait a minute," she said.

She tapped Ramos on the shoulder, knowing the look of triumph on her face would be better suited to a cat who had just eaten the biggest canary in town.

"It wasn't the pool," she said. "It was the car."

"But who did it?"

"You saw him," Dena said. "Or, rather, you didn't."

THE CRIPPLED FLOATCHAIR had limped back to the penthouse at about half-speed. It listed at a drunken angle, but Dena tried to look dignified and stern from its depths. She felt like an armchair detective from the old vids. She was tempted to affect a foreign accent, but it was too late for that. And Ramos made a terrible sidekick.

Thompason, Tamm, and Ramos stood behind her. The four inhabitants of the luxury apartment and Mrs. Sesman sat on velvet-covered divans facing her. The infinity pool glinted to Dena's left.

"This is absurd," James Longmore said, glaring at Dena. "Do you think this is some sort of drawing room mystery in which you assemble the *suspects* and lay out your case until one of us confesses?"

"Yes, sir," Dena said. "That's exactly what this is."

"Oh, honey," Margan said, clutching her husband's arm. "How thrilling!"

"Enough, Margan," Obed Amini said, with a glare at his wife. "One of us is about to be accused of murder!"

"I know! I hope it's me. I'll be the envy of everyone on my social network circle!"

"Did you kill him?" her husband demanded.

"No. I liked him. But think of the headlines! They'd trend from here to Saturn."

Anita Longmore gave a distasteful glance toward the pool. "Do we have to sit here next to that thing? It killed our friend!"

"We've done our research," Ramos said. "The pool had nothing to do with it. It was an innocent bystander, just like you."

"Then what caused the catastrophe?" James Longmore demanded.

"His Circo XIII," Dena said. "For it to have caused that reaction on contact with the pool's forcefield, it had to have been loaded with superdense materials that upset the wall's balance. The load in it had to exert the pull of almost half a gee of extra gravity to trigger the reaction."

"But that's impossible," Laila Sesman said. "We flew here in that car. There was nothing that heavy in it, unless you count my cosmetics case. How could it possibly carry that much weight? Wouldn't we have felt it?"

"The car couldn't have levitated if that mass was on board when you arrived," K't'ank said. "My calculations are precise. The addition had to be placed within after."

"But you couldn't put a moon's worth of mass in a *car*. Where did it come from?"

Thompason had assisted the police in every way since the

investigation had begun. Dena saw no reason to hang him out to dry.

"Mr. Thompason purchased a number of items for the hotel in case its clientele might request it," she said, careful of her phrasing. "One of the things on the list was an antigravity generator. This chair has an antigravity generator. They're really small these days. Gravgens are used on starships to create Earth-type habitats. For a small ship, they don't have to be big, but it's a lot more powerful than a lift for a floatchair."

"But that would have lifted it, not sunk it," Amini said.

"It was set on reverse," Dena said.

"How could it hold that much?"

"There are practically no limits on the heft the Circo XIII could lift," Ramos said. "If you could fit them in there, you could take everybody in the hotel for a ride, but it'd be like a clown car. It could carry the drive for a while until the gravity it was generating overwhelmed the Circo's engine."

"How much more? Enough to overload the infinity pool's forcefield?

"Absolutely," K't'ank said. "More than forty percent over enough."

"But why didn't he notice it when he got in?"

"If the car didn't have to levitate, then you might not notice it at first," Dena said. "But as it warmed up it would haul you back toward it, hard. Driving it on a surface, the Circo didn't have to use the antigrav engine, but it could still move forward."

"That was why he couldn't control the car," Longmore said, horrified. "He was fighting gravity in the storage compartment."

"He might not even have been conscious when he went into the pool," Ramos said. The others all shivered.

"Is that why the chair is damaged?" Thompason asked, pointedly.

"Exactly," Dena said. "We, er, tested our theory. Sorry about that."

"But why did Sesman do it?" Longmore asked. "Why did he go along with a stunt that killed him?"

"He didn't know it would be fatal," Dena said. "He only thought it would be funny."

"He was betrayed by the person he roped in to help him with the joke," Ramos pointed out.

"Who was that?" Anita Longmore asked. "Surely not one of us. I don't know how to reverse the polarity on an antigravity generator."

"And we all liked him," Amini pointed out.

"It does not appear that the problem is with those who know him now," K't'ank said.

Dena nodded. "It was with people who knew him before. He seems to have a great reputation among his current circles. But perhaps not with those who have known him in the past."

"None of us sabotaged the car!" Longmore insisted. "I want to see the security footage. It must show us the person who is responsible."

"You're right about that," Dena said. Thompason gestured toward the wall to his right. The projected artwork shimmered and vanished, to be replaced by the videos that Dena and K't'ank had watched nearly a thousand times now.

"There's no one there," Margan Amini said.

"That's right," said Dena, feeling smug.

"But we saw no one!"

"Exactly!" Dena said, feeling more like an armchair detective than ever. They liked to make those obvious-sounding exclamations. "And why did you see no one?"

"Because there was no one to see?" Amini suggested. "The garagebots were the ones who sabotaged the car?"

"No. Because the recordings were tampered with. And who has override codes?"

"Well, I do," Thompason said, shrugging. "And Tamm, of course. But we both have alibis. Don't we?"

Suddenly, Tamm grabbed the back of Dena's floatchair and raced it in the direction of the infinity pool. Dena was thrust back against the chair's thick padding, unable to wriggle out of it and free herself. He was going to throw her in! The antigrav engine might trip off the forcefield. She would be crushed!

"Malone! Reverse polarity!" K't'ank shouted.

That was it! Dena clapped her palms down on the padded controls. The chair lurched backward, almost throwing her out of it. It knocked Tamm sprawling. She steered it in a tight turn over his body, turned off the antigravs and made the heavy piece of furniture drop down onto his chest. Ramos leaped forward and slammed cuffs on the man's hands, almost the only parts of his body sticking out from underneath the floatchair.

"He doesn't have an alibi," Dena said, to the stunned inhabitants of the room. "Because no one saw him."

"Brilliant!" K't'ank crowed, when they were back in the station house. Tamm was stowed in a cell awaiting his legal representative. "I mean, I am brilliant. I found the data that led to the solution of the crime."

Dena didn't contradict him.

"Why him?" Captain Potopos asked. "How would he know what kind of damage he could do with a drive, and why did he have it in for Sesman?"

"K't'ank found it in his records, Captain."

"He has an advanced degree in astrophysics from Alpha Centauri University," K't'ank announced. "He applied to ANCHOR for a grant to do field emissions research. I gleaned thousands of records until I found the notation of the interview. Sesman was the one who turned him down. He probably recognized the instability of Tamm."

"Mrs. Sesman confirmed it," Dena said. "He wasn't able to get funding anywhere. He took a job with the hotel because he has the necessary security clearances and technical know-how. Sesman liked people. He probably recognized Tamm and asked if he'd help him with a prank. Tamm saw it as his chance."

"Nice work, both of you," Potopos said, then glanced toward Dena's bracelet. "I mean, all three of you. I'm giving a briefing to the press in an hour. I want you there. K't'ank's a big hit with the press. They want to ask him questions."

"I am glad they appreciate my wisdom," K't'ank said. "It is good relations for Salos."

"Can I run home for a little while first, sir?" Dena asked, eagerly.

"What for, Malone?"

She grinned. "My husband just messaged me to say that my floatchair's been delivered. I want to take it out for a test spin. I'll be back ASAP, sir, I promise."

Potopos looked hopeful, but drew himself up.

"Just don't dunk it in any pools on the way back," he said.

Jody Lynn Nye

Best-selling science fiction and fantasy author Jody Lynn Nye describes her main career activity as "spoiling cats." When not engaged upon this worthy enterprise, she has published over forty books and novels, largely humorous, some in collaboration with noted writers in the field, such as Anne McCaffrey and Robert Asprin, and over 110 short stories. Her latest books are *Myth-Quoted*, nineteenth in Asprin's Myth-Adventures series; and *View from the Imperium*, a sort of Jeeves and Wooster in space.

Her web site is www.jodylynnnye.com

About the Editor

Alex Shvartsman is a writer, anthologist, translator, and game designer from Brooklyn, NY. His short stories have appeared in *The Journal of Nature, InterGalactic Medicine Show, Daily Science Fiction, Galaxy's Edge,* and a variety of other magazines and anthologies. In addition to the UFO series, he has edited *Coffee: 14 Caffeinated Tales of the Fantastic* and *Dark Expanse: Surviving the Collapse* anthologies. His web site is www.alexshvartsman.com

Acknowledgments

We'd like to thank everyone who pitched in to produce this book: associate editors James Aquilone, Cyd Athens, James Beamon, Frank Dutkiewicz, Michael Haynes, and Nathaniel Lee; copy editor Elektra Hammond, book designer Melissa Neely, graphics designer Emerson Matsuuchi, cover artist Tomasz Maronski and many others whose talent and hard work made this a better book. Special thanks to Anne Roberti and Bryant Happ for their invaluable support of this project.

**Explaining Cthulhu to Grandma
and Other Stories**

A short story collection by Alex Shvartsman

Coming February 2015.
Pre-order at www.ufopub.com

Unidentified Funny Objects
An annual collection
of humorous science fiction and fantasy.

Also enjoy additional stories published at
www.ufopub.com

Unidentified Funny Objects 2
Available at www.ufopub.com and from fine booksellers everywhere.

UNIDENTIFIED FUNNY OBJECTS 4—coming in 2015

14 Caffeinated Tales
of the Fantastic

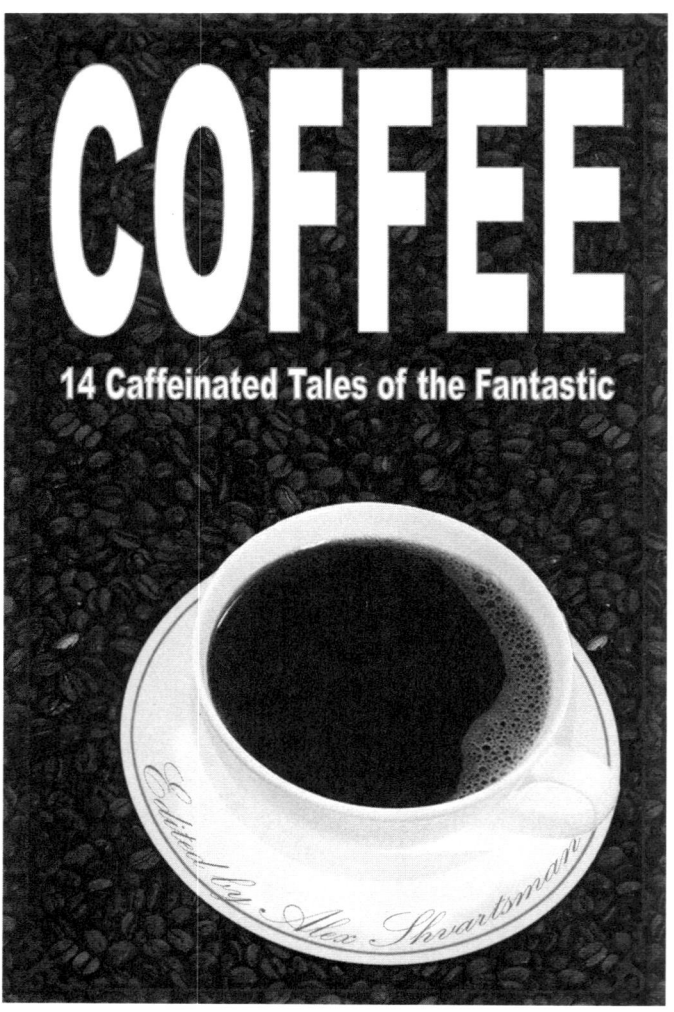

Order at ufopub.com
or from your favorite bookseller.